Barrington Street
Blues

The Collins-Burke Mystery Series

Sign of the Cross
Obit
Barrington Street Blues
Cecilian Vespers
Children in the Morning

Barrington Street Blues

A MYSTERY

ANNE EMERY

ECW Press

Published by ECW Press
2120 Queen Street East, Suite 200, Toronto, Ontario, Canada M4E IE2

LIBRARY AND ARCHIVES CANADA CATALOGUING IN PUBLICATION

Emery, Anne
Barrington Street blues : a mystery / Anne Emery. -- Pbk. ed.

ISBN 978-1-55022-906-6

I. Title.

PS8609.M47B37 2010   C813'.6   C2010-902775-2

Cover and Text Design: Tania Craan
Cover Image: Bojan Brecelj / CORBIS
Typesetting: Mary Bowness
Production: Rachel Ironstone
Printing: Webcom 1 2 3 4 5

Mixed Sources
Product group from well-managed forests, controlled sources and recycled wood or fiber
www.fsc.org Cert no. SW-COC-002358
© 1996 Forest Stewardship Council
FSC

99%

ANCIENT FOREST ™
FRIENDLY

This book is set in AGaramond

The publication of *Barrington Street Blues* has been generously supported by the Canada Council for the Arts which last year invested $20.1 million in writing and publishing throughout Canada, by the Ontario Arts Council, by the Government of Ontario through Ontario Book Publishing Tax Credit, by the OMDC Book Fund, an initiative of the Ontario Media Development Corporation, and by the Government of Canada through the Canada Book Fund.

 Canada Council   Conseil des Arts   Canadä    ONTARIO ARTS COUNCIL
for the Arts   du Canada   CONSEIL DES ARTS DE L'ONTARIO

PRINTED AND BOUND IN CANADA

ECW PRESS
ecwpress.com

For
Ann Copeland
Friend, Lawyer, Master of Disguise

Acknowledgements

I would like to thank the following people for their kind assistance: Joe A. Cameron, Rhea McGarva, Joan Butcher, Helen MacDonnell, and Edna Barker. As always, PJEC. All characters and plots in the story are fictional, as are some of the locations. Other places are real. Any liberties taken in the interests of fiction, or any errors committed, are mine alone.

I am grateful for permission to reprint extracts from the following:

Same Old Loverman, by Gordon Lightfoot. c. 1971 & 1999 (renewed) Early Morning Music. Used by permission.

Sunday Mornin' Comin' Down.
Words and Music by Kris Kristofferson
© 1969 (Renewed 1997) TEMI COMBINE INC.
All Rights Controlled by COMBINE MUSIC CORP. and Administered by EMI BLACKWOOD MUSIC INC.
All Rights Reserved   International Copyright Secured   Used by Permission

GUILTY
RANDY NEWMAN
© 1973 & 1975 WB MUSIC CORP. & RANDY NEWMAN
All rights on behalf of RANDY NEWMAN administered by WB MUSIC CORP.
All Rights Reserved   Used by Permission of ALFRED PUBLISHING CO., INC.

Every effort has been made to locate the copyright owners of material quoted in this book. Any omissions are sincerely regretted, and will be corrected in subsequent editions, if any, if brought to the publisher's attention.

Chapter 1

"Two Dead in Barrington Street Shooting"
— Halifax *Daily News*, January 13, 1991

"It's the end of the road. The dark end, down by the train tracks, where Barrington Street peters out after running its course through downtown Halifax. One man lies face down on the pavement, his canvas field jacket stained with blood, a Rolex watch glimmering on his wrist. The other, dressed in sweatpants and a windbreaker advertising Gatorade, lies on his side, a gun still gripped in his right hand. The first homicides in Halifax in 1991. The city averages eight murders a year. If, as police believe, this was a murder-suicide . . ."

My client looked up from the newspaper clipping. "What's all this about their clothes? How's that news? They make it look like Corey was a bum, and him bein' dead doesn't matter as much as the guy with the watch."

"It's not a news story, it's an opinion piece," I told Amber Dawn Rhyno. "But never mind that. Your husband's death matters to us, so let's talk about him."

"Corey's not — he wasn't my husband."

"Common-law husband. How long did you live together?"

"You mean when he wasn't in jail or the treatment centre? Me and

Corey were together on and off for nine years. Ever since I had Zachary."

Zachary was her son. The whole time they had been in my law office, the boy had been sitting on my side table and falling off, sitting and falling. Each time he fell, he took a stack of my files with him to the floor. I tried to ignore him.

"All right, Amber. Tell me what happened when you first heard about Corey's suicide."

"I wasn't surprised at all. Not one bit. He blamed that place. Or, like, he would've if he didn't die. If he came out of it, he woulda said it was all their fault."

I studied Amber Dawn Rhyno, imagining her on the witness stand in a damages suit against the addiction treatment centre where Corey Leaman had been staying before he was found with a bullet in his brain. Amber Dawn was a short, skinny woman in her late twenties. She had a hard-bitten face, and thin brown hair that was straight for about six inches, frizzy at the ends. An acid-green tank top revealed a tattooed left shoulder.

"Who's Troy?" I asked her.

"Troy?"

"The tattoo."

"Oh." She shrugged. "Just this guy."

"Someone you were involved with?"

"We weren't really, like, involved."

I let it go. It was not as if I would allow her anywhere near opposing counsel — never mind a courtroom — in a sleeveless top.

"Zach!"

The child had picked up my radio, and was trying to pull the knobs off it.

"Put that down," I told him. "Now."

"You can't make me!"

"Yeah. I can." I got up and wrenched the radio from his hands. He began to howl.

"It's not his fault," his mother said. "The social worker says he has a problem."

"I'm sorry, Amber, but I have another client coming in. We'll get together again. In the meantime, I'd like you to write up a little history of your relationship with Corey Leaman, including what you recall about the times he was admitted to the Baird Treatment Centre."

"But I already told you everything."

"There's a lot more that you'll remember when you sit down and think about it."

My clients would never sit down and write. But I would worry about that later. Zachary's howling had reached a new, ear-splitting pitch. Time for them to go.

"Call me if you need anything. You have my number."

"Yeah, okay. Thanks, Ross."

"I'm Monty. Ross is the other lawyer working on your case."

"Sorry. Can I have your card? I already got Ross's."

"Here you go."

She read the card: "Montague M. Collins, B.A., LL. B. Right. Okay, bye."

I watched Amber drag her son out the door and thought about her case. Corey Leaman, her common-law husband, and another man, named Graham Scott, were found dead of gunshot wounds at five o'clock in the morning of January 12, 1991, in the parking lot of the Fore-And-Aft. This was a nautically themed strip joint situated across from the Wallace Rennie Baird Addiction Treatment Centre. The two buildings are the last structures at the bottom end of Barrington Street, which runs along the eastern edge of the Halifax Peninsula, from Bedford Basin in the north to the train tracks that traverse the south end of the city. The street had seen better days, and would again, I knew. But that was neither here nor there for the two men who had been found sprawled on the pavement at the end of the road.

The gun was in Leaman's right hand. He had apparently dispatched Scott with two bullets in the back of the head, then put a bullet in his own right temple. Leaman's drug addiction had landed him in the Baird Centre; he had been released shortly before his death. The police were keeping the file open even though the medical examiner had declared the case a probable murder-suicide. Now, three months after the deaths, my firm was representing the families of Leaman and Scott in a lawsuit against the Baird Centre. We claimed the treatment facility had been negligent in releasing Leaman when it knew, or ought to have known, that Leaman presented a danger to others and to himself. It was by no means certain that we could pin the responsibility on the treatment centre, but we would do our best.

†

The following night, Tuesday, I had left the world of drugs and guns and was seated in the choir loft of St. Bernadette's Church. Next to me was another unlikely choirboy, Ed Johnson. Ed and I were more accustomed to wailing the blues in our band, Functus, which we had formed in law school more than twenty years ago; the St. B's gig was something new. A much purer tone of voice was expected here. That wasn't going to be easy, given that Johnson and I had spent the previous night in a succession of bars around the city. But the choirmaster had ordained that we be present, and so we were.

"I hear you've got the Leaman case, Collins," said Johnson. "How much do you expect to rake in?"

"No idea. I've barely looked at the file."

Johnson claimed to hate working as a lawyer but, in reality, the law courts were mother earth to him. He was tall and thin with light brown hair and a bony face; his lips were set in a permanent sneer. Every guy has an old friend that his wife doesn't trust, someone she thinks is going to lead her husband astray in the world of wine, women and song. Or, as we know it today, sex, drugs and rock 'n roll. To all appearances, Ed Johnson filled that role nicely. But in fact, behind the seen-it-all, done-it-all façade, Ed was as tender-hearted as anyone I'd ever met. And, as far as I knew, even his own wife had nothing to worry about.

Ed was still talking about the Leaman case. "Well, I don't imagine you're talking big bucks for lost future income. It wasn't two brain surgeons who shot each other's lights out in the Foreign Daft parking lot."

"No, from what I understand, the families just want —"

"Don't tell me." He put his hand up. "Let me guess. It's not about the money. It's the principle of the thing, right? The families just want justice. So, is it going to be more trouble than it's worth, or what?"

"Could be. But I've got Ross Trevelyan working with me. He's a certifiable workaholic, so I won't be knocking myself out."

"Yeah, I heard. Rowan finally managed to reel him in. Well done."

Rowan was Rowan Stratton, the senior partner at my law firm, Stratton Sommers. Rowan had been trying to woo Ross away from Trevelyan and Associates, his father's firm, for years. Ross was the son of John Trevelyan, one of the city's most eminent barristers, who had recently been appointed a justice of the Nova Scotia Supreme Court. John was considered Supreme Court of Canada material, and the betting was that he would soon be elevated to the Court of Appeal, where he would sit until a place opened up on the country's top court in Ottawa. The Trevelyan name was like gold.

"I thought Ross would be full of shit," I said, "but he isn't. He offered to help me with the Leaman case, among others, and he's doing all the discoveries for Rowan on the Sherman Industries file. So it's worked out well."

"Better him than you. I don't envy you trying to pin those two shootings on Wally Baird's detox. So they released Leaman; they thought he was all right. What else were they going to do, keep him in for the rest of his life? Defence counsel will stop at nothing to keep the floodgates closed on that one. And it definitely won't be about the money for them. Because there won't be much of a claim. They'll just want to avoid setting a precedent for every Tom, Dick, and —"

We heard a whisper hiss its way through the ranks of the boy sopranos on the other side of the choir loft. They straightened up and fell silent as the choirmaster appeared before us.

The Reverend Brennan X. Burke was tall, stern, and immaculate in his clerical suit and Roman collar. He had black eyes, black hair flecked with grey, and an Irish-looking mouth, from which emerged a voice tinged with the accent of the old country whence his family had come when he was but a lad.

"Good evening, gentlemen."

"Good evening, Father!"

"Welcome to the first rehearsal of the St. Bernadette's Choir of Men and Boys. Let us bow our heads and pray. *Exaudi nos, Domine sancte, Pater omnipotens . . .*"

"It's still in Latin?" Ed whispered. "I thought they switched —"

I kicked Ed somewhere between the ankle and the shin to instill in him the proper attitude towards prayer, and he lapsed into silence. Burke communed with God in Latin; that's all there was to it.

St. Bernadette's was a small neo-Gothic church at the corner of Byrne and Morris streets in the southeast part of Halifax, near the harbour. The light of a spring evening shone through the stained-glass windows, giving the church the appearance of a jewel box. More to the point for us, the acoustics were magnificent, which made it the ideal location for the choir school run by Father Burke.

We sight-read our way through a musical history of the Catholic Church, from thousand-year-old Gregorian chant to the multi-layered sound of the Renaissance to the *Ave Verum* of Mozart. The choir director listened to voices and the way they blended, and shuffled people around to get the sound he wanted. I was surprised at how good the younger boys were; their sight-reading and vocal abilities spoke well for the choir school. Johnson and I had the croakiest voices in the loft — no surprise there — and we were the subject of damning looks from the priest as a result.

But all was forgiven when we adjourned for a post-choral pint. Brennan Burke and I had become friends over the past year after I defended him — successfully — on a murder charge. He and Johnson had met the odd time, usually when the priest came to hear our blues band perform. We left the church and got into my car. There was no discussion of where to go; it was a foregone conclusion that we were headed for Grafton Street. The Midtown Tavern & Grill, with its familiar red and green sign and its unpretentious appearance, was an institution in the life of the city. Three draft were on the table before we'd settled in our seats, and the waiter didn't waste our time telling us about himself or about anything with raspberry *coulis* in, on, or around it.

"Can you believe the sound coming out of that little Robertson fellow?" Burke remarked. "He's only nine years old. A little hellion but he's cute as a button."

"You're fond of young boys, are you, Brennan?"

"I am, Ed." Burke took out a pack of cigarettes, lit one, and blew the smoke away from the table. "Young girls, too. And grown women. I tolerate a few obnoxious middle-aged male companions as well. You sounded great, I have to say. A bit rough around the edges, but I may have a solo for you if I can catch you after an early night."

"Could happen."

"How long have you and Monty known each other?"

"Long time," Ed replied. "When I met Collins I wanted his parents to adopt me."

"I can't imagine why they didn't."

"Neither could I at the time. Though it might have had something to do with my debt load in law school."

"Ah."

"Yeah, I was a little out of the adoptable category by the time I met them. I hear they took in a kitten instead."

"So, why Monty's parents?"

"Well, look at him! Did you ever see anybody more placid than this guy?"

"I don't know. I've seen him a little perturbed on occasion."

"Notable because so rare, am I right? His mother was always in pearls, and his father always had his head in a book. 'I dropped in to borrow the car, all right, Dad?' 'Sure, dear, go right ahead.' Dear! To his twenty-two-year-old son."

"He called us all dear. He was a sweetheart."

"See? What did your old man call you, Brennan?"

"'You little gobshite,' most of the time. But he meant well."

"My old man called me 'kumquat.' And he didn't mean well."

"He called you a fruit?"

"No, he called my brother a fruit. He called me 'kumquat' because he's such a dumb fuck he thought it meant something dirty. Probably still does. Ole Vinny ain't never going to be asked to serve on the Greater Halifax Literacy Council."

"Is your father here in town?"

"I hope not. So. Monty's working on a suicide case. Those guys can't be buried in consecrated ground, right?" Father Burke started to reply, but Johnson kept on: "I wonder if you can ratchet up the damage claim because of that. Mental anguish for the family."

"I've met the wife. I can't quite see her wailing and gnashing her teeth over a religious rejection."

"Then you're not doing your job, Collins."

"Moooooo." I looked up the next morning to see Ross Trevelyan standing in the doorway to my office. "Our milch cow just walked in the door."

"Oh?"

"The girlfriend and, unsuspected until now, the wee tiny daughter of Graham Scott. Graham Scott who, his parents insist, was getting off drugs —"

"Scott was on drugs too?"

"*Off* drugs, Monty, *off* drugs. Unlike Leaman, Scott was going clean and was practically on the road to medical school when his untimely death occurred outside the Fore-And-Aft."

"You say he had a daughter? How old?"

"Two."

"Well!"

"And — *and* — any day now, the girlfriend is going to be delivered of a second little calf who'll never know her daddy."

"No!"

"Yes. Dependency claim for millions. Two little girls who lost the guidance and financial support of a father who was almost certainly going to win the Nobel Prize for medicine. So, Monty, do you want to meet them, or would you like me to handle it?"

"You go ahead. Thanks, Ross."

"No problem. And his parents are coming in this afternoon. You may have heard of them. Alastair Scott is a clergyman, but they live well. They're sitting on a pile of old money. I'm going to be in court and may not be back in time for their appointment."

"I'll see the parents."

"Great. Meanwhile, I'll draw up the contingency agreements." We were required to register with the court the agreement between us and our clients to take thirty percent of whatever we recovered in our lawsuit against the treatment centre. Which, as Ross had pointed out, could now be millions.

Ross was in his late thirties. Short, trim, and handsome with thinning dark hair and a winning smile. He was one of those people who look better with eyeglasses than without; his tortoiseshell frames gave him an air of distinction. I had never met anyone who worked harder. He confided to me when he joined Stratton Sommers that he had never felt appreciated when he was toiling away in the middle ranks of his father's prestigious law firm. He was ready when Rowan made his latest offer of a partnership. I walked out to the waiting room and told Darlene, our receptionist, that I would be seeing Mr. and Mrs. Scott when they came in later in the day.

†

I had not even opened the Leaman and Scott suicide file yet, but, as I expected, Graham Scott's parents were not looking for information from me. They were determined to set the record straight about their son, and all I had to do was listen. Canon Alastair Scott and his wife, Muriel, were both tall and slim with blondish hair beginning to turn white. He appeared in a well-tailored business suit, but I could easily picture him in clerical collar and vestments. He was an Anglican priest with a doctorate in divinity. Muriel Scott wore a pale blue dress with a light tweed jacket and a string of pearls. I knew they were friends of my senior partner, Rowan Stratton. I doubted they had even been aware of the Fore-And-Aft before their son was found dead there.

"Our son has been portrayed in the press as a drug addict and a criminal," Canon Scott began as soon as we had introduced ourselves. "In fact, he was not an addict. He was a recreational user of cocaine, not crack cocaine, and he was able to go for long periods of time without it. He had a minor criminal record, for drug possession and common assault. Graham got in with an unfortunate set of companions in high school. I don't put the blame entirely on others of course. Graham was responsible for his own actions, and should have known better. Indeed he did know better. Notwithstanding all this, he got through high school without repeating any grades and, with some interruptions and backsliding, he managed to complete three years of a science degree at Dalhousie U. Graham told us he was planning to go back this September and finish his degree. After that, medical school. It was his dream — to be more accurate, it was his intention — to become a cardiologist. There is no doubt in my mind that eventually he would have achieved that goal."

"Graham comes where in the family? You have other children, I know."

"He's — he was the third of four. Boy, girl, boy, boy. None of our other children got into trouble, but Graham was a bit of an adventurer. I always felt he would sink the lowest and, in the end, rise to the greatest heights."

"Canon Scott, Mrs. Scott, where was Graham living just before his death?"

Muriel Scott answered. "He had recently moved back in with us. He had been rooming with some friends, but that arrangement was a trial to him. I think he saw moving home as a way to begin getting his life back in order."

"Did he ever speak to you about Corey Leaman?"

"Never heard of him, until this happened," the canon said.

"So you don't know whether he was acquainted with Leaman before his death." They shook their heads. "Did he talk about his friends, the people he went around with?"

"The only friends he talked about to us were people we knew, youngsters he had been with at the Halifax Grammar School. These other people, he never alluded to them."

"How old was Graham?"

His mother started to speak, cleared her throat and tried again. "Graham died one week before his twenty-second birthday. He had his whole life — I know it's a cliché, but Graham had such a future ahead of him. Despite the trouble he'd been in, and the rough characters he'd taken up with, he never lost his essential goodness. His quality."

"Now, about Graham's girlfriend. And his child."

"Yes?" They both spoke at once.

"Did you know the girl, and your grandchild?"

They exchanged a glance. Eventually, the father replied: "No."

"Had you been aware that he had a child?"

The exchange of glances, the shaking of heads.

"Have you since met the girlfriend and the little girl?"

"At the wake and the funeral for Graham," his mother answered.

"And since then?"

"No."

"Did she tell you, or were you aware, that she is expecting a second child?"

Silence. Not even an exchange of glances.

I would have to check the law on paternity tests, specifically, who could apply to the court to order one. Graham Scott's children would be the key to the damage award. His parents would be entitled to something, as would Corey Leaman's family. But it was Graham's kids who could claim to have lost a lifetime of support from a (hypothetically) high-earning father.

After the Scotts left, I made a pass by Ross Trevelyan's office, but he wasn't there. I saw the file on his side table, picked it up, and took it to my desk, where I dictated a memo on my conversation with the Scotts. I was just finishing up when Ross came in.

"Hi. Court just wound up. Were the parents in?"

"Just left. The long and the short of it is: Graham was going straight to a residency in cardiology." Ross beamed. "He had never mentioned Corey Leaman, but he never talked about any of the other lowlifes he ran around with either. And he never told his parents about the existence of their grandchild. Or of the pregnancy, if he knew of it. The girlfriend was not included in any Sunday dinners with the vicar."

"A respectable family like his, he kept his other life a secret. Having met the girlfriend, I can't say I'm surprised he hid her in the shadows. She's a bit, well, 'not our sort, darling,'" he finished in a posh British accent much like that of Rowan Stratton. Ross looked at my desk. "You've got the file? Good. You may want to read through it before you meet Doctor Swail-Peddle."

"Who?"

"A very favourable witness."

"Oh?"

"Or he will be, if his telephone call is anything to go by."

"You mean he called you?"

"Yes. He heard about the case, and gave me a call."

"What's his interest?"

"He was a psychologist on staff at the Baird Addiction Treatment Centre."

"Was."

"Yeah. I don't know what the story is, except that he's willing to help us out. I've pencilled him in for tomorrow afternoon, late. You may want to sit in if you're still around at six or so."

"Sure."

He waved and went off.

I opened the file and began to read. The first thing that leapt out at me was that the police had initially regarded this not as a suicide, but as a double murder. There was no known connection between the two men, no known motive for Leaman to kill Scott. They each had a history of drug use and trafficking, but Leaman would hardly have executed Scott for a drug deal gone wrong, then killed himself immediately afterwards. Then again, Leaman had a psychiatric history and had occasionally been violent in the past. Who knew what might have provoked him to kill Scott and turn the gun on himself?

That was another thing, the gun. There had been no indication that Leaman had ever used or possessed a gun. The police had not been able to trace it. It was an unusual weapon in this day and age, a German Luger P-08, which was already being replaced by another weapon before the end of World War Two. This one was almost certainly stolen, but no collector had stepped forward to claim it. There were no complete fingerprints on the weapon apart from Leaman's. There were smeared prints, which could have belonged to Leaman or somebody else. This, to me, served to support the suicide theory. Typically, if someone wanted to commit murder and make it look like suicide, they wiped the gun free of prints, then placed it in the victim's hand. Guns used by people like Leaman tended to be passed around; if his had been the only prints on the gun, that would have struck me as suspicious. There was no detectable gunshot residue on Leaman, but there was a handwritten note in the file, probably scribbled by a detective after conversation with an expert: "Recoverable residues generally do not persist on skin for very long . . . residues may be absent for any number of reasons." I knew there had been freezing rain the morning the bodies were found.

In the end, the police had left the file open. With no witnesses and no evidence of a third person at the scene, they could not establish a double murder. The medical examiner's and autopsy reports were meticulous in describing the gunshot wounds; they did not come to a definitive conclusion as to whether or not Leaman's wound was self-inflicted, but the M.E. put it down as a probable suicide. That was good enough for me. And it would remain good enough, as long as we weren't faced with a witness popping up later to say there was somebody else at the Fore-And-Aft that morning.

†

"Collins. Have you forgotten?" It was the Undersigned, the most pompous partner in our firm, who never referred to himself as "I" or "me" but as "the Undersigned" in his correspondence. He had slicked-back fair hair and a perpetually irritated expression on his face. He was vibrating impatiently at my door in his imitation English suit of clothes. Our founding partner raised a condescending eyebrow at the Undersigned's back as he passed by in his real, and threadbare, English tweeds, which he had probably brought over with him when he immigrated in 1945.

I had indeed forgotten. It was Thursday, April 18, the day my firm was taking me to lunch to celebrate what they considered to be my finest achievement. I had just been named a Queen's Counsel. I hadn't even applied for the honour; the Undersigned had. He — his real name was Vance Blake — had taken it upon himself to cobble together my curriculum vitae, and some kind words from references, and submit an application on my behalf after shoving the forms on my desk and having me sign them when I was distracted. I had promptly forgotten all about it. But Blake had not. In his view, the more Queen's Counsels the firm had on its letterhead, the better.

So we all trooped down the hill to the waterfront, to Wigginstaff's, a self-consciously upmarket bar and dining room favoured by certain members of the Nova Scotia Barristers' Society. We took up all the tables overlooking the harbour and ordered drinks. I watched through the window as a sailboat bobbed along like a toy on the choppy water; it was dwarfed by a massive container ship heading up the harbour to the Ceres terminal. Once the pre-luncheon drinks were in our hands, a toast was raised to me.

"To Montague M. Collins, Q.C."

This was met by the insufferable "hear, hear," which I always associated with mutton-chopped Victorian pomposity. "Speech, speech," they chanted.

I rose to respond: "Our clients come to us because they need a voice. We speak for them in places where they otherwise might fail to be heard or understood. I stand in that proud tradition and I am humbled by the opportunity to do so." I hoped to be even more full of shit when I got wound up. "When the taxman cometh to take his pound of flesh," I declaimed to another round of "hear, hears" from the solicitors in our tax department, "our clients want to be assured —"

"— that they won't have to pay one red cent!" a partner called out.

I continued: "— that their tax dollars are not being squandered on yet more ill-advised attempts by the state to come down on the backs of the citizens and to further grind down —"

"Risk-takers and entrepreneurs who are the engine of the economy in this country, and who are fettered at every turn by —"

I ignored Vance Blake's corporate passion and soldiered on: "— further grind down the poor, the disenfranchised, the marginal and the crazed, those who come before the criminal justice system, propelled there by the misfortune of their birth and their assigned place at the bottom of the heap in our society. Guilty they may be, in the eyes of the law, yet it falls to us, Stratton Sommers, Barristers and Solicitors, to implore the courts for understanding and mercy. Can any one of us, in his or her most private moments, honestly say he has not, at some anguished moment of his life, shared the murderous fury of my recent client who took an axe to the pale and trembling flesh of —"

"We don't want to hear it!"

"Sit down, Collins!"

"I cannot possibly say how much it means to me to have the might and prestige of Stratton Sommers behind me as I go to the wall for these hapless denizens of the criminal courts. To be honoured by you as I am today —"

Rowan Stratton had turned a deaf ear to the protests of certain members of the firm when I was hired to set up a criminal law practice. It was still, evidently, a sore point for some.

"You're an asshole, Collins," Blake hissed as I passed his table at the end of my speech.

"It's an honour and a privilege to be on your enemies list, Vance," I replied, sending a wink in the direction of Monique LeBlanc, who shared my view of the Undersigned.

I sat down beside Monique and picked up my beer. She leaned over and asked: "Who's going to defend you, Monty, the day we find Vance slumped over in the boardroom with a knife in his back?"

"I bear him no ill will."

"I cannot believe the way you let all this run off your back."

"You have distinguished yourself," my very British senior partner muttered from my other side, "as a cad and a blackguard among your partners. For that I salute you."

We finished our celebratory lunch and walked up Salter Street to our office, just around the corner on Barrington. We occupied the seventh floor of a ten-storey glass box recently erected between two old ornate buildings that I much preferred to ours. The firm used to be in one of them, a four-storey Italianate building that I admired; unfortunately the firm had moved to its more modern quarters just before I joined up. The new building struck a jarring note in this block of nineteenth-century structures.

†

I wanted to devote my time to the Leaman case when I got back, but first I had to deal with my other clients. The first in line was Yvette, a hooker and crack addict who was charged with assaulting another woman in a fight over a boyfriend. She was an old client from my Nova Scotia Legal Aid days. She couldn't pay my regular fee, so my partners were never happy when her name came up at the office. We would meet in court the next morning. I went over the statements given by patrons of the Miller's Tale, the bar where the fight had occurred, looking for any indications I could find that Yvette was acting in self-defence when she hit Doris Pickard over the head with a chair.

At nine on Friday morning I was standing with my client outside the provincial courthouse on Spring Garden Road. It was muggy and warm. Grotesque stone faces, fanged and wild, looked out at us from the facade of the Victorian court building. Yvette was wearing purple leggings that might have fit my eight-year-old daughter. A black tube top gave partial cover to her emaciated upper body. Her hair, a startling orangey blonde, was long in back and short in front, the bangs and sides curled away from her lined, olive-skinned face. She took a desperate drag of her cigarette as if, in the unhappy event of a conviction, she might not be able to score any drugs, including nicotine, in jail.

"So, Yvette, before we get in there —"

"Why-vette, not Eve-ette. How many times do I gotta say it for you, Monty?" she asked in a weary voice.

"All right, Why-vette." Why, as in why had her mother chosen the name "Yvette" if she did not even know how to pronounce it? But we were far from Yvette's christening day now.

"Doris's statement says you came at her with the chair because Bo was going to stay with her instead of you when he was released from the Correctional Centre."

"Bullshit! She said Bo got a tat on his arm with her name on it when he was inside. I said she was a lyin' slut, and she held up a bottle of Blue Typhoon and was gonna hit me." She barely got through her story; she seemed ready to fall asleep on her feet. Caution: coming down from this medication may cause drowsiness.

"Don't fade on me, Why-vette. This bottle of — what did you say it was?"

"Blue Typhoon. She was gonna bash me in the head with it, so I hit her in self-defence."

"Right. Let's go inside."

When the trial got under way, one of our witnesses, another hooker named Wanda Pollard, switched loyalties and backed up Doris's allegations. Yvette glared daggers at Wanda and repeatedly gave her the finger. I tried to undo the damage with my next witness, but Yvette had her own ideas of where the case should go. When she took the stand, she told a story completely different from the one she had given me. She decided, on her own, that a defence of drunkenness was her best legal strategy. Yvette did not deny that she swung the chair and smashed Doris in the face with it. But now she claimed she herself had guzzled the bottle of Blue Typhoon. After that, in a drunken rage, exacerbated by a rare medical condition that had not been disclosed until that moment, Yvette had lost it and attacked the other woman. On and on it went, a story I heard for the first time as I stood there poleaxed. Yvette was convicted and remanded into custody; sentencing would follow in a couple of months' time. I had to prepare for a bail hearing, so I clomped down the staircase to the basement cells, pressed the button, and waited for the sheriff to let me in.

I met with my client in a small room. But I didn't stay long. Her conviction, and her need for a hit of crack, had soured her mood. "You're no fuckin' good, Collins. You said you'd get me off. I want another lawyer. You're fired."

"What I said, Eve-ette, was that if the judge believed you and not Doris, your chances were good, but if the other version was more believable, you'd have to pack your jammies. Speaking of your story, Eve-ette, imagine my surprise when I heard it for the first time."

"You fuck off. You're fired. I want Saul Green."

I waved her off and headed for the door. I had planned to get a bite of lunch on Spring Garden Road but I decided to return to my office, grab Yvette's file, and deliver it personally to Green's office before she had time to phone, weeping with remorse, and hire me back. This happened all the time: client changing story or otherwise screwing up case, blaming lawyer, firing lawyer, calling to beg lawyer to represent him or her again. I liked to ship the file out before that pleading phone call, one less thing to worry about. I was known in some circles as the fastest courier service in Halifax.

But not fast enough this time. The message was waiting for me when I walked in. Could I call Yvette? She wanted to apologize and she had something to tell me. Well, she could work on her apology for a while in her cell.

†

I had to pick up an obscure legal text at the Sir James Dunn Law Library, so I drove to the law school on University Avenue. I collected my book, then steeled myself for an encounter with one of the professors at the law school.

"What now, Collins?" Maura MacNeil's brow was furrowed in a scowl.

"Did I catch you at a bad time? Again? Should I come back in, say, the year 2000 when you might be on an upswing?"

"Come back when you've taken the trouble to remember my schedule. I have a class in ten minutes. The way I always do this time on Friday. What are you doing here?"

"I was in the library and I was wondering if you'd had lunch."

"I plan to have lunch after my class. But what's that got to do with you?"

"That's just it. I don't want to have lunch at all. I think I'm eating too much lately and I figured if I stopped by here, two minutes with you would put me off my food. Mission accomplished."

Maura and I had two children together; we'd been separated for nearly five years and shared the kids week on, week off. She still lived in our old family home downtown on Dresden Row. I felt I had made more of an effort than she had to reconcile our many differences. Now, as I hovered unwelcome at the threshold of her office, I wondered for the thousandth time why I didn't just pack it in.

"You're not eating too much," she said. "You're drinking too much. I'm the one who's going overboard with eating. I've gained ten pounds."

Maura was one of those very attractive women somewhat above society's ideal of the perfect size for females. A wide mouth, upturned grey eyes, creamy skin, and shoulder length brown hair. Normally she didn't give a damn about her size so maybe she had gained a few pounds. She looked fine to me. "You look fine to me."

"Thank you."

"What do you mean, I'm drinking too much?"

"I don't know how else I can put it so you can understand, Collins, but let me try. Whenever I've seen you lately, you have a glass in your hand, which you raise to your lips and —" she put her right hand up and mimed someone tipping a glass of liquid down his throat "— guzzle. And that glass always seems to contain, or so I suspect, the chemical compound designated variously as ethanol, ethyl alcohol, or just alcohol, chemical formula: CH_3CH_2OH."

"You rarely see me, so how would you know?"

"I know. The fact of the matter is your drinking has increased ever since you started hanging around with Brennan Burke."

"Am I hearing you right? I must be the only man in the world being castigated by his wife for spending too much time with a priest!"

"I'm just saying you've —"

"Had enough. I'm taking the kids to the Rankins concert. Don't wait up."

"You got tickets?"

"I got tickets."

Silence, as she considered the consequences of being obnoxious to me once again. Then: "How many tickets?"

"Three." She knew I was lying about the number, but I didn't care. I would give the fourth to somebody else.

I retreated from her office but decided that, since I was at the law school, I might as well do a bit of research into the possible liability of the Baird Centre. I went back to the library and gathered some typical medical malpractice cases. Then, with an eye to Graham Scott and the dependency claims of his children, I looked for cases in which people successfully sued institutions for harm done by inmates who were released when they should have been kept inside. I started with a well-known case in which some Borstal boys in England escaped from custody, boarded a yacht, and soon thereafter rammed into another vessel. The question was whether the Home Office and its Borstal officers owed a duty of care to the owners of the damaged boat. Lord Reid considered an American case in which it was held that such a heavy responsibility should not be imposed on the New York State prison system. Distancing himself from the skittish Americans, His Lordship stated that "Her Majesty's servants are made of sterner stuff," and could bear up very well under the duty of care owed to the plaintiffs. I hoped our local courts would feel the same way about the Baird Treatment Centre. But Corey Leaman had not escaped; he had been released. I would hit the books again another day. Before I left, I checked the indexes to see if there were any reported cases in which the Baird Centre was named as a defendant. There was one: a visitor had sprained her ankle when she tripped in a depression in the front walkway, and was awarded two thousand dollars in damages. I went from the library to the Law Courts building, where I looked in the records for any recent litigation in the works. The only case coming up against the Baird Centre was a claim by a contractor who had not been paid for repairs to the building's foundation. Nobody had ever sued the centre for anything resembling malpractice.

†

Before I could go to hear the Rankins, I had to put in an appearance at a house-warming party at Ross Trevelyan's. He had recently moved from a duplex on Lawrence Street to a much grander abode on Beaufort Avenue in the city's south end. The story was that his wife, Elspeth, had put an offer on the place when Ross was out of town, confident that Ross would fall in love with it the way she had. In my experience, men did not fall in love with houses with the same passion women did, especially when those dwellings cost four times as much as the past digs. But Ross must have been impressed by the place, because here they were.

It was big, multi-gabled and vaguely Swiss in style. A nice residence anywhere, a very expensive one on this street. Mrs. Trevelyan greeted me at the door. "I don't believe we've met. I'm Elspeth."

"Monty Collins."

Elspeth was tall and slim with a shoulder-length blonde pageboy. She peered behind me. "Are you alone?"

I followed her gaze then turned back. "Quite alone. We're safe now."

"Ha ha. You're the one who does criminal law, do I have that right?"

"I'm the one."

"No offence, but I'm glad Ross doesn't do that kind of work anymore. He did criminal cases when he articled. That was back before I knew him, but every once in a while we'll be downtown and some really tough character will say hi to him. We go to St. George's Anglican — you know, the round church — and there are a couple of prostitutes who hang around that area. If we go to a function at night, we hear: 'Hey, Ross!' It's embarrassing, let me tell you. Did the firm ever think of phasing out the criminal practice?"

"They're just phasing it in, actually. Or they have been since I arrived a few years ago."

"I see."

"Are you going to phase me out or let me in?"

"Oh! I'm sorry. Come in, come in."

I stepped into the foyer and then the living room, where I spied Ross, red-faced and sweating, working at some sort of gadget by the large stone fireplace.

"What are you doing there, Ross?"

"Oh, hi, Monty. I'm trying to get this fireplace insert to work but I'm not having much luck."

"Just as well. It's too warm for a fire anyway."

"I know, but she wants it. Looks homey. You know how it is." He shrugged and went back to his labours.

"Ross, honey, Daddy said there's an easier way to do that. Don't you remember?"

"No, I don't."

She turned to me. "My father says Ross finds the hardest way to do everything. So, what would you like first, Monty?"

"A beer would be good."

"Oh, right, of course. But I meant would you like a tour of the upstairs, or the main floor? Everyone else is up in the master bedroom."

"Perhaps we shouldn't interrupt."

"No, no, I meant they're just having a look around. Oh, good. Renée. This is Monty Collins. He's one of Ross's partners at Stratton Sommers. This is my sister, Renée. Why don't you take Monty upstairs and show him around?"

Renée seized me by the elbow and led me towards the stairs. We met Rowan Stratton coming down. Stratton was no stranger to fine houses. "The woman whisked me upstairs before I even had a chance to greet young Trevelyan," he said. "And I haven't caught so much as a whiff of Scotch."

Rowan's wife, Sylvia, descended the stairs behind him, looking pained. She whispered in my ear: "I've never seen such an elaborate nursery. One is always astonished at the array of products available for babies these days. Do they have triplets?"

"No kids. One rumoured to be on the way."

The sister was waiting for me on the stairs, so I followed. She took me gently by the hand and drew me towards the sound of other voices. Surely it was only my imagination, but I thought for a moment she made a quick check of my ring finger, which had been bare ever since Maura and I had separated.

By the time a beer found its way into my hand I downed it with what must have looked like unseemly haste, and made my excuses to the host and hostess.

†

When I pulled up at my old house on Dresden Row I could see my daughter, Normie, staring out at me from the living room window. Her real name is Norma, after the heroine of the opera by that name, but don't ever call her that; she answers only to Normie. My son, Tommy Douglas, is more than content with his name. My wife decided to call our son after the leader of the first socialist government elected in North America. I was a fan of Douglas too. He was a great wit and, because of him and his introduction of medicare, I didn't have to pay whopping medical bills for the birth of my children. Tom joined my daughter at the window, and I waved. The grey wooden house had two storeys and an attic with Scottish dormers. Every time I saw the place I felt a pang of regret that I no longer lived there. The kids came out, with their mother at their heels. All three piled into the car for the Rankins concert. I raised a questioning eyebrow, and my wife just smiled. When we arrived at the Metro Centre I handed the kids their tickets, and they bolted ahead.

"And how is it that you are at my side this evening?" I asked her.

"Easy."

Right. She knew that any excursion with our son and daughter would not be shared with another woman, if there was another woman in my life, which my wife always believed there was. So I would have offered the fourth ticket, if there was a fourth ticket, to a friend. First guess would be Brennan Burke.

"Burke just rolled over for you and gave up his ticket?"

"I know every line of every song the Rankins ever did. Brennan Burke doesn't. I promised him another evening of entertainment in return."

"Oh? And what kind of entertainment would that be?"

"There's no need for such an insinuating tone of voice. My usual brand of entertainment, involving me prancing around simpering and naked in a pair of shag-me shoes, is just not on for him, is it? Given that he's a celibate priest."

"How come that brand of entertainment was never on for me?"

"I guess that's because you're not one of the sailors in port with the NATO fleet. So, as I was saying, I'll just have to think up something else for Father Burke. Like dinner at home with the kids. Or lunch at home with the kids. Or a movie and popcorn at home with the —"

"All right, I get it."

The opening band was warmly received, the Rankins were great, and Maura was directing the occasional comment into my ear as if we had never been apart. At intermission I asked what everybody wanted, and I headed out to the canteen to stand in line.

Old Monty wasn't doing too badly at all. Maura couldn't possibly know how I treasured these rare nights when we went out as a family. Well, maybe it was time I laid it on the line. Gave it another try. If we made an effort to get over the mistakes we had both made, the recriminations and resentment we had each generated in the other, and if we were both willing to start all over . . . I would make the first move. Apologizing for things I had done, forgiving her for things she had done. Maybe as early as tonight.

"Monty! How are you doing, babe?" No! Not this, not now. I turned to the voice and found myself grabbed by the belt and pulled towards —

"Bev. Hi."

Bev drew me closer and said: "I've missed you, Monty. In more ways than I can say here in a public place. But I'm willing to ditch the lump I'm with if you'd like to spend intermission out back with your pants around your knees. And that's just for —"

"I hate to be the one to break this to you. Whoever you are." My wife had appeared with appalling timing. She went on: "But the last time Collins stood outside with his pants down, it was thirty below zero, he was too drunk to know the difference and, well, he's just not the man he used to be. Now, if you'll excuse me, I'll escort the poor thing back to his seat."

Bev was a woman I had spent a few raucous nights with, usually following a night of blues with my band, Functus. Due to my stupidity,

Maura had walked in on us one day in my living room. That day, I thought things couldn't get any worse.

Bev released her grip on my belt and melted back into the crowd, leaving me to fall into the abyss and keep falling for all eternity. I had simply ceased to exist, as far as my wife was concerned. She did not speak to me or look in my direction for the rest of the night. Tom and Normie were intent on the show and didn't seem to notice. They gabbed all the way home, covering the frigid silence in the front seat. They got out in a noisy cacophony of "thanks" and "see you soon." MacNeil slipped away without a sound.

†

I was still brooding over my latest marital fiasco when I pulled up outside the Halifax County Correctional Centre on Saturday morning. Yvette had a coy smile on her face when I sat down to speak to her in one of the lawyer–client meeting rooms. "I'll do something for you if you do something for me, Monty."

"I don't bargain with my clients, Eve-ette."

"Why-vette."

"Why-vette. If I came all the way out here, I'm going to do your bail hearing, so there's no need for bargaining. We'll have the hearing on Monday, and you'll be out. Now, should I even ask what you were offering to do for me, or should we move on to discuss your bail application?"

"You don't even want to hear what I got to say?"

"Go ahead." I hoped it would not take long, so I could get home.

"I know somethin' nobody else knows."

Yeah, whether the mayor likes to be the lamb or Little Bo Beep when he —

"I know somebody who was there when that murder happened."

"What murder?"

"At the Fore-And-Aft."

Not a muscle in my body moved. I stared at her.

"You know, when that guy got shot."

"Two guys were shot."

"The Leaman guy."

Leaman? It was Graham Scott who got shot: he took two bullets to the head. Leaman put a bullet in his own brain — I would not have described that as getting shot. "That was a murder and suicide," I said. Did she know I was involved in the case? I doubted it. Ross Trevelyan's was the only name that had been mentioned in the media, as far as I knew.

"Yeah, right." Yvette snickered. "The *suicide*."

"That's the way the medical examiner saw it."

"That's 'cause the medical examiner wasn't down on his knees in the parking lot doing some young dude when Leaman got iced."

Oh, Christ. What was she saying? She sat back, triumphant, arms folded against her scrawny chest. I took a deep breath.

"Tell me."

She made a "maybe I will, maybe I won't" gesture, but I sat tight. It wasn't long in coming.

"That bitch Wanda is gonna be sorry she fucked with me at my trial. She thinks nobody knows she was there. But she didn't count on me doin' my duty as a good citizen, just like she done on the witness stand. Wanda was with this guy —"

"Who was the guy?"

"Beats me. Anyway she was doin' him around the back of the bar. They just finished when they heard voices and then a gunshot. The guy she was with zipped up his pants and took off. She vamoosed in the other direction. She didn't want to see nuthin'. And didn't want nobody seein' her. She was on probation for a whole lot of charges, and she was breachin' her probation just bein' out at that time of night. Let alone bein' high. Eckcetera, eckcetera."

"Let me get this straight. What exactly did she hear?"

"Guys hollerin' and a gunshot."

"A shot or shots?"

"A shot, I think she said."

There was one bullet in Leaman, two in Scott. Did this mean Leaman was shot first and Scott appeared some time later? Or did Wanda hear the first round fired at Scott? If so, what accounted for the gap between the shots?

"And you said guys were shouting?"

"Yeah."

"What were they saying?"

"I don't fucking know. I wasn't there."

"What did Wanda say?"

"Just that they were hollerin' and then blam! End of conversation."

"What time was this?"

"Late. Three, four in the morning." She fixed me with a slightly wall-eyed gaze. "So I figure the killer don't know there was a witness. Witness Wanda. And she sure as hell ain't talkin'. And there's the john, too. Whoever he was."

"How do you know this?"

"She was bombed one night and started blubbering to me about it. Scared the killer knew she was there and would come and get her. Guess she got lucky. 'Cause she's still walkin' around. Let's hope for her sake her luck don't run out."

Chapter 2

This is the day I'm gonna roll the dice.
— Mel "Snake Eyes" Rooney

The conversation haunted me all the way home. I decided not to add to the obvious stresses in Ross Trevelyan's life until I had to. He was counting on this case as an account receivable, and as a beacon sending out the signal that Ross was a lawyer who specialized in the potentially lucrative business of plaintiff-side personal injury litigation. I would leave him in peace for now and do a bit of investigating on my own.

First thing Monday morning, I retrieved the file from Ross's office and read through it again, trying to find a starting point for a quiet probe into the shooting. The police had canvassed people who worked at the bar, but nobody had seen or heard anything. The shooting happened after hours. None of the staff had seen Leaman or Scott in the place that night. Nobody in the file could, or would, identify any connection between the two men. If either of them had been selling drugs to the other, there was no reference to that in the material we had before us. There was a police report indicating that Leaman and Scott had never been incarcerated in the same institution at the same time. Leaman had spent considerable time in the addiction treatment centre; Scott had never been treated there. I scribbled a note about Wanda Pollard being a possible witness. But something else struck me while I was reading through the file: the one piece of hard evidence that might be traceable was the gun. The Luger was an antique. It had almost certainly been stolen. The police had tried various gun collectors but had not found the owner. I wondered whether it was a souvenir brought over from Germany after World War Two.

I picked up the phone and dialled. "Up for a game of darts tonight, Burke?"

"Darts? You're at loose ends for something to occupy yourself, I'm thinking."

"A beer then. I want to head out to the Legion for a bit of detective work. Thought I'd start with the one on Cunard Street."

"And what do you hope to find out at the Legion?"

"I'd like to trace a piece of German weaponry. Namely the Luger that was used in the Fore-And-Aft shooting. I'm hoping to reassure myself this was really a suicide."

"I thought it was one of your partners who was doing the work on this."

"I'm doing a little sleuthing to convince myself we have a case. Ross is a true believer, if you'll pardon the expression. He sees gold within his grasp. I, however, tend to think *fortuna vitrea est; tum cum splendet frangitur.*"

"Is that you, Collins? I thought I heard someone speaking to me in the language most dear to my heart."

"Why should that surprise you? Have you heretofore regarded me as an unlettered buffoon?"

"Not at all, at all. So. Fortune is like glass; it glitters just at the moment of breaking. That's how you see your case?"

"That's how I see all my cases, Brennan. But, yes, I'm particularly suspicious of this one. I intend to investigate a little further."

"Ah. Come by and pick me up around nine-thirty. I'm giving a seminar at the theology school before then. High Christology in the Gospel of John. I didn't see your name on the registration list."

"So give me the crib notes."

"That would be a start. See you tonight. How were the Rankins?"

"The Rankins were great. You should have hung on to that ticket."

"Nah. You know how it is when MacNeil wants something."

"No, I don't actually. All I know is when she doesn't want something."

"Don't be telling me that. You banjaxed it again?"

"Later."

I had just put the phone down when Ross Trevelyan called, to remind me that we had a witness coming in. I picked up the file and headed for Ross's office. We chatted about other matters while we waited for the psychologist who had treated Corey Leaman at the Baird Centre. Ross's secretary brought him in, and we stood to greet him.

"Doctor Swail-Peddle? Nice to meet you. I'm Ross Trevelyan. This is my partner, Montague Collins."

"Hi. Call me Gareth."

I shook his hand. Gareth Swail-Peddle was short and slight with a small face nearly hidden by his salt and pepper beard. Tiny dark brown eyes were magnified by huge glasses. He sat in the chair beside mine, and relieved himself of a large canvas shoulder bag.

Ross sat behind his desk. "So. Gareth. Thanks for coming in. I'd normally say 'how can I help you?' but I guess in this case it's 'how can you help us?'"

"Well, let me be upfront with you, Ross. And Montague. I'm what you would call a disgruntled former employee! That's not always a positive indicator of credibility. True, I was unjustly dismissed from the Baird Centre, and my relationship with that organization is conflictual. But I'm here to tell the truth and do whatever I can to help the survivors of Corey's suicide."

"Monty and I are most appreciative, Gareth. What can you tell us about Corey?"

"Well, as you probably know, Corey was admitted to the facility on more than one occasion. He struggled with an addiction to cocaine and of course he had family issues as well. So many people do. During his most recent, and final, admission I was of the view that his recovery had not progressed to the point where he should have been discharged. Our director did not share my view."

"The director is Doctor Edelman?" I asked.

"That's right."

"And your position was what?"

"I am a clinical psychologist. I was on staff as a therapist."

"What happened?"

"Well, Corey's recovery was —"

"No," I interrupted again. "I mean, what happened with you? How did you end up leaving the centre?"

There was a quick tightening of the lips but, if Swail-Peddle was annoyed at the change of subject, he did not let on. "Doctor Edelman and I had what might be called a personality conflict. He is a fine psychiatrist. But he is very controlling. He could not accept that my treatment methods were as valid as his, and he made my situation there untenable. It's all for the better. I have opened my own practice, and the self-actualization I am able to achieve now is something I could never have achieved as a staff psychologist. So, as bitter as the parting was, I really should thank Edelman for his unintentional role in my self-fulfilment as a therapist! Back to Corey, though, it was Edelman who had the final say in discharging Corey prematurely from treatment. His methods were very orthodox; he failed to see that they were ineffective. Corey should have been admitted to our Phase Two program, which involves a much longer stay and a more intensive course of therapy. But no. Corey was out, and you know the result."

"I take it you'll have no trouble facing off against Doctor Edelman if and when this goes to court?" I asked, thinking that he probably lived for the day he could castigate the psychiatrist in a public forum.

Swail-Peddle smiled and held out his hands in a nothing-to-hide gesture. "No trouble. I won't conceal from you the fact that I was frustrated in my efforts to get a hearing before Doctor Edelman. Now perhaps I will. Though I imagine he will become quite unpleasant, through his own lawyer, if I challenge him in public."

"Yes, I would say the Baird Centre will mount a vigorous defence," Ross put in, "but we intend to counter it."

"I don't suppose you have any notes or a chart relating to Corey?" I asked. "The records would have stayed at the centre, I presume."

"His chart, his medication records, and so forth would still be on file at the Baird."

"We can subpoena those."

"But I believe I may have some notes of my own. I kept a diary and some of the entries may relate to Corey."

"If you could provide those, we'd appreciate it."

"I'll call and let you know what I've found. And if there's anything else I can do for Corey's family, don't hesitate to get in touch."

"So, what do you think?" Ross asked me when the psychologist had departed.

I leaned across his desk and said, *sotto voce*: "Maybe he pulled the trigger himself."

Ross reared back: "What are you saying?"

"You know what the police always say about overly helpful witnesses, people who insinuate themselves into the investigation."

"No. I don't."

"You should have kept up with criminal law, Ross. Cops always suspect people like that."

"But we're not in the business of suspecting people, are we, Monty? And neither are the police on this one; they're not looking for a killer. As for us, we are in the business of establishing that Leaman's *suicide*, and his regrettable decision to take Graham Scott down with him, was in fact the fault of the Wallace Rennie Baird Addiction Treatment Centre. And now we have Doctor Swail-Peddle."

"At least we can be fairly sure he's not using an alias. Name like that, he didn't make it up."

"Be serious, will you, Monty? We have the good doctor providing inside information that supports our case. He was utterly candid about his dispute with the centre. He has nothing to gain by helping us. I think we should be grateful."

"Nothing to gain but revenge against his former employer."

"Which he — again, candidly — admits will sour for him once he is forced to undergo cross-examination by the centre's counsel at trial."

"You're right. If he's on the level, his evidence will be very helpful indeed."

†

I drove downtown to St. Bernadette's that evening to pick up Brennan Burke for our excursion to the Legion. He was just getting out of his car when I pulled up. "Give me two minutes to get rid of this collar if we're going to be lifting a few." I told him to go ahead.

"How was the seminar?" I asked when he joined me in my car.

"Sure, it was brilliant. How could it be otherwise with myself at the head table? So, what exactly are you trying to find out?"

"If there are any genuine war veterans on hand, I'll be asking whether they know of someone who brought a Luger back with him." He looked skeptical. "It's worth a try. It's the only place I can think of to start."

The Cunard Street Legion, Branch 25, was noisy and full of smoke. I was surprised at the size of the crowd until I noticed a bunch of tables grouped together. A party of some sort. All the participants were a couple of decades short of WWII vintage. Burke and I went to the bar. A beer for me, a Jameson for him. The bartender was young, but I asked anyway: "Is there anybody here tonight who served in World War Two?"

"The only one I can see is Mrs. Dryden over there. She was with CWAC, Women's Army Corps."

I approached her table. She had the wrinkled face of a lifelong smoker; her cigarette burned forgotten in her hand as she perused the baseball scores in the *Chronicle Herald*. "Excuse me, Mrs. Dryden. I'm hoping to speak to someone who's a veteran of World War Two; the bartender pointed you out."

"I'm a veteran, yes. How can I help you?"

"I'm trying to find the owner of a German pistol, a Luger that was used in a shooting here in the city. The owner's not in any trouble; I suspect the gun was stolen. I thought it might have been brought back after the war, and it would sound familiar to somebody."

"Ha! Good luck, kiddo. I bet that would sound familiar to a lot of people. More than a few must have come over in forty-five. I wouldn't know; my war was in England."

"All right. Thanks anyway."

"You might try old Bill Groves, though. He's a collector."

"Where would I find him? Does he come in here?"

"He'd love to come in here. But he's in an oxygen tent in Camp Hill Hospital."

"Oh."

"Go and see him. Bill loves visitors. His family never goes near him."

"I will. Thank you."

"And don't go empty-handed. Bring him a pack of Craven A."

"For a man in an oxygen tent?"

"You young people are too serious about this stuff. Bill smokes in there all the time. What's he got to lose?"

An entire wing of the hospital if he blows it up, I thought, but kept it to myself. I thanked her again and joined Brennan at our table.

"She spent the war in England. But she gave me the name of somebody else."

"Good."

I would drop in to see Bill Groves. I also had to find Wanda Pollard and see whether Yvette's story checked out. I hoped it wouldn't, but I could not just sit on it. Prior to the Blue Typhoon affair, I had seen Wanda in court numerous times on drug and fraud charges, usually represented by Legal Aid and at least once by Ed Johnson. Perhaps he knew where she might be found. I took Burke on a detour on our way from the Legion.

Ed and his wife, Donna, lived in a condo on Coburg Road, a block away from the law school. I punched in his number and he came down to meet us in the lobby.

"You guys out on a tear? Or taking part in a second-hand smoke study?"

"We were at the Legion. The ones who didn't die in combat are being felled by nicotine poisoning."

"Legion, eh? Going anywhere now?"

"No, heading home. I have a question for you. You represented a hooker named Wanda at one time, didn't you?"

"Yeah, and I'm representing her again next month. Wanda the Wand Whacker." Brennan rolled his eyes.

"Any idea where I might find her?"

"You're not that desperate, are you, Collins? Good-looking guy like you? Speaking for myself, I'd rather —"

I cut him off: "Spare us the details of what you'd rather do."

"Livin' the blues," Johnson said, "that must be it. You weren't born on Tobacco Road or blinded by a brutal stepfather, so cruisin' hookers would be the —"

"I find him utterly convincing when I hear him play the blues,"

Burke put in, "so he's either lived the life at some point or he's able to identify wholly with those who have."

"Funny you should say that, Brennan. Of course maybe Collins got plastered one night and confessed to you about his road trip."

"His road trip."

"Right. Our Monty spent a year on the road with a band. Did you know that?"

"No."

Ed leaned towards Brennan and said in a mock-conspiratorial whisper: "Let's just say there are certain jurisdictions in the United States of America where Collins, or whatever he was calling himself during that episode in his life, is *persona non grata.*"

"Can it, Johnson. I was asking you about Wanda Pollard. I want to talk to the woman, that's all."

"What in the world do you want to talk to old Wanda about?"

"A case I'm working on."

"What case?"

"Just tell me where the woman lives, will you?"

"She works Hollis Street near Cornwallis Park. Lives close by, in a dive on Mitchell Street. Unless she's in a drug-induced coma somewhere, you'll eventually be able to pick her up."

Wanda was nowhere in sight when Burke and I cruised down Hollis Street. I decided to come back the next day and call at her building. Since we were in the neighbourhood, though, one thing we could do was check out the scene of the shootings. I couldn't remember the last time I had been inside the Fore-And-Aft. That may have been because it was long ago, or it may have been that I literally could not remember my time in there. It was that kind of joint. You didn't go there to sip Frascati and discuss the latest art film. You went there to get pie-eyed and watch the jaded strippers grinding away on the makeshift stage. Burke and I drove down to the tag end of Barrington Street, parked, and stepped out in the fog. We gazed over at the east side of the street. The Fore-And-Aft was a low yellow brick building with fortified plate-glass windows. Its main item of decor was a ship's wooden figurehead, a bikini-clad woman with cascades of golden curls, enormous lips and breasts, her face turned in a come-hither posture towards incoming patrons. Her aft end was bulky and rounded. She had a white sailor cap perched rakishly on her head, and somebody had painted extremely dilated pupils in her turquoise eyes.

"I didn't even know this place was here. Are we going in?" Burke asked. Even the Fore-And-Aft would be a cozy shelter from the fog that chilled our bones, but I didn't want to waste my time in there.

"No point. The place was closed when the shooting occurred."

The bodies were found in the parking lot at the side of the building. We walked around and saw that there was an extension, kind of like a back porch, at the end near the parking lot. Wanda could well have been servicing somebody on the other side of the porch, unseen by passersby. The only neighbouring buildings were the Wallace Rennie Baird Addiction Treatment Centre, the old Foundry Building, and some small businesses that were open only during the day. At this time of night the area where Leaman had been found was in shadows cast by large bright lights up the street. Scott's body had been farther out in the parking lot, beyond the shadowed area. I could see how someone bent on a murder-suicide would have felt confident that he could accomplish his aim in the dark hours of the morning without being interrupted. The only people who could have seen the event were night-owl patients or staff looking out the windows of the Baird Centre across the street. That may in fact have accounted for the choice of location, a point we would stress if our lawsuit survived the new information relayed to me by Yvette.

"Let's go across the street and take a look from there," I said to Burke.

The Baird Centre was a nondescript brick building constructed in the sixties for offices. I suspected the Baird people had been able to buy it on the cheap and renovate it to their own specifications. It was set back from the street with an optimistic little garden in front and a driveway running along the side. As soon as we set foot on the property a floodlight came on. I continued to the entrance, went up the front steps, and looked at the Fore-And-Aft. I could see nothing but blackness in the parking lot, which was well out of the floodlight's range. People on the upper floors may have been able to see a bit better, but I didn't think so.

"We're not going to learn anything here. Let's call it a night."

I could not keep Yvette's story to myself. If the shootings were murder, and if there was a witness, I had to inform the police. I would give it one more night, then I would call the investigating officer and give him the tip. But, as it turned out, I met up with the police sooner than planned. On Tuesday night, at the Hotel Nova Scotian, there was a fundraiser for the homeless. It was hosted by one of the city's most prominent do-gooders, Kenneth Fanshaw. Fanshaw had made some serious money in real estate development. And although — or perhaps because — he did not fancy street people lounging around outside his downtown condo developments, he had proposed the building of a new, fully-staffed shelter near the railway station and the hotel. This would complement shelters already in place in other parts of central Halifax.

Fanshaw was greeting people at the door. A short, compact man with smoothly coiffed dark brown hair, he was dressed down for the occasion. He was usually spotted in pricey European-cut suits; tonight he had on khaki pants, a comfy sweater, and loafers. His wife, Bunnie, was at his side, her perfect teeth bared in a grin, her short blonde hair sprayed up in birdlike tufts.

"Hey, there!" Kenneth beamed at me. "Your face is familiar, but —"

"Montague Collins."

"Come right on in, Montague, and lay your money down!"

"I'll do that."

There were casino tables and other booths run by various service clubs and organizations including, I saw, the Halifax Police Department. Fate had delivered me into their hands, so I headed in that direction. I greeted the uniformed cop at the booth, Phil Riley, and we engaged in a bit of banter. Then I delivered my message.

"I'm representing the families of Corey Leaman and Graham Scott in their suit against the Baird Treatment Centre. I received a tip that there may have been a witness. One of the local hookers. Ever come across a girl named Wanda?"

He nodded. "Wanda Pollard?"

"Yeah. If it checks out, this may in fact be what you guys suspected in the first place."

"This isn't shop talk, I hope, gents!" Fanshaw had come up behind me. "Phil," he said to the officer, "I have you down for a little spiel later on. About the police presence downtown, and their support for the project. That okay with you?"

"Sure, Ken. As you know, the chief had hoped to be here."

"I know. Family crisis. I wished him all the best. Don't tell him I said so, but you're a better after-dinner speaker than he is! Must be all that Irish blarney."

"Hey, you just let me know how thick you want me to lay it on."

"Thanks, Phil." Fanshaw turned away, and was greeted by another guest.

"So, Monty," Phil said, "Wanda may have seen something at the Fore-And-Aft. I'll get on that first thing tomorrow morning. Appreciate it, especially since —"

"Right. If it's true, it blows my case out of the water."

"I'll let you know what we come up with."

"Great. Thanks."

I made my way around the room, lost a few dollars at the crown and anchor, wrote out a cheque and was given a receipt by Bunnie, then stopped for a slice of pizza from a merchant I recognized from Blowers Street. I spied one of my law partners in rapt conversation with the owner of Wigginstaff's, the trendy, expensive bar and restaurant where I had made my maiden speech as a Q.C. Felicia Morgan laughed up in Chad Heath's face, touching him lightly on the arm with a hand still brown from a recent trip to Cuba. Felicia had a cloud of black hair and wide-set green eyes; she spent a fortune on her clothes. Another woman approached and hailed Heath. Felicia, without turning to acknowledge the newcomer, shifted her body so the other woman would have to make an obvious effort to break in to the conversation. I recalled that our firm had handled Heath's divorce from his second wife. He had managed, with our kind assistance, to hang onto the bulk of his assets. I avoided family law myself, but there were some who thrived on it.

Felicia caught sight of me. "Good evening, Monty! You know Chad, I'm sure."

I shook hands with him, and Felicia continued the introduction. "As you know, Chad is the proprietor of Wigginstaff's. I suspect you've spent a few nights there sampling his exquisite selection of wine and spirits."

"Caused a scene in there one night," I allowed.

"There are no scenes in Wiggie's, surely. Monty is a partner of mine at Stratton Sommers. He handles some pretty unsavoury characters, Chad. Nobody you know, I'm sure. I concentrate on mergers and acquisitions myself. Then, when I've had enough of that, I peel off the pinstripes, wriggle into my bikini, and jet off to the islands for two weeks of sand, salt and, well, whatever else comes up. Now, Chad, I heard that you —"

I eased myself out of earshot and headed for the door.

†

Bill Groves was out of his oxygen tent and sitting in a wheelchair when I appeared the next morning in his Camp Hill Hospital room. His hair was sparse, his face drawn and grey.

"Mr. Groves? My name is Collins. Monty Collins. I'm a lawyer working on a case, and I'm wondering if you can help me."

His head, body, and chair turned as one unit. "Eh?"

I repeated my introduction and got on with my question. "I was in the Legion looking for someone who fought in Europe in World War Two, and a Mrs. Dryden suggested I look you up. She asked me to give you these." I handed him a carton of cigarettes, and his eyes lit up.

"Thanks. How can I help you?"

"I'm hoping to learn something about the Luger P-08."

"The Luger? I have a few of those myself. What is it you want to know?"

"One of those pistols turned up at a crime scene. We think it was stolen, and we'd like to trace it."

"Better not be one of mine! Hand me that phone, will you, Colin?" I didn't correct him on the name. I picked up the telephone and set it on his right knee. "My son lives at my place now. Might as well, eh? I can't keep the place up if I'm stuck in here. He never paid any attention to my gun cabinet, but I'll get him to check. Christ knows, he's not doing anything else. Just sitting on his arse,

38

waiting for his ship to come in. Well, there's no ship coming in to Lower Sackville."

The old man stabbed at the numbers, and the phone teetered precariously on his knee. "Willie!" he shouted down the line. "Willie! Yes, fine, fine. Why wouldn't I be? Listen. Go down to my gun cabinet and tell me if all my — tell me how many Lugers are there. Never mind that, just do it for Christ's sake!" He held the receiver away from his ear and shook his head in irritation, then rolled his eyes as he endured the long wait for his son. This had become, instantly, the most important thing in his life. "What? Well, speak up! Yeah? Good. No reason." He banged the receiver down, and the phone clattered to the floor. I picked it up and replaced it on the table.

"They're all accounted for. I have four of them."

"Do you know any other veterans who have this kind of gun?"

"Not any more."

"Collectors?"

"Wayne Turpin is the only one I can think of. Out in Hatchet Lake. That doesn't mean there aren't collectors out there with Lugers, just means I don't know them."

"Where were you in the war, Bill?"

"I was one of the Water Rats! Bet you never heard of them, eh, kid?"

"Scheldt Estuary, 1944."

"Well, well, well! And do you know where we got that name?" I did. "Ever hear of a fellow by the name of Monty, Colin?"

"I've heard of a fellow named Field Marshall Bernard Montgomery."

"Good old Monty! He gave us the name, you know, the Water Rats. So, are you a military buff?"

"Can't say I'm up on the military, but I'm a history buff. So, were you there right through until the liberation?"

"I sure was, and I never met finer people than the Dutch. The welcome they gave us, you can't imagine."

"Tell me about it."

"Well, when we went through the streets —"

"No, go back. Clearing the Scheldt."

I was there for two hours. Spellbound.

There were other things I should have been doing, but they struck me as irredeemably dull after listening to Bill. So I cranked up Dutchie Mason on the stereo and went for a drive, west on Quinpool Road through the Armdale Rotary and out through the countryside to Hatchet Lake. I eventually found a shabby brown wooden house with a built-in garage. A ferocious-looking black dog planted itself in front of the garage door and barked, baring its fangs. A man with a shaven head, a goatee, and tinted aviator glasses came out of the house.

"Help you?"

I opened the car door a crack and set my left foot on the asphalt driveway.

"Don't worry about Biff; he's all talk." How often had I heard that? The man turned to the dog and bellowed something at it; the dog sat and panted.

I approached the garage and patted the dog on the way by. "Nice kitty," I crooned. The aviator glasses turned and glinted at me, as if to say: *What kind of nutbars are coming out from that city now?*

Turpin had two Lugers of his own; they were still in place, and he didn't know who else owned a Luger P-08.

†

I was at Video Difference that night, picking up a couple of movies to watch with my daughter, Normie, and I noticed a new National Film Board production about Canada's role in the liberation of the Netherlands in 1945. I tried to remember whether Bill Groves had a VCR in his room. I didn't think so, but surely there was one available in the hospital. It was a seven-day rental so I decided to get it. Normie and I watched our shows, and bloated ourselves with popcorn.

I stopped by Camp Hill Hospital the next morning. Bill was lying on his bed, staring at the ceiling, when I arrived.

"Morning, Bill."

He turned and looked at me blankly for a few minutes, then wheezed: "Hi, kid."

"I brought you something."

"Oh, yeah? What?"

"A new documentary on Holland. Would you like me to ask somebody to set it up for you? No hurry. It doesn't have to be back till next week."

"Sure."

"I checked with Turpin about the pistols, but no luck."

"The Lugers, right. That's too bad."

"When you brought those guns over here, did you have to —"

"Not guns. Gun." He paused to take a few desperate breaths. "I only brought one over myself."

"Is that right? I thought you had several of them."

"Yeah, I do. But that's because I bought them off other guys."

"Oh. Other soldiers."

"Yeah. Frank MacInnis, Archie Campbell, another fellow I can't remember now. MacInnis traded for another piece I had. Campbell sold me one. He had two. Used to twirl them on his fingers and aim them like in the westerns. 'Stick em up, pardner,' he'd say with a German accent. What a card, old Archie." Bill went into a fit of laughter, which exacerbated his breathing difficulties to the point where I considered calling a nurse. But he recovered. "Dead now, him and Frank. Archie died back in the seventies, Frank just last year. Dropped dead in his driveway. Nobody even knew he was sick. Poor old Frank."

"Campbell," I asked him, "wasn't he the father of Darren Campbell?"

"Who?"

"Darren Campbell, the lawyer. Everybody called him Dice. Was Archie his father?"

"Yeah, the son was a lawyer. Full of piss and vinegar, that kid. A bit of a bad actor, caused Archie and the wife to pull their hair out sometimes. But at least he wasn't a deadbeat, sitting on his arse all day collecting pogie."

"Bill, I'm going to leave this video and I'll ask one of the nurses about playing it for you. I'll come by to pick it up next week. See you then."

"Sure. Thanks, Colin."

Darren "Dice" Campbell was a bit of a legend in legal and party circles in Halifax. He was a couple of years younger than I was, which would have made him forty-two if he hadn't leapt to his death from his tenth-floor office back in 1985. If he had inherited his father's Luger, somebody might remember it. I called Ed Johnson. His secretary told me he was out of the office, and he had a trial at the provincial courthouse in the afternoon.

Johnson was slouched against the wall of the courtroom when I arrived. He looked hungover.

"Ed. You're not a well man."

"A long night of booze, smoke, and bad cards. I get the shakes just thinking about it. Maybe I'll plead my guy guilty and go home for a snooze."

"You might be doing him a favour."

"For sure. So, what's up?"

"You knew Dice Campbell, didn't you?"

"What do you mean?"

"What do you mean, what do I mean? You knew the guy, right?"

"Didn't everybody?"

"Well, didn't you do some cases with him?"

"Yeah, a couple."

"You guys did some partying together?"

"Early on."

"Early on in what?"

"I mean Dice's parties got a little, well, I don't know. I wasn't there."

"You're not making any sense, Johnson. Maybe your client should throw himself on the mercy of the court before it's too late."

"It's just that, yeah, Dice and I and some other people used to drink and party together once in a while but then I heard the parties got a little out of hand."

"And a blushing wallflower such as yourself would not want to be present for anything too *outré*." *Or you wouldn't want your wife to know you were there.* "But it's not Dice's party escapades I'm interested in."

I thought I could read relief in his thin, pallid face. "So, what's all this about Campbell?"

"Did he have a gun?"

42

"Whoa! Where did that come from?"

"Just, do you know whether he ever had a gun?"

"He did have a gun. Or I heard he did. Dicey all looped up, waving a gun around. I was just getting over the shakes and now I have to deal with an image like that."

"What kind of gun was it?"

"How the fuck would I know? Do I look like some kind of gun goon?"

"You do, actually, now that I think of it."

"Well, I'm not."

"But you'd know a handgun from a long, pointy thing like a rifle or a shotgun."

"What I heard, it was a handgun. No idea what kind. Why this interest in Campbell and his weaponry?"

"The Leaman case. The weapon was an old German pistol, a Luger. Dice Campbell's father had a Luger that he brought over from the war."

"I gotta go, Collins. You're making even less sense than I am. Tramaine?" Johnson had spotted his client. "Get rid of that headgear and divest yourself of all that gold. Lose the pager. We're claiming you're *not* a drug dealer. Remember? *Not* a drug dealer." Johnson waved me off and advanced on his client.

So Dice Campbell had owned a gun. It may or may not have been his father's Luger. Until I learned otherwise, I would proceed on the assumption that it was. That left me with a big coincidence: a murder-suicide effected by the same type of German handgun that had been owned by someone who had also, a few years back, committed suicide. Of course, Campbell had not used the gun to kill himself. Why not? I couldn't recall any questions being raised about the lawyer's death, and I had no reason to raise any now, but it did strike me as odd. And I wanted more information about Dice Campbell's gun.

†

Mavis Campbell was a real case. Until that Thursday afternoon I had known Dice Campbell's widow only by reputation. Now I was sitting across from her in the bar of the Holiday Inn on Robie

Street. We were at one of the low tables along the bar's enormous windows overlooking the Halifax Commons. She was obviously a regular; when I called her she said: "I assume you know where to find me when the five o'clock whistle blows." She was already in place, with a double Scotch in front of her, when I arrived. I ordered a beer.

"So. Mavis. I'll try to explain why you might be able to help with this murder-suicide. You didn't want to meet in my office."

"Do you keep a bottle of Glenfiddich in your desk drawer?"

"Used to, but I just couldn't keep it in stock."

"Yeah, that's what I figured." She sipped her drink, and sipped it again.

The widow was about five feet four inches tall, with a hefty build that must have been voluptuous a few years back. Mavis's hair was an unlikely shade of red and was pouffed to look as if it had been blown by the wind. Her eyes were done up with gobs of mascara, her large mouth painted a fire-engine red. She had an elaborate scarf draped over her shoulders.

"I know who you are," she announced, after lighting up a smoke and appraising me for a few moments. "You used to play in a band with Ed Johnson and those guys. Blues, right? I used to go listen to you sometimes with Dice, at the Flying Shag." That was the nickname for a dive called the Flying Stag, where my band used to have a weekly gig. "We were usually pissed by the time you came on, but I think you were good."

"Yeah, our band is called Functus. We still play, at least for ourselves."

"Functus, that's it. Some legal word. What's it mean, anyway?"

"It comes from *functus officio*, which means that a judge is without further authority or legal competence because he's finished with the case. But we just liked the sound of it."

"Okay. I thought it was Fucked Us. For years. But, as I say, I was piss drunk every time I was at the Shag. You always wore faded jeans and worn-out T-shirts. You were really cute. Still are. You were finishing law school when Dice started. Yeah, it's coming back to me now. You married?"

"Well . . ."

"Yeah, right, never mind. Dickie!" She called to the bartender without turning around. "Did somebody come in and break your arms when I wasn't looking?"

"Coming right up, babe."

"What do you do, Mavis?" I asked her, when Dickie departed after delivering her fresh drink. "Where do you work?"

"I'm a fed. Tax auditor."

I tried not to show my surprise but I was obviously unsuccessful. She looked at me, laughed, and raised her glass before downing half her Scotch.

I decided to get to the point before it was too late. "I was just wondering about Dice."

"Weren't we all!"

"Did he have a gun?"

"Oh, yeah, he had a gun. I was a little worried about it, that we might be in a fight some time and it might escalate to armed conflict. With me unarmed."

"You were seriously worried?"

"Well, not really."

"So he had a gun. What kind was it, do you know?"

"Something his dad took off the Hun during the war. A Luger, I think it was."

"Where is it now?"

"I haven't a clue. Why?"

"You don't have it."

"No. Why?"

"Because a gun just like it turned up at the scene of a murder-suicide I'm looking into."

"Really. Well, I never saw it again, after . . ."

"After he died?"

"Yeah. I don't know what happened to it. He kept it in a drawer in his office. Brought it out once in a while to use as a prop at party time." Here, she let out a loud squawk of laughter. "Pointed it at people as a joke."

"Was it loaded?"

"Yeah, at least sometimes it was, because one night he fired it at the wall of his office. The bullet's probably still there."

"His office? Why?"

She gave an elaborate shrug. "Who knows?"

"Well, were there people with him at the time?"

"Couple of friends. We stopped in there after the bars closed."

"You say you never saw the gun after your husband died."

"No. I never found it when I cleaned out his things. It wasn't in the house and it wasn't in the office."

"Can you remember when you last saw it?"

"Oh, yeah. This office wall performance was shortly before he died. Maybe a couple of days before."

"So the gun went missing between then and the time he died."

"Must have."

"Did you report it stolen?"

"No, I didn't know if it was stolen or if he gave it away or what. And I didn't give a shit one way or the other."

I had to wonder about the timing: the gun disappearing just around the time of his death. He certainly didn't die of gunshot wounds, but perhaps there was some question about his suicide after all. I might as well ask his widow.

"When you heard about Dice's suicide, where were you?"

"I was standing right behind him going 'ha ha ha, it's all mine now!' Asshole!"

"Who?"

"Who what?"

"Who's an asshole?"

"Dice!"

"You and your husband didn't get along?"

She looked at me as if I were demented. "Get along? Who gets along? Do you get along with your wife?"

She was asking the wrong guy. Or the right one. "There were problems in your marriage, then."

"Depends what you mean by problems. We fought. A lot of pricey china got smashed. He whored around behind my back. I cheated on Dice to get back at him but I passed out with the guy still on top of me. But what the hell? I liked old Dice; he was a few laughs."

"When you heard about the suicide, did that make sense to you? Did you think he would take his own life?"

She shrugged. "Why not?"

"Let's look at *why*. Were you aware of any reason he would have wanted to end it all?"

"He had money troubles, big time. That would be the only thing that would push Dice over the edge. It wouldn't be a lost love, or a guilty conscience, or anything like that. But money would do it. If anything would."

"What was the source of his money problems?"

"What do you think?" I didn't answer so she continued. "It all went up his nose. Or he gambled it away. He mortgaged our house without telling me; took some chick in to forge my signature. I let him have it when I got wind of that. What a jerk."

"Did Dice have any enemies?"

"Enemies?" She turned towards the bar. "Dickie! I'm going to need an IV here to replace my fluids if you don't hop to it!"

"On its way, Mave!"

"You have to keep these guys on their toes. So, Monty, you think somebody pushed Dice off that balcony. Who would have done that?"

"Well, you say he had a big cocaine habit. And serious gambling debts. That opens up a few possibilities."

She waved my speculations away with a bejewelled hand. "That was just for fun. He always came up with money for his coke. And as for his gambling debts, nobody was coming around to break his legs. He knew which creditors to pay first! Nobody cared about his lack of money but Dice himself."

"How was his law practice going?"

"Down the toilet."

"It was a one-man practice, right?"

"It was a no-man practice. He was a good lawyer but he just let it slide."

"Do you think he ever did anything desperate in relation to his law practice?"

"Like what?"

"Like dipping into his trust fund, his client's money, to cover gambling debts?"

"Not that I know of. But he wouldn't have told me anyway."

"So, no problems with the Bar Society? An investigation or any-thing of that nature?"

"The only investigation he was ever subject to was a raid on one of our parties!"

"Really."

"I just took the whole thing as a joke. These two grim-faced cops showed up. I yelled out something like 'Scatter, everybody, Vice Squad!' Or 'Panty raid!' Or something. They weren't amused. But they didn't find any blow, or illegal games, or corrupted minors, or anything else. They left with a warning to keep the noise down. But hell, when you're on the tenth floor of a downtown building, who's worried about noise? Stuffy pricks, the two of them."

"Who were the cops? Did you know them?"

"No. One was named Tulk. I remember that because my brother had just got married to a girl named Tulk. No relation; she's an American. But we never saw the plods again."

"How were you left financially after your husband's death?"

"Do you mean, did I just take out a great big fat insurance policy the day before he got splattered all over the pavement?"

"Right."

"No, neither of us ever bought insurance. We had no kids, we were fairly young. We didn't want to waste any money on insurance. I was fine afterwards. My salary was good. I sold the big house in Clayton Park and bought a fixer-upper downtown."

Mavis was still at her table when I left the hotel.

I wasn't a ballistics expert, though I could certainly find one. But lawyerly caution told me that any evidence, whether it was related to my case or any other matter, had better be collected and logged by the police. If it was significant and somebody like me or my expert tampered with it, the evidence would be useless. So I made a call to Constable Phil Riley and told him there might be a bullet lodged in the wall of Dice Campbell's old office. A bullet that might or might not prove to be of interest in the Leaman-Scott double shooting.

†

Ross Trevelyan appeared flustered when I stopped by to discuss the case with him Friday morning.

"Rough day at the office, Ross?"

"Oh, hi, Monty. No, I . . ." He glanced at his watch.

"I'll come back another time. It's nothing urgent."

"No, no, come in. I'm just reading this article in *Canadian Lawyer*. It's about the superior court judges across the country, which ones have been most influential in taking the law in new directions. I've been trying to get to it all morning. I was hoping to have it finished before I —" He looked at his watch again. "Shit. My father is coming by and we're going to the Halifax Club for lunch. Well, you know how it is."

I wasn't sure I did. The Halifax Club had been catering to the business elite since 1862; I rarely entered the elegant Italianate building. And lunches with my father had not been occasions I felt I had to prepare for. I decided to let him cram for his noontime encounter and turned away, nearly bumping into John Trevelyan as I did.

"Good morning, Justice Trevelyan."

He was tall and broad, dressed in an immaculately tailored suit. His head was large and crowned with wavy hair that was going from auburn to grey. The judge peered down at me. "Do I know you?"

He should. I had spent three days trying a narcotics case before him two months before. Well, if he didn't know me now, he'd know me later. I had filed a sixty-eight-page factum with the Court of Appeal, citing fourteen grounds for overturning his decision. He was a very good judge in the civil courts, but he was inexperienced in the world of criminal law.

Either he read my mind or he suddenly decided to acknowledge my existence. "Oh, yes, Mr. Collins. Excuse me. Ross! Aren't you ready? So this is where they've put you. Is there a shortage of office space on this floor? I'll speak to Stratton."

His face reddening, Ross answered: "They offered me an office with a harbour view but it was on the south side. Sun streaming in all day. I'd bake in there, so I took this —"

"Is that a piece of jewellery I see on you?"

Ross looked at his right wrist. "It's a Medic-Alert bracelet, Dad. You know, for my peanut allergy. Elspeth wants me to wear it."

"That girl has you whipped."

I looked at Ross, who wouldn't meet my eyes. "Let's go," he said.

"Good news," the father announced, as I made way for them.

"Oh, yeah? What's that?"

"Your brother's coming home."

"Great," Ross lied. Was the brother a lawyer too? No, I remembered, he was some sort of international finance wizard who had bought a large country house outside London. It had been in the papers.

I suspected that my ruminations on the Leaman case would not be greeted with enthusiasm by Ross that day — and perhaps not any day soon — so I decided to continue my own discreet inquiries. If it was going to be tilt, game over, I wanted to know about it sooner rather than later. There was no point in adding to the stress in Ross's life unless things took a clear and unmistakable turn for the worse.

Chapter 3

Now the only thing a gambling man needs is a suitcase and a trunk.
And the only time he is ever satisfied is when he's on a drunk.
— Traditional, "House of the Rising Sun"

"Collins was a son of privilege."

"Hardly."

Ed Johnson, Brennan Burke, and I were at the Midtown on Friday night for a steak and a pint. Ed was rewriting my biography.

"His dad was chairman of the math department at Dal."

"You make it sound like His Lordship upon the Woolsack."

"Well, your mother came from money. A real lady. Good thing she didn't know some of the stunts you pulled, eh, Collins? You didn't spend your youth with Mummy and Daddy looking on at the tennis club. You knew there was a better time to be had hanging around dives listening to the blues. And then when you took to the stage yourself, well, the less said the better."

"I don't know what you're talking about, Johnson. I'm a fine upstanding citizen just like everyone else at this table."

"He could get away with anything, Brennan. Just look at him. Face of an angel. Every night of dissipation and debauchery shows up on me, but not him. Even after that road trip."

"Ah. The road trip," the priest remarked.

I flapped a hand at Brennan to indicate that it was of no importance, but Johnson ignored me.

"This was the band our Monty was in before we got together as Functus. From what I hear, he was lucky to be in one piece at the end of their U.S. tour. Got out of the country with little more than the T-shirt on his back, if my information is accurate."

I had to get him off that subject. "I thought you were extolling the virtues of my family for Father Burke; now you've got him thinking I need an emergency trip to the confession box."

"Oh, your family, right. What was that story about your parents' marriage? Your father piloted a plane back from wartime England to claim his bride? What was it?"

"You're exaggerating again. He sent a telegram."

"Oh. But I know there was a whiff of scandal."

"Apparently. That's why my mother never alluded to this herself. Her parents had somebody else in mind as a son-in-law, someone more —" Johnson butted in by saying "Right" and rubbed his fingers together in the commonly understood sign for money. I went on: "Someone with more certain prospects, let's say. Dad was a graduate student in math while he was courting my mother. When he went over to Cambridge for his doctorate, she told him, no doubt at her parents' prompting, that he should not expect her to wait. He said she might not be waiting for him but he would be waiting for her. And off he went into a cloud of equations. He got his Ph.D. and ended up working at Bletchley Park, the code centre in England, during the war. Anyway, the news reached him that my mother was about to be married to her other suitor, and he sent a telegram. But it didn't arrive until the day of her wedding, and was not read until afterwards, at the reception, with the other congratulatory messages. The telegram said: 'Dear Evelyn Stop Marry me Stop Yours Marshall.' And she did. She flew over to England to tie the knot. But not before a big fuss with the church, annulment proceedings, whatever. Her family was scandalized. Dad's family all had Cheshire Cat grins on their faces over the whole affair."

"What a sweet guy, your father. You wouldn't hear boo from him, then he'd come out with a sly little remark that would crack you up."

Brennan turned to Ed. "I take it from our previous conversations that your own father was something of a —"

"Apart from the odd sneering comment, we don't hear anything about your dad at all, Johnson," I interrupted. "Nobody's ever met him. Bit of a shadowy figure, it seems."

"And the more fleeting the shadow, the happier we were. The best times at our house were when he was off on a binge somewhere. Let's just say the old man had some bad habits."

"How bad?"

"Trash. We were trash."

On that note, we all turned our attention to our beer and drank in silence for a few minutes.

Then I brought up a new topic of conversation. "Ever hear of a cop named Tulk?" I didn't want Ed to know why I was interested, but I wondered if I could track down one of the cops who had raided Dice Campbell's party, see if he knew anything about the gun.

"Warren Tulk," Ed replied. "He's nuts."

"What do you mean?"

"They drummed him out of the force after he got religion."

Brennan rolled his eyes heavenward and picked up his draft.

"Got religion how?" I asked. "What was the problem?"

"'Why aren't Baptists allowed to fuck standing up? Because it might lead to dancing.' That kind of religion. He joined some wacky sect that outlaws everything, and so everybody he saw when he was on the job was a sinner. Arrests went way up, but convictions went down. The Crowns wouldn't prosecute half the stuff he brought in. Really petty drug offences — one joint — or liquor offences, or questionable solicitation charges. He busted a card game and it turned out the police chief's brother was sitting there with a big pile of chips in front of him. They eased Tulk out. He became a preacher or a Bible salesman or something. I think he's the one who runs that Christian bookstore a few blocks over. Why are there so many nutbars among the religious, Brennan?"

"I have no idea." He smiled across the table. "I can't speak for those who are not adherents of the one true faith."

"Well, at least old Tulk has the courage of his convictions," Ed retorted.

"As so many nutbars do," Brennan replied.

"Come to think of it, you're kinda slack, aren't you, Brennan?"

"What do you mean, slack?"

"Isn't it your job to spread the word?"

"Yes, that's part of my job."

"Well then. You've got an unrepentant atheist singing the best parts of the repertoire in your church choir, and you don't lift a finger to try to convert him."

"They say a stiff prick has no conscience, Ed. Well, neither does the prick who runs the St. Bernadette's men's choir. You've got the best bass voice, you get the bass solos."

†

It was my first time inside the door of the His Word Bookshop on Blowers Street. The shelves bore titles like *Free Your Inner Evangelical!* and *Deviants in Power: Liberals on the Court.* But the man behind the counter on Saturday morning was not the sour-faced pilgrim I had been expecting. True, he had his blonde hair in a style bordering on the blow-dried confection of a TV evangelist. But he was casually dressed in tan pants and a yellow sweater, and his expression was welcoming. I could not quite picture Warren Tulk as a cop.

"Good afternoon. If there's anything I can help you with, just let me know. Otherwise, I'll leave you to browse all you like."

"Actually, Mr. Tulk, I was wondering if I could have a word with you."

"Yes? What about?"

"My name is Montague Collins. I'm a lawyer and I'm looking into a death that happened a few years ago. An apparent suicide." He had begun to look a little wary. "Darren Campbell, the lawyer."

His face registered distaste but only fleetingly. "I remember Mr. Campbell. Why is his death under investigation?"

"It isn't, except by me. I've discovered that he had a gun in his possession before he died, and that gun has turned up in a case that I'm involved in."

"What kind of case?"

"Another suicide. I'm just wondering how the gun got from there to here."

"And how do you think I can help you, Mr. Collins?"

"I understand that you were a police officer in the past."

"That's correct. I retired to take up another calling."

"Right. And I heard from someone that you participated in some kind of raid at an office building on Barrington Street, where Mr. Campbell and some friends were having a party."

"It was not a raid. I was responding to a complaint from a citizen, about a group of people disturbing the peace. I issued a warning and left them to it."

"So, what was going on? What kind of party was it?"

"The usual. Gambling, loud music playing, liquor flowing, people groping each other."

"No sign of a gun on the premises?"

"Not that time."

"Do you mean you were there on other occasions too?"

"No, I wasn't there. Thank the Lord. I had heard rumours of a gun. A gun being fired into the air off a balcony. But it never became a police matter. As I say, a rumour."

"Who was there when you showed up at the party?"

"Campbell. His wife. She was drunk. A couple of people I recognized as lawyers. Most of the others I didn't know."

"Who made the complaint?"

"I can't remember now. It may have been one of the other tenants in the building. Or somebody in one of the apartment buildings downtown."

"Who was your partner that night?"

"Lorne Balcome. I'd have to say Lorne was less than enthusiastic about our approach to Campbell and his gang. I don't know why. Maybe he just didn't care about the noise and the possible offences being committed."

"These parties of Campbell's. They were legendary, weren't they?"

"They were depraved!" Tulk snapped. "I happened to catch them on a good night. From what I heard there were goings-on at that place that would curl your hair. But nobody seemed to care. Let the lawyers disport themselves as they please! That seemed to be the attitude."

"The attitude where? In the police department?"

"Everywhere."

"So what kinds of things were going on? You say they were depraved."

"All I have is innuendo, Mr. Collins. I'm not going to pass on rumours. Lest I inadvertently bear false witness."

I knew I wouldn't get anything more from Warren Tulk, so I thanked him for his time and had a look around the shop. I spied a book on statuary depicting angels and cherubs, which I bought for Normie. Even since she had seen Father Burke at a wedding, dressed in white vestments and — she claimed — surrounded by spirits, she had been on a quest to determine whether he might in fact be an angel. Perhaps this book would assist in her research. I would present it to her on Wednesday, when she would be hosting a dinner party with me and Burke as guests. Normie was choosing the menu, cooking the food, setting the table and, given that my daughter had proven herself to be a bit of a seer, maybe conducting a seance.

†

Having met Dice Campbell's flamboyant and hard-living wife, Mavis, I tried to form a mental picture of the woman he would turn to for recreational fun, his mistress. I had been on the verge of imagining a Swedish masseuse or a Brazilian porn star, but I was way off track. Dorothy Mellish had a master's degree in early childhood education and ran her own daycare centre. I had spent a day and a half trying to find somebody who could identify one of the rumoured "other women" in Campbell's life. Here I was on Tuesday afternoon in the Poplar Street Preschool. Dorothy escorted me into her office after the last child had been picked up; she cleared off a seat and offered me tea.

"None for me, but you go ahead."

"I will. It'll just take a second." Dorothy busied herself with the tea things, and I looked her over. Small, with glasses, pale skin, and light brown hair tucked behind her ears, she could almost be described as mousy. She was dressed in a light blue jumper over a flowered shirt. When she was seated, she said: "You're here about Darren."

"Yes. As I explained on the phone, I'm wondering whether there might be a connection between Dice's — Darren's — death and a

56

case I'm working on. The possibility may be remote, but if there's a link, it may raise questions about what happened to Darren in 1985."

"You mean there is some doubt about whether his death was really a suicide."

"Right. What did you think when you heard about it?"

"I was broken-hearted. But it never occurred to me that it was anything but self-inflicted."

"Why was that?"

"Because Darren's life was a shambles. And it was destroying him."

"How did you meet him?"

"When I was doing my master's at Mount Saint Vincent, Darren was teaching a law course to undergraduates. It wasn't part of my curriculum but I hoped to start my own business some day, my own preschool, so I sat in on the course. Thought it would be useful."

"Was it?"

"Yes, I'm glad I took the course. And Darren was a good instructor. He made the subject come alive. Of course, he was most entertaining. I was a few years older than the other students; Darren and I got talking after class. I resisted his flirtation, I suppose I'd call it, for a long time. I knew he was married. And I don't approve of that. Eventually, I came to know he was unhappily married. How many people use that excuse to justify themselves? I turned out to be another one of those. I fell in love with Darren against my better judgment."

"So you began seeing each other regularly?"

"Yes. Once or twice a week."

"Where?"

"At my apartment."

"What was he like on those occasions?"

"He was very sweet and very serious. Talked to me a lot about his life and his problems."

"What problems did he describe to you?"

"Darren wanted children. His wife did not."

"I see."

"He thought they both wanted kids but were unable to have them. He tried, for years, to get Mavis to go with him to a doctor.

She kept stringing him along, putting him off. 'It will happen when it happens, don't worry about it.' He finally found out she had been on the pill all along and had no intention of getting pregnant."

"Do you think what Darren really wanted was to divorce Mavis and settle down with — someone else? Was that the real Dice Campbell?"

She gave a quiet laugh. "No, Mr. Collins, I think the real Dice Campbell lived to party and raise hell. He just got tired; I was his relief. He cared about me, I know. But I doubt there was a future in it. I would never, ever have accepted the wilder side of his life, and we both knew it."

"Did Mavis Campbell know about you?"

"Not for a long time. But eventually, yes."

"How did that come about?"

"That followed hard upon the heels of the pill revelation."

"A confrontation?"

"There was a confrontation between Darren and Mavis every time the driveway needed to be shovelled, or one of them failed to get to the liquor store on time. So, yes, there was a confrontation. A major blow-up."

"When was this?"

"Not long before he died. Two or three weeks maybe. I'm not sure now."

"Did he stomp out of the house and come to you after the fight?"

"No. She got to me first."

"Really!"

"Yes, the quarrel took place in the morning when Darren was on his way to court. I was at work with the children. We had just sat down for story circle when the door burst open and Mavis came charging into the room, scarves flying, eyes blazing. She ranted and screamed at me like someone in an opera. I stood up to try to shield the children from her wrath. They were terrified. One of the other teachers shepherded them into the kitchen. Anyway, Mavis called me every name in the book and some I'd never heard, warned me to keep my hands off her husband, and flounced out."

"You must have been frightened."

"I was initially. I was appalled for the sake of the children; all during her tirade I was calculating how to explain this to the children and their parents. But I quickly realized it was only going to be verbal. And do you know, I'm sure I saw a glint in her eye that wasn't only rage. I think she was enjoying the scene. I wasn't the only woman Darren had ever seen on the side, and Mavis knew it. Maybe I was a more serious threat. But that woman was enjoying herself!"

"Was she drunk?"

Dorothy looked thoughtful. "I don't think she was. From what I heard, she was inebriated most of her waking hours. But I got the impression she wasn't that day. Of course, it was morning."

"What did she say to you? Apart from the name-calling, I mean."

"Just that Dice was her man and I was a little so-and-so who would never win him away from her. 'He'll never leave me. Never. Dice and I have a love you can only dream of. So find yourself a nice little furniture salesman, get married, produce a couple of rug rats, and disappear.' Darren didn't get out for a while after that! I only saw him a few more times before he died. He didn't even hide from her where he was going, so I was a little nervous about another attack from Mavis, but it never happened."

†

I was asking questions and getting answers. But all I really had were a number of isolated facts. Three men were dead. The deaths may all have been connected — the gun raised that possibility — but I had no idea how. If anybody was present when Dice Campbell died, that individual had never surfaced. Which wasn't surprising if Dice's death was a homicide. How was I going to smoke him out, if there was such a person? I did know there was somebody on the scene when Leaman and Scott met their demise — Wanda, the world's most elusive streetwalker — if Yvette could be believed. How was Wanda earning her living if she wasn't out on the stroll? It was time to go cruising again.

I didn't see her in Cornwallis Park, but there was a girl down on the corner of Hollis and South streets, so I called her over. Her face fell when I said I was trying to find Wanda.

"Wanda isn't here, baby. I am. So, what would you like?"

"I just want to talk to her."

"Yeah, right. Well, I haven't seen her." She shrugged and walked away.

I tried again the next night, with the same result. So I knocked at the door of the flat where she lived on Mitchell Street, down by the grain elevator. The old wooden apartment building had been quite stylish at one time, if the bracketed doorways were any indication. Now a tattered Confederate flag drooped in the front window, and the mailbox I took to be Wanda's overflowed with junk mail. Nobody answered any of the doors.

†

"Mummy, listen to this!" Normie burst in upon us, wide-eyed, brandishing a tattered cookbook. "Brains! Brains are supposed to be pink and plump. You should only buy them when they're fresh, and you have to cook them immediately!" She looked up. "Otherwise, they'd be rotten and stinky, right? Are you okay, Father Burke?"

I glanced in his direction. He gave her a wan smile. "Fine, sweetheart."

It was Wednesday night, the first of May, and I was sitting in my old family home on Dresden Row with my wife scowling at me from across the room. Brennan and I were having dinner with the family. Brennan, as usual, affected to ignore the tension, and chatted away about a fellow priest's trip to Ireland. Normie plunked herself down on a footstool in front of his chair and delved further into her cookbook.

"It says here you can eat the brains of calves, pigs and lambs. Lamb brains only weigh a quarter of a pound. Not too smart, eh? You have to remove the membrane — mem-brain, get it? — anyway, you do it with a knife and wash the blood off, then put the brains in a pan and boil them —"

I heard some kind of murmur from Burke's direction and looked over again. He had put his drink on the table and was massaging his temples with one hand. His face, what I could see of it, was the very whitest shade of pale.

"Am I grossing you out, Father?" she said, her concern not quite

60

masking her delight.

"I'll get you for this, you little maggot," he said to her, lightly pulling on one of her auburn curls. She grinned at him.

As it turned out, the meal was beef Stroganoff, which she brought off successfully enough to earn a compliment from her brother, Tom, before he left for a party of his own. Beef Stroganoff struck me as an unusual choice, but there was something familiar about it. She remained tight-lipped but sported a telltale blush.

Her mother spoke up: "I was cleaning out some old letters and photos. Normie came in and found a menu I had planned years ago. She thought it would be nice if —"

"It was the first dinner she cooked for you!" my daughter burst out. "When you were her boyfriend!"

Maura rolled her eyes as if the memory of us as boyfriend and girlfriend was too tedious to bear, but I said: "Let's have a look at it."

"Okay." Normie rose and stomped upstairs. She must have squirrelled it away somewhere. A minute later she was back. "Here it is!"

I unfolded the yellow paper and smoothed it out on the table. The menu was there with all the ingredients, and page references to the cookbook.

"Why beef Stroganoff?" I asked Maura.

"I didn't even know what it was, but the name 'Stroganoff' sounded impressive."

It was the other notes she wrote to herself, however, that were so arresting. I read them aloud:

> "Use Fannie F. Read recipes all thru first in case surprise at end, e.g. soak overnight.
>
> "Call landlord, fix stuck window. If burn anything, need air thru.
>
> "Slice onions BEFORE shower and make-up!
>
> "Use metal measuring spoons — plastic warped, may be inaccurate. Smooth off top with wide blade knife before dumping in.
>
> "Dessert: bring into conversation somehow — if he makes face, don't let on I made them."

"Awww," Brennan was prompted to say. "That's sweet. She wanted to do everything right to impress you."

"Young and delusional," she replied.

"What did you mean about the dessert?" I asked. "You don't have the ingredients down."

"How the hell am I supposed to remember that?"

"Come on."

"I think it was cupcakes. With Smarties stuck in the icing."

"Why did you think I'd make a face?"

She shrugged.

"She must have thought you came from a family of cordon bleu chefs," Brennan suggested.

"I figured they probably had some kind of soufflé every night at his house. But I wasn't going to attempt that and have it fall flat."

I read out the final note, which was marked by an asterisk at the bottom of the page: "'If he brings wine/flowers/candy, bring out candles. If no, save for P. Unless!!!'" I looked up at her. "What was this? You were planning another dinner with P? Pierre, I suppose. And you were going to the highest bidder? Whoever showed up with the biggest box of chocolates?"

"No! It wasn't like that. Though leave it to you to draw that inference. It was just that if you arrived with flowers or candy, I would take that to mean — this is corny but — a romantic dinner. As opposed to you stopping by for a quick scoff and then going out with the boys, in which case candles would have been embarrassing."

Brennan cut in. "So, did he bring wine or flowers or candy?"

"He brought all three."

"A success then, was it?" he asked.

"Back to Pierre," I interrupted. "I always wondered just how long he stayed in the picture after we got together."

Burke cut me off. "She said 'unless.' Unless what, MacNeil?"

"None of your business!"

Burke smiled at her over his wineglass.

We were all silent for a while. Normie, not hearing any more old tales, drifted off to her own amusements, but not before she took one last look at Father Burke and wrote something in a small notebook she carried in her pocket. Angel research, I assumed. Maura got up and went behind my chair on her way into the kitchen. I caught her by the hand. "Since you went to all that trouble to win my heart, why don't we —"

"Buzz off!" She slapped my hand away and continued into the kitchen.

Maura, Burke and I sat in the living room afterwards and spoke of other things. But Burke, who had been playing the matchmaker ever since we met, brought the conversation back to the past.

"Ah, the poor wee child, slavin' over the hot stove to feed her da and her mam. Sure, didn't she think her efforts tonight would re-kindle the —"

"Piss off," I responded.

"Now there was obviously something about this fellow you liked at one time, MacNeil."

"Sure. I liked him wailing on that harmonica till three in the morning. And then getting up next day and whipping everybody's arse in debates at the law school."

"What was he like then? Tell me."

"What was he like, or what did I think he was like?" Burke didn't answer, and, after a while, she deigned to speak of the old Monty she once knew. "He was in third-year law, while I was a lowly first-year student; he was nice-looking; and he played in a band. Therefore, I concluded he was one of the cool people, which, to me, meant he must be an arsehole. And I would hate him if I got to know him. But lo and behold, he wasn't one of the cool people. He tended to go his own way. He seemed to be sweet and funny and considerate. I dared hope — for years! — that he wasn't, indeed, an arsehole."

"And you were right."

"You may think so, Brennan, but that's because you were never married to him and never had to see him, in a public place, being pulled by another woman by the front of his pants —"

"That again!" I remonstrated.

"I know it's a minor everyday occurrence in your life, Collins. But I try to live my life on a higher plane than that, if I can. So such an event, to me, is emblematic of everything that went wrong, and remains wrong, between us."

"No. It isn't. I never looked at another woman the whole time you and I lived together. You're the one who decided I had to go, when I got stuck working nights and weekends and had to miss that vacation we planned when the kids were small. I was out working my tail off —"

"I didn't split up from you because of work. There were other problems."

"— working, not picking up women. In fact, even now when guys like Al MacDonald head out to the Twa Corbies for 'Scotch and Skirts Night,' as they put it, I don't go along because I *don't* want to be a middle-aged jerk cruising for girls in a bar. All I have to do is think of Normie being in bars a few short years from now. I really am tired of this posturing of yours, whereby you paint me as some kind of woman chaser like these other guys."

"Oh, so when this broad came up to you at the Metro Centre and grabbed you by the belt, if indeed it was your belt and not something else, it was a case of mistaken identity, was it? Maybe she doesn't recognize any of her male acquaintances face to face. Maybe you guys all look alike to her from the waist up."

"She was an occasional date. There have been very few women in my life, contrary to what you claim."

"Date! Now there's a euphemism if I ever heard one. That's like calling Al Capone a tax evader."

"He *was* a tax evader."

"And you are trying to evade, or should I say weasel out of, the fact that you and this . . . this tawdry —"

I was about to counter with Maura's relationship, whatever it was, with a much younger male companion called Giacomo, but I remembered my earlier resolve: to be conciliatory. And forgiving. I veered on to another topic, without any of the finesse of a law school debater.

"How about that first trip to Cape Breton?"

"Are you brain-damaged, Collins? How could you leap to Cape Breton from where our conversation was going?"

"I don't blame him," Burke interrupted. "Let's hear about Cape Breton."

"It must have been after that dinner," I said.

"Very soon after."

"Right. The dinner went well so I was emboldened to offer her a

64

ride to Cape Breton to see her family. I figured if I could get on their good side it would give me an in with the daughter, who, despite her efforts on my behalf in the kitchen, was playing hard to get. I had told her I loved her but she would not so much as acknowledge that she found me tolerable. So I would go along, impress the family, and then she'd see what a great catch I was."

"Went like clockwork, did it?"

"How did you know? I had just bought a car and I wanted to take it on a road trip. This was going to be ideal. I got it all tuned up the day before. I went for a haircut. Bought some treats for the drive. I was to pick her up at nine in the morning. I went home for an early night, to get lots of sleep so I'd be sharp next day. But then some guys called to say they were having a midnight hockey game; they'd rented ice time at the Forum. Did I want to play? Well . . . maybe just the first period. So I went to play hockey. There was alcohol involved. Near the end of the second period I got checked into the boards and broke my left tibia and thought I was going to lose one of my front teeth. I ended up in emergency at the Victoria General, and had to wait for hours to get my leg set. I was in agony and half-corked. The tooth was loose. The hours ticked away. I begged them to get it done, and to get somebody to save my tooth.

"I won't get into it all. It was nine-thirty in the morning before I got out of the hospital. I needed a shower and a shave. but if I went home for that, I'd be even later. I was nearly crying by the time I got into my car. Then I realized I couldn't use the clutch with my leg in the cast. I lurched along in the car and somehow made it to her place. Got out and hobbled to her door. She looked at me as if I were a bug that had just crawled out of her salad. I tried to smile at her but I kept my tongue over my loose tooth and, well, it just went downhill from there. She lit into me for being late, for being hungover, unreliable, and irresponsible. I told her I had to go home first to clean up, and she said we either got going right then or forget it. I insisted on shaving at her place, with her rusty razor, so I had cuts all over my face along with everything else. Then I had a shower with the cast on, and fell in the tub. I feel as if I'm living through it again. When we finally got going, she had to drive, but she wasn't used to a standard shift, so she kept stalling the car. I was afraid she'd strip the gears. I barked at her about it, and she barked back. It took eight fucking hours to get to Cape Breton. Since I hadn't eaten, I was feeling increasingly sick and at one point had to ask her to pull over so I could throw up at the side of the road. At least I still had my tooth. Anyway that's how I presented myself to her family."

"My relatives were damned impressed. 'Oh, you've done well for yourself there, Maura. You went all the way to Halifax for the likes of that? You could have got something like that over in Reserve Mines, saved yourself the time and expense.'"

"And yet, you ended up at the altar."

"Yeah," she said, not without a spark of humour. "I wonder if we can sue the priest. Have you ever been named a defendant in a sacrament-gone-wrong lawsuit, Father Burke?"

"But, when you look at it," I suggested, "if we made it through that day, surely we can —"

"Go home, Collins, I'm tired."

"Oh. Uh, you don't happen to know where I can score a box of Ganong's dark chocolates at this time of night, do you, sweetheart?"

"*Go!* Do I have to scream it into the side of your head? Go home. Normie! Come down and say good-night to your dad. He's leaving."

Burke and I stood in the front hall waiting for Normie to say goodbye.

"So, Brennan, the bachelor life must be looking pretty good tonight, eh?"

"It has its blessings. What's this?" He picked up a postcard of the Roman Colosseum from the little table in the hall. "Someone you know is visiting the Eternal City?"

"I don't know who it's from. It arrived in the mail at the office this morning. Take a look at the message — the sender says 'Ask.' Took the trouble to use a calligraphy pen by the look of it, but just wrote the one word."

"Ask what?"

"I can only assume it's from the plaintiffs in a lawsuit over the shoddy construction of their condominium. We're defending the contractor who built it. But why send it to me? Maybe they think their lawyer's pleadings weren't eloquent enough. They're either saying: 'It should have been built to last two thousand years,' or: 'It's a ruin.' I don't know. 'Ask'? I don't have to. I've seen the place. If we can't pin it on somebody else, we'd better cut our losses and settle. Anyway, I brought it over for Normie; she's studying Rome in school. I forgot to give it to her."

Brennan stared at the postcard. "Next time I go to Rome you'll have to come with me. Ever been there?"

"I had a short visit there. Too short. You lived there for what, three or four years?"

"Four, when I was studying at the Greg and the Angelicum."

"Those are the Pontifical something or other?"

"Pontifical Gregorian University, Pontifical University of St. Thomas Aquinas. Thomas is called the Angelic Doctor; hence, the Angelicum."

"Sounds lofty."

"We'll go over some time, and I'll show you around." He replaced the postcard on the hall table. "Is there a club called the Colosseum here in Halifax?"

"No."

"Was there ever such a place?"

"Not as far as I know."

"Or a sports stadium?"

"No. Why?"

"I'm thinking of a fellow I know who sleeps rough. Have you ever run across the Gladiator in court circles?"

"The Gladiator?"

"This homeless fellow. He sleeps in the park across from the Hotel Nova Scotian. Comes to the rectory once in a while for a bite to eat. Calls himself the Gladiator."

"No — I've had guys who think they're being monitored by aliens, or the KGB, or the CIA, but I've never had anyone from Roman times."

"There but for the grace of God go you and I. Anyway, he performed or fought — it's never the same story — at the Colosseum. Says he can take me there but then he gives me a sly look and says I wouldn't like it. I got the impression he was talking about a place here in the city."

"Nope. It may be real to him but not to the rest of us. Here's the little chef. Good night, angel. See you soon."

Brennan and I took our leave and went our separate ways.

†

I finished a chambers application at the Supreme Court building the next morning, then stood in front of the windows chatting with one of the other lawyers on the case, Glen Crocker. I peered through the gloom and saw what looked like a fellow barrister leaping about the plaza in front of the Law Courts. "Is that Al MacDonald doing a step dance out there on the pavement?"

Glen joined me at the window.

"Probably."

Another lawyer became visible in the fog. He machine-gunned MacDonald in the manner of a hot-dog hockey player who had just scored the winning goal against the Russians; then they high-fived each other and made "We're number one" gestures to a non-existent TV camera.

"What's that all about?" I asked.

"Big bucks, that's what it's about. Remember the humongous development project that was halted out there on Highway 103? Well, it's on again. Shopping centre, office tower, condos."

"But it was more than that, wasn't it? Weren't they practically building a small city?"

"Right. The consortium designed an entire community, not just a strip mall with some shoddy housing nearby. They were making a genuine effort to do it right. The part closest to the water, out on the point and along the ocean, would be residential. The commercial stuff would be closer to the highway. It was all supposed to blend in."

"Yeah, I heard they were ambitious. They wanted houses, shops, parks, trees, a school, doctors, dentists, a city square, everything within walking distance. The people would live and work in the neighbourhood. They wouldn't have to commute to the city to work."

"Sounds too good to be true, doesn't it?"

"Yeah. But it used to be the norm."

"Thought I might move out there myself," Glen said. "Where you've got people and businesses, you need lawyers! The biggest thing was that a couple of federal and provincial departments were going to relocate there. A government building. Jobs leaving downtown and going out to Bromley Point."

"That was the name — I'd forgotten. But did it ever got off the drafting table?"

"Oh, it got a lot farther than that. Then it came to a screeching halt. And I do remember the screeching. They were crying in their Corona at Wigginstaff's. The project was halted because of environmental concerns, land-use problems — there was probably an old Indian burial ground to top it all off. Anyway, as I'm sure you know, it's been on hold for six years while a whole tangle of legal issues wound their way through the courts. Supreme Court of Canada heard it, sent it back here. Our court just gave it the go-ahead with some modifications."

"So we've got a big development that's going ahead, after years of delay. You're right: big bucks for somebody," I remarked.

"Yep. MacDonald and company, and a few other firms, stand to make a pile. Some lawyers worked on it and never saw a cent; now they will. Money that's been held in trust, earning interest, is about to be released. It's been a long wait for some of them. You're obviously not in on it, so don't go near Wigginstaff's tonight. I hear there's a big party planned. Poor old Albert Farris never lived to see it; guess his partners will reap the benefits."

"I never knew Albert."

"You must have known Dice Campbell. His ghost will be hovering over the gathering tonight. Old Dice loved a party!"

"Dice was involved?"

"Oh, yeah. Big winnings for him if he'd stuck around. Poor bastard."

"Is that right. Who took over Dice's files when he died, do you know?"

"Jamie McVicar."

†

Jamie McVicar and I had gone to law school together. When I returned to the office I gave him a call and asked him whether I could go through Dice Campbell's files. I told McVicar about the Luger P-08, which suggested a connection between the Campbell suicide and the putative murder-suicide of Leaman and Scott. I didn't mention what I had just heard about Campbell and the Bromley Point development. McVicar told me to come right over.

As I was leaving, though, I saw someone wheeling our television and vcr into the boardroom, and that reminded me I had not yet retrieved the Netherlands Liberation video I had lent to Bill Groves. So I took a detour over to Camp Hill to pick it up. I didn't recognize the man in Bill's room. When I tracked down a nurse, she told me Bill had died early in the week.

"I'm sorry. You didn't know? Are you a relative?"

"No. I just met Bill a few days ago." But I felt the loss all the same. The nurse found the video for me, and I decided the least I could do in memory of Bill was watch the film about Canadian soldiers in Holland. I put it on my dashboard to take home that night, and continued on to McVicar's law office.

Jamie led me to a boardroom, where he had stacked the dusty boxes containing Dice's files. A cup of coffee, a pen and a notepad were in place on the table. I thanked him, and got to work. With even a cursory review of the files, in chronological order, you could plot the rise and fall of Dice Campbell on a graph. He started with the usual storefront practice: low-end property transactions, wills, divorces, a bit of commercial work. And he was obviously well-regarded in the profession. Rowan Stratton had sent some work his way. Even the lordly John Trevelyan had selected Campbell for a little job, namely to amend a lease, write to the Canada Pension office, and prepare a will, all for a woman named Matilda Lonergan. If Mrs. Lonergan had been in a nursing home, Trevelyan's hourly rate for the trip out to see her would have been three times the fee he could decently charge her for the work. No wonder he handed it off to a younger, cheaper lawyer. I flipped to the last page of the will, which was a list enumerating every teacup, china poodle, and knickknack the old lady owned. The lease was for a duplex she owned in a rundown area of central Halifax. But it was not long before things began looking up for Dice. I saw that one of the largest insurance companies in the city had directed a healthy portion of its defence work his way. He began to get more and more criminal work as the years went by. I found the correspondence file relating to a large and complicated drug trafficking trial he and Ed Johnson had worked on for over a year; they represented two of the five accused men. Ed told me he and Dice had done some cases together. I didn't recall hearing anything in particular about this one, but no doubt there was a story; Dice's performances in the courtroom were still the subject of boozy reminiscences in the legal fraternity.

I moved on to duller things. Agreements of purchase and sale, mortgages, minute books for small companies, file folders with sheets of handwritten notes attached. One caught my eye because I recognized the name Debbie Schwartz, a highly regarded psychologist I called upon from time to time to assist my clients. Had Dice used Debbie's services too? I didn't learn much from his note: "Asked Debbie Schwartz re: fruitcake from DT; yukked about house call, says don't pay him time & 1/2 or might come back! Name familiar but doesn't know him; suggests try again, call Drug Dependency." Aside from the drug reference, the note was obscure, and I put it back in the file.

Dice kept a file of press clippings. Some were about his courtroom triumphs. Others seemed to be cases Dice found interesting. One stood out because of the unusual weapon involved, a food blender. The kid, whose identity was protected by the *Young Offenders Act*, had been sentenced to three months in jail for assaulting one of the workers at the group home where he was residing at the time. I imagined sharp blades whirling, and I pushed the thought from my mind. It was a Legal Aid case, and I noted that even the kid's mother did not show up to support him. The judge gave her a blast *in absentia*.

The deterioration in Dice Campbell's law practice seemed to coincide with his increasing involvement in criminal work. But there was nothing in his files to suggest this was anything more than coincidence. The papers showed unreturned phone calls, missed appointments and even court dates, and escalating harassment from clients, fellow lawyers, and courthouse staff.

Among the papers Jamie McVicar had given me were Campbell's account books. I dug them out and took a quick look at the books reflecting the latter years of his practice. I didn't see anything out of the ordinary except declining revenues. Nothing to suggest improper dealings with his trust accounts, which can lead to a lawyer being disbarred. But I couldn't be sure. I was not an accountant.

The biggest surprise was what was *not* there. There was not a word about the delayed and recently revived Bromley Point property development out on Highway 103. Glen Crocker had told me Dice was involved. The scheme promised — and would now belatedly deliver — a big chunk of fees with interest compounding at generous rates over six years. Why was there nothing in his files?

†

By the time I got back to the office, it was early evening. The staff had left, and only a few lawyers were still at work. My desk was piled with correspondence to be signed, and messages to be returned. I started to slog through the pile. One of the messages, I saw, was from Constable Phil Riley. I got him on the phone.

"Evening, Phil. You called? I was out for the afternoon."

"Hi, Monty. I've got some news for you. It's the same gun. The bullet lodged in Darren Campbell's old office wall matches the ones that killed Leaman and Scott. Which may just mean Leaman stole Campbell's gun. Or somebody else stole it and it made the rounds, ending up with Leaman. I went through what we have on the Campbell suicide. Looks like we did a pretty thorough job of canvassing his friends and acquaintances, other tenants in his office building. The medical examiner's report shows the injuries were consistent with a jump or a fall from a great height. You know the building. It's twelve storeys high, and some of the upper floors are stepped back so the corner offices on those levels have small terraces. Campbell had one of those, on the tenth floor. The terrace door was open. There was nobody else around. If there was another individual involved, we found no evidence of it. Of course the offices were all closed for the night, except his. My partner and I went back to the building the other day and took a look around but except for the bullet we didn't come up with any new insights. We'll keep an open mind, but we don't have much to go on at this point."

"I understand."

"One more thing. You got lucky with Wanda Pollard. We can't find her. So, still no witness who can contradict the murder-suicide theory. But we're going to maintain a lookout for her."

"Thanks, Phil. Keep me posted."

The cop's information left me, for the time being, with the appearance of a good case of suicide. Which was the whole point. Ross Trevelyan and I wanted to build a case for damages against the Wallace Rennie Baird Addiction Treatment Centre on the grounds that the centre had been negligent in releasing Corey Leaman before getting his drug habit under control; Leaman, still suffering from drug-related problems, had killed himself and, for some reason, had killed Graham Scott before putting a bullet in his own brain. If this wasn't a suicide — if the two men had been murdered by somebody else — our lawsuit on behalf of the victims' families was a non-starter. I was trying to rule that out. Phil Riley's information about Wanda didn't hurt us. But where was she? Her absence could mean many things: she was out of town; she was the victim of revenge by or on behalf of Yvette; word had spread about Wanda's presence at the shooting, and she had been frightened off or taken out by the killer. If there was a killer.

The gun connection was disturbing. In my mind, I pictured not an old German pistol but a time bomb ticking away in the background, set to go off at any moment and blow my case to bits.

†

Saturday morning, the fourth of May, was beautiful and warm. After I completed a few long-neglected chores, I stopped by the house on Dresden Row to see if the family wanted to head out to Lawrencetown to walk the beach and admire the surf. I saw that congratulations were in order: my daughter had a thriving little garden of daffodils and paperwhites in front of the house. The door was open, but nobody was downstairs, so I skipped up the stairs to Normie's room. When I glanced out the window overlooking the backyard I saw Maura, and was about to call down to her when I noticed two strong-looking legs sticking out from under the shed. A repairman? With bare legs? Then I saw that her chair and the one next to it each had a glass in the cupholder. Was this Giacomo, the young bit of stuff my wife had on the side? I wouldn't have thought his legs would be that long. I waited, staring. The legs began to emerge, followed by gym shorts and a naked torso.

The man turned away from her and wiped dirt off himself. Then he reached for a white T-shirt lying by the shed, and put it on. It was — when he turned to my wife, I could see it was Burke! What the hell? He looked at her and shrugged. Whatever he was supposed to do under there, he hadn't done it. No surprise there. He was even less of a handyman than I was. But never mind that: what was he doing with her on a Saturday morning and how long . . . I stopped myself in mid-thought. I was acting the way I had on a couple of occasions when Burke first came into our lives as a client. I had got myself all balled up wondering whether there was something going on between the two of them — or, at the very least, whether he had his eye on her. Unfounded suspicions that reflected badly on only one person: me. I had put it down to the stress of Burke's trial. Thinking back on it now, I had to laugh. But here he was with her again, drinking and half naked. I told myself to get a grip. The man had become my closest friend; he was a friend to Maura and the children as well. And he had made it his own personal mission to get our family reunited.

He put his arm around Maura's shoulder and said something. She bolted up and hooted with laughter. He got up, drained his glass, and headed to the shed. He slipped his feet into a pair of sneakers. I knocked loudly on the window and waved. Burke looked up, squinted, and raised his hand. I met him downstairs. He didn't look any more guilty than if he were standing at the back of his church, wearing a cassock and clutching the Word of God in his hand. But then, he wouldn't look guilty. He was the type whose expression wouldn't change if his butt were on fire.

"What's up?" I asked him. Nothing, I hoped.

"Why don't you tell her to spring for a new shed?"

"What do you mean?"

"The floor's rotten in that one. So the plank I tried to wedge underneath is going to let go, and she'll still have a great gaping hole in the floor."

She came in then. "Collins. To what do I owe this pleasure?"

"Try to contain yourself. I came to see if anyone wants to take a drive to the beach."

"Oh. Well, the kids aren't home. Normie had a sleepover at Kim's."

"Again?"

"What do you mean, 'again'?"

"You may as well rent out her room, she spends so little time in it. At least on weekends."

"Really. You're conveniently forgetting that she spends half her nights at your place. Do you rent out her room when she's not there? Or is it just your own bedroom in which money changes hands? Of course, I shouldn't judge your entire stable of female companions by the impression made by just one, who certainly looks like —"

"Jesus the Christ and Son of God!" Burke exclaimed. "My work's cut out for me here, I'm thinking. Ministering to the determinedly estranged. I have to go. Should I leave you two alone in the same room?"

I knew I would say a great many things that I would regret if I stayed behind, so I turned without a further word to my wife and left with Burke. I wasn't in the mood for him either but I could not justify being uncivil.

"How did you get roped into fixing that floor?" I asked him.

"Came by at the wrong time. And now I'm overdue at the church."

"See you later then." I made ready to leave.

"I meant to ask you," he said, "did you ever hear anything more about the Colosseum?"

"No, I didn't. But I imagine the postcard was someone's way of drawing attention to those crumbling condominiums my clients built. When you think of it, the word 'condominium' is Latin. Roman, in other words. Maybe this is the beginning of a campaign by a very literate consumer advocate."

"But why would someone write 'ask' in reference to that? You already knew the place was in ruins, didn't you?"

"Oh, yeah. We have shelves full of photos and engineering reports detailing just how badly the place fell apart."

"Well then."

"Well then, what?"

"I just think there's something else going on. I told you about the Gladiator, the homeless man who comes to us for a meal now and then."

"Right. The guy who fought at the Colosseum."

"His name is Vernon. He was on about the Colosseum again yesterday."

"Uh-huh." Part of my mind was replaying the scene between Burke and my wife in the backyard; another part was castigating me for being a flaming idiot.

"Said the cops had been there." Burke was waiting for my reply.

"What?"

"Vernon said the police had been there."

"Where?"

"At this Colosseum. Have you been listening, Collins?"

"Sorry. All right. Vernon, the Gladiator, did something at this so-called Colosseum, and the cops showed up. Did he give you any other information?"

"No, but he was agitated. Said he might want to come to confession some day. But he's not a Catholic, so he doesn't know what to do. Said he wasn't the only one, but then he got all mysterious and shut his gob. Literally. Pressed his lips together and flapped his hands at me to go away."

"So, what do you think is going on?"

"I just think there's something wrong. And somebody sent you a photo of the Colosseum."

"Well, it wasn't this guy. It arrived in the mail with a stamp and a typed address label. But, if you like, we'll track Vernon down and ask him about it."

"Good."

Since Tommy Douglas and Normie weren't around, I decided I'd better spend the rest of Saturday in the office catching up on work, including the condominium case. Sunday I had the kids with me all day, and we had our trip to Lawrencetown Beach. We hit it at a good time; the waves were enormous. When we got back to my place, we had a little Collins family jam session, with guitar, keyboard, harmonica and vocals. Dinner was *spaghetti con le vongole*, prepared by Tom, and we had cupcakes with Smarties on top, lovingly designed and crafted by Normie. A good time for all of us. On Monday, I worked a twelve-hour day and hit the sack as soon as I got home.

†

Tuesday morning, Burke and I took a stroll to Cornwallis Park, the one-block square between Barrington and Hollis streets, across from the venerable Hotel Nova Scotian. The park was dominated by a statue of the founder of Halifax, Edward Cornwallis, who gazed out over the harbour with his tricorne hat clutched in his hand. There were two men in overcoats sleeping on benches. We struck out with the first, but the second was the Gladiator. Brennan put his hand on the man's shoulder, causing him to jump up and look wildly around him. His light brown hair was long and matted, and he had a straggly beard. He could have been anywhere from thirty-five to fifty years of age.

"Morning, Vernon."

"Father! What happened?"

"Nothing happened. Get yourself awake there, and we'll go for breakfast."

It took him a while to get focused and to relieve himself of something clogging his throat; the sound brought a greenish tinge to the face of the fastidious Father Burke. Then we walked across the park together. I noticed Vernon had a slight limp. We sat at the counter in the South End Diner, the priest and I with our guest between us. After the waitress took our orders, Burke introduced me to the Gladiator.

"This is Monty. Monty, Vernon."

His watery pale eyes took me in, and then he turned to Brennan. "Was he one of them?"

"One of whom?"

Vernon spun around on his stool and leaned towards me, his breath nearly knocking me flat. I resisted the urge to move out of range.

"Did I have sexual relations with you?"

"What?" I reared back suddenly, nearly falling off my stool.

"He looks like the type," Vernon said to Burke.

"How do you mean, Vernon? He looks like what type?"

"The type they had there."

"Where?"

A sly look. "You know."

"The Colosseum, you mean?"

"Don't, don't, don't," Vernon pleaded. He put his head down and covered it with his hands as if he were ducking for cover.

Breakfast arrived, and we busied ourselves with knives and forks, coffee and cream.

"Vernon?" He gave me a wary look. "Do you know a girl named Wanda, who works around the park at night?"

"Who wants to know?"

"Just me."

"I haven't seen Wanda for a long time. Coincidence?" He raised his eyebrows.

"How long has it been since you've seen her?"

"Time, time . . ." He shook his head. "It marches on."

"What did you mean by 'coincidence'? Coincidence between what and what?"

He gave me a blank look. Either the remark had been meaningless or it had already been forgotten.

Brennan spoke gently. "Vernon, I know you were a gladiator. Can you tell us something about that?"

"Oh, no. Oh, no. No, no."

"All right," I said. "We'll leave you out of it. Would you just tell us where the Colosseum was?"

He wagged his finger under my nose. "The constabulary have it under twenty-four-hour guard."

"The police are there now?" I asked him.

"They're there. But you can't see them."

"How do you know?"

"Because I saw them."

Brennan looked at me, then asked Vernon: "What makes you think you had se — something to do with Monty here?"

"I never!" With that, he jumped up, fell against the counter, righted himself, and stumbled out of the diner.

Burke pushed his plate away and reached for his wallet. Only then did I realize he hadn't touched his meal.

"Well! What lesson can we take away from this, Father?"

"That you and Vernon once got it on at the Colosseum, and

somebody sent you a postcard to remind you of it. Maybe your anniversary."

"Father?"

"Yes, my son?"

"Piss off."

Chapter 4

Wake up late and I walk down to the square
Man sellin' cocaine standin' there.
— Maynard T. Maitland, "Cocaine Blues"

Back at the office Tuesday morning I looked through the file we had on Corey Leaman. Several drug convictions, theft, break and enter, assault, the usual breaches of court orders. And one assault with a weapon. Which was what again? I turned to the page. The weapon was a food blender, but it was not as gruesome as it had seemed when I first read it. He had not set the blades whirling and stuck someone's hand in the jar; he had picked the whole machine up and thrown it at a counsellor at the group home where he was living. *When I first read it?* Where had I seen a reference to this blender assault case? It was just the other day, but I had never read through Corey Leaman's file. Dice Campbell's clippings file, that's where it was. What was Campbell doing with a news clipping about Leaman? I recalled he had a lot of news stories. Maybe he kept a file of odd cases. I made a note to follow it up. For his kitchen appliance assault, Leaman had been represented by Bob Mahoney, an old crony of mine at Legal Aid.

†

"My boy didn't do nuthin', and he's goin' to jail. Because you didn't do your job. If you were any good as a lawyer you woulda proved to the judge that the police been pickin' on my boy since he was ten years old."

"Your boy went to jail, Mrs. Craig, because he broke into the home of an elderly man, tied him up, slapped him around, stole his pension cheque and his dead wife's jewellery, and then tried to cash the cheque at the old fellow's bank. And it was his fifth offence. I got your boy eighteen months. The Crown was looking for seven years. The maximum sentence is life in prison. I didn't rob the man, your son did, and that's why he's in jail."

"I'm gettin' a real lawyer next time."

"You do that. Now, I really must go. Hey, Monty!"

"Some things never change, eh, Bob? How many times in my Legal Aid days did I live through that scene?"

"Yeah, this guy should be going away for years. I get him eighteen months and I have to put up with this."

"I know, I been there. I caught up with you because I want to ask about another old friend. Corey Leaman."

"Oh, right. Corey took a bullet in the head a while back." ·

"Yeah. I'm representing his family in a suit against the Baird Centre."

"Good luck."

"I'm up against it, I know."

"Poor Corey. Never had a hope."

"Assaulted a group home worker with a food blender, right? Just how much of a badass was this guy?"

"It wasn't as serious as it sounded. Honestly. And Corey wasn't that bad a guy. Compared to some, and all things considered. I always had the impression that, for all his faults and rotten luck, he really wanted to better himself. He wasn't stupid. He knew he was headed towards a black hole if he didn't shape up. The time I had him for the blender assault, the judge reamed him out because his mother didn't show up. Or rather reamed out the mother. She didn't hear it because she was in the clink herself for some grievous offence."

"How about a father?"

Bob cupped his ear and leaned in towards me. "How about a what?"

"Right. No point looking in that direction."

"Nope. You've been out of Legal Aid too long, Monty. If it hadn't been for old Tilly, the record would be bare of any kind words on Corey's behalf."

"Old who?"

We were interrupted by a shabby-looking man who came up to Bob and stood there shuffling his feet. "Hey, man," he finally said.

"Hey, Ralph. I thought you were on your way home."

"I was but, like, I don't got no money to get home."

"I gave you a bus ticket, remember?"

"Yeah, but, like, I sold it."

"Sold your bus ticket? For what?"

"A smoke."

"Okay, well, here." Bob gave the man a couple of dollar coins. "Get yourself home now."

"Thanks, man."

I watched him shuffle out. "You know you've been away from Legal Aid too long when you forget what counts for legal tender in the local economy. You were telling me about someone who spoke up for Corey Leaman."

"Right. Tilly was an elderly neighbour. Leaman used to do odd jobs around her place in Lower Sackville."

"Maybe I should look her up. What's her last name?"

"I don't remember it off hand, but I'll call and let you know. If I forget, prompt me."

"Sounds good. Thanks, Bob."

†

The next day, I was in provincial court, in a room with dark wainscoting and wooden beams across the ceiling. Our deliberations took place before a portrait of the queen. My client, Keisha, was charged with assaulting another girl at a high school dance. Keisha was eighteen but looked several years younger with no makeup and her hair in pigtails.

The complainant, a girl around the same age as my client, was on the stand, and I was cross-examining her. When the police arrived at the scene, she had not been able to describe the person who hit her. A point I was trying to make for the court.

"You weren't able to give the police a description of the person who attacked you, is that correct?"

"I know who she is."

"But my question was, you couldn't give the police a description at the time. Isn't that right?"

"I don't know what I told the cops. But it was her!"

"Her?"

"Yeah, her!" And she pointed a finger at my pigtailed client. "Her, with the blow handles."

I turned my head to hide my unsuccessful effort to keep a straight face and found myself looking into the eyes of a highly amused Father Brennan Burke.

When it was over, and my girl convicted, I spoke to Burke.

"What are you doing here?"

"I came for the entertainment. And I wasn't disappointed."

"No shortage of laughs here."

"Actually, I'm here to collect my fee."

"Fee for what? You guys charge now? If you think I'm going to pay you to hear my confession, and then have to kneel down and say three Hail Marys afterwards —"

"I can't imagine what would pour out of you in the confessional after all these decades but, whatever it would be, three Hail Marys wouldn't even grant you a preliminary hearing with the Man Above. But that's not why I'm here. I've been doing your work for you. And I know you'll show your appreciation, if not by paying me a private investigator's fee, at least by treating me to a pint at my local."

So we repaired to the Midtown for lunch. On me. When he had his draft in front of him, and a cigarette lit, he filled me in: "The Colosseum." I rolled my eyes and picked up my glass. "If you're connected to this in some way — or, I should say, if someone thinks you are — you'll be wanting to watch your back."

"I told you, Brennan. I've lived here all my life and I've never heard of anything called the Colosseum."

"Yet somebody sent you a postcard. The Colosseum was the nick-name given to a private club, or a gathering, that used to meet in an office building here in downtown Halifax. And what went on there was so vile that anyone who participated is loath to speak of it. I got the impression there were threats, violence perhaps, against anyone who ever spoke out."

"You heard this from Vernon? So, who was in this club? Squatters using a building after hours?"

"Not squatters. 'High mucky-mucks' was the phrase used by our man Vernon."

"That sounds kind of funny with an Irish accent."

"I take it that is the vernacular for 'the quality,' — well-heeled, prominent citizens who found a way to keep themselves amused in the small hours."

"What were they doing?"

"Here. Read Vernon's description. He'll never talk to you."

"How did you get him to talk to you?"

"I'm a man of the cloth, Collins."

"But you said Vernon isn't a Catholic."

"Like the pope, I have an influence that extends beyond my own cult following. This is a transcription of my notes of the interview."

He handed me two pages of typed copy. As I read, I imagined I could hear the voice of the dishevelled homeless man I had met in the diner.

They had us up in there. They were scared of the cops so we went there one by one. There was this girl. Her father used to beat her up. Stepfather, like. She used to sleep up against the library. Everybody did it to her. Like, she was on every time. Whatever they wanted, 'cause they had the shit. Can you get me a drink?

Now, Vernon, when you say "they" had you up there, who do you mean by "they"?

Oh, can't say, can't say. High mucky-mucks. Oh, yeah.

All right. What did they do?

They wanted us to fu — have sexual relations.

Sex with whom?

Oh, with us, with each other. People from the street. They wanted to watch us doing it to each other. They laughed. Or some of them would — one guy would — you know, do it to himself. I saw him on TV.

Getting a medal. He was in the Colosseum with his hand in — Like, he should have to give that medal back, right? They made that girl do it with the guys off the street. Dirty guys. They gave her so much shit she was out of it, you know? Like, they had rocks of crack, and blow, and they even had some H, you know, and all that shit.

So. A group of men —

Ladies too. Oh, yeah.

A group of men and women. Sort of well-dressed people? That type? They gathered together some of the people from the street, the homeless, and got them to have sex with each other, and these men and women looked on.

They watched and laughed or did other stuff.

And one of these men you recognized.

No! No, no, no! Don't know his name! Never knew, never!

But you had seen him on television, being presented with some class of medal or award.

Oh, yeah. He got the kid to give him — what's that word? A queer word. French. No, not French. Handsome kid. Light hair, blue eyes. Little-kid face. Like that guy we saw at breakfast time, your buddy. Maybe him. No, not him. They liked this kid. Dressed him up. One of the mucky-mucks took him in the shower. Made him his boyfriend. Not me. I was the Gladiator. They got me drunk. I couldn't fight. I said later. But I fought this guy 'cause they said I could have a quart of rum and, besides, I thought I could win 'cause the other guy was old. But I got beat up. Bad kidney. Blood coming out in the toilet. It went away but I got nerves damaged in my leg. That's why I got the gimp. The Romans said: "Vern, you could fight a lion." A lion, eh? They showed me a picture of a big dog. Said I could have a forty-ouncer. I said: "I don't know, man." Like, if that man beat me up, and him an old guy, maybe a big dog would kill me, eh? But I never saw any dog. Then this other guy came in and sang. Good singer. And he took the older guy away, the guy that put the beating on me. The singer shoved him out the door. Thanks, Father. Oh, that's hot. I'll wait till it cools.

Vernon, these people sat around in the Colosseum and watched homeless people have sex and fight with each other. Do I have that right? Who gave it the name Colosseum?

I don't know, I don't know. Somebody said: "Welcome to the

Colosseum. Thumbs up, thumbs down, which way did it go?" They
argued about that. They were all coked up.

Is it still going on?

*No, no, no. Nobody says it now. It stopped. They came around at
night with lots of shit and booze. Told me to keep quiet. Tell nobody. Told
us they'd cut us off. No more drugs. Put us in the hospital. With the crim-
inally insane!*

I looked up from the notes. "Jesus Christ!"

"And somebody sent you a photo of the Colosseum and said:
'Ask.'"

"If somebody thinks I was involved in this, he's barking up the
wrong tree. I never even heard a rumour of this. So I don't see —"
Then I did. "Did you find out where the Colosseum was?"

"Yes. Vernon and I walked there. He pointed at it. Number 1803
Barrington Street."

"Dice Campbell's office building."

"You've been developing some skill in the field of investigation over
the past couple of years, Collins, but you're slipping. If you need any
more assistance, give me a ring. Now I'm off to feed the multitudes."

He was on his way out when I called him back: "Brennan, next
time you see Vernon, try to find out what kind of medal the guy was
receiving, or who was awarding it."

"What would you do without me, Collins?"

†

Without him I would have remained in the dark about the goings-
on at the Colosseum. But now that I knew, I could try to corroborate
Vernon's story. Warren Tulk, the cop turned preacher who raided one
of Dice's parties, said the activities there were "depraved" but was
unwilling to say more. Tulk had his partner with him that night, and
I remembered his name: Lorne Balcome. I tracked him down on
Thursday. He was working in Dartmouth, and we met at a Tim
Hortons on Portland Street. Balcome was an enormous man with
thick black hair brushed back from a low forehead. He sat hunched
over a large coffee while we chatted.

"Warren got a little excited."

"When you raided a party at Dice Campbell's office?"

"It wasn't a raid, by any stretch of the imagination. We got a call."

"From?"

"No idea. I can't remember. Anyway, we arrived at the office —"

"Was this the law office itself?"

"Yeah, one of the top floors. They had a bar set up in the board-room. More like a permanent fixture, I guess. Anyway, it was just a bunch of lawyers and their friends partying."

"When was this, Lorne?"

"Spring or summer of '85."

"So what got Warren so upset?"

"Well, they had some girl dancing on a table. A stripper, I guess. They were all pissed. Campbell's wife gave us a hard time. But you know, it was a private party. I didn't give a shit. I told Tulk to lighten up."

"What was his reaction to that?"

"He said he'd heard stories about parties a lot more crazy. Sick stuff going on. Minors and drugs, perversion, I don't know what all. But I never heard anything like that from anyone except Tulk. I just forgot all about it. Warren went to Jesus, and I concentrated on busting bad guys."

When I got back to the office there was a stack of pink message slips on my desk. One was from a Detective Burke, with a familiar phone number. I dialled and, when he answered, I said: "Getting a little full of yourself, aren't you, Burke? A little too immersed in your role?"

"Just eager to be of service. After all, you've solved a few thorny problems for me in your time. I had a word with Vernon."

"Yes?"

"The way he remembers it, he was watching television somewhere and saw one of the mighty Romans, one of the Colosseum people, being handed some sort of medal by the Grand Poobah. Mixing his metaphors a bit there. But anyhow, it seems the Grand Poobah is the mayor."

"When was this?"

"He couldn't tell me, but I got the impression it was a few years ago. Vernon remembers thinking he would take it to the *Daily News*."

"But he didn't."

"No. He thought the story was too hot — his words — that they would know who leaked it, and he would be silenced with extreme prejudice if he uttered a word. But in the same breath he told me he tried to tell a police officer."

"Who?"

"No idea. All the cop said was: 'Don't call us, Vern. We'll call you.'"

"I wonder whether this medal was the City of Halifax Esteemed Citizen Award — the CHECA. Somebody pointed out that the acronym sounds like the old Bolshevik secret police, the Cheka, but the mayor's office didn't bother to change it. Nobody knows history anymore. The CHECA was initiated fifteen or twenty years ago. If that's it, then it wouldn't be hard to get a list of all the recipients. Booster types, gung-ho city promoters, you know the sort of thing."

"I'm not sure how much the names would mean to our man Vernon."

"I suspect there's no shortage of photographs of these people. I'll see what I can find, and maybe we can put together a little photo lineup for him to examine."

I decided to put a bit of distance between myself and my request for the photos of the esteemed citizens of Halifax. I asked my secretary to go over to City Hall the next morning and obtain copies of photographs of the medal recipients for my daughter's school project.

Then I sat back and considered what I had learned. Criminal activity had been going on at Dice Campbell's office. Drugs were involved. Someone sent me a postcard about it after I started to ask questions. Corey Leaman had a history of drug offences. Dice had kept a news story about an assault with a blender; the young offender was not named, but Corey Leaman's file revealed that he was the assailant. Dice Campbell's gun was used in the shooting. All I could do was quote Vernon: "Coincidence?"

†

That evening, May the ninth, was so mild you might have thought it was July. I wiped down the Adirondack chairs in the back yard of my house in Armdale, and sat with Brennan, Normie, and Tommy

Douglas, gazing across the water at the Halifax peninsula. Our conversation was punctuated by the sound of tiny waves lapping against the shore.

"I wonder when that bottle's going to wash up. You haven't seen it, have you, Tom?"

"Nope. No sign of it, Dad."

Looking at Tommy Douglas was like looking in a mirror, a kind, forgiving mirror reflecting my younger self. He and I had the same dark blonde hair and blue eyes. My daughter had thick, curly auburn hair and hazel eyes, magnified by a pair of delicate glasses.

Normie's eyes were sparkling now, as they always were when there was a story featuring her as the main character. "I'll go down and look." She trotted down to the shoreline. "Nothing here!" She came back and curled up in her chair, an expectant look on her face.

"When Normie was a baby, we had her over at the Dingle. You can see the tower to the south of us there. She was in her carriage, in a bright red jacket and a little knitted hat with kitty ears. And we were out on the dock. I handed her her baby bottle, and what did she do?"

"I flung it out into the water!"

"She flung it out to sea. Have you any idea how much those plastic baby bottles cost? We've been looking for it ever since. Hoping it will wash up. Or hoping some sailor, far from home, will spy it bobbing out there on the Atlantic."

"I was bad!"

"Och, you did a mortaller there, Normie. Pegging your bottle out to sea. And I thought I'd heard it all in the confessional," Burke said, shaking his head.

"I know. Daddy! We have a picture of me that day in my kitty hat. A slide. Let's look at them. Please?"

"It's not dark enough for slides, sweetheart."

"Yes, it is. Downstairs, with the curtains closed."

"Slides?" Burke asked.

"Yeah, my father took a whole pile of our photos, ones when the kids were little, and had them made into slides. He was a real slide buff. Had the projector, the screen, all the gear. This was before videos."

"That much I know."

"So I have all that stuff now. Every once in a while they demand a slide show and they make me lug all this antique equipment —"

"Retro, Dad," Tom offered. "I'll go set it up. Come on, Klumpf." Tommy knew he could always get a rise out of his sister by calling her Fräulein Klumpenkopf, for the unmanageable clumps of hair that adorned her head after a night of twisting her hair while she slept.

"Don't call me Klumpf! I'm coming with you."

"We're in for it now. Call us when you've got it going."

They had it going twenty minutes later, and we all got seated in the family room, facing the enormous white screen. My daughter was at the controls. "Ready?"

"Roll it."

"Jazes! Is that you, Monty? How old were you when you fathered this child? You don't look any more than seventeen."

I thought for a minute it was Tommy I was looking at, but it was me, years ago, with a humongous smile on my face. Tommy was the bundle in my arms. All you could see of him was blue blankets and a little fist.

"Oh, I was a good ten years older than that. I started aging fast once this little bugger came into my life."

Normie clicked the button, and we were looking at a family shot. I was in an armchair leaning over a golden-haired toddler while he took baby steps towards the camera, a proud grin on his little face. Maura was behind the chair, with her arms around my neck, her face resting against mine. Burke gazed at us in silence. This was followed by me, naked from the waist up, standing in the bathroom with a razor in my hand.

"A picture of you shaving?"

"Yeah, well, she was making fun of me. When we had Tommy, I was worried. His skin was so soft and delicate I was afraid that when I kissed him or put my face against him, I would hurt him, so I got into this habit of shaving twice a day. New father, what did I know? Maura, coming from a big family, thought it was hilarious."

"Really?" Tommy asked.

"Did I have soft skin too, Daddy?"

"You? I had to shave hourly for you, Normie."

"I thought so. Let's call Mummy!"

I reached over and dialled her number.

"Hello?"

"Hi."

"Oh."

"Settle down, MacNeil. Didn't your mother ever teach you to play it cool when a guy calls?"

"I'll try to control myself."

"Good. What are you up to? I was just looking at a very lovely picture of you."

"Let me guess. You're about to ask me what I'm wearing, and then you're going to tell me that you have nothing on and —"

"You obviously have me confused with one of the lower life forms that make up your circle of admirers today, but no. This is the father of your children speaking and we are all sitting here watching slides of the kids as babies."

"We haven't even got to me yet!" Normie complained. "It's all Tom!"

"So I thought maybe you'd like to join us."

"Uh, well, I can't."

"Other plans, have you? Maybe I should have asked what you're wearing after all."

"I'm sitting here wrapped up in cellophane, barely held together with duct tape, and a big pink bow on top, just waiting for someone to come in and claim the prize."

"I take it that if I show up, all I'll get is the consolation prize."

"Yeah. For you, I'll put on a baby-poop yellow velour track suit."

"So I'm hearing a *no*."

"Your intellectual growth astounds me."

"Brennan's here too."

"And he's been *listening to this conversation?*"

"No, until you raised your voice to an operatic shriek, he could only hear me. Now everybody can hear you."

"Tell the kids I'm sorry, and I'd love to watch the slides another night."

"I am in possession of the slides."

"So you're part of the deal. Well, I'll just have to grit my teeth and bear it."

"I'm looking forward to it too. Good night, my love."

Brennan looked at me with his eyebrow raised.

"I've got her eating out of my hand," I told him. "Next slide there, Normie."

She clicked through the slides at warp speed until we got to her, then resumed a more leisurely pace and lingered over every image of her babyhood. The kids drifted away when the show was over.

"You and herself looked happy enough in the early days," Burke remarked.

"We were."

"So, tell me. Not in excruciating detail, but what in the hell went wrong?"

I sighed and put down my beer. "Where to begin? MacNeil and I had planned everything out. We would not let work rule our lives, we would devote our time to each other and to the six children we intended to have. We spent a year in London, where she got her master's degree in law and I worked in a storefront legal clinic in the city's east end. We had the time of our lives. We came back, and I joined Legal Aid; she was teaching at the law school. We had Tommy Douglas. We were ecstatic. A few years of Legal Aid work and I was starting to burn out, or so I thought. Sometimes I had two trials in a day, plus arraignments, sentencings, client appointments, on and on. Rowan Stratton, after my brother married his daughter — well, you know Stephen and Janet — Rowan began his campaign to lure me into private practice. He wanted me for civil trials but offered to let me take on criminal clients as well because he knew I wouldn't move otherwise. You know how popular that has been in the firm. Anyway, I left Legal Aid, a move I question to this day. I was on the billable hours treadmill and ended up working evenings, weekends, and holidays. We had two children, and I hardly ever saw them. The tension between me and MacNeil grew in inverse proportion to the amount of time I was able to enjoy at home.

"We spent a year looking forward to a vacation in New Brunswick, to get ourselves back on track as a family. We had rented a cottage and we lived for the day we could get out of town and have three whole weeks with the kids on the beach. It ended up I had to work; had to fly to Toronto at the insistence of a client. That was it for Maura. Either I cared more for work than I did for her and the children — not true — or I was a pathetic lackey who didn't have the balls to tell the firm to stuff it. I like to think that wasn't true, either. I cut down my hours, with a corresponding reduction in pay, so I could spend time with my family. Who by then were living without me in my beloved house on Dresden Row. But at least when it was my week for the kids I had the time for them, time I have jealously guarded to this day."

"So why couldn't you work it out, once you'd cut back on your hours?"

"Because by that time, which is par for the course in these things, we had both done things that we are still throwing in each other's faces to this day. Everything turns into a shitstorm. Everything. It all came to a head when I went away for a weekend and came back to find she'd taken all my belongings from the house and put them in storage."

"She what?"

"After that, I cleaned out our joint savings account."

"You what?"

"We had a special high-interest account in both our names, and after she gave me the boot, I cleaned it out."

"That doesn't sound like you, Collins."

"It's not as bad as it seems. It all started when I went away for a weekend. I had tickets for some Expos games in Montreal. This was a long-planned getaway for me, Ed Johnson, and a couple of other guys. But coming on the heels of the missed summer vacation, it was not a popular move. Which I can understand. And she thought that, with Ed along, it would turn into a weekend of boozing and going to strip joints and Christ knows what else."

"And did it?"

"No. We went to the games, we did some bar-hopping. It was all quite civilized. But when I got home there was nobody there. All my things were gone. All I saw was an envelope saying Collins. That's all she wrote, as they say. And in it was a key to a storage warehouse in Dartmouth. She had kicked me out. Of my own house."

"The family home."

"You're getting wild all over again."

"So would you. And don't bother to deny it; I know you too well.

Anyway, it's a good thing she made herself scarce. She'd taken the kids to Cape Breton for the week. I rented a hotel room and went house-hunting the next day. The day after that, I found this place. Instead of getting a mortgage, which she would have been required to sign, I went for the savings account. That and some investments I had on my own were enough to pay for the house. By the time she showed her face in town again, I was the owner of a new house, and the money was gone."

"Mother of Christ!"

"The thing about this bank account was that it was meant for the children's education."

"This is getting worse by the minute."

"Not really. It just sounds it. The way my wife grew up, money was a scarce commodity, never to be squandered. Her dad was a coal miner with seven kids. They didn't have much. And she was determined to put aside every cent we could spare for Tom and Normie's future. This money to her was sacred. Untouchable."

"You knew it would be devastating to her, and you stole it!"

"I didn't steal it. It was half mine, and I merely reinvested it. She went thermonuclear when she found out. But she knew there was no loss of the kids' money. The money was now in this house, which would increase in value. Which it has, greatly. As long as we were still married, I couldn't sell it without her signature. If we divorced I would have to settle with her. If I died, it would all go to them anyway. Plus I had other money stashed away for the children. She knew all that but wasn't about to admit it during the firestorm over the bank account. To this day, if you want to get her wound up —"

"No, thank you."

"And since then, it is I — old faithful Monty, patient, shit-eatin' Monty — who has made all the efforts to reconcile."

"This Bev must be a bit of a stumbling block," Brennan suggested. "MacNeil walks in on the two of you here at the house, and then Bev shows up and makes a grab for you at the Metro Centre. This woman has been nothing but a jinx for you, Collins, when you think of it."

"Maura blows it all out of proportion. It's not hearts and flowers with Bev, on my part or on hers. It's physical. Period. And MacNeil took up with that Giacomo character —"

"All right, all right. How's the investigation coming along?"

It took me a few seconds to calm down and refocus. I told him about Dice Campbell's gun. "And," Brennan said, "Campbell was tied in with the Colosseum."

"Right. My secretary is picking up the CHECA award photos tomorrow. We'll present them to Vernon, see if he recognizes any of Halifax's top citizens from his time as a Gladiator."

†

The next morning, Friday, I dialled the rectory at St. Bernadette's, but Burke wasn't in, so I left a message with the priests' housekeeper, Mrs. Kelly. "Get Father Burke to call me right away. Tell him I have the negatives."

He called me in the afternoon. "Jazes, Murphy, and Jameson, would you ever be drivin' an oul woman into an early grave? Poor Mrs. Kelly looked as if her heart was going to give out when I got in and she rushed me at the door. She usually avoids me like the Antichrist. 'You had a call, Father! He says he has the negatives!' So, what have you got?"

"I've arranged all the esteemed citizen photos in a little package. I glanced at them. The usual suspects. Where can we find Vernon?"

"At his regular table, I imagine."

Brennan met me at the door of the rectory, and we set out on foot to Cornwallis Park, where Vernon had taken up residence.

We took him once again to the South End Diner, got him seated, and then I spread out my sheets of photos. I knew a number of the people who had received the CHECA award, and I recognized most of the other names. Rowan Stratton, my boss, was there, and his wife, Sylvia. Our other founding partner, Adrian Sommers, was one of the earliest recipients; he died shortly after he received the honour. I saw Angus Rennie Baird on the list; he would be the son, or perhaps the grandson, of the Wallace Rennie Baird for whom the treatment centre was named. Justice John Trevelyan was there, real estate developer Kenneth Fanshaw, a local newscaster, a rabbi, Canon Alistair Scott, and a number of Rotary and Chamber of Commerce stalwarts.

"All right, Vernon, you know what we're trying to do," Brennan said. "Monty will show you a series of photographs. Take your time with them, and tell us if you recognize any of these people from the Colosseum."

The photos were four to a page, with short biographies, presented in alphabetical order. I passed the first sheet to Vernon. No reaction. Next page and the next, same thing.

"Looks like you struck out, young Monty!" Vernon announced, with a superior smile. "We're wasting our time here, gentlemen! If there's no further business, I suggest we adjourn!"

I flipped a couple more pages at him. He had his arms folded across his chest; he shook his head at each sheet of pictures. Then his face went rigid.

"Do you recognize someone?"

"Oh, no. No, no. This won't work."

"Let me see the picture, Vernon." He reached over and swept all the pages off the counter. "Vernon, show us who it was."

"It was the whole bunch of them! They were all in on it! Don't try to find me!" And with that, he fled the diner.

"Jesus Christ. What do we do now? I didn't count the number of pages I gave him before he reacted. But even if I had, they're all —"

"Settle yourself down, young Monty," Brennan said, as he bent under the counter and gathered up the pages. "It was this one." He handed me a page.

"How do you know?"

"Because this woman's name caught my eye when Vernon was looking at it. Maude Gunn. I noticed it because of Maud Gonne, a well-known figure in Irish history."

I looked at the page he'd given me. "Maude Gunn. She must be seventy. Gilbert Fraser. He was a judge on the Court of Appeal. Dead fifteen years. Rabbi Abraham Greenberg. Abe Greenberg? I'd suspect you before I suspected him."

"I wasn't even in town."

"You'd still be guiltier than Abe. That leaves us with only one suspect, real estate mogul and man about town Kenneth Fanshaw. Well! Are you sure this was the page that set him off?"

"This was it."

I knew my fellow barrister Al MacDonald had lunch at the Lower Deck every day he could manage it. I was hoping Al would be useful in two ways. He knew everyone in the city, and he might tell me something about Kenneth Fanshaw. He might also do a bit of boasting about his involvement in the Bromley Point project. On Monday I found him in the pub, sitting with a young lawyer named Bruce Ferguson at one of the long lacquered tables.

"Al! How's it going?"

"Hey, Collins. Just coming in for lunch? Have a seat."

"Hi, Bruce."

"How're you doing, Monty?"

We gave our orders and made small talk for a few minutes. It was not long before Bromley Point was on the table for discussion: Bruce asked Al whether he had any cases on next door in the Law Courts that afternoon.

"Nope. I'm taking a drive out Highway 103 to hear the music of jackhammers and piledrivers. Going out to view the scene."

"Ogle the scene, he means, Monty. Al eats, sleeps, and dreams — I don't even want to think about what else he does — the Bromley Point development."

"Yeah, I've seen a lot of smiling faces around here lately, yours among them, Al. You finally got the green light, eh? How long was that thing on hold, anyway?"

"Six years, Monty." He began speaking in a heavy Scottish accent, rubbing his hands together in a parody of the happy miser. "Interest rates have been close to ten percent on average over the past few years, and when you compound it . . . A lot of lawyers are owed a lot of money in back pay, and a happier few invested money of our own. It's the future profits that have us in thrall."

"Who was in on that? Lawyers, I mean?"

He rattled off a dozen names.

"I heard Dice Campbell was representing one of the contractors," I prompted.

"Oh, yeah, big time. Not one of the contractors, one of the developers. Poor old Dice. If only he'd hung on, he'd be sitting in clover today."

"Well, somebody must be. His partners?" Bruce asked.

"Dice didn't have any partners. This was all before your time, Bruce. Dice was a solo act. Looks like widow takes all. Good time to buy stock in Glenfiddich Company Limited. Ever see that woman drink? Man, can she slam it back! You weren't there for any of the chugging contests, were you, Monty?"

"If I was, I don't remember."

"A bunch of them used to go to the Bulb and get blitzed. They had these chugging contests — you'd think they were a bunch of frat boys — and Mavis would be the last one standing every time. She even drank Ed Johnson under the table. Literally. The way I heard it, he just slid down in his chair and under the table, out cold. Women obviously have even more biological advantages than the ones we know about. Well, now she's got a financial advantage — she'll never draw another sober breath. Which, strange to say, may be good news for those who know her. You've heard of mean drunks? Not Mavis. But she's damn nasty when she isn't oiled up."

"Was Dice his real name?" Bruce asked.

"Nope — it was Darren. Got the nickname in high school. Even then he was a black-belt gambler. Poor bastard. I heard gambling debts were the reason he took a leap out his window. One way to cancel your debts to the kind of people who can't legally enforce them. When you think of it, a big chunk of the Bromley Point windfall would have gone straight into the pockets of some very unsavoury people if Dice had lived."

But he hadn't. "Will these people try to collect from his widow, do you think?"

"I doubt it. If they were going to go after her, they would have already. It's not as if she's been penniless. She's got money, and no troglodytes have come down from Montreal to break her legs in all this time. So I'd say Mavis will be doing the Merry Widow Waltz from here on in."

The waiter brought our plates, and we turned our attention to lunch. After a few minutes, I eased into the subject that had brought me to the pub.

"Somebody told me Kenneth Fanshaw has a big piece of the Bromley Point action," I remarked. I had no idea whether he did, but the odds were in my favour.

"Oh, yeah, he's all over it," MacDonald confirmed.

"I don't really know the guy. What's he like?"

"He's excellent!" Bruce exclaimed. Al took a twenty-dollar bill from his wallet, rolled it up, and pretended to snort a line of cocaine. Bruce was oblivious of Al's pantomime. "Mr. Fanshaw has done so much for this city. And the business community. Three new businesses —"

"Did somebody say 'biz'?" Al interrupted. "Know what he called his first boat?"

"No."

"The *Biz-Mark*. There was a lot of Johnny Horton karaoke happening around the yacht club scene in those years."

"Who's Johnny Horton?" Bruce asked.

"You're a child in a man's clothing, Bruce. Johnny Horton was a famous historian."

"Really?"

"Yeah, he made history accessible to the common folk by singing about it. One of his songs was 'Sink the Bismarck.' Fanshaw was too proud to change the name, so he got rid of the boat. Time to trade up anyway."

"As I was saying," Bruce resumed, "three businesses in as many months have decided to relocate here on the strength of Mr. Fanshaw's powers of persuasion."

"He's your client, Brucie. What else are you going to say?"

"My firm's client, not mine. But seriously, he's a great guy. And Mrs. Fanshaw is one of Halifax's brightest stars when it comes to charity."

"You're starting to believe your own press, there, Bruce. Are you guys their publicists? 'Metro's Hottest Couple,' 'Halifax's Rising Hostess,' 'This Year's Must-Have Invitation.'"

"Where are you getting all this bullshit, MacDonald?"

"I guess you don't read the social pages, Collins. You probably tune it all out."

"You got that right."

"I, on the other hand, read every word of our local papers even if I have to choke on some of it. It's entertaining. And sometimes it points to new opportunities in the form of billable hours."

"Speaking of Fanshaw *et al*, I have to get back to the office and do some work on the public hearing about the homeless shelter," Bruce announced. "There's always somebody bitching whenever somebody tries to do good." He pushed his chair back and dropped some bills on the table. "See you gentlemen later."

"Enthusiastic young lad," I commented after he was gone.

"Ah, for the days when we believed in our clients, eh, Monty?" We shared a laugh.

"So, is Fanshaw everything Bruce cracks him up to be?" I probed.

"He's probably no worse than any other self-made tycoon. Though I know there's a wrongful dismissal suit against him. Saw the papers in the prothonotary's office. And he's not too popular with the contractor who built his house. That wound up in court too, from what I hear. You've seen the house, I take it?"

"No."

"Do a drive-by. Or, better still, a sail-by. Best view is from the water. Mad Ludwig's Castle, the neighbours call it. But don't blame the builder! It wasn't his idea. Ken probably drafted the plans himself when he was all coked up. Well, I gotta go and view my retirement property."

Chapter 5

"Pick Me Up On Your Way Down"
— Harlan Howard

The next morning, I was working on a malpractice case and losing track of time when the receptionist buzzed my office. "Monty, Mrs. Carter is here for her appointment."

"Thanks, Darlene." I put the phone down and wondered who Mrs. Carter was. I hadn't recognized the name when I checked my list of appointments. I went out to the reception area where I found a short, heavy woman in light green sweatpants and a matching top. A black nylon windbreaker sought in vain for closure in the front. A patch on her left arm displayed a bowling pin and the name Vonda. Her dark curly hair gave off a metallic glint. I put her age at fifty or a hard-luck forty-five.

"Mrs. Carter?"

"You Collins?"

"I am. Come into my office." She followed me, wheezing. She was nearly out of breath when we completed the short walk to my door. "Have a seat. What can I do for you, Mrs. Carter?"

"Nothing," she said, and pulled an inhaler from her jacket pocket. She took a couple of puffs, then spoke again. "There's nothing you can do."

"I don't understand."

"There's nothing anybody can do to bring my boy back. All the money in the world can't bring him back."

"Your boy would be . . ."

"My Corey." She dropped her head, and I heard the sounds of sobbing.

"I'm sorry. This would be Corey . . ." I run across a lot of Coreys in my work.

"My son, Corey Leaman." She looked up at me, dry-eyed.

"You're Corey's mother?"

"Who'd ya think I am, the tooth fairy?"

"No, I just didn't make the connection. I'm very sorry about your son, Mrs. Carter." Where had she been all this time? Was she really Corey's mother? "I'm glad you've come in. You'll be an enormous help in presenting his case. I'd like to see Corey's school records, find out what sports and activities he was in, that sort of thing. Get a picture of his life before his troubles began." *And you'd better be able to produce something if you want to jump on this bandwagon.*

"I don't have nuthin' like that."

"No?"

"I ain't been into his stuff for years."

"His stuff is where?"

"At my place."

"Have you been away?"

"You might say that."

"How long?"

"Four years."

"P4W?"

"That dump. I wouldn't put animals in there."

The Kingston Prison for Women. What had she done to get sent up there?

"I haven't had a minute's peace since I heard about Corey. Can't sleep, can't eat. It's a shame, a goddamn shame." She looked away from me and bit down on her lower lip.

"Is Corey's father still alive?"

She shrugged.

"Would that have been Mr. Leaman?"

"No, Leaman was my husband. That piece a shit."

102

"I just wondered. No one has come forward to make a claim, except for Corey's common-law wife and his —"

"Who? First I heard of it."

"Why don't you give me a few details, Mrs. Carter? Your full name, address, phone number, and then gather up whatever you can find at your place relating to your son."

She gave me the details, but her mind was on other things. "Who's this here girlfriend?"

"Oh, that can wait for another time. We'll get everyone together in the office once we have more information from you. When did you first hear of your son's death?"

"A while back."

"What was your reaction?"

"I freaked. They had to hold me down!"

"Did you ever think Corey was someone who would take his own life?"

A cagey look came into her eyes. "What're you drivin' at?" What she meant was: Is there money in it if it's not a suicide?

"Did you believe it when you heard it? That it was a suicide?"

"Yeah, I guess so," she equivocated.

"And that he would shoot another man first, then turn the gun on himself?"

"Who was this other guy?" And was his family going to split the winnings?

"His name was Graham Scott. Had Corey ever mentioned him?"

"Never heard of him."

"I understand your son had a long history of drug use and other problems."

"He got in with a bad crowd. But nuthin' woulda happened to him if that detox centre didn't throw him out on the street."

"Had you been in touch with Corey during the years you were in Kingston?"

"Sometimes."

Never, I was willing to bet.

"Why don't you go home, see what you can find relating to Corey, papers or whatever you have, and call back for another appointment."

She pushed herself up from the chair and got stabilized before commencing the walk to reception. At my office door she turned to face me.

"These guys have gotta pay for what they done to my boy. So, like, let's make them pay up front."

"There's not much chance of that, Mrs. Carter."

"Why not? I sprained my back a few years ago. Got rear-ended. It still hurts somethin' terrible. And they paid in advance."

"The insurance company made an interim payment."

"Yeah."

"That's not going to happen here."

She gave me a disgusted look. "Maybe if you were doin' your job, it would."

"No. It wouldn't. But we'll discuss the case more fully next time. Bye for now."

She lumbered out to the elevator, and I scribbled some notes, then shoved them in the file. I included a reminder to call if I didn't hear from her in the next couple of days.

†

It was Tuesday night, and Ed and I were choirboys again.

"How's your hopeless case this week?" he asked, as the young boys clomped up the stairs to take their places in the choir loft.

"Which one?"

"Death at the Foreign Ass."

"We have a new plaintiff."

"Oh yeah?"

"Yeah. Somebody turned up claiming to be Leaman's mother."

"Really. You think she's on the level?"

"Could be. Nobody else has come in claiming Corey as a son."

"Are we on for the Midtown after this?"

"Tradition demands it, I should think."

Our attention was directed to one of the boy sopranos, who had risen to stand at the railing of the choir loft. Left hand on his heart, right hand flung out to an unseen congregation, he embarked on an oration for the amusement of his fellows. "I, Rrricharrrdd Rrroberrrtson, was rrrecently instrrructed by the Rrreverrrend

Brrrennan O'Burrrke to make morrre of an efforrrt to rrroll my Rrrs when singing in the choirrr." Richard's performance was greeted by giggles from his fellow students; encouraged, he went on: "To prrrove that I am rrright and Brrrennan is wrrrong, I shall rrrecite Rrrudolph the Rrrednosed Rrrein —" Richard's voice halted as suddenly as if he had been garrotted. Burke, footsteps unheard on the stairs, stood before us. Poor Richard stood gaping, white-faced, at the choirmaster, who affected to take no notice.

"Let us pray. *In nomine Patris et Filii et Spiritus Sancti. Amen.*"

Richard slipped into his seat, stared down at his clasped hands, and prayed with deathbed fervour.

"We are going to give a concert. The music will reflect the entire liturgical year and the entire range of music we do, from Gregorian chant to Renaissance to Baroque and Mozart. Over the next couple of weeks I want to see what voices we have for parts of Handel's *Messiah.*"

"Father? Is that the orange book?"

"You should be assigned the task of writing the concert program, I'm thinking, Kevin. Where was the Messiah first performed, Kevin?"

"Dublin, Father."

"Consider yourself redeemed. Now, I intend to find a balance between the slow, majestic interpretations of the past and the trendy, chirpy ones being produced these days, as if they're trying to zip through it and get to the bar for last call. As I'm sure you know if you've listened to various recordings of this, there are some parts that sound ridiculous — to the point where they lose their meaning — if they're sung too fast. We'll try to avoid that, without sounding too ponderous at the other extreme. So. The choruses will be 'And the Glory of the Lord,' 'All We Like Sheep,' and 'Behold the Lamb of God.' David and Emmet, I'd like you to try 'He Shall Feed His Flock.' I prefer a bass to an alto for 'Who May Abide.' Tony?"

"I'm going to be missing a lot of time, Father. My son's in hockey."

"Ah. How about you, Ed? Would you like to make your solo debut?"

"I'm not sure what to tell you, Brennan. I'm probably the only guy here who doesn't know any more of the *Messiah* than the 'Hallelujah Chorus.'"

"That's why Mr. Handel provided us with a score, Edward. Some would say a number of scores but we won't get into that. So, Johnson, all that will be required of you is to read the notes and sing them to the best of your ability. With my gentle guidance, of course. Rrrichard Rrroberrrtson!" he barked suddenly, causing the little boy to jerk spastically in his seat. "Something tells me you are now ready for 'I Know That My Rrredeemerrrr Liveth.' Does that suggestion meet with your approval?"

"Y-yes, sir. Father."

"Good. Make it your own. Now, gentlemen . . ."

The rehearsal began, and I enjoyed losing myself in the music. It had the power to make me forget the aggravations of the workday. Apparently I was not the only one.

"I've had a hoor of a day," Burke remarked as we followed the last of the boys down the stairs from the loft. "A pint would go down like liquid gold."

"Are you Reverend Burke?" The voice came from the semi-darkness of the nave. Burke didn't challenge the improper form of address.

"I am."

The woman had a pugnacious face and black hair cut in a severely geometric style. "I'd like a word with you, please. And I warn you, it won't be pleasant."

"Ah. In that case we'd better take it outside."

"What do you mean?"

"I mean: let's not have any unpleasantness in the presence of the Blessed Sacrament." He nodded towards the altar.

"I don't hold with all that."

"I do."

"Very well." She turned on her heel and marched from the church, looking back once to make sure Burke was behind her.

The four of us stood in the parking lot. The woman cast her eye from me to Ed, but we were not about to budge before the scene had played itself out.

"You don't seem to recognize me, Reverend."

He looked at her intently, then he had it. "Good evening, Mrs. Robertson."

"I'll get right to the point. My son tells me you subjected him to an ethnic slur."

"That doesn't sound like Richard."

"Are you calling me a liar?"

"Why don't you tell me what Richard said."

"He said you told him that for a Scotchman — the correct term is Scot or Scotsman, by the way — for a Scotchman, he certainly was tongue-tied when it came to the letter R."

"That's it?"

"What do you mean?"

"That's the slur?"

"You engaged in a stereotype based on his ethnic background. As if all Scots speak in the same kind of brogue!"

"I fail to see what's got you so vexed, Mrs. Robertson."

"Then you are a most insensitive man."

"Was Richard upset about this?"

"He's too young to understand. He thinks it's all a big joke. But I don't. And I have to wonder whether that is why he was not given a solo at last month's school recital."

"Well, he has a solo now."

"Don't patronize me, Reverend. Don't stand there and say my boy has a solo just to placate me, because I am not that easily placated."

"I can see that. I assigned Richard a solo part earlier this evening, after he gave us a lovely recitation of one of the standard works of the secular repertoire. I'm sure he'll tell you about it. Where is he, by the way?"

"I asked Richard to wait for me in the car." Burke looked around, trying to spot him. Mrs. Robertson spoke again. "It's over there, behind the police cruiser and the paddy wagon. Really, this neighbourhood —"

"The *what* wagon, Mrs. Robertson?"

"The paddy wagon. They pulled in just before I —"

"You mean the wagon they throw all the drunken Paddies in?" She looked at him in growing consternation. He leaned towards her with a confiding manner, and said in a brogue straight from the quays of Dublin: "Sure, we prefer to call it the *Patrick* wagon."

The woman moved uncertainly towards her car. Inside we could see Richard staring out, mortified. The priest gave him a friendly salute. Brennan was nearly grinning as he made his way to the car for our weekly jaunt to the Midtown.

†

I decided to make a detour to pick up a Tomaso pizza on my way home from the tavern, so I drove to Young Street and chatted with the guy while he made up my order. On the way down Gottingen Street, the pizza filling the car with the scent of a great feast to come, I had to swerve suddenly to avoid a group of people out in the road. I pulled over and looked back. It was a brawl that had spilled out from Cuzzin Lucy's, a greasy dive that sought in vain to recreate the days of Cousin Brucie's, a strip club that had its heyday back when I was in law school. Lucy's promised "Girls, Girls, Girls!" and "Topless Waitresses!!!" I recalled a cartoon someone had pasted on the bullet-proof window, showing a body without a head or a torso; the lower half of the body was dressed in black with a frilly white apron; a tray of draft was perched on its truncated upper surface. I spotted one of the topless waitresses at the fringe of the mob; she was all there except for the contents of her stomach, which were being violently ejected on the sidewalk. Two police cars came roaring up the street, sirens wailing.

Out of the corner of my eye, I saw somebody dart between two buildings across the street from the club. I squinted and saw a woman smoking a cigarette and watching the scene with dead eyes. I thought I recognized her but I hoped not. Candace McCrea had left home at fifteen to live with a boyfriend who — same old story — turned out to be a pimp. She developed a crack habit, went out to work for him, and came to me when she was charged with shoplifting. Her criminal activity expanded along with her drug habit. Finally, when she was arrested for armed robbery committed against a couple of high school girls on their way home from band practice, she was ready to be helped. A co-ordinated effort by her parents, social workers, probation officers, and others in the system culminated in her admission to a residential treatment centre in Ontario. She came out and began studying for a psychology degree at Dalhousie. Everything was fine.

Or so I thought. But there she was, loitering across from a strip joint on Gottingen Street, dressed in a pair of tight white pants and a low-cut black tank top. She looked wasted.

I pulled up at the curb, leaned over, opened the passenger door. She sauntered over and began her spiel: "You looking for a good —"

"Get in, Candace."

"Mr. Collins!"

She reluctantly got into the car with me.

"What in the hell are you doing, Candy?"

"What's it look like?"

"It looks as if you're right back where you started five years ago. You should be sitting in the Dal SUB, eating bad food and moaning about how tough your psych exams were. What happened?"

"I'm going to start again next year."

"How did you end up out here again?" She shrugged. "Where are you staying?"

"With a friend."

"Don't tell me you've taken up with another boyfriend like the last one."

"Just a friend, okay?"

"You look worn out."

"I need a hit."

"Do your parents know where you are?"

"I'm all grown up now. Not their problem."

"How about something to eat?"

"I'm not hungry."

"Not even a slice of pizza?"

"I couldn't."

"Timbits and a coffee." A shrug. I turned right on Cornwallis Street and headed in the direction of the Tim Hortons outlet at Young and Robie, known to aficionados as Headquarters. My companion ordered a large double double and two Boston cream doughnuts. I asked for a small black coffee. I drove up to Needham Park so we could look over the harbour while she ate. I took the opportunity to ask a few questions.

"Did you ever hear of something, say a club, known as the Colosseum here in the city?"

She shook her head. "I never heard of it. And if it has a cover charge, I can't afford it."

"I've heard that some of the street kids were lured, or enticed, to go to this place."

"Okay, so no cover charge."

"It wasn't a nightclub; it was really a group of adults who picked up some of the homeless people and brought them to —"

"You mean that cop?"

"What cop?"

"A guy who used to come around acting religious. He even brought this lady with him — she looked like she ate too much of her homemade bread. Or she worked slinging buns in a bakery all day. I remember she smelled like bread. She must've weighed a hundred and eighty pounds, easy. I forgot all about that till now. I used to think of her as the gingerbread lady. You know, that kid's book, I forget the name of it now. But the girls all knew he was a cop. The street bums probably didn't know the difference."

"What did these people want?"

She gave me the look of someone who has been around the block over and over again for decades, even though she was barely twenty-one. "What do they all want?"

"Did they come out and ask for sex?"

"No. I just told you. They pretended to be religious. Said they wanted to help."

"Help how?"

"By taking people off the streets. They'd take the kids home, they said."

"Meaning they'd take them back to their parents?"

"No, to some other home, I think. The gingerbread lady's house maybe."

"Did anyone ever go with them that you know of?"

"I saw this guy — he was stoned — he got in the car with them."

"What kind of car?"

She shrugged. "An old man's kind of car. Big, dark, boring, you know."

"So this guy got into the car."

"Yeah, and the lady drove and the cop got into the back seat with the dopehead, and they took off."

"Where was this?"

"It was downtown. By that shitty-looking parking garage. What do they call it?"

"Tex-Park?"

"Yeah, that's it."

"When did this happen?"

"I don't know. Years ago."

"Who was the guy they took with them? Any idea?"

"Just some little loser who was always hanging around in front of that cool old building on Barrington Street, with the turret. The Khyber."

"Did you see him again after that?"

She thought for a minute. "No, I never noticed him again."

"Where do you want me to drop you off?"

"Same place you found me."

I resisted the temptation to lay into her about what she was doing with her life. It would have been pointless.

"Take care of yourself, Candy," I said when I let her out.

"Yeah. See you in court."

"Without question."

The pizza would need reheating anyway so I further delayed my homecoming and made a detour downtown to the squalid, graffiti-covered parking structure at the corner of Sackville and Granville streets. I approached the attendant, a heavy-set man with jet black hair and the face of a boxer, and introduced myself.

"I'm hoping you can help me. I'm trying to track down a young guy who went missing a few years back."

"Good luck."

"How long have you been working here?"

"I been here eight years."

Now what? *Did you ever see a boring dark car with a coppish-looking man and a plump woman in it?*

"You see hundreds of cars a day, right?"

"Oh, yeah."

"Did you ever see anything that looked like a couple cruising for young kids in here?"

"You're puttin' me on. People drive in, they park, they drive out. What's to notice?"

"Did street people ever curl up here for the night?"

"Not if I could help it."

"Did they though?"

"Once in a while I'd see one drift in or out. I told them to move on."

"Who else used to work here? You aren't here twenty-four hours a day, seven days a week."

"It just seems like it. But if you're asking who else works here now that also worked here years ago, the answer is nobody. I'm the only veteran in this operation. We used to have students in here working part-time. One of them got so caught up in his homework, he missed some shitball who broke into nearly forty cars. What a genius. I was glad I wasn't his old man, footin' the college bill for that egghead."

"Do you remember the names of any of these students?"

"Nah, they came and went. Well, I remember the bozo who missed the break-in. 'Cause his name was Dudley. Dudley Douth-wright. Fit him to a T."

Dudley did not sound promising as an eyewitness, but he might have known other students who worked at the place. Or, he might have failed to notice them. I thanked the attendant and headed home.

There may have been a legion of God-fearing cops in the city, but the guy I pictured in that big dark sedan was Warren Tulk. When I got home I called Brennan. "Up for some more detective work?"

"It could be arranged."

I relayed what I had heard from Candace. "So I'm more curious than ever about the Reverend Warren Tulk. I told you he has a book-shop."

"Right. His Word."

"Why don't you drop in and do some shopping?"

"I'll ask him for an unabridged edition of the *Summa Theologiae*."

"You already have a copy of the *Summa*. I saw the volumes in your room."

"I have one of my own, yes. But I'm tired of lending it out. Comes back all dog-eared and covered with beer stains. Sure, the works of

St. Thomas make a lovely gift for those hard-to-buy-for individuals we all have in our lives."

"And while you're at it, get him talking about kids, street people, that kind of thing."

"I will."

I said goodbye and heated up the pizza.

†

"Monty!"

I was coming up from the cells in the Spring Garden Road courthouse on Wednesday afternoon when I was hailed by one of my wife's closest friends. Liz was tall and athletically built with uncontrollable shoulder-length blonde hair. She attracted attention wherever she went; if she noticed, she never let on. "Liz. Should I even ask what you're doing in this courthouse?"

"As opposed to divorce court, I suppose you mean. My divorcing days are long behind me," she sang out. "It got too expensive." She explained her presence: "Speeding ticket."

"City or highway?"

"Highway."

"Well done. I didn't know she had that much power."

"She certainly does. And it's the original engine."

"I know. Have you got her outside?"

"Want to go for a cruise?"

"Yeah."

Liz was well aware that I coveted her auto. The funny part was I generally had no interest in cars and bought whatever I could get a deal on when I needed a change. But this was a 1954 Chevy Bel Air, lovingly painted in pale, creamy yellow with white trim. The mid-May sunshine blazed from the car's glossy finish. She was parked around the corner beside the Sebastapol monument in the Old Burying Ground. Liz and I got into the Chev, rolled down our windows, and headed out on Barrington Street. We were the object of admiring glances as we cruised through the south end of Halifax. Inevitably, the name of our mutual acquaintance came up. "I was out with Maura the other night," Liz said.

"Mmm."

"Not in the best of cheer."

"When is she ever?"

"She's usually a million laughs when you're not around." How encouraging. "I'm sure it's the same for you," she added, as if that might take the sting out of it. "Of course, it probably had something to do with the jerk who accosted us at our table."

"Who do these waiters think they are?"

"I'll ignore that. Fanny, Maura, and I went out for dinner, then we repaired to one of the local establishments for our port and cigars. Gabbing away, having a grand old time, when this Romeo came over and said: 'What are you girls doing out alone on a Saturday night?' Alone! Of course, you know what he meant by that." She gave me a sidelong glance.

"Alone as in, not with him."

"Right. Three women in a bar without a man. That constitutes 'alone' in his lexicon."

"Would I be right in assuming you discouraged his advances?"

"Maura did. By the time she finished with him, I don't imagine he was able for any more advances that night. My point is: maybe the single life isn't all it's cracked up to be. For Maura, I mean. It suits me fine. I don't mind telling these clowns where to get off."

"But you think Maura's grown weary of telling people off? Is that even remotely possible? If so, we'll all be the better for it. More to the point, is she unattached these days?" Was she still seeing someone called Giacomo, is what I wanted to know.

Liz shrugged. "You know Maura. If there is someone, the experience is complete in itself; she's never felt the need to blab that kind of thing to her friends." As we pulled up in front of the courthouse, she added: "We're all coming to see your band tonight at the Flying Shag. She's looking forward to it."

"How do you know that?"

"Because she said: 'I'm looking forward to the Shag.'"

"Shag as in the nickname of the Flying Stag, or shag as in —"

"Get out of my car."

Looking forward to the evening? With me? That, from Liz, was the equivalent of any other female friend putting her hand on your arm, looking soulfully into your eyes, and spending an hour telling you she thinks there's hope for your "relationship" if you make the right moves in the wife's direction. I knew years would go by before Liz would ever get this personal again. Of course, maybe Maura was looking forward to the night out for reasons that had nothing to do with old Monty. But I wouldn't dwell on that.

I opened the door and got out, then caressed the car's gleaming finish. "I've got a gentle touch if you ever need someone to polish your rear panels there, Liz."

"Piss off, Monty. See ya!" I waved, and she purred away. I walked from the courthouse to my office, buoyed by the conversation but still cautious from long years of experience with my estranged spouse.

Chapter 6

I'm not some long-lost someone, just dropped in to say hello.
It's the same old loverman, baby, lost so long ago.
'Cause I was born to believe
I never could deceive.
— Gordon Lightfoot, "Same Old Loverman"

Maura, Liz, and Maura's other best friend, Fanny, were putting back the draft and whooping it up at the Flying Stag. The Stag — we called it the Shag — was a low-ceilinged bar located at the end of a suburban strip mall that also boasted a cheque-cashing service, a laundromat, and a pawnshop with a grimy, barred front window. My blues band, Functus, still played here on occasion, of which this was one. I looked upon my wife's presence as a sign of hope. In two more days she would be flying to Geneva for an international conference on poverty law. She would be out of the country for three weeks. The fact that she would spend one of her last nights in Halifax listening to old Monty and his blues harp had to mean something, did it not? I got the impression, from the mellow look on her face, that she had been lifting a few before her arrival. I, too, had a glow on from a couple of hours with my fellow Functi, at Comeau's on Gottingen Street.

"No, you don't," Maura said, seemingly out of the blue. When I followed her glance, I saw she was responding to Ed Johnson's sweatshirt, which said: "Do I fucking *look* like a people person?" She was right: he didn't.

But he had the people on his side during our first set. "House of the Rising Sun," with Ed on vocals and organ, was spellbinding. Not for the first time, his impassioned take on the old standard made me wonder just how close he was to the truth when he dismissed his family with the comment that they were "trash." Charlie Trenholm, our drummer, caught the mood and gave us an insistent, heavy drum beat that underscored the hard-luck drama of the song.

I alternated between guitar and harmonica for the set, then Ed and I sat down with Maura, her two pals, and Ed's wife, Donna. The person who had freely chosen to sign on with Ed Johnson for life — for better or for worse — was a handsome woman with an angular face, long dark hair, and stylish glasses. She had the air of one who sits back and watches the whole circus go by, making her own observations and not sharing them with the wider world. One thing she knew without any doubt was that Ed, although he would rarely admit it, would be lost without her.

But I was intent on my own wife; when we had finished the set, Maura had looked me up and down with eyes made lazy by intoxicants.

"Should I increase your spousal support payments, Collins?"

"Sure, go ahead." What payments? Neither of us was making any payments; we shared the expenses relating to the kids, but there were no other financial complications.

"A clothing allowance at least. How old are those jeans? They look as if you put them on when you were seventeen and grew into them over the ensuing decades. Can't be very comfortable."

"Is that a blues harp in your pocket or are you just glad to see me?" This from Fanny. In contrast to the tall, blonde Liz, who had gone through two divorces, Fanny was short, dark, freckled, and married to her childhood sweetheart. They had a houseful of kids.

"You've got her where you want her now, Collins," Ed chimed in, "eyeballing your fine masculine form."

"And the T-shirt," Maura continued, as she so often did, as if Johnson hadn't spoken. "Is that a picture of Dutchie Mason circa 1975? It's so faded I can't make it out. And then there's your face. They make disposable razors now. They're cheap."

The truth was I had about eight loads of laundry stacked up at home, and I had not been able to get to them. I hadn't shaved in the morning because I had overslept, had a quick shower and rushed off to work. I didn't bother to explain.

"Maybe she'd like you better if you looked more like an opera conductor," Johnson offered. "Didn't you name your daughter after some opera queen? I don't know what you guys see in all that screeching and melodrama, but who knows? Give it a try. Appear before her in a coat and tails, your golden locks swept back, your face the very portrait of artistic disdain. That's what she wants, Collins, not a scruffy-looking blues guy in a torn T-shirt. So tart yourself up and next thing you know, you'll be playing her like a violin."

"You mean he's going to take something long and rigid and move it back and forth, and back and forth, while I make sounds that people describe as almost human?"

"Yeah!"

"Nah, wouldn't want to wake the neighbours. Sorry."

"Bagpipes," Johnson tried.

"Let me get this straight. Collins would be dressed in a plaid skirt and he'd have me hiked up in his armpit somehow, squeezing me and —"

"Are you people barristers of the Supreme Court of Nova Scotia," Fanny asked us, "or white trash what just don't know how to act?"

"I'm both," Ed answered. "I won't speak for the other two."

"You're getting me nowhere, Johnson," I said to him.

"I never said it would be easy. Here, have another brew and try to hit on somebody else. How about Liz here?"

"Thanks, Ed, but I've gone off men," Liz replied. "Not worth the trouble. But you, Maura, come on. Look at him." She pointed to me. "He's so sweet. Kinda like a shopworn altar boy. How can you resist?"

She could resist, as I knew all too well. I turned the conversation to other matters, and drank too much beer. We did our next set and, because we had an extra horn player, ended it with a big number, namely Chicago's "South California Purples," with myself as lead vocalist. This performance was directed towards one end, namely pleasing my wife; it was one of her favourite songs. At one point during the piece I saw her big grey eyes on me. She looked away when I caught her. Did I have a chance after all?

"That didn't sound half bad," she conceded when I returned to the table. Her speech was a bit slurred. She got up to go to the wash-room and stumbled over her chair leg. Perhaps the sacrament of marriage could be renewed. I followed at a discreet distance and, when she emerged, I was ready.

"Come outside for a minute."

"Whatever for?"

I grabbed her by the hand and pulled her along till we were stand-ing in the shadows against the outside wall of the bar. She put up only token resistance, and I didn't want the opportunity to pass us by.

I said to her in an urgent whisper: "Let's get in the car and —"

"The car!"

"No! I meant get in the car and drive to my place where we can be alone and —"

"We can't leave our friends, and the band! And we're too blitzed to drive. You're like a god-damned teenager."

"I feel like one."

"Yes, you do, now that you mention it. Oh, Monty, this is prepos-terous. Back off."

"We won't be gone long. Just —"

"We won't be gone at all. Monty, I'm heading inside. I'm going to order a glass of ginger ale. And I am never going to drink this much again. Ever."

She stalked off to the entrance of the bar, and I followed behind, dejected.

My last set was the blues personified, and I was the object of inquiring glances from everyone but my former wife. She did not look in my direction again.

†

She had to face me the following day, however, because she was one of the organizers of a conference on criminal law being held at the Lord Nelson Hotel. I was giving a talk on "*Mens Rea*, Murder, and Fundamental Justice." To be taken seriously by the judges present, I had a shave and a haircut, and wore my most serious navy suit with my whitest white shirt, and a sombre tie. My presentation was scheduled just before we were to break for dinner. I discoursed upon the law and wove in some criminal court war stories. Given the attention and laughter accorded my presentation, I counted my performance a success.

"No more skin-tight jeans, I see," Maura remarked, as the waiters began serving pre-dinner drinks.

"They got a little uncomfortable last night. Quite suddenly."

"Yes. I remember. Your talk went over well."

"Maura, listen. I apologize for last night and for any disrespect I seemed to be showing you. I was an idiot."

"No more than I was!"

"Well, you had a higher blood alcohol reading than I did."

"I won't try to hide behind that," she said. "I don't want to waive my right to vilify all the other arseholes who do stupid things when they're drunk."

"So. Are you staying for the dinner?"

"Not much choice, given that I'm on the committee. But the last thing I need is another dinner with mashed potatoes. I can barely fit into some of my clothes."

"Well, you're pleasing to my eye, in or out of those tight, constricting garments."

"*Pòg mo thòn.*"

"Somebody told me that means 'pleased to meet you' in Gaelic," one of our fellow barristers chimed in on his way to the head table. "Do I have that right? I'm going over to Scotland for a conference on constitutional law next month, and I'd love to open with a Gaelic phrase. *Pawk ma hawn, Pawk ma hawn*, I'll have to remember that."

"Good idea," Maura agreed, all innocence, as she sent the president of our local Bar Society off to Scotland with the greeting *Kiss my arse*.

"You're bad," I told her. "So. Why don't you come sit with me and abuse me all through the meal?"

Abuse me she did, but I felt her heart wasn't in it. Emboldened, I put my arm across her shoulders and leaned in to deliver a few words of intimacy.

"Let's go get a room," I urged her.

"What? Now?"

"It's a hotel. Let's get a room."

"And leave in the middle of the banquet?"

"You'd rather sit through a bunch of after-dinner speeches than get naked in a great big king-size hotel bed? Come on."

The fates were smiling on old Monty at last. It took some effort to wear her down, but there we were, together in a hotel room for several hours of rapture.

Afterwards, I was spent and exhausted, and still I could not bear to relinquish her.

"Monty, let me go. I have to get home. I need some sleep and I have to finish packing for the trip tomorrow."

"I'm coming with you."

"No. You're not."

"Well, I have to check out."

"What for? You paid for the room. Stay in it."

"No, I'm leaving."

"You're not making any sense, Montague."

I wasn't about to admit that I wanted to leave just so I could tack on another five minutes in her presence, from the hotel to the house on Dresden Row. She would be in Geneva and I would not see her for three whole weeks; June 7, 1991, seemed as far off as the year 2000.

We went down to the desk. "I'd like to check out."

"Check out? Now?" the clerk inquired. New on the job, obviously.

†

I was in a daze as I sat in my office Friday morning not even pretending to do any work. I was capable of nothing more taxing than reliving the previous night in my head, over and over and over. I finally had to snap out of it — only temporarily, I promised myself — when Brennan called to say he had spoken with the Reverend Warren Tulk.

"Let's meet for a picnic," I suggested. The warm, golden spring day only enhanced my euphoria.

"Eat outside like a pack of squirrels, you're saying."

"Maybe the odd pigeon; this will be a downtown picnic."

So we bought sandwiches and joined the lunch-hour office workers in the city's Grand Parade. "Choose your view, Brennan. God or

Caesar." At one end of the parade square was St. Paul's Church, the oldest Protestant church in Canada; at the other end was City Hall, a sandstone Victorian building whose north-facing clock was stuck forever at 9:04, the time of the Halifax Explosion in 1917. We sat at the foot of the signal mast, and he gazed in the direction of the little Georgian church. I stared across Barrington Street at Dice Campbell's old office building, with its corner terrace on the tenth floor, from which he had jumped — or been pushed — to his death.

"Warren Tulk and I are pals now," Burke said. "Brothers in the Lord. I went to His Word Bookshop, ostensibly to buy a copy of the *Summa Theologiae*. But not one of St. Thomas's works was on offer. There was nothing in the shop to indicate that the church fathers had ever given their reasoned consideration to the great questions of revelation, theology, or metaphysics. No ancient texts, no modern theologians. I just can't accept the notion that any old yokel can read the Bible and come up with his own interpretation, and that is considered just as legitimate as —"

"You're such an RC. Why would you expect to find Catholic writings in a Protestant bookshop?"

"Why not? Wouldn't you want to cover the subject from as many angles as possible? I read Jewish theologians and philosophers. Why wouldn't a Protestant have a look at some of the great Catholic scholars?"

"All right, so you didn't find anything to your liking in the shop. What about Tulk?"

"He's a nice enough fellow. He spoke of this group he's associated with. Very evangelical by the sound of it. Almost speaking in tongues, I suspected."

"You mean like the early Christians whom everyone took to be drunks, but really they were filled with the Holy Spirit?"

"Monty! You give me hope. Your ignorance is nowhere nearly as profound as I have always feared. So much work to do here, I've always been thinking."

"Get to the point."

"Warren is concerned about social problems in the city or, as he also said, a complete moral breakdown. He blames the schools, the courts, the news media, et cetera, for the plight of so many young kids today. The schools because they have given up prayer and discipline, the courts because they are too lenient, the politicians for pandering to I forget whom, and the laws aren't strict enough. Oh, and sharp lawyers are a big part of the problem, for getting criminals off on technical defences. You get the picture."

"What's the solution, from the Tulkian perspective?"

"For one thing, a pressure group composed of clergy and lay people from various Christian churches in the city."

"Just Christians?"

"In his words, 'our Jewish brethren' are well-meaning, but too liberal on the issues."

"I see. What else?"

"We were interrupted. Some sort of crisis came up. A woman burst through the door. 'Warren! We had visitors. Jordan called me, and I just told him to stay inside. But —' That's when she spied the Papist lurking in the background, and the flow of words came to an abrupt and untimely halt. Significant glances were exchanged, and I knew the tactful thing would be for me to withdraw. So I stayed. But I wasn't able to suss out what was going on."

"This woman. Tell me about her. Was she his wife?"

"No."

"What did she look like?"

"A little roundish, with grey curly hair. Plainly dressed in a skirt, blouse, and cardigan sweater. Sensible shoes, as my sisters would say. A pleasant face. But she had something up her arse that day. He closed up shop and left with the woman."

"Did you go the extra mile and follow them home? You want that gold detective shield some day, and you're not going to earn it sitting on your butt reading the life of Billy Graham."

"I confess I did not. But they weren't going home, or not to his house anyway."

"Oh?"

"Tulk lives in Lower Sackville. This woman, or Jordan, or somebody, lives outside the city."

"How do you know that?"

"She didn't want to say anything with me there, so she engaged in a bit of subterfuge. She took out her wallet, which had a little pencil holder in it and a small notepad. She wrote out something for him to read. I couldn't see the note but I did get a quick glimpse of her driver's licence. I could not make out much in the short time I had, but her first name is Sarah, her last name starts with the letters MacL, and all I could see of the address was 'County, Nova Scotia.' Now I realize she could have been talking about a business or a shop of some kind, visitors showing up there, and Jordan being told to stay inside. So we may be talking about two locations, her home out in the county and this other place. Or it may be one."

"Why did you conclude this crisis was not at Tulk's house?"

"Oh. Right. Because he called his wife, Jill, and told her something had come up, and he might miss dinner. It was obvious she was asking him what was going on, and he was putting her off."

"Did he mention the other woman's presence in the phone call to the wife?"

"No."

"Did he ever say anything about having a son named Jordan?"

"He mentioned children, but I don't know whether he told me their names. So. What now, Lieutenant?"

"We track her down, Sergeant. Too bad her name doesn't start with Z, instead of MacL. Have you any idea how many MacLachlans, MacLarens, MacLeans, MacLellans, MacLennans, and MacLeods are in the phone book?"

"Have you any idea how tiny and insubstantial your phone directory looks to someone who is accustomed to the multiple tomes of the New York City white pages?"

"Very well, then. That wee tiny task is yours. Let me know when you've found her."

"Then what?"

"Then we go out there, wherever it is, and find out why they don't like visitors."

"I've already blown my cover."

"I'll go in alone. If anything happens to me, you run in from the bushes and give me the last rites."

"Sounds like a rational plan. Do you think all this is getting you anywhere?"

"Not yet, obviously. But I can't proceed with litigation over a suicide if it's going to turn out to be murder committed by someone else."

"And you're thinking of Tulk as a suspect?"

"I don't know if I'd go so far as to call him a suspect."

"Then why are you looking into him? Because you believe there's a link between Leaman and Campbell, and Tulk raided one of Campbell's parties?"

"He raided the party, he's known to have very strong views on people he considers degenerates, he got turfed from the police force for his attitude. And didn't you tell me sharp lawyers are on his black-list? Finally, as I told you, I heard about a couple sounding very much like Tulk and this woman Sarah cruising, or at least looking, for young people in a rundown old parking garage downtown."

"Looking for them for what purpose?"

"That's what we have to find out."

When our picnic was over, I walked back to the office for my last appointment of the day: Corey Leaman's mother. I waited for her, but she didn't show up. I would give her ten more minutes, then I would slip the surly bonds of office life, pick up the kids and head over to my brother Stephen's for what I knew would be a sumptuous dinner. His wife, Janet Stratton, was the daughter of my senior partner. She had overcome her British joint-on-Sunday heritage and had become a superb cook. Janet hosted the dinner every year to kick off the Victoria Day long weekend in May. The kids and I looked forward to stuffing ourselves and playing with Steve and Janet's two small children. The minutes passed, Leaman's mother didn't show, and I was off.

†

By mid-morning Saturday, Tommy had left to see his girlfriend, Lexie; I had dropped Normie off to play with her best friend, Kim; and thoughts of work began to encroach on my day; I wondered why Corey Leaman's mother had failed to keep her appointment. Had I seen the last of her, once she learned there would be no advance pay-ments from the Baird Centre? If she was legit — if she really was Corey's mother — I wanted whatever information she could give me about her son. I was headed downtown anyway, so I went to the office and retrieved the file from the cabinet in the back corridor. Yes, she had given me her number.

I reached her on the phone. "Yeah?"

"Mrs. Lea — Mrs. Carter?"

"What."

"This is Monty Collins. You had an appointment with me yesterday. Did you forget about it?"

"Oh, yeah, right. I had other things on my mind."

"I see. Well, I was wondering if we could schedule another appointment so you can bring in whatever information you have about Corey."

"Kinda hard to find anything in here today."

"Is there a problem?"

"I'd say it's a problem when somebody breaks in and tears the place apart and makes off with my personal belongings!"

"You had a break-in?"

"Oh yeah, big time."

"When was this?"

"Night before last."

"Were you home at the time?"

"If I'da been home, don't you think that fucker woulda had a fight on his hands before he lifted my brand-new TV and remote?" She was wheezing just telling the story; I couldn't quite imagine her fighting off a burglar.

"Have the police been there?"

"It was prob'ly them."

"Probably them what?"

"That done it."

"Why would you say that?"

"They always had it in for me and my family, that's why."

"Still, I doubt they would burglarize your place. Do I take it you didn't report it?"

"They're useless."

"Listen. Hang on there and I'll come over."

"Suit yourself."

The Leaman/Carter family home in Lower Sackville was a run-down bungalow with avocado-green siding, which was coming away at the corners and around the door.

Vonda Carter was in a purple track suit this time. She invited me inside. The living room had a soiled rust-brown carpet and a suite of furniture covered in orange, gold, and green floral fabric. A print of a garish yellow and pink sunset was the only decoration; it appeared that a plaque had been wrenched off the bottom of the frame, giving rise to the inference that the print had been swiped from a motel room. Things had not yet been put to rights after the burglary. A number of bowling trophies and other objects were strewn across the floor; a set of metal shelves stood empty. Vonda sat in front of a black plastic table on which there was an overflowing ashtray with a cigarette burning in it, and the scrapings from a collection of scratch-and-win lottery tickets.

"Look at this dump. What kind of animal would do that?"

"Don't you think you'd better call the police?"

"Fuck it."

"When did you get home and discover this?"

"Around ten in the morning."

"You'd been out all night?"

"Yeah, I was out all night."

"Do you think it might have been somebody you know?"

"Nobody even knows I'm back in town yet!"

"Well, the person you spent the night with knows."

"Like, I wouldn't notice if he got up and left for two hours, then came back with the stuff he stole outta my place? Gimme a break."

"I meant if he knows you're back in town, he may have told somebody else. Word may have got around." No reply. "Was there any trouble here when you were away?"

"Never."

"Was someone living here in your absence?"

"Most of the time."

"Who?"

"My cousin."

"Where's the cousin now?" She shrugged. "Did the cousin report anything suspicious?"

"More like the neighbours ratted on him, than him reporting on anything else."

"What did the neighbours say?"

"Called the cops on him for a couple of parties. They came, but they didn't find nuthin'."

"As far as you could tell, when you got back from Kingston, was everything still here?"

"Like what?"

"I mean, did you notice anything missing when you got home from prison?"

"There was nothing missing."

"When had your cousin moved out?"

Another shrug. "Months before that."

"So, what was taken in the break-in?"

"My TV, remote and VCR, a set of knives, and other stuff," she said, then added: "and a picture!"

"What kind of picture?"

"By that guy. You know, he's Canadian."

"His name?"

"I don't remember his name, but he did that picture with the binoculars."

"You don't mean Alex Colville?"

"Alex! Yeah!"

I didn't bother to respond to that and neither, I guessed, would the claims department of her insurance company.

"What do you think they were after?" I asked her.

"Beats me. The fucking pricks."

"What are you going to do?"

"Well, I've got that back."

"Hmm?"

"I've got that back that hurts. When it gets better or if I take a couple of Tylenol Threes, then I'll put this mess back together."

What could I say? "Do you want me to help you?"

She looked ready to jump at the idea, then had a change of heart. All of a sudden she didn't like the idea of me going through her things.

"Nah. Thanks anyways."

"While I'm here, though, could you put your hands on anything you have relating to Corey?"

"No, I can't."

"Why not?"

"Because whoever was in here took all my personal papers."

"What kind of papers?"

"I had a box where I kept all my bills, prescriptions, letters, old probation orders, the usual shit."

"Did these papers include things relating to Corey?"

"I guess. I never looked at them for a long time."

"What might have been in them?"

"Old pictures he drew, maybe a couple of report cards, stuff about his treatments, I don't know."

"Do you have any other children?"

"Yeah, Shonda Lee. But I never seen her for years. I think she's out in Vancouver."

"Did the burglar take stuff about her too?"

"All my papers," she repeated.

"How about family photos? Do you have any of those?"

"I suppose so."

"Could you check?"

She heaved herself up from the chesterfield and made her way into a back room. I got up and looked around. I saw an old Bacardi box in the corner with a couple of papers in the bottom. But they were just credit card receipts. A cable television bill and an old Lotto 649 ticket were caught in one of the carton's flaps. This may have been the vault. I heard her chugging in behind me.

"Is this where you kept all your papers?"

"Yeah."

The burglar didn't want to lug the box out; he must have had a sack with him.

"Here's some pictures."

She handed me two photographs. One was a school picture of Corey in grade two; he looked like any other dark-haired kid with a tooth missing. The other must have been Corey, though it was impossible to tell. All I could see was a small person in an enormous helmet, sitting on an all-terrain vehicle.

"Where was this taken?"

Vonda shrugged. "Beats me."

On my way downtown I considered the break-in. Judging by

what was left in place at Vonda's, I suspected she had not had a collection of valuable silver or electronic items. She had just been released from Kingston Penitentiary. I didn't think it likely that expensive goods survived the four years of her absence, only to disappear as soon as she returned home. I tended to believe the television and VCR really existed; they would have been the first items she acquired after being sprung from P4W. She may also have picked up a supply of drugs or cash on her arrival. Wouldn't she have taken them — drugs at least — with her when she headed out for an all-nighter with the boyfriend? If it was a straight burglary, carried out by somebody looking for items to sell, why would the guy take her personal papers? It seemed far more likely that the papers, whatever they were, constituted the real reason for the break and enter. But what had been in that box? Were the papers related to Vonda, or to her son? Was it coincidence that the break-in occurred shortly after she got back in town? Unlikely. Had she brought papers home with her? If so, did they have something to do with our case? Did she really not know what the burglar was after? I hadn't had any luck in my interview with her. I decided to call Leaman's girlfriend in for another talk.

I wondered what kind of friction might develop between the girlfriend and the mother. Maybe it already had. Amber Dawn Rhyno was unavailable when I called; I left a message on her machine.

†

Tom, Normie and I spent a fun, relaxing Sunday, which I appreciated all the more because I knew I could not take Monday off even though it was a holiday. Too many cases coming up that week. I would have to join the other nerds working Monday.

When the morning came, I was not in the mood for Corey Leaman's common-law widow. I had just received some bad news in a phone call from Ed Johnson.

"Remember that old hooker who used to get all liquored up and hit on you at the Flying Shag? The one whose false teeth fell out when she choked on a piece of pepperoni, and she just put them in her pocket and —"

"I know, Ed. She's been a client of mine for years. Ronette Gammon. What about her?"

"Let's just say lemon gin sales are down, the penicillin market has taken a permanent dive, and there's a new set of dentures in the organ donation registry."

"For Christ's sake, Ed. What happened?"

"She's dead. Beaten to death by some lowlife boyfriend."

"Oh, God! The poor little thing. She never had a hope. Some of these people, you read their files going back through their lives and you try to figure out the point where some kind of intervention or assistance might have made a difference. With some of them, you realize, there was nothing that could be done. The course was set at conception. This father, that mother, you could predict everything that would happen in the kid's future. None of it good. I think she was one of those."

"A doomed zygote."

I agreed. When I got off the phone, I thought about Ronette Gammon, her miserable life, her predictable death, and the unfairness of life in general. I looked up when Amber Dawn Rhyno and young Zachary were ushered in. The kid was yelling "Ninja! Ninja!" over and over and over again. Every once in a while he leapt off his chair, and every time — every single time — the chair tipped over with a crash, causing him to shout an obscenity while he struggled to set it upright again. This did not prompt him to vary his routine. Amber Dawn sat there picking at a scab on her thumb and ignoring her son. I took a deep breath and got on with it.

"Amber," I began, "did you notice anything unusual about Corey's demeanour just before his death?"

"His what?"

"His death."

"Yeah, but what did you say before his death?"

What? Oh. "His demeanour. The way he was acting, the way he was talking. His mood. Anything different around the time of his death?"

"Well, he was pissed off."

"About what?"

"I mean upset. You know, about being sent home from the treatment centre." She was sticking to her lines, but I needed more than that.

"You said he was pissed off. Tell me about it. I'm not the judge. I need all the information I can get in order to do my job here."

"Somethin' happened. It got him all worked up."

This was the first time I had heard about something happening. "Worked up how?"

"He was bouncin' off the walls, he had somethin' on his mind."

"Did he give you any idea what it was?"

"He wouldn't tell me but he said he had to take care of it."

It sounded as if another nail was about to be driven into the coffin of *Leaman and Scott v. The Wallace Rennie Baird Addiction Treatment Centre.*

"When did this happen?"

"Like, a couple of days before he got — before he committed suicide." She sat forward and spoke with urgency. "I figured it had something to do with the treatment centre. Like, maybe he found some papers or talked to a doctor or something and found out they made a mistake. Proof they shouldn't have let him out. And they were trying to cover it up."

"What makes you think that?"

She shrugged. She had reached the limits of her imagination.

"You mentioned papers, Amber. Did you see any papers?"

"Not really."

"Well, yes or no?"

"I said no."

"You qualified it. You said 'not really.' So, did you see any papers?"

"No."

"Did he mention papers of some kind?"

"I thought he was just tryin' to make me jealous, you know?"

"No, I don't know. Tell me."

"Zach! Get over in that fuckin' corner and be quiet or I'll cut it off!"

"Cut what off?" I asked, startled. The boy set up a wail that went on and on, up and down, like a siren.

"He knows what I mean. Don't you, Zach? I told him if he's bad I'll cut off the cable TV and he'll have to watch the CBC or the French. See how long he lasts with that!"

"Amber. What did you mean about jealousy?"

"Corey said he heard from an old girlfriend. But I didn't believe him."

"Why not?" Another shrug. "Who was the old girlfriend?"

"I dunno. I think he was lying. Not lying, but you know. It did-n't mean nuthin', I know that, 'cause me and him were going to get married."

"All right. What exactly did he say?"

"He come home that night and —"

"Home from where?"

"He went out to his old house. His mother's house."

"Was that somewhere he went regularly, out to the house?"

"No. Like, there was other people living in it."

"Who?"

"I dunno. Some uncle or something."

"But Corey went out there on this occasion."

"They were movin' out. His uncle and them. So Corey said he was goin' out there to see if there was anything he could, like, use."

"What, for instance?"

"Furniture and stuff."

More likely looking for things to sell before his mother returned from Kingston. "All right. He went out to the house in Sackville. Then what?"

"Then he come home and I was like: 'Did you get any stuff?' And he was like: 'I found somethin' else.'" She brought the scabbed thumb to her mouth and began to gnaw. I couldn't watch.

"Amber. What did he say he'd found?"

"He was raggin' me about this letter or whatever it was. Sayin' it's great to go to the old homestead once in a while and read letters from your old girlfriends."

"Did he bring any letters home with him?"

"No. I asked him and he said he didn't bring it because it was safer where it was."

"Safer? What did he mean by that?" She didn't answer. "Safer in that you wouldn't see it?"

"I don't think that's what he meant. He seemed like he wanted to hide it from somebody else."

"So you've never seen it?"

"No. I searched his pockets and all his other stuff that night but he didn't have it."

"And it was after this that he was worked up?"

"Yeah, whatever it was, he wanted to do somethin' about it."

"So, what happened after that?"

"You know."

"No, I don't."

"He died."

"What was the timeline? His body was found on the twelfth of January. His death occurred that morning, several hours earlier. Had you seen him the night he died?"

"Uh-uh. He never come home that night."

"At all?"

"He went out that morning, first thing, and I never seen him again." She looked away.

"I'm going to look into this, Amber, and I'll be in touch."

"He wouldna been so worked up about all that shit, whatever it was, if he got the treatment he needed at the centre. His head wasn't on straight."

"Did you ever meet Corey's mother?"

"Huh?"

"Corey's mother, Vonda."

"I never seen her."

"Okay. I'll talk to you later."

She grabbed Zachary and dragged him from the room. He set up a cry: "Don't cut it off, Mama, don't cut it off!" Once again, one of old Monty's clients draws unwelcome attention in the waiting room of Stratton Sommers.

So. A letter from someone in Leaman's past. An old girlfriend, Amber thought. Whatever it was, he had left it at his mother's house for safekeeping. The question was: would the letter still be there? Had Vonda Carter found it? Had the burglar taken it? And what was in the letter that set Corey off so soon before he was found with a bullet in his head?

Chapter 7

All we like sheep have gone astray.
We have turned every one to his own way.
And the Lord hath laid on Him the iniquity of us all.
— Isaiah, 53:6 (Handel, *Messiah*)

After reaching a settlement in a personal injury case late Tuesday morning, I was sitting across from Dudley Douthwright in his office at Dalhousie University. I hadn't really expected Dudley, assistant professor of statistics and quantitative methods, to look like his name, but he did. Or perhaps he was trying to live up, or down, to the name. He had the appearance of an unassuming, fairly handsome man of forty-five, but he probably wasn't past his late twenties. He wore glasses, a white shirt, navy tie, and pale blue cardigan.

"Thanks for seeing me, Doctor Douthwright."

"You're welcome. With classes over for the year, I have a little more time to spare."

I explained why I was there.

"Tex-Park. Oh, my. Not my most exciting employment opportunity."

I resisted the temptation to ask where he had succeeded in finding vocational thrills.

"Did you ever see any homeless people sleeping or hanging around there?"

"I suppose I saw people who did not seem to correlate with a vehicle. They must have been using the facility for something other than parking. But I can't say I paid much attention."

"Do you remember the names of any of the other part-time attendants?"

"I was there in 1985 and 1986. What year are you inquiring about?"

"I wish I knew."

"When did the person go missing?"

"Again, I'm not sure."

"I don't know what you can expect to learn from such nebulous data, Mr. Collins."

"I know. It's a long shot."

"All I can give you are the names of a couple of students I worked with during the summers I ingested all those exhaust fumes at the parking garage. I can still taste it." He shuddered. "I knew a Donny somebody who put in a few hours a week there. And Chaz Thurber. He worked several summers there while doing his sociology degree. He spent much of his time making what he no doubt considered insightful comments about the people and their choice of vehicle."

"Where's Thurber now, any idea?"

"Still labouring away at his Ph.D, as far as I know."

"Here at Dal?"

"He's studying here and teaching part-time at the Mount."

"Thanks for your help."

"You're welcome. I hope you're not wasting your time."

I called Mount Saint Vincent University to make sure Chaz Thurber was there, then decided to have lunch before heading out to the campus. The death of my old client, Ronette, weighed on my mind, and I wanted to be alone. I drove home, fixed myself a sandwich, and sat out in the sunshine. I wondered whether there was anything I could have done beyond getting her out of her various legal predicaments. But I knew the answer: nothing I could have done would have altered her fate. One thing this tragedy did, though, was bring into stark relief how petty my own troubles were; I resolved to pull out all the stops to get my family back together when Maura got home from Geneva.

While I was sitting there, one of the neighbourhood kids came by, weighed down by a rake, a hoe, and some other gardening implements.

"Hi, Mr. Collins. You don't mind if I cross here, do you? It's quicker this way, and this stuff's heavy."

"I don't mind at all, Ian. Any time. Have you taken up gardening?"

"I'm helping out at Mrs. Fancy's; she can't do it herself. Gives me a bit of spending money. You know."

"Great. I may have some things I need help with too."

"Sure."

That reminded me: I had never heard back from my former colleague, Bob Mahoney, about Corey Leaman's neighbour, the woman he'd helped by doing errands and odd jobs. She might be able to give me some insight into Corey. Would she have known him well enough to say whether he seemed the type to take his own life? Perhaps not, but it was worth a try. I didn't have much else to go on. I sat for a few more minutes, then hauled myself out of my chair and called the office of my old employer, Nova Scotia Legal Aid. I got Bob's secretary on the line.

"How are you these days, Monty?"

"Great, Trudy."

"Do you miss us?"

"Yes, I do, as a matter of fact. How are things?"

"Fair to middling. Bob isn't here. He's in court all day. But I know he was trying to reach you. Don't know what it was about. I'll tell him you called."

I then called my own office and found out Bob had left a message for me that morning.

"Good thing you asked, Monty. I forgot to write you a message slip."

Why didn't that surprise me? My secretary, Tina, was far, far out of her depth in a law office. "What did he say?"

"He said: 'Tell Monty the name of the woman he's looking for is Mrs. Lundrigan.'"

"All right. Thank you, Tina. And try to stay on top of those messages."

The phone directory did not identify anyone by the name of

Lundrigan in Leaman's area of Sackville, so I decided to take a little jaunt out to the Leaman-Carter neighbourhood to ask around. I got the impression nobody was home chez Vonda, which was good; I wasn't about to tip my hand to Leaman's mother about my search for Mrs. Lundrigan. I began my canvassing at the house next door. But the harried young mother, with one baby on her hip and a naked toddler clinging to her leg, had never heard of Mrs. Lundrigan. Across the street were two new jerry-built apartment blocks. I did not expect any joy there, but I made the rounds anyway. Only at a house a block away did I come close to enlightenment.

"I don't know."

"All right. Thanks anyway."

"But my grandmother might."

"Oh. Could I speak to her?"

"No."

"No?"

"She's not here."

"I see. Where could I find her?"

"She's in a home."

"Tell you what. I'll leave you my card. If you're speaking to your grandmother, you might ask her, and you can call me if she has any information about Mrs. Lundrigan."

"Okay."

I drove back along the Bedford Highway and dropped in at Mount Saint Vincent to speak to the former sociology student who had made comments about the customers and their cars during his nights as an attendant at Tex-Park. I parked my car and took a moment to enjoy the spectacular view from the campus, which overlooks the waters of the Bedford Basin. I found Chaz Thurber in his office examining a long accordion-pleated computer printout. After seeing how well Dudley Douthwright fit the popular image of a statistician, I was expecting a tweedy, bearded academic in the sociology instructor. But Chaz Thurber looked more like an Argentinian soccer star, with wavy long black hair and a strikingly handsome face. I introduced myself, gave him a short spiel on why I was there, and asked when he had worked at Tex-Park.

"Summers of '84 to '86."

"Did you notice any street kids hanging around the place?"

"Oh, sure. I used to rap with some of them."

Rap? Were we back in the seventies? "Perhaps you can help me then. Was there any talk about a man and a woman driving around, or parking at Tex-Park, and picking up street kids in their car?"

"There was no talk about it, but I had my own suspicions."

"Oh?"

"I had seen the same car there at the same time of night, off and on for a few weeks. There wasn't anything unusual in that by itself, but I remember thinking I never saw the occupants come down the stairs and go out. It seemed they parked and stayed up there, then drove out later. There was just something about them that didn't jibe. He looked fairly young and fit, and she was older. She was like an archetype of the homely peasant: heavy, round-faced. They didn't seem like a couple. They had some kind of religious totem dangling from the rear-view mirror."

"What kind of car was it?"

"A Crown Victoria. I knew the licence number at the time, but I can't remember it now."

"Why did you feel strongly enough about this to memorize the tag number?"

"Because one night they had this girl in the car with them. And I thought maybe they were exploiting these marginalized young people."

"Who was the girl?"

"Someone I'd seen hanging around in the parking garage."

"And then she was with this couple? Did you get the impression she had gone into the car willingly? Or had she been abducted?" He shrugged and looked away. "What is it?" I prompted him.

"I don't know what she was doing with them. She may have known them, or —" Again, a reluctance to continue.

"What's the matter, Chaz?"

"It's just that I had tried to connect with this girl, do some dialoguing, She wouldn't open up. When I saw her in the back seat of the car, I made kind of a questioning gesture as if to say: *What are you doing there?* Or: *Are you okay?*"

"And?"

"She gave me the finger."

"And then what?"

"Nothing, really."

"So you didn't follow it up?"

"No."

"Why not?" But I knew the answer. She had given him the finger, brushed off his attempts to "dialogue." So the hell with her, even if she was being exploited. "Did you see the girl again?"

"No. Right then was when a group of stowaways was found on a ship from the Middle East. I got involved in that issue and I left my job in the parking garage."

"So you have no idea what happened to the girl."

"No. But the way she looked at me when she left was not, like, *Help me, I'm being kidnapped.* It was *Fuck you.* So, she didn't look as if she was in fear of her life."

"Not at that point, anyway," I said.

I left him and drove downtown.

When I got back to my desk, I scribbled some notes on that day's interviews and put them in the file. Graham Scott's name caught my eye. I didn't have much information about him. It occurred to me to ask his family for a photo. Not that it would serve much of a purpose, but it could provide an excuse to see his parents and perhaps learn more about his life. So I picked up the phone, called his mother, and invited myself over to pick up a snapshot.

The Scotts lived in a large, elegant old house on Larch Street, across from Kings College. The entire front yard was a garden of spring flowers. Muriel Scott, wearing an old canvas jacket and a straw hat, was pruning a shrub; it looked as if it was just past flowering.

"You're handy with a pair of secateurs," I said to her.

"That's a word we don't hear much these days," she replied. "Come inside."

She ushered me into a living room done tastefully in pale blue and cream.

"How are things progressing?" she asked.

"Oh, these matters tend to move at a stately pace."

"I see. Well. Let's choose a photograph of Graham. You need this for what again?"

"We want to come as close as we can to an accurate account of what happened that night," I improvised. "It would help if we could trace Graham's movements."

"I thought the facts were quite straightforward, Mr. Collins. This Leaman fellow was released prematurely from the Baird Centre. His problems were such that he took my son's life, and then shot himself with the same weapon."

"Yes. But the fewer loose ends we have heading into the litigation, the less likely we'll be tripped up by opposing counsel. We want to be in possession of all the facts, as painful as they might be. A picture may assist us in finding people who may have seen Graham that night."

"Very well. Have a seat, Mr. Collins. Can I get you anything? Tea, coffee?"

"No, thank you, Mrs. Scott. I won't keep you."

She left the room and came back a few minutes later with two large photo albums. "I don't suppose there is much point in showing you this one. It depicts Graham's earlier life, his teen years. This is the more recent collection." She fell silent as she reverently turned the pages of her son's short life. I picked up the earlier album and saw a handsome, sandy-haired young boy on the tennis court, on the golf links, and on a modest-sized sailboat. I could see only part of the boat's name: "— *ark*." In his late teens, Graham began appearing on a series of Japanese motorcycles, starting at about the 350 cc size, moving up to a Goldwing 1000. A series of girlfriends stood at his side; the girls seemed to get less and less preppy-looking as the years went by. I could have sworn one was an old client of mine.

Mrs. Scott turned to me and drew my attention to some pictures in the later album. Graham on the Dalhousie campus, Graham at a church event with his father in his vestments, Graham clowning on one of the *bateaux-mouches* on the Seine, Graham with his arm around a black-haired beauty on the deck of a sailboat. Not the "— *ark*" this time, a larger boat with a crowd of revellers on board.

"Quite the sailor, was he?" I asked his mother.

"Oh yes, Graham loved the water. That's my brother's boat. Graham was on board every chance he got."

I looked at the background. The photo must have been fairly recent. Mad Ludwig's Castle was visible on shore. "Do you know the Fanshaws?" I asked, pointing to the garish house.

Her mouth tightened into a severe line, but she said in a level voice: "No. Well, we have met them at various events around the city, but we don't know them personally." Not our sort, darling, I suspected.

"Then I imagine you're glad you're not in sighting range of the palace."

"Mmm. They do a lot of good works," she said dutifully.

I thought of something then, a remark I had heard about a boat. "That boat Graham was on, the smaller one — do you know the name of it?"

She cleared her throat. "Yes. That was Kenneth Fanshaw's boat. He called it the *Biz-Mark*. Prompting some to question his grasp of history."

"So Graham used to sail with Mr. Fanshaw."

"I believe that was an isolated incident. Now if you look at the more recent photos, you'll see Graham as he was shortly before his life was taken from him."

The albums showed a privileged young man enjoying his life. I wondered whether he had possessed a photo spread of his own, detailing the seamier side of that life. His mother and I agreed on a close-up, which showed him to great advantage, and I headed back to work. I would probably never have occasion to show his picture to anyone because I couldn't think of anyone to show it to.

I got to the office just in time to receive a call from a Mrs. Pottie. "Hello."

"Are you the fellow's been asking after poor Tilly?"

"Um, I don't —"

"Speak up! They've got the darn television turned up so loud you'll have to shout. Half the people here are deaf! I'm at Shady Dale, you know, the nursing home. Ever since I took a turn."

The Shady Deals nursing home. Poor soul, whoever she was. "Mrs. Pottie? I'm sorry. I'm not sure what you're calling me about."

"Weren't you out in Sackville earlier today asking after Tilly? My granddaughter — God knows, she's thick as two planks — she was just here. A red-letter day when I get a visit from that one. She gave me a business card and said some man was on the doorstep."

"Oh, yes. Tilly Lundrigan. So, what can you tell me about —"

"I can start by telling you you've got her name wrong. I thank my

Lord and Saviour that I still have my hearing. Maybe you're not so fortunate. Tilly's name was Lonergan, and I don't know how many times I've heard people say it like *Lundrigan*. Tilly Lonergan. Now, what is it you want to know?"

"I'd like to know where I can reach her."

"Is that some kind of joke?"

"No. Oh, is she —"

"Tilly's been gone ten years now. Heart. If I told her once, I told her a thousand times. I said: 'Tilly, get your medications adjusted. They've got you on so many pills, they're probably cancelling each other out.' But Tilly was the type, doctors are God. Well, she's with God now and if she could be here to give us a revelation, she'd probably tell us He's not a quack in a white coat writing prescriptions for pills that the drug companies are out to get rich on even if they kill you."

"You were a good friend of Mrs. Lonergan, I take it."

"Well, neighbourly friends, you know. See each other at the bus stop on the way in for our appointments, or her going to that food bank or wherever it was she helped out. Though why Tilly took the bus when she could easily have afforded a taxi, I couldn't tell you. Same with that house. She never put a cent into it. They tore it down, and slapped up a bunch of apartments. Instant slum. But anyway, that's the way things are. We'd see each other in the street and say hello."

And knew each other's prescriptions. Well, I supposed that was bus chat for some people. "Did Mrs. Lonergan ever mention a young guy by the name of Corey Leaman?"

"I know that scoundrel used to work around Tilly's house, but she never spoke of him to me. Maybe because she knew what I thought of him."

"You knew Corey?"

"I didn't know him. I knew *of* him. Drugs and loud cars, and God knows what else. A jailbird in the end. Well, you could see that coming."

"Well, thank you, Mrs. Pottie. I appreciate your call."

"You're welcome. Now, if you'll excuse me, I have to get after this bunch of incompetents to turn down that squawk box so some of us can have a moment's peace. Goodbye."

So. No kindly neighbour to reminisce with me about Corey Leaman. But the name Tilly Lonergan had struck a chord in a distant chamber of my mind. I would have to give it some consideration. Meanwhile, I had thought of someone else who had known Leaman. It was quitting time, but I would try for one more interview before I left. Doctor Gareth Swail-Peddle, who worked with Corey at the Baird Centre, had promised to come in if he found his notes about Corey's treatment. I called his office, but was told he was out of town, attending a "codependency" conference in Las Vegas. I left a message asking him to call me.

†

"Are you into the candies again, Normie? I told you no candy before your supper." I had just walked into my living room to find both my kids with their hands in the candy bowl. They ignored me.

"Is there real fruit in these ones?" Normie asked her brother. "I should be allowed three if it's real fruit."

"I think we can count anything made of sugar as fruit," Tom answered. "Sugar grows out of the ground. It might even be a vegetable."

"Four then," Normie muttered, and she scooped them up in her hands.

"You got a problem with that, Dad?" my son asked me.

"Nah. Supper's just frozen lasagna anyway."

I stuck the lasagna in the oven, and we all went downstairs where I kept my instruments. I took out one of my harmonicas and played some shuffles, with Tom keeping up on guitar, and Normie plinking along on the keyboard.

"We're going to a *ceilidh*, right, Daddy?"

"Hmm?"

"When we go to Cape Breton."

"Yes, right." Maura and I had made plans, during our night of détente at the Lord Nelson, to take the kids to Glace Bay the weekend she got back, to visit her family. This had not been presented as a second honeymoon by any means; it was, if I remembered accurately: "You may as well come too, and Brennan. He'll enjoy the music. There's a *ceilidh* that weekend." Still, I was hopeful.

"Grandma called the other night and said she'll have the tea on."
So, it had been confirmed. All the better.

I sat there smiling at my children. I remembered the feeling of Normie's soft little arms curling around my neck when she was a toddler. I remembered Maura coming by in the car to pick me up at the office, our baby girl in the car seat; the little chubby legs would start kicking when she saw me, and a big grin would spread across her face. Tommy was the same at that age. Nobody ever loves you like that again. Makes you believe human beings are basically good. Or at least they start off that way.

We ate our lasagna, and Tom settled down to a chemistry assignment. It took some effort, but I got Normie started on her math homework. Then I put some tunes on the stereo and did nothing but anticipate the weekend in Cape Breton.

The Leaman case must have been percolating just below my consciousness, though, because when I turned my mind to it, I remembered where I had seen the name Matilda Lonergan: in Dice Campbell's papers. And one of Dice's news clippings was about an unnamed offender who turned out to be Corey Leaman. I had not yet decided whether to regard that as a coincidence or a finding of significance. Bob Mahoney had told me Mrs. Lonergan had spoken fondly of Leaman at one of the boy's court hearings. Was it the relationship with Leaman that accounted for her name in Dice's records? I sat back and closed my eyes, trying to bring an image of those files into my mind. A lease, that was it. And Campbell had handled the woman's will along with some other little job, a pension problem or something. But why not? A lawyer practising alone tended to do a bit of everything. If it put a hundred dollars or so in his pocket, that was better than zero. Perhaps later, when the practice grew, a will would not — I remembered it then. John Trevelyan, before his elevation to the bench, had passed the little assignments on to Campbell. Not worth his time, I supposed. Why not get a junior lawyer in his own firm to handle it, though? The person who could answer that question, of course, was Justice Trevelyan. But there was no need for me to endure the insufferable man myself when I had his long-suffering son in my office. Ross was probably still bent over his desk on a Tuesday evening, toiling away to pay the humongous mortgage he must have taken out for the house on Beaufort Avenue.

"Hello?" Even two syllables gave him away. The man was frazzled.

"Ross. It's Monty. You sound a little tense."

"Oh, Christ. I took the long weekend off. Worst thing I ever did. The whole weekend I was in a panic about what was waiting for me at the office. And sure enough, it's come down on me like a ton of bricks. I've got discoveries tomorrow and I haven't even read the file. That's because I have a factum due —" I heard a crash and shot the phone away from my ear. "Sorry, sorry. I had the phone on top of the appellant's factum, which is the size of, well, a phone book, and when I reached . . . Never mind. What can I do for you, Monty?"

"This won't add too much to your workday."

"Whew! So, what gives?"

"I was just wondering if you could have a word with your father for me."

"A word about . . ."

"Not about a case in his courtroom, needless to say. A name has come up in connection with the Leaman case. A woman called Matilda Lonergan." Silence. "Ross? Are you there?"

"Sorry again, Monty. I'm half reading what's in front of me here. You'll have to forgive me. What was the name again?"

"Matilda Lonergan."

"Never heard of her."

"No, well, the connection was with your father."

"Oh. Okay."

"I remember seeing something about her in Dice Campbell's old files."

"Dice Campbell."

"Yeah, your father must have been tossing him a bone once in a while. Stuff your father didn't want to bother with. Was your dad a friend of Campbell's?"

"I doubt it! Well, could have been, I guess, if you say he gave him some work. What kind of work was it?"

"Her will, a lease for a small building, some other thing."

"I see."

"The papers are in a file that makes reference to Trevelyan and Associates, and she also has a connection with Leaman. She was a neighbour of his and was apparently quite fond of him."

"Where's this will now?"

"In with Dice's old files."

"What does it say?"

"I didn't read it. I just remember flipping to the last couple of pages and seeing that Dice's secretary was one of the witnesses. Looked to me like the usual little-old-lady will, teapots and knick-knacks lovingly divided among her nieces. You know the kind of thing."

He laughed. "Sure. And what else was it, a lease?"

"Yeah. She was the landlord of a little place that would not, I suspect, bill itself as 'executive living.' So, I was hoping you could ask your father about this woman, whether by any chance she ever mentioned Leaman. He probably won't even remember, but why not give it a try."

"No problem. I'll ask him and let you know as soon as I've spoken with him."

"Great. Now I'll leave you to your factum, and the discovery, and whatever else is making your life a living hell right now."

"You said it. Monty?"

"Yeah?"

"Did you ever think of just chucking it all, working in a bar, selling your house and moving into a little comfy flat somewhere?"

"Gets to you, doesn't it?"

"It wouldn't be so bad if — don't get me wrong. Elspeth is the most wonderful wife a guy could ever hope for. But we just bought the big place on Beaufort, and now she wants to put an addition on it."

"Whoa!"

"Yeah. I'm hoping the city won't give us a building permit. Maybe I'll rent a backhoe, set it up in the yard, and let the neighbours start fretting about what we're going to do. Get them riled up so they'll oppose it!"

"That may be your best hope. I'll let you go, Ross. Don't work all night."

"Right."

Well, I had negotiated for my nights off years ago, and this particular evening would be devoted to the music of the heavens. I said goodbye to the kids, grabbed my choir binder and headed downtown to St. Bernadette's.

†

"All right, gentlemen," Father Burke announced after the usual opening prayer, "the group favourite, 'All We Like Sheep.' Yes, it's great crack to sing it. Until the end, when it is very solemn, and you have to make that transition seamlessly. It is one of the most moving passages in all of the *Messiah*. 'And the Lord hath laid on him the iniquity of us all.' What does iniquity mean, Richard?"

"Sin, Father?"

"Right. Sin. Wickedness. That's what the Lord took upon Himself when He came down to earth. The wickedness of us *all*."

"All except you because you're a priest. Right, Father?"

"Sadly, I cannot claim exemption. But I'm sure you little fellows can. When we grown-ups sing it, though, we do so in full recognition of our iniquity. Handel underscores that for us in his final, sombre chord. Basses, bring out that F and lean on it. Let's hear you beginning at bar seventy-six. And needless to say we want to hear every *q* and every *t*. Consonants like the crack of a rifle."

The choirmaster was pleased with the sound, and we sang several other Handel choruses. Even Ed Johnson got into the baroque spirit, doing a great job on the long vocal runs so typical of Handel.

Burke and I headed over to the Midtown afterwards, as usual. Ed said he had a quick errand to run, but would be joining us shortly.

Our beer arrived, and Brennan asked: "So, what's the word from the MacNeil?" He lit a cigarette and sent the smoke up to the ceiling.

"I haven't been talking to her."

"What, she hasn't called?"

"She's spoken to Tom and Normie. She always seems to call before I get home from work."

"Time difference."

"I've tried to reach her a couple of times but missed her. Things are going well, according to the kids. A lot of work, but she's seeing the country too. She hopes to get down to Italy for a couple of days."

"Mmm. That fellow Giacomo must be out of the picture now, do you think?"

I shrugged. Giacomo was my wife's sometime paramour. He had been in Halifax on some sort of visa; had he returned to Italy? I didn't know and, these days, I wasn't going to brood about it.

"So she gets back when?" Brennan asked.

"Two and a half weeks from now, the Friday we go to Cape Breton. You still on for that?"

"When does who get back?" Ed asked, arriving with a waiter in tow. "Leave the tray," he instructed.

"Speak for yourself. I'm not drinking a tray of draft."

"Nobody said you were, Collins. I am. Padre, you can help me out. So, who's away?"

"Maura."

He groaned. "She's been away for years. What else is new? How did you ever let that out of your grasp, Collins? You loser. The lush, the creamy, the soft flesh of Maura MacNeil writhing beneath you. The sassy mouth silenced at last, except for little murmurs of delight. God, just to think of it gives me a — sorry, Father. I don't want to put sinful thoughts in your mind."

"You're not an occasion of sin for me, Ed. But thanks for your concern."

"I tried to jump her bones in law school. She treated me to a vituperative — one would almost say emasculating — diatribe from which it took me eons to recover."

"You seem to have recovered quite well."

"Yeah, I moved on to less challenging targets. Then Maura met Babyface here, and her icy heart melted at the sight of him. But somehow he fucked up and she fucked off. Maybe she's lonely. Maybe I should try to hit on her again. Nah, somebody must be keeping her happy."

"Go fuck yourself."

"Such language in front of your priest and choirmaster."

"He took the words right out of my mouth, Johnson," Burke remonstrated. "How would you like it if Collins was talking about your wife that way?"

"I'd love to think other guys lust after my wife, but nobody ever does."

"Not that you'd ever know, pinhead. Donna is a very attractive woman, Brennan, and, as you must have inferred, very, very tolerant."

Ed got up to say hello to someone on the other side of the tavern, and Brennan looked at me, his left eyebrow raised. "Tolerant doesn't begin to describe what his wife must be, putting up with him. Is he like that with her?"

"He's like that with her when they're with us. With her alone, I suspect he isn't. He's harmless. In fact, he lives in fear that his wife will leave him, that Donna will wake up some day and realize he's not good enough for her, and that will be it. Get him really loaded, and he'll work himself up to the point where he has to rush home to assuage his fears."

"Ah," Brennan said.

"So, powerful stuff from Mr. Handel tonight," Ed remarked when he got back to the table. "The arrival of Jesus in the world doesn't seem to have had much effect on the iniquity quotient, Padre."

"Certainly seems that way," Burke agreed. "It's one of the standard arguments against belief."

"I bet you'd lose your religion pretty quick if you saw what we see every day of the week in court."

"Are you telling me all defence lawyers are non-believers? Should I be starting a new ministry?"

"Well, no. But they should be. How anyone can believe in a God who is all good, after hearing what these depraved psychos and bottom-feeding lowlifes do to each other, day in and day out, is beyond me. Sometimes I feel like throwing the cases, sitting on my ass, and not doing any work for them; let them rot in jail. Who gives a fuck?"

"Now, don't be sending any more of them out to the Correctional Centre. That only makes more work for me."

"That's right. You've got some kind of chapel going out there. So you do see them. Come on, Brennan, 'fess up. Aren't you ready to pack it in? Give up the collar and find yourself a nice little hausfrau?"

"Sounds to me as if you're more ready to pack it in than I am."

"Nah. It's just that some of them . . . well, let's just say the world would be a better place if they suddenly ceased breathing."

"So? What's stopping you?"

"What do you mean?"

"Why shouldn't you go and choke the breath out of them?"

"Huh?"

"There's no reason not to, is there? From your point of view, the materialist view. There is nothing transcendent in the universe, nothing exalted about the individual. The human person does not belong to God because there is no God. We're just animals like, say, the hissing cockroach. And it simply doesn't matter if we kill each other off. 'Without God, everything is lawful,' to paraphrase the Brothers K."

"Who?"

"*The Brothers Karamazov*. Don't you read anything but case law, Ed?"

"Don't you read the papers, Brennan? I see a lot more people being killed by religious zealots than by, say, Atheists for a Caffeine-Free Café Society."

"You seem to be forgetting the Reign of Terror during the French Revolution, the millions who died under Stalin and Mao, and all the other officially atheist horrors. But fortunately the non-believers of my acquaintance are some of the least murderous people I know, and I admire them precisely because as far as they're concerned they have no reason to be so forbearing. Why aren't they out there blowing away the miscreants who have breached the social contract or otherwise pissed them off? I don't know. I guess they just act the way they do out of the goodness of their hearts. And of course they don't agree with me as to where that goodness comes from!"

"Whatever happened to talking about chicks and cars?" Ed wondered. "How did we get into a deep discussion of moral theology, or whatever this is?"

"We haven't even grazed the surface of the topic," Brennan declared. "Anybody else having another draft?"

"Don't mind if I do. Collins?"

"Why not?"

†

The next couple of weeks were taken up with an armed robbery trial and a series of discovery examinations in the crumbling condominium case. I made no progress at all in the Leaman investigation.

My free hours were spent with Tom and Normie, and we had a grand old time together playing music, going to movies, and having picnics in Point Pleasant Park. We were all in a lather of anticipation for the return of wife and mother Maura, and the long-planned weekend in Cape Breton.

Chapter 8

Do you prefer to drink alone?
— Alcoholics Anonymous Questionnaire

June 7 finally arrived. Maura's plane was delayed by fog, and we said quick hellos at the airport before heading out on the Trans Canada Highway for Cape Breton Island. Brennan was driving his own car, so I travelled with him. Maura and the kids were in my car behind us. The fog lay over the highway, and we needed our headlights at four o'clock in the afternoon. Brennan kept checking his rearview mirror, as if he thought MacNeil couldn't keep the car on the road without divine intervention.

It was eight-thirty by the time we arrived in Glace Bay. The MacNeils had departed for the *ceilidh*, but had left the doors of the two-storey family home unlocked. Perhaps they were never locked. We unloaded the car, cleaned ourselves up a bit, and left for the Legion Hall on Union Street downtown. We entered to a set of jigs and reels played by an assortment of fiddlers crowded together at one end of the room. They ranged in age from eight to eighty, and many of them did a step dance as they played. The applause was uproarious when they wound up and announced a short break for a little gillach. People flocked to the bar. A group of card players immediately coalesced around a table and began, or resumed, a game of tarabish.

"I told him his arse was suckin' wind! He was no match for District 26 of the United Mine Workers of America!" At the sound of her father's voice, expounding in the strongly Celtic accent of Glace Bay, Maura led us to the table where he was holding forth. He turned and saw us approaching.

"Ach, here they are now! And high time, too." He rose to greet the latecomers. Alec the Trot MacNeil got his nickname from his devotion to Leon Trotsky's theory of permanent revolution. Back in his working days, when he wasn't miles under the sea hacking at the coal seams, Alec was above ground organizing the miners to take on Big Coal, Big Capital and their Big Lackeys in Government. He was six feet in height, big boned and strong, but stooped with arthritis from a lifetime of bending under the low ceilings of the mines. His thinning white hair was brushed wildly back from his forehead.

"What time did you leave Halifax?"

"Dad, you've asked me that same question every time I've come home since I was eighteen years old!" She let herself be enveloped in the big man's embrace. Her mother, Catherine, came over and joined in. She was a stout, pretty woman with short grey hair and laugh lines etched deeply into the skin around her eyes. She and Alec made a big fuss over the two grandchildren and allowed as how it was good to see old Monty as well. I introduced them to Brennan.

"So! A man of the gospel," Alec said, eyeing him with suspicion. "Social gospel, I hope."

"Mr. and Mrs. MacNeil," he said, shaking her hand and then his.

"Have you got your dancing shoes on, Father?"

"Always, Mrs. MacNeil."

"Call me Catherine."

"Call me Brennan."

"An Irishman, are you?"

"Yes, with a long layover in New York."

"Lenin thought the revolution might take place first in Ireland. Why do you suppose it didn't?"

"I don't know. But Stalin was later of the opinion that we were too 'Mexican' to be good revolutionaries."

Alec barked out a laugh at that and clapped Brennan on the shoulder.

The musicians returned, fortified for another set, and Normie, after a few minutes of bashfulness, joined some cousins in a step-dancing group at the front of the room. Tom, whose bashfulness was more prolonged, eventually approached a young girl with fiery red hair and dark eyes, and asked her on to dance. I was captured by an old friend of Maura's, leaving Brennan to make conversation with Maura and the in-laws. It wasn't long before his head was thrown back with laughter, so the stories must have been as entertaining as I remembered. As soon as I got free of the friend, I tugged on my wife's hand and brought her to the dance floor, just in time for a slow number, which allowed me to whisper in her ear.

"I've missed you."

"Mmm-hmm," she replied, seemingly distracted by the sight of old friends and foes in the Legion Hall.

"You were kept occupied during your stay in Geneva? I didn't hear much from you."

"Quite occupied, yes."

"But now that you're home, we'll be able to take up where we left off. Tonight, with any luck."

Was that a blush I saw on her face? Now there was a rare sight. I pulled her closer to me, but she managed to wriggle away. "There's Meg! Let's go over and say hello." She manoeuvred herself out of my arms and headed for her old school friend. I had my work cut out for me. But it was early yet. The room suddenly erupted in cheers and whistles, and I looked around. A lovely girl with long blonde curls had joined the band.

"Natalie!" the crowd called out. Had Natalie MacMaster been retained as a surprise guest performer, or had she just dropped in on her way through town? She began to play, and not a toe was still. Maura was teaching Brennan the rudiments of step dancing and she seemed to have lightened up. After a few lively reels, Natalie slowed it down, and I looked on as Father Burke took my wife in his arms for a slow air called "If Ever You Were Mine." He smiled down at her and whispered something in her ear; she responded by cupping his face in her hands and saying no and something else I couldn't lipread. What's that about, I wondered. Then they danced. For the first time, I became aware of a woman sitting with her back straight against the wall. Catherine's ancient mother, Morag, was dressed head to heel in black, the only way I had ever seen her. She held Maura and Brennan in the beams of her intense black eyes. The old woman gave me the willies; she always had. I looked around for distraction and caught my daughter's eye. Natalie had introduced what she called a strathspey.

"Let's show them a thing or two about dancing, eh, Normie?"

"All right!" she squealed. "Let's go, Daddy!"

I did not get to enjoy my wife's company that night; she was tired from her trip, and took to her bed in the room she was sharing with Normie. The next day, Brennan and I and the kids went on tour with Alec. We saw various landmarks in the workers' struggle in Cape Breton and went down into the Ocean Deeps Colliery, a mine that was open for tours, beneath the Miners' Museum. Maura spent the day visiting old friends. A night's sleep seemed to have done her good; when we got home for dinner she was a little more talkative than she had been the night before. The house was filled with people, and we drank and told tales until we sat down for a big scoff in the dining room.

The table was virtually sagging in the middle, there were so many platters of food. A roast of lamb, a turkey, countless plates of vegetables and loaves of bread, bottles of red and white wine. Rum and whiskey were within easy reach on the sideboard. There was a cooler of beer just inside the kitchen door. Crowding around the dinner table were Brennan, Maura and I, our two kids, Alec and Catherine, the grandmother, Morag, Maura's sister, Lucy, her husband, Donald, and their three children, Allan, Laurie, and Grace. Four people I didn't know were at a card table off to the side. The liquor flowed freely, and the conversations overlapped.

Lucy was filling Maura in on an old acquaintance. "So they pulled little Gaetan-Philippe out of school."

"Gaetan-Philippe? They grew up in Sydney Mines, for Christ's sake. They don't speak two words of French between them!"

"Ah, but zey have been to Paree!"

"Well, *zut*-freaking-*alors*! I've been to Moscow, but I didn't name my kid Igor."

"Anyway they pulled him out so they could home-school him, because he's gifted."

"Gifted, my arse. Everybody's kid is gifted now, have you noticed that? That little peckerhead is no more —"

"So she signed up for this home program and bought all the books, and the little turd behaved so badly, and threw so many tantrums, that she desperately wanted to dump him back in the school system but she was too mortified to admit it."

"Mortify *this*, Gaetan!" Maura's brother-in-law had tuned in just in time to tune out again. "Crack me open a beer, dear! What was that you were saying about the army, Alec?"

I switched channels to catch a rum-fueled dissertation by Maura's father.

"In aid of the civil power," he exclaimed, "that's how they put it when they sent the army in. Bull*shit*. In aid of corporate capitalism, is what they meant. In aid of corporate greed. And when I came over in 1925, as a lad of five short years, I saw for myself what they were up to, the British Empire Steel Corporation and its company thugs. Well, the miners showed them! But not before William Davis was shot down in the prime of his life by company police. Murderers!"

"Don't get yourself in a lather over it now, Alec," Catherine MacNeil said gently. "I suppose you'll want to attend Mass with us tomorrow morning, Brennan."

"I used to go to church when Andy Hogan was doin' the Mass," Alec said. "A fine priest and a good socialist. The early Christians were socialists; you can't disagree with that, Father Burke!" The old man turned his ferocious glare on Burke. "It's right there in the Bible."

"I'm sure Brennan has read the Bible, Alec," Catherine said.

"I have," Burke assured them.

"Well?" Alec challenged him. "Am I right?"

"You're not far wrong, I'm thinking, Alec. The early —"

"How can there be such a thing as a right-wing Christian? That's what I'd like to know." Maura had interrupted herself in mid-sentence to turn from her sister and join the politico-religious discussion. "Piling up a personal fortune at the expense of the poor; where's the authority in the gospel for that?"

I usually did my best to participate in these multi-level talks, but I was on my way to being half-corked and I had other things on my mind. Namely, how many hours would I have to wait until I could get Maura by herself and continue our newly resumed marital relations. The MacNeils had their room, the old lady had hers, Brennan had his, Maura and Normie were in the fourth bedroom, and Tom and I had a couch and a cot in the basement. Things must have been crowded when Alec, Catherine, and their seven children shared this house in earlier times. But, then, who had more than four bedrooms? Alec had built this place himself; it was a palace compared to some of the houses in the area, particularly the company houses, owned by the coal company.

As long as Normie didn't get too wound up tonight, I could count on her falling asleep by nine. Could Maura and I both beg off whatever entertainment was planned so we could be alone? Maybe Alec would take Brennan out to a tavern, and — I realized someone had asked my opinion on something. "What?"

"Never mind, Montague," Alec said. "He talked himself out at the courthouse this week, did he, Maura? Or do you two not talk at all now? If not, why is he here? We were hoping you two were finally going to get back under the same roof."

I smiled. The in-laws were on my side.

I went back to my calculations. I wasn't the only quiet one at the table. Maura's spooky grandmother sat across from me. Old Morag rarely spoke and, when she did, it was usually in Scottish Gaelic. She was regarding me with her glittering black eyes, which she then trained on Maura and on Brennan. She shook her head, as if in disagreement with an utterance only she could hear.

"Alec, get your fiddle out after dinner and give us a tune, why don't you?" Catherine suggested.

"I may do that." The old man's voice had softened. "If our little Normie will do a step dance for us. You were kicking up your heels with your dad last night, weren't you, little one?"

"That was fun!"

"Do you make music yourself, Normie?"

"I can play four songs on the piano. Tommy Douglas plays the guitar and saxophone."

"So you just need a few more kids in the family: a fiddler, a drummer, and a singer. Then you'll have a family band. Like the Barra MacNeils."

"Any relation?" Brennan asked.

"No," said Donald.

"Yes," countered Alec.

"Distant," declared Catherine.

"And the Rankins. Whatever happened to the big families?" Alec demanded. "That's what I'd like to know!"

"Everybody's telling the church to get stuffed when it comes to birth control, Dad," Maura answered. "And rightly so. The pope's own hand-picked commission came out in favour of relaxing the ban."

"People can't afford them, that's what," the old man declared. "Big families are a luxury only the rich can afford, and they don't want them. Hiring nannies to watch the children while the parents cavort on the tennis court! And all the while, working people are being squeezed and cheated to the point where the thought of another child —"

"We're having a baby!" Every tongue was stilled. Every eye locked on to my little girl. She beamed at her mother. Maura sat staring at her, speechless at last. The old grandmother was rocking and nodding her head, the terrible eyes shining at my daughter.

"Is she right, Maura?" Catherine asked.

"Ach, she is right," the old lady intoned. "The child has the sight." My wife nodded dumbly.

"Mummy didn't tell me. But I know there's a baby in there. I'm so excited!"

I, thunderstruck, could no longer hear what was being said around me. We were having another child? How many weeks ago was it that we were together? The tests they had now were amazing in their ability to confirm a pregnancy so early. Well, not so amazing. I was just out of step. As the news sunk in, I was filled with a joy that almost made me delirious. I could see it all: me as the solicitous husband, my wife's belly growing, the birth of our new baby, the walks around the old neighbourhood with the baby carriage, the five of us together in the old house, everything falling into place at last. I could feel a grin spreading across my face and I didn't even try to contain it.

"And you're due when, darlin'?" my mother-in-law asked.

Silence. Then, reluctantly: "The third of October."

What? This was the eighth of June. The third of October was less than four months away! That meant she was already more than five months gone, and I hadn't been with her until — I stared across the table at her, and she stared back, unable to turn away, horror written all over her face. My eyes turned to Brennan, whose normally unreadable features had been blasted into an expression of shocked disbelief.

Everyone at the table, as if in answer to an unspoken command, turned to me.

With one last look at my former wife, I got up from the table, grabbed my wallet and keys, and walked out.

†

Roaring down the Trans Canada at roughly twice the speed limit, still half-lit from the booze in Glace Bay, I cranked up the car radio and was mocked even by that. It was a song by Free Movement about a guy who gets the bad news, rises from the table, stubs out his cigarette, and walks away from his marriage. I scrabbled around the glove compartment until I found a George Thorogood CD and rammed it into the machine. I was the personification of the word *greaser*. But I didn't care. As long as I lived, I would never get over sitting there at the dinner table, with her family all around us, me with a big fucking grin on my face, thinking we were going to be together again, counting the hours till Normie would fall asleep so I could get in there with MacNeil, anticipating it like a sixteen-year-old kid, and all the while she knew she was carrying a child that wasn't mine and that everybody was going to know it. She didn't even care enough about me to give a thought to what this would do to me; she didn't have one shred of residual feeling for me. Warn me off from the trip to Cape Breton? Why bother? Who cares? And just who was Mr. Wonderful, that she would risk a pregnancy at forty-two or whatever age she was; wasn't it more dangerous after forty? I didn't fucking know.

So, who was it? Her Latin lover, Giacomo? I hadn't heard his name or caught sight of his dark curly locks for months; I thought he'd gone back to Italy. Or he'd fallen out of favour with Her Worship. But if it wasn't him, who was it? The look on Burke's face when she made her announcement! You usually couldn't read his expression if your life depended on it, and there he was looking as if he'd taken a musket ball to the heart. I'd wondered about the two of them before; in fact, I'd come close to pounding Burke one night during a drunken row in which he'd told me to smarten up or I'd lose her. But I realized I was being ridiculous. Or was I? I knew he had taken a shine to her, but I always told myself he liked her as a friend.

Think about it, though. The guy had taken a vow of celibacy. No, it wasn't a vow. A vow was made to God. This, he explained, was a promise. Of chastity. To his bishop. I knew he took it seriously; he lived up to it nearly all the time. But not entirely one hundred percent of the time. This wasn't a delicate little virgin when he entered the seminary; he'd been getting more tail than any three of the rest of us put together until he went into the sem. And he'd had the occasional fling since then, as I well knew. Very rarely, to be fair to him. But still. And how many times had I seen him and her sharing a little laugh? And dancing together? Like last night. And what exactly had been going on that Saturday morning I'd popped in at the house unannounced and found Brennan there half naked? The more distance I put between myself and her, and the faster I did it, the happier I would be. But by the time I reached New Glasgow I was falling asleep.

I pulled off the highway, stopped at a convenience store for toothbrush, paste, and some other overnight supplies, and signed in at the Heather Hotel in Stellarton. No sooner had I flopped down on the bed than I was wide awake again and restless. I went down to the pub, sat at a table, and ordered a double whiskey. A party of young women was whooping it up in the corner. Businessmen and Westray miners took up most of the rest of the pub. I knocked back my drink and got another. And started brooding about Burke again. He was always trying to get MacNeil and me back together. What if he had another motive in trying to shove us together? Part of it was genuine, I had no doubt. He counted us both as friends; he wanted the best for us. But did he also want her with me because this way he could be sure of seeing her fairly often? And was there something else too? I remembered the time he had put the run to this Giacomo, saying mysterious things to him in Italian on the phone. What had that been about, really? Was he doing it for me, or for himself? Was it that he couldn't stand the thought of Giacomo or any other guy having Maura if he couldn't have her himself? Did I not count because you don't miss a slice off a cut cake? I was her husband; he was not jealous of me. But with other guys — I was tired of myself and my deranged reasoning. I ordered a beer and surveyed the pub.

One of the young ones from the girls' night out came up to the bar and asked the bartender for a Singapore Sling. She chatted flirtatiously while she waited; she had obviously known the guy forever. As she was about to return to her table, she was greeted with shrieks of joy when two of her long-lost friends burst into the bar with elaborate excuses for the lateness of the hour. It was clear that there was no room among the party at the back; they asked if I would mind sharing my table. What could I say?

"You're not from here!" one of the new arrivals said to me.

"No, I'm a come-from-away."

"With Sobeys, I bet."

"Mmm." I imagined it was a common sight, personnel from the grocery chain appearing in Stellarton for a conflab at headquarters. I wished I were there for something as routine. "Right."

The first girl, who had been at the bar, offered to stand me a drink for my generosity in sharing my table, so I started on yet another beer that I did not need. It was all a blur after that.

†

I woke up the next morning with an agonizing headache and a feeling of squeamishness in my stomach. The smell of stale smoke and stale beer was overpowering. Must be from my clothes. Had I been in a bar? Where the hell was I? The horrible evening came back to me, Maura's pregnancy and the excruciating humiliation of her announcement in front of everyone. Or had she announced it? Wasn't it my daughter who blurted it out? And the witchy old grandmother. And Burke sitting there. And then I had bolted and driven home. But I wasn't home. I went to a bar and passed out. The image of a glass of whiskey rising to my mouth — I rocketed out of the bed and into the bathroom just in time to eject the foul contents of my stomach into the toilet. A couple more sessions of that and I stood and looked at myself in the mirror. Jesus! I had to get out of here. Where was I? I couldn't bring myself to shave; my hand was too shaky for that. I peed for what seemed like five whole minutes, brushed my teeth for an equally long time, and took a leisurely hot shower. My stomach was better, but the headache was still paralyzing. I walked into the bedroom.

"Sorry I fell asleep before you finished." I nearly jumped out of my skin, which was all I had on. I turned my bleary eyes to the bed and saw a young woman sitting with the bedspread up to her neck. She had a plump, pretty face and short brown hair sticking up all over her head. Who the hell was she?

"What did you say?"

"I just said I fell asleep before you were done because you seemed to be taking a while and I was really tired."

Before I was done? What happened? Was I having sex with some-one who wasn't even conscious? Was there something in the *Criminal Code* about that? Did loss of consciousness nullify consent? Would this constitute . . . I tried to clear my head.

"Sorry," I said finally, "that's what too much alcohol does to me. Things take a little longer to, uh, come to a conclusion. So, any-way . . ." What was her name?

"Should I get dressed, or . . ."

"Whatever you like, sure."

"Or did you want . . ."

I'm some guy — an older guy — she doesn't know, I was such a lousy lay last night that she fell asleep, and she wants to know what I want to do? I fervently hoped my daughter would not grow up to be such a pleaser. But how could she, with MacNeil at the helm? Strong mother, strong daughter, I'd always been happy to think. The thought of MacNeil, who didn't care about pleasing anyone but her-self, whose body was now —

I forced my mind to the here and now. What I was about to do with a person I didn't even know was out of character, or so I liked to think. But if all around me were losing their heads, why not me too?

"Let me in there between the sheets with you, sweetheart. Let's see if I can keep you awake this time."

"Jake?"

Jake! "Uh, yeah?"

"Maybe I should, like, brush my teeth. I have my cosmetic bag with me, and it will only take a minute."

"Go ahead, take your time."

She stayed awake and became positively chatty afterwards. I still didn't know her name. All I wanted was to get out of there and back to Halifax. As soon as the girl was gone, I'd be on my way; I'd grab a burger at a drive-through and boot it for home. She got dressed and headed to the bathroom, then emerged shortly afterwards with her makeup on and her hair somewhat tamed. She gave me a shy smile and busied herself with her handbag. My urge to get moving was visceral.

But I heard myself ask her: "Are you hungry?"

"Yeah, kinda."

"Let's go have breakfast."

"Okay!"

We sat in the restaurant, and she resumed what must have been our conversation the night before. "So, like I was saying, I told him: 'No, I'm not going to let the fries just sit there swimming in grease, and then serve them to somebody an hour later. I'm going to put new fries in, and if the customer has to wait an extra two minutes, fine, he'll be grateful for fresh-tasting food.' Now, you can imagine how that went over. So I came up with a compromise, because I'm not a troublemaker. Well, you understand what I'm saying, Jake, in your own job — you don't grind up a big hunk of meat and let it sit there for two days on the counter, getting all brown and old, right?"

Meat? What was she talking about?

"Hey, Monty! What are you doing out here in the boonies?"

Christ! I turned to the sound of the voice, and saw a lawyer I knew sitting a few tables away. "Hi, Don. How's it going?"

"Great. Probably run into you in Halifax next week."

My companion was looking at me over her omelette, her face the very portrait of pained accusation. "Monty? You mean your name isn't Jake?"

"No, it's Monty."

"And I suppose you're not really in town to receive the top-selling meat manager award either? I'll bet Sobeys doesn't even give out that kind of award! You just made it up to impress me!"

"I'm sorry. I was loaded. Not that that's a good excuse, but —"

"You probably don't have a job at all. At Sobeys or anyplace else. You're probably on pogie! And you were just looking for someone to go to bed with, and then you got lucky. Because not only did you get that, but you figured with my job you'd also get a free cheeseburger and fries! Didn't you? Well, I'm not like that! The day you'll get a free French fry offa me is the day the moon turns blue!"

"I understand. I won't try anything like that with you."

"Good. And I suppose you're married too. Using a fake name because you don't want your wife to find out. If I'da known that —"

"One thing I can tell you in all honesty: I couldn't care less if my wife finds out."

"That's sick!"

"No, it's just that she doesn't care. Our marriage is over."

"That's what they all say, I bet."

"It probably is. But in my case it's the painful truth."

"Looks like somebody's got you on the stand for a change, coun-sellor, and you're not holding up too well. Maybe they should rescind your Q.C.!" Don was beside our table, making my life just a little more miserable than it already was.

"I'm taking a shelling, no question," I agreed.

"Good luck!" He leaned in and whispered in my ear. "Checkout time's not till noon." He continued on his way.

"What did he say?" my companion asked me.

"Nothing."

"I asked you what he said!"

The witness will answer the question. "He said checkout time's at noon."

"Why would he say that?"

"I guess he's hoping you and I can patch things up."

"Patch what up? You're a total stranger and —"

"I was a total stranger last night."

"I didn't think so. You gave me a whole life story. Your name was Jake, you had worked your way up to meat manager at the Cole Harbour Sobeys, you're like me being too shy to sing karaoke unless you have six beers first, and you share my love of snowmobiling. Now that I think of it, there's not a lot of snow in Halifax. You've probably never been on a snowmobile in your life, have you?"

"Once."

"Or an all-terrain vehicle, like you said."

"Doom buggies, never."

She crossed her arms over her chest and glared at me. I felt like a heel. I was a heel.

"I've been a real prick, haven't I?"

"Yes, you have."

"I'm sorry. Honestly. Let's go."

"Let's go where?"

"I'll drive you home. Unless you have a car here."

"No, I don't. But I'm going to call a friend to come get me."

I didn't know what to do, besides give her a quick kiss goodbye.

"You're never going to be stopping by here again, are you?"

"No. I'm sorry."

"Well, at least you're finally telling the truth!"

†

Was that someone knocking at my door? Well, they could bloody well keep knocking. I was home in Halifax, it was Sunday night, and I was putting back the whiskey and fretting about my fate. Knocking again. Get lost! Obviously whoever was at the door had never heard the song about the guy who would rather be by himself when he's drinking alone! The last thing I wanted was company, or the obligation to sound neighbourly at the door. Good — the knocking ceased. I poured myself another drink and tried to get my thoughts in order. I did not want to see the face of Maura MacNeil ever again. How was I going to arrange that? I wanted to see my kids as often as I always did, but without her in the background. Especially her getting more and more visibly pregnant with someone else's baby. Whose ever it was. Whoever's? I was losing my grasp of the English language. And when the baby was born, well, that didn't even bear thinking about. I'd have to get the divorce proceedings over before then. That Giacomo had better not cross my path. If he was still in town. Or maybe her old flame Pierre was back. Or if it wasn't either of them —

"Monty! Are you in here?"

Burke! The last person in the world I wanted to see. Or the second last. Though maybe they were on the same level. Why was I thinking that? The way they danced together in Cape Breton? And the look on his face at the table . . .

"What are you doing here?"

"You really shouldn't leave that key out. If I know where it is, everybody else must —"

"Get out of here, Burke."

"You're legless! How much have you had to drink?"

"Fuck off."

"I just got back, and I brought you your things."

"You just got back from Cape Breton? Now? You stayed for a leisurely visit with her family, did you?"

"Well, she was in no hurry to come back here. And we only had the one car."

"All right. You've delivered my stuff. Now get lost."

"She feels terrible about all this."

"She's never felt terrible about anything in her life. Certainly not about anything she ever did to me."

"This isn't something she's done to you."

"Oh no? Then why was I the odd man out last night? She didn't have the decency to tell me before I got there, so I was set up, like an idiot. In front of my son. In front of my little girl. In front of her family. And you sitting there. If you could have seen the look on your face —"

"Hold on there. Give me a drink."

"Get your own fucking drink."

He did, and stood facing me in the kitchen. "She obviously didn't intend to get pregnant, so really —"

"Really what?"

"She hasn't done anything more than you've done, when you think about it."

"What are you talking about?"

"Well, do you take precautions every time you're enjoying a bit of the how's-your-father?"

"Huh?"

"Who knows, there may be some woman out there carrying a little Monty around in her belly, and you don't know it. So I'm saying that what MacNeil did is no worse than —"

"She should have fucking told me! Instead of climbing into the sack with me and leading me to believe we had a chance together."

"She told me she didn't know about the pregnancy till she went to a doctor in Geneva. I thought women would know these things but . . ."

But she never had a regular cycle in her life, so she wouldn't necessarily suspect anything. She just thought she was gaining some weight.

"So she sat down and told *you* all this? Why would she do that?"

"Because she was beside herself about what happened at the dinner table. She had no intention of letting the secret out until she had time to speak with you in private. But Normie, with her intuition —"

"MacNeil could have fucking called me from Geneva, instead of keeping me in blissful ignorance till she got back and then letting me make my pathetic appearance in Cape Breton."

"You're not the only one who was sitting there gobsmacked!"

"And just why would you be gobsmacked at the news?"

"Because it was painful for everyone. For you, for your son, for . . ."

And for Burke too. Despite all his efforts to lobby on her behalf, it was clear: he thought it was a disaster. Either out of sympathy for me. Or out of what I suspected before, his own jealousy of the little weasel Giacomo, helping himself to what Burke could never have. Or could he?

"Get the fuck out of my house, Burke."

"Ease up on the booze, Monty. I'm not the problem here."

"How do I know you're not?"

"What's that supposed to mean?"

"I mean I know you haven't exactly lived the life of a monk since you entered the priesthood."

"Damn near!"

"Yeah, right. I know your sexual history."

He laughed. "No, you don't."

It was the laugh that did it. Before I knew what I intended to do, I had launched myself at him. I drove my fist into his left eye and knocked him backwards. The kitchen table broke his fall, and I landed on the table on top of him. I grabbed him by the collar of his sweater and smashed his head down on the tabletop. It was only then that I came to my senses. I stood back. He lay there looking up at me. It was only then too that I realized he hadn't made any effort to fight back. If he had, I don't know what would have happened. He was taller than I was, and heavier. And from what I knew of his earlier life, he had a lot more experience with his fists than I did. But then, I had rage on my side. I had never struck another human being in my life, except in self-defence. Now this. I was too weary and disgusted with myself to pursue my usual course of drunken reasoning: that is, what did it mean that he didn't fight back? I just couldn't think about the whole catastrophe anymore.

Burke rolled off the table, stood up, and headed for the bathroom. I heard water running, then he came back. There was a bit of blood below his eye; I must have broken the skin. Assault causing bodily harm. He walked to the refrigerator and opened the freezer door, brought out some ice cubes, rummaged in my kitchen as if he lived there, found a plastic bag, and made an ice pack, which he applied to his wound. He didn't say a word, but made no move to leave. I couldn't bring myself to speak. The telephone rang. It could only be one person, waiting for Burke to soften me up, then calling to try to justify herself. I picked up the receiver and immediately replaced it on the hook. He just shook his head in exasperation.

He showed no signs of taking the hint that he was not welcome; in fact, he looked as if he didn't have a care in the world, aside from the swelling in his face. I was overwhelmed with fatigue and couldn't even face the challenge of walking up the stairs to my room. I staggered into the living room and collapsed on the chesterfield.

The sun was streaming in the kitchen windows when I awoke. I had a quilt over me so I must have — Burke. He was going to kill me with kindness. I had no idea what time he left. My mind was flooded with memories of the night before, and the weekend, and then . . . a new thought. My poor little daughter, who had been so excited about the baby, had to sit there and watch her father walk out on his family. How was I going to make that up to her? What kind of explanation — I lurched to the bathroom and, for the second time in as many days, was violently ill.

†

I wasn't much better Monday. I spent an agonizing day in the office bent over paperwork, hiding from everyone, and I was still there long after the staff had left for the day. MacNeil called; I hung up on her. Tuesday wasn't great either, though I did manage to reach Normie on the phone after school and offer a bogus explanation of why I walked out of the MacNeil house in Cape Breton. "A new baby is a very big event in a mummy and daddy's life. I was taken off guard and upset that I hadn't been told. But then I calmed down and realized Mummy wanted it to be a surprise. She probably knew you had figured it out, and she wanted you to be the one to announce it." I had no idea what drama had followed my departure but, whatever happened, the family must have succeeded in reassuring Normie that she was blameless. She didn't sound as if she was suffering any ill effects.

I was at my desk long past closing time, preparing questions for a discovery examination. A siren wailed outside, and I tried to shut out the sound. I jumped when I heard another noise, then looked up to see Ed Johnson standing in my doorway.

"Who let you in here?"

"I come like a thief in the night."

"That sounds faintly biblical. Did you get religion or something?"

"No, I just come like a thief. There's not a building in this city I can't wangle my way into. I can't believe I'm saying this but I'll get used to it: are you coming to choir practice?"

Shit. I had forgotten all about it. Every time the image of Burke had come into my mind I had forced it out. I couldn't imagine seeing him in the company of Johnson and the rest of the choir. But if I skipped the rehearsal without a valid reason, and if Burke had any visible injuries, Johnson would come up with a scenario even more bizarre than the one that had unfolded in my kitchen Sunday night.

"Yeah, have a seat till I finish up here."

Half an hour later we were sitting in our places in the choir loft of St. Bernadette's. The buzz of young voices went on around us.

"I thought you were sick, Benny. How come you weren't at school?"

"I'm better now."

"You just want that solo!"

"Ha ha. You sing it. I don't care."

"So you haven't seen Burke, have you?"

"How could I see him if I wasn't at school? Duh!"

"Well, he looks like he got —" The little boy stood up and swung an imaginary punch just as Burke appeared in front of us. He grabbed the child by his upper arms and placed him on his chair. The boy stared fixedly at his closed hymn book.

"Good evening, gentlemen."

"Good evening, Father."

"What happened to *you*?" Ed's voice went up an octave.

"Would you like to sing with the boy sopranos tonight, Johnson?"

"How'd you get the shiner?"

I couldn't bring myself to speak, let alone make any kind of comment on the priest's swollen, discoloured eye. I could feel Ed's gaze on me as he sensed significance in my silence.

Burke raked the choir with his eyes, the damaged and the undamaged, and said: "Let us pray. *Confiteor Deo* . . . I have sinned exceedingly in thought, word, and deed, through my fault, through my fault, through my most grievous fault."

Hadn't they changed that, and shortened it? Leave it to him to choose the version that had me reiterating my guilt three times. It was going to be a long night. The runs in the Handel were beyond me, but I took some comfort in the Palestrina.

We settled in at the Midtown afterwards.

"Better start picking on altar boys your own size, eh, Brennan?"

"Looks that way, Ed. Though I have to tell you, this altar boy wasn't much smaller than I am. And usually the most even-tempered fellow you could ever meet." Ed turned to me but spoke again to Burke. "Oh yeah? What brought this on?"

"The fellow questioned the doctrine of transubstantiation."

"What's that?"

"Don't get me started, Ed. So I got a little hot under the collar and gave him a shove. And he drew off and clocked me. He'd obviously never heard the command 'Touch not the Lord's Anointed.' Set us up, Joe," he said to the waiter.

Ed gave me a searching look, then changed the subject. Or so he thought. "I saw Don MacKinnon in court this morning. In town for an interlocutory application. Said he saw you in Stellarton on the weekend. I thought you were in Cape Breton."

Jesus Christ. I may as well have stayed in Stellarton, if Halifax was such a small gossipy town.

"No, I was in Stellarton."

Burke was eyeing me but kept quiet.

"Yeah, Don had a bit of a smirk on his face but he wouldn't tell me what was so funny." *Good.* "Just said: 'I saw Collins on the weekend. My lips are sealed.'"

I shrugged and affected not to see their curious gazes.

Brennan finally turned to Ed: "How are you getting along with 'Who May Abide'? Will we be hearing it next practice?"

"Sure. I'll work on it at home. Scare the piss out of Donna."

Fortunately, the conversation never veered from the subject of music, allowing me to avoid dealing with Burke's injury and my culpability.

†

Work came as a relief the next day. There was nobody looking at me out of a damaged eye, nobody casting curious glances between the priestly victim and me, nobody who knew my world had recently blown apart. The only problems I allowed myself to consider were those of my clients. Like the guy who was going on trial for armed robbery the next day, and who refused to consider a plea bargain even though his uncovered face was clearly visible on the video camera at the credit union he held up. And his accomplice called him by name during the getaway. I wouldn't be losing any sleep over him, or over his trial next week. I yawned and got up to fetch a cup of coffee in the lunchroom. In my office again, I turned to the deaths of Corey Leaman and Graham Scott. And Dice Campbell. I was still trying to find a connection among all the people involved in the two incidents.

I decided to prevail upon Jamie McVicar, the keeper of the files, one more time. He was out of town, but his secretary set me up in a small conference room with the boxes of Dice's papers, a jug of water, and a bowl of Smarties. Things were looking up. But I found no new references to Leaman, or at least not any that I recognized as such. An elderly neighbour of the Leamans had a will and a lease done by Campbell, but that could hardly be considered a connection. Where were her papers? I couldn't find them in the boxes the secretary had brought in, so I poked my head out of the conference room and called her name.

"Is this everything, Cheryl?"

"That's it."

"I seem to recall something else in here but I don't see it now. Has anyone else been through these files lately, do you know?"

"Nobody here, I don't think. Except for the — a property development file. Jamie needs that once in a while."

"When you say 'nobody here,' are you suggesting someone else has come by to see Dice's papers?"

She laughed. "Well, I was sick for a couple of days. There may have been a parade of people coming in to see the files then. But seriously, aside from his wife, I don't imagine —"

"Mavis comes in to look at them, does she?"

"Not usually, but she stopped in the other day."

"Did she take anything with her?"

"Not that I noticed. Wait now. I think Jamie may have given her some updated material on the — on a matter that's come to life again." Bromley Point, I assumed. "But I didn't see her when she left."

†

Mavis Campbell was holding court at her regular table in the Holiday Inn bar. A near-empty glass and an overflowing ashtray indicated that she had been in place for a while.

"Afternoon, Mrs. Campbell."

"Mr. Collins. To what do I owe this pleasure?"

"I imagine you'll have all kinds of unexpected company when the money rolls in."

"What money would that be?"

"The money that's been collecting interest since the Bromley Point development was put on hold. The money that will soon be released into your safekeeping."

"Your cynical, insinuating manner doesn't go with the boyish looks, Monty. I have that right, don't I? Monty?"

"You have my name right, yes."

"Dickie! Have you diverted the water of life to irrigate the parched nations of the world, or have you saved a drop for the needy here on your own doorstep?"

"Sorry, Mave! Be with you in two shakes."

"It can't come soon enough, Dick. I don't want things to get ugly for you."

"Here you go, doll. Anything for you, sir?"

"No, thanks. I'm not staying."

"Poor little me. Alone alone, all all alone, alone on a wide wide sea. I hate the sea. I've lived here all my life and I hate the sea."

"Water, water, everywhere, nor any drop to drink."

"That must be it." The woman was loaded, but she carried it well.

"It must have been frustrating for Dice to know that the Bromley Point money could be held up indefinitely, while he struggled to pay his debts."

"Must have been."

"Have you ever been approached by any of his less reputable creditors?"

"You're not talking about the Canadian Imperial Bank of Commerce, I assume."

"No, I'm talking about knuckle-draggers coming down from Montreal to collect on his gambling debts."

"That's never been a problem for me, Monty. I know goons here who know goons in Montreal. If I thought there was going to be any knuckle swinging, I'd call these guys and send them up there. But if this is a lead-in to offering me your services as a bodyguard, I appreciate your concern."

"I'm not available for such close surveillance, unfortunately, Mavis."

"Pity. I guess you'll just pop in here from time to time to observe my spending habits."

"Yes, I'll be interested to see whether there's a change in those habits any time soon."

"Do I look like a killer to you, Monty?"

"Do I look like a bluesman to you, Mavis?"

"Dice took a flyer on his own initiative. Get over it and leave me alone."

"Does the name Matilda Lonergan mean anything to you?"

"Should it?"

"Does it?"

"No."

"Did you ever know Corey Leaman?"

"Is that the other stiff you're trying to prove was murdered?"

"Actually, I'd rather prove he did it himself."

"So, then, why all this bullshit about Dice? I don't get it."

"The police have confirmed that the bullets in Dice's old office wall match those in my two victims."

Mavis went perfectly still. She left her drink untouched, and did not seem to notice when I slipped away.

†

I had managed for several days to avoid the sight and sound of my former spouse, but my luck was about to run out; I could hardly have her banned from our daughter's school play, *Return of the Glass Slipper*. Normie was playing Cinderella's evil stepmother, Mergatroid. Her teacher was greeting parents at the door of the auditorium.

"Evening, Mr. Collins."

"Evening, Miss Dunphy."

"Normie has been looking forward to this, and it's finally here!"

"I can't wait to see it. She's been rehearsing her lines and being most abusive to me in my role as Cinderella; I'll be happy to relinquish that role to someone more petite and feminine."

"I'm sure you did your best."

"But maybe there's a campy version of this somewhere that would give me free rein to develop my inner Cinderella."

"Now I see where Normie gets her sense of the absurd! I'd better let you find a seat."

"Are you going to speak to me tonight, or are we going to carry this feud right into our child's schoolyard?" Here she was.

I didn't look at MacNeil. "As far as I am concerned, you no longer exist; *ergo*, it would be a highly irrational act for me to speak to you."

"This is ridiculous. Are we going to sit apart and ruin this night for our child?"

"We are going to be sitting apart for the rest of her life. Thanks to you." I went outdoors and left her inside. It was all I could do to avoid going up to someone and bumming a smoke, a habit I had given up with great difficulty when our son was born. And here he was now, with his lovely girlfriend, Lexie. Tom gave me a questioning look, and I nodded towards the building. *Yes, Mother is here.*

"Is Father Burke coming?" Lexie asked. She wasn't yet out of her teens but she had a small church choir of her own. "I have to ask him something about William Byrd."

"He told me —" before the incident "— that he's going to try and make it." After lights out, I hoped, unless that black eye had healed.

"Let's go. I want to sit real close so I can make faces at her," Tom claimed.

"Don't listen to him. I wish my brothers treated me the way he treats Normie."

We all went inside to face the music. The nonexistent MacNeil was in the third row, with several (other) empty seats beside her. Ever the gentleman, I ushered Lexie and Tom in ahead of me and sat in the aisle seat. The lights were extinguished and the chattering subsided. The curtain went up and the show went on. Normie hammed it up shamelessly as the nasty mother, but we in the audience lapped it up.

When it was over, the other three chatted as we waited for Normie to get out of her costume and join us. We heard someone come up from behind and we turned as one. I saw Lexie's eyes grow big as pie plates. MacNeil and Tom asked in chorus: "What happened to *you?*"

"Downtown parish. You know how it is."

"No. We don't." MacNeil stared and waited for an explanation. None came. "What kind of a life do you live when that collar comes off, Brennan?"

Normie came flying from the wings. We all congratulated her on her performance, and she beamed, but her eyes were on the battered priest. Battered angel, perhaps, depending on how her research was going.

"Father Burke! *Who beat you up?*"

He leaned towards her. "Somebody tried to say you weren't mean enough to play Mergatroid. I said you were. And he hit me."

"Did you hit him back?"

"Not allowed to. Have to turn the other cheek. Meek, mild Christian that I am."

I was on my way home when I remembered that some of my fellow lawyers were getting together at the Twa Corbies on Spring Garden Road. I hadn't planned to attend, but suddenly I felt the need of a few stiff drinks and the companionship of people who knew nothing about my latest, and final, marital meltdown. Or my assault upon the Lord's Anointed. We partied for a couple of hours, then my drinking buddies left for home. I stayed on for a few more shots of whiskey. Afterwards I stood outside, disoriented, wondering where my car was. A late-night sax player across the street was doing "Don't Explain" the way I had heard Grover Washington do it in Montreal back in 1974. If ever there was an end-of-the-affair piece, that was it. I went over and put some bills in his case, then hailed a cab for home.

†

Thursday morning I was putting the final touches on a factum due in the Court of Appeal that afternoon. My head was pounding and my stomach was half-sick from the night before. It was good to give my full concentration to the intricacies of a legal argument that had nothing to do with me personally but would make or break the case for my client. My position was that the wiretaps on my client's phone contravened Section 8 of the *Charter of Rights and Freedoms* and should never have been admitted in evidence at trial. Under Section 24(2) —

"What's this now?" I looked up at the sound of the Irish voice and saw Burke standing by my desk.

"Who let you in here?" He affected not to hear me, engrossed as he was in the private papers sitting on the desk.

"Montague Michael Collins, petitioner, versus Maura Anne MacNeil, respondent. No, this isn't right."

Fatigued and hungover, I had no patience for him. "What the fuck are you talking about, 'not right'? What are you doing?" He had folded the divorce papers and was putting them in his pocket. "Put those back. I'm waiting for the bailiff to pick them up and serve them."

"I'll take care of it."

"Fuck off! Give me those. They've been issued by the court."

"Settle yourself down, Montague. Why add more stress to the woman's life? What's the rush?"

"Burke, you hypocritical prick, I just do not need any aggravation from you."

"How am I hypocritical?" He sat and made himself at home, helping himself to one of the new Stratton Sommers fountain pens we had just received. Then he took a second one.

"You're hypocritical because if it was your wife — if you had a wife — and she got pregnant by another man, your behaviour would make mine look like bowing-and-scraping, hat-in-hand acquiescence in comparison. I would be the Brit who came home and found his wife in bed with three men and all he said was: 'Hello. Hello. Hello.' Compared to you. I've come to know quite a bit about you over the past year, Brennan, don't forget. And I've met your old flame in New York. And she told me that when she had, temporarily, ditched you for another man, you saw her attending a concert with the other guy — not getting knocked up by him — attending a concert. And you staged a major scene in the theatre —"

"Montague, Montague. You are speaking of events that occurred in the long distant past. Before I was called to God's holy priesthood. Before I became a man of infinite love, wisdom, and forbearance."

"Let's move to more recent times, then. How about the night you intercepted a phone call from my errant wife's Latin lover, Giacomo, and you — not me — you set about discouraging his advances and hung up the phone without passing it to her."

"I merely slagged him a bit. If he couldn't stand up to that, he's hardly a match for MacNeil."

"Well, he was good enough to provide her with a child. Or somebody was. Who knows who? And, for some unfathomable reason, you expect me to overlook this. You wouldn't stand for it at all, if it were you, so don't give me any of this tiresome crap about adding to her problems. Give me those goddamned papers."

"You need a bit of time to cool off."

"What, I'm going to get cool, calm, collected, and giddy with joy as the time of her delivery approaches? I just don't need you pissing me off right now."

"This is not what I came for. Are you all right? Did you drink yourself stocious last night? You don't look well at all."

"Get on with it. What did you come for?"

"The latest from Vernon."

"Yes? Go on."

"It took some doing on my part but I got a couple of names from yer man. Literally. Two names were all he could come up with. And even then he whispered them to me as if we were being watched. Which we were not. But Vernon warned me: 'Beware the mighty Romans!' One participant was a fellow by the name of Fred Tolliver."

"Tolliver! He was a cabinet minister in the previous government. Minister of Justice! Are you sure you heard him right?"

He didn't deign to answer. "The other was Negus. First name Vince but they called him Vegas Negus. Quite the man for the gaming tables, it seems."

"Like Dice Campbell."

"This fellow apparently gambled for the favours of a young girl at the party. They played cards to see who would have, well, first crack at this poor child, who was brought there blindfolded under the promise of drugs and dinner."

"Jesus Christ. I can't believe I never heard whispers about any of this."

"Perhaps somebody tried to tell, and nobody took it seriously."

"Or they were intimidated into keeping their mouths shut. I have no trouble seeing this as the kind of secret someone would kill to protect."

"True. Well, I've delivered my message, Monty. Now I'm off to spread more joy amongst my flock."

"Yeah, you've done wonders for the mood in this office. Forgive me if I don't see you to the door." I rested my head in my left hand and returned to my factum, trying to get back to the *ratio decidendi* of *R. v. Duarte*, but my concentration was broken. It didn't help matters when I looked up and realized Burke had really had the gall to keep — to *steal* — my divorce petition. What were the chances he was going to act as process server and deliver the papers to MacNeil? They were probably crumpled up in a waste can already. I was going to cut a very impressive figure with the prothonotary: "Good morning. This is Montague M. Collins, B.A., LL.B, Q.C. calling. You remember those divorce papers I filed with the court? Right. Well, I, uh, like, lost them. Or somethin'." I would deal with it later. I went back to my arguments for the Court of Appeal.

When I finally looked up from my work I was famished. I needed nourishment to get me through the afternoon, so I decided to take a run across the street to the Athens.

"Off for a little bite to eat, Monty?" My *femme fatale* law partner, Felicia Morgan, had stepped into the elevator with me.

"Uh-huh."

"Where are you going?"

"Athens."

"Oh, I love the pastitsio there. Maybe I'll join you."

"Sure."

On the way to the restaurant she talked shop. "You and I should work together, Monty. We could team up on some of my major files."

"Well, I'm not much of a team player, as they say."

"You're working with Ross Trevelyan."

"Yeah, but . . ."

"Let's hope he can handle it."

"What do you mean?"

"He had a breakdown, you know. Had to be hospitalized. Didn't you hear?"

"I never hear these things, Felicia."

"It was a long time ago. In his early days working with John."

"John?"

"Justice Trevelyan."

"I'd have a breakdown too, if I had him lording it over me every day."

"His brother, Ian, didn't have any trouble dealing with the father. Look where he is now."

"Where?"

"A big country estate in England. Consorting with the best people, don't you know. I heard there are a couple of royals in their circle!"

"There you go. Ian moved three thousand miles outside the old man's jurisdiction."

Felicia kept up a stream of conversation while we waited for our orders and ate our pastitsio and moussaka. She didn't seem to notice that I was distracted by the appearance of a hugely pregnant woman at the next table. I began to stew once again about Maura's pregnancy. When we finished, Felicia ordered a cappuccino. I was anxious to get back to work but was not rude enough to get up and leave.

"Monty?"

"What was that? Sorry."

She leaned over and put a manicured hand on my arm. "I was telling you about the night at Ken and Bunnie's."

"Oh. Right." Something about the Fanshaws' swimming pool.

"Anyway, as I was saying, there was something wrong with the indoor pool, so they had filled the outdoor one. Everybody went out for a swim even though it was only the middle of May. But I hadn't brought my bathing suit. Bunnie offered to lend me hers but, well, Bunnie's so nice and slim — almost boyish, isn't she? — and I knew her suit wouldn't have covered me very well. So, good girl that I am, if I couldn't be decently covered, I wasn't going in. Everyone else had an absolute blast in the pool while little Felicia sat on the sidelines with her J & B."

I tried to sneak a glance at my watch but I knew she'd notice. She went on: "I drank too much to drive home so I stayed over. At about seven in the morning the temptation of that glistening water was too much for me. So, with everyone else fast asleep, I slipped out of the house for a little skinny-dip in the pool. I'm sure you know how delicious cool water feels on those parts that don't usually get exposed!"

"I do." Was there anyone who didn't?

"So there I was paddling around in nothing but the birthday suit the Lord gave me, and you'll never guess who turned up!"

"No. Who?"

"Come on. Try. You know where Ken and Bunnie built. Not far from the Waegwoltic Club. Tore down, was it two or three old houses? Anyway, near the Waeg. And what else is near there?"

I shrugged and caught the time. One-fifteen. Time to wrap this up.

"I looked up from the pool and saw the archbishop! The Catholic one. The bishop's residence is right along there, and apparently he goes out for a walk early every morning. He just nodded, wished me good morning, and kept on walking!"

"The old get-a-picture-of-herself-naked-in-his-mind trick again, eh, Flayshe?"

"Drop dead, Ed." Ed Johnson had made an appearance by our table. "Contrary to your crass interpretation, I was just telling Monty —"

"Save it, sister." To her annoyance, he sat down with us and grabbed a menu from the next table. "You don't need this anymore, do you, dear?" he asked the expectant mother.

"No, you go ahead."

"When's the big day?"

"Two more weeks."

"Great."

"Do you have kids?" she asked Ed.

"No. My wife thinks the gene pool will be better served if my kind dies out."

"Oh! I'm sure she doesn't mean it."

"I'm sure she does," Felicia insisted. "I cannot imagine why she puts up with you."

"She feels sorry for me," Johnson answered. A waitress stopped by, and he ordered a Keith's, then continued. "She knows if she dumped me I'd be at the mercy of some of the man-eaters who are out there on the singles circuit. I'd be defenceless. Barracudas, she calls them."

"I think you have unresolved issues about women, and I'm not going to sit here one minute longer and listen to your ravings. Sorry, Monty. See you back at the office." With that, Felicia got up, turned on one stiletto heel, and walked out of the restaurant.

"What was all that about, Johnson?"

"That old campaigner. I can't stand her."

"That much was obvious, but was it necessary to be so rude?"

"It's necessary, Collins. Trust me. I've seen her in action before. The stories of herself naked, which she just happens to drop into the conversation: oldest trick in the book. Next it will be a pair of tickets to some pricey event that she was handed at the last minute. 'Would you care to come along with me?' Or: 'Here, you take both tickets. Have a great time.' Of course only a cad like me would take the two tickets and leave her standing there. Remember when Malcolm Finlay's wife died? Malcolm didn't even get through the funeral reception before old Flayshe was all over him. The hand on his arm, the look of concern: 'If you ever feel the need to talk.' Now she's glommed onto you. She's obviously heard that you and Maura have really hit the skids; she smells a divorce. She's desperate for a husband, but he's gotta have money, which she must think you have. Don't tell me you can't see through her."

I could, and I had. I assumed Felicia had spied the divorce papers in the office. But I couldn't quite bring myself to give her a pre-emptive warning to back off.

"You're too much the gentleman, Montague. You gotta be brutal with her, or she'll be on you like a tick."

"She's a good-looking woman. I wonder why she hasn't snagged some rising entrepreneur and got him to build a palace for her."

"Because guys can't stand her once they get to know her. She never lets up. Except in the sack, where she slacks right off. Sex is only the means to an end for her. Even Chad Heath, who'd screw a rattlesnake if somebody held it down for him, even he stopped returning her calls. You know, Felicia Morgan's not even her real name. It's Phyllis Mosher or something. But enough about her. You look like something that was sent for and couldn't come. Were you boozing it up last night?"

"Yeah, with MacDonald and his ilk at the Twa Corbies."

"You should have called me. Get lucky?"

"I got blitzed."

Ed turned to another topic of conversation, but I was distracted again by the pregnant woman at the next table. Her husband came to pick her up. Wrapped his arms around her and hugged her tight, with a big happy grin on his face.

†

That night I had to make an appearance at the Dresden Row house to pick up Normie for a movie. She had gone out to the car to wait, and Tom wasn't home. That left me alone with MacNeil. It didn't take long before we were into it.

"You're a real shit, Monty."

"Oh yeah? When did I become a shit?"

"That's just what you are. Get out of here."

"No. I intend to stay here while you describe in precise detail the moment when I became what you say I am. Let's hear it."

"Piss off."

"Let me help you then. We were in Cape Breton, were we not? At your family's dinner table. A few short weeks after our impetuous, impassioned rendezvous at the Lord Nelson Hotel, which for me was a prelude to a reconciliation but for you was nothing but a toss in the hay. But let's get back to dinner with the family, shall we? There was you near the head of the table, me at the other end, and all those other people who are dear to us. Remember it now?"

Were there actually tears in those eyes? Not likely.

"I was sitting there with a big, goofy, happy, deluded, cat-got-the-canary smile on my face, directed at you. And then what happened?" She put her hands on my chest and shoved me away from her. I grabbed her arm and turned her around. "I asked you a question. What happened?" Silence. "Since you're suddenly bereft of words — for the first time in your long and loquacious life — I'll fill it in for you. The moment I became a shit was the moment when I, in the presence of my son, and my daughter, and my friend, and my in-laws, learned for the first time that you are pregnant with another man's child. Have you any fucking idea what that moment was like for me? I am not going to stoop so low as to stand here and call you a bunch of names. I don't want to be in your presence that long. If it weren't for Tom and Normie I would never speak to you or look at your face again. Don't you stand there and tell me what a shit I am. This situation is solely, entirely, totally, one hundred percent your fault. Not mine. And I will never, ever forgive you. Got it now?"

She stood looking up at me wide-eyed, slack-jawed, dumbstruck. As if these were the first words she had ever heard come out of my mouth. And for all I knew, they were. I turned and left her standing there.

Chapter 9

You been another man's woman, I can see it in your eye.
You been another man's woman, baby, I can see it in your eye.
You tellin' me you're sorry, that ain't nothin' but a lie.
— Maynard T. Maitland, "Other Man's Woman Blues"

"Oh, Monty! Hold on a second, will you?" It was Felicia, bustling towards the elevator at closing time the next day with a bunch of shopping bags. I held the door open so it wouldn't crush her and her parcels.

"Thanks."

"What's the occasion?" I asked, though I doubted she needed an occasion to go on a search-and-destroy mission in the shops on Spring Garden Road.

"As if you didn't know!"

"I don't. Sorry."

"Oh no, maybe it's my fault. Didn't you get your invitation?"

"Invitation to what?"

"To the Fanshaws'."

"The Fanshaws' what?"

We arrived at the ground floor, and I helped her with the packages.

"They're having a party Saturday night. The twenty-second. They've invited me and asked me to bring along some of my partners. You didn't get my note?"

"No. Anyway, have a good time. I have to —"

Her hand shot out and stopped me from turning away. "I'm such a klutz sometimes but I kind of told Ken that I'd bring somebody from the firm. I think they're shopping around for new counsel, to tell you the truth. We do some work for them, but I think it's time we pushed for a more lucrative solicitor-client relationship with Ken and his companies."

"Well, then, I hope you invited Vance Blake. He'll rope them in."

"Between you and me, Monty," she whispered, putting her face close to mine, "I can't stand Vance. He's so vulgar."

"*Excusez-moi, vous autres.*" Our associate Monique LeBlanc had just come in the door and stopped to have a word.

"Hi, Monique," I said. Felicia didn't greet her but gave me a look, as if the interruption must be painfully unwelcome for both of us.

Monique didn't notice. "Did you see Alyre up in the office? We arranged to meet, but I'm late. I wonder if he's up there waiting."

"I didn't see him, but that doesn't mean he's not there."

"Felicia, you didn't see Alyre, did you?"

"Who?"

"Never mind."

She got into the elevator, and the doors closed behind her. Felicia rolled her eyes. "That boyfriend. Have you met him?"

"Alyre? Sure."

"Do you know what he does?"

"No."

"He's a plumber."

"Really?"

"Really!"

"Great. I should get his number. I need a whole lot of work done at my house but I tend to put things off. If Monique says he's got some time open soon, I'll —"

"Right. The boyfriend with the crack of his ass showing in your bathroom and Monique sitting on the edge of the tub drafting a factum for the Court of Appeal. Can't you just see him making conversation with the Strattons at the next firm event? Do you think that French accent of Monique's is put on?"

"Why would it be? She's from Caraquet, like Alyre."

"If you say so. Anyway, back to Ken and Bunnie's thingy on Saturday night. Can you make it?"

Normally the last place I would want to be on a Saturday night was Ken and Bunnie's thingy. But these were not normal times. Three men were dead under questionable circumstances, and Ken Fanshaw had known two of them. One he had sailed with; the other he had partied with. The sailing may have been innocent — although, if my memory served me, Graham Scott's mother looked as if she had swallowed a bitter pill when she saw the photo of her son on Fanshaw's boat in her album. The Campbell parties were decidedly not innocent. If Vernon's reaction to Ken Fanshaw's photo meant what I thought it meant, Fanshaw was one of the Romans in attendance at those parties. An evening in Fanshaw's company would give me the opportunity to observe him without having to manufacture a reason. The drawback of course was Felicia Morgan. Long red fingernails were tapping me on the chest.

"I'm waiting, Monty!"

"Right. What time is this affair at the Fanshaws'?"

"The *affair* starts at eight-thirty. Or we could start it earlier. Why don't you come up for a drink first?"

"We'd better make it eight-thirty. I have some things to do before then."

"Fine. Dress is casual." That at least was good news. "Okay then. I'd better get all this stuff out to my car." What could I do but carry some of her bags? After that, I was away.

†

Saturday night, with a heavy heart, I pulled up outside the upscale Summer Gardens condominium tower to pick up Felicia. She got into my car, showing a lot of leg, and we drove down Spring Garden and Coburg roads to the Fanshaws' palace on the Arm.

The house was everything I had dreamed of — when I was five years old. The exterior was an extravagance of late Victorian turrets, a mix of Gothic and Palladian windows, and a Georgian-style clock tower aping the one on Citadel Hill. If this was the castle of Mad Ludwig, he had a mad wife who ran riot through the inside of the house. The interior was a pastiche of decorating fads, with faux marble columns, frescoes, jarringly mismatched wallpapers, and bad modern art hung for some unfathomable reason in rococo frames.

This was to be an evening of games. I detest being invited to someone's house and made to sit and play games. Of course that is usually because I want to engage in free-wheeling conversation with the other guests; at the Fanshaws', it was probably not much of a loss. I chose Scrabble for my first game and ended up with three people I had never met. Felicia chose backgammon. I contemplated phoning my brother and having him make a fake emergency call to get me out of there. The sole reason I had agreed to come was to learn whatever I could about Kenneth Fanshaw. But the only way to do that would be to tag along after him and play the same aggravating games he was playing. I couldn't work up the ambition. I did notice, and I cannot say I was surprised, that every game he played, he played to win. There was no casual conversation from Fanshaw that night. His only comments were "fuck" or "fuckin' A," depending on how he was doing. We occasionally heard him speak when he barged into somebody else's conversation — nearly always a woman's — to issue a correction or pontificate on the subject under discussion. I had seen the type before, a man — nearly always a man — who could not bear to lose, and could not bear to let anyone else's remarks stand as the last word on a subject. Other people addressing a topic? If Ken didn't jump in, somebody might think he knew nothing about it! For my part, I made words up or deliberately misspelled them, but none of my opponents noticed. Bunnie fluttered around, sat on laps, played a hand or a round for other people, and generally caused them to lose points at whatever game they were playing. I was tempted to get looped on Ken's whiskey, but I had to keep a head on my shoulders in order to deal with Felicia. I had one drink of Irish, then switched to ginger ale.

"Are these real gold, Bunnie?" I heard a woman ask. She was holding up a pair of large, heavy-looking dice.

"Yeah, I got them for Ken last Christmas. They came in a set: gold, silver, and bronze."

"Aren't you afraid somebody will put them in their pocket when they leave?"

"Oh, I think we know our friends better than that, Trish! I trust you!"

"I saw a pair of those," said the man sitting with Trish. "Dice Campbell had them. Poor Dicey, eh? They didn't bring him any luck."

"I didn't know you played cards with Dice Campbell, hon," Trish said. "I wouldn't have been too happy if I'd known that. You might have lost the house!"

"It was only once, Trishie."

"Dice Campbell was my lawyer," another woman said. Her earrings appeared to contain as much gold as the dice. "I kind of wondered about him. He was really nice. And good-looking! But, Trish, you remember when I bought the apartment building on Inglis Street —"

"Yeah, I was wishing I could win the lottery so I could afford to outbid you for it, Leona! Such a beautiful building. And you'd never have trouble finding tenants so close to the universities. I figured it would be a gold mine."

"Yes, and it was priced like a gold mine! I retained Dice to search the title and do all the related work. Lawyers get a percentage of the purchase price, so there was a good bit of money in it for him. Turned out he was already representing the vendor, the company that was selling the building to me. That's kind of a conflict of interest, wouldn't you say? If there's a problem with the title, or the foundation — or if there's a disagreement — whose side is he on? He sure wouldn't have wanted the sale to fall through, no matter what. Anyway, he told me I should have independent legal advice and he gave me the name of another lawyer to go to. But the guy was a friend of his, so I didn't know what to do. Dice kind of pressured me to go to this guy. I got the impression he was a little too interested in the large amount of money involved! Anyway, I didn't like the feel of it, so I went to somebody else."

I couldn't help but ask: "Who was the lawyer he tried to send you to?"

"I don't know. The name was familiar at the time, but I can't remember now."

"Yeah," Trish's husband chimed in. "I heard there were times when Dice was pretty desperate for money. He had a lot of expensive habits."

"When was this?" I asked.

"Nearly ten years ago. I bought the building in 1981."

"So, Leona," Trish said. "Tell us. Is it a gold mine?"

"I've done well with it. Now I'm thinking of doing major renovations."

"I can help you with that!" Bunnie exclaimed. "I have lots of ideas that could brighten up that place."

Leona and Trish exchanged glances, then Leona replied: "Thanks, Bunnie. I'll let you know."

Finally, it was time to go. I shook hands with our hosts. "Thanks, Ken, Bunnie. Great time."

"You're welcome, Montague. Drop by and see us any time. And you, Felicia, of course."

"Of course, Ken. Bunnie, call me!" She thrust her face on one side of Bunnie's and then the other, kissing the air beside her ears.

When we were seated in my car, Felicia said: "I could tell you stories about those two!"

"Oh?"

"Why don't we have a nightcap at my place, and I'll fill you in."

Here it was. I wanted to find out anything I could about Fanshaw, but a stint in Felicia's condo was the price to be extracted. Sighing inwardly, I said: "Sure." I drove towards my fate like a hostage in a carjacking incident.

"Have a seat and relax," she purred when we were inside. "I'll fix us something to drink."

I sat on a crimson crushed-velvet love seat and looked around. The living room was done up in a mix of traditional and modern furniture, all of it top of the line.

Felicia returned with a multicoloured drink of some kind and leaned way over to hand it to me. "What is this?" I asked her.

"It's a secret potion, Monty, what do you think? Actually, it's something I learned to make when I vacationed in Haiti last year."

Chances were it had nothing to do with Voodoo, but it didn't look like my kind of libation.

"Have you got a beer?"

"Boring! Oh, all right. Keith's?"

"Perfect."

She poured me a beer, came back, and curled up beside me on the love seat. Let the haggling begin.

"What did you think of Ken and Bunnie's house?"

"Big-Pot-at-Bingo Baronial."

"Isn't it! They're so tacky. I've tried to guide them, gently, but they don't take the hint. I guess when you grow up with nothing, that's the way it is."

"Uh-huh."

"But they're wonderful people. Great friends. Not everyone would agree."

"Is that right?"

"There's no accounting for friendship sometimes, wouldn't you say, Monty?"

"There's something in that, I suppose."

"For instance." She leaned in close, making contact on a number of fronts in the process. "I have some real dirt on your friend Ed Johnson. And if you —"

"I don't want to hear it."

She looked at me in genuine surprise. "Sure you do."

"No. I don't." I twisted away to place my glass on the table beside the love seat, moving slightly away from her as I did so.

"I'll bet Johnson would be all ears if I said I was going to tell him tales about you."

"There are no tales about me . . ." No tales that I would want to reach the ears of Felicia or anyone else involved in the legal system here or abroad.

"That's not what I heard, you outlaw!" She wagged her finger at me like a cartoon schoolmarm. I said nothing in reply, and she finally relented. "Okay, we'll leave your misdeeds for another day. Or another night. Now, you say you don't want to hear a word against Ed Johnson. But surely you want to hear about the Fanshaws. Everybody wants to know about them."

"I don't care about the Fanshaws. Say whatever you like."

"But you do care about Ed. Isn't that sweet? I'm sure he'd be touched."

"I'm sure."

"Well, anyway, Ken Fanshaw is lucky to be where he is, even if you and I agree his house is hideous, because if he hadn't been a very clever little operator, he might be serving time in prison instead of hosting parties and heading up charity wingdings."

"Why? What did he do?"

She smiled and reached up to brush a strand of hair behind my ear, again moving in overly close to do so. Were her arms shorter than normal?

"Why don't we get comfortable and discuss this on a more level playing field, as they say?"

"Oh, I think we're fine here."

"Playing hard to get, are you? I like that in a man. A nice change from the way they usually behave, charging at a girl the minute the door is closed."

"Fanshaw? You were saying?"

"He's not hard to get, let me tell you! The question is, who would he like better, me or you?"

"I don't see much of a future for me and Ken. Our decorating styles would clash frightfully, and that alone would drive us apart."

"Ha ha, very amusing, Monty. Anyway, about Ken. He likes a little snort once in a while. And I don't mean that the way our fathers did. We're not talking a shot glass full of Scotch."

"Right."

"I have it on good authority that Ken financed a big shipment of cocaine. The stuff started to make its way around the streets, and the police caught Ken's co-conspirator for trafficking. Ken paid him handsomely to take the rap and keep his mouth shut. Ken put the guy's money in an account for him, gave him the papers; it was there waiting when the guy got out of jail."

"Who was the co-conspirator?"

"I have no idea."

"When was this?"

"A few years ago."

She went to the kitchen and came back with another beer. The narrative resumed. "Now Bunnie, believe it or not, doesn't know any of this. Bunnie's in line to receive a not inconsiderable sum from her father whenever he kicks the bucket. The father's nothing but a sawmill operator. But guess where?"

"Where?"

"He is the owner of lands contiguous to and abutting on the Bromley Point development."

"I see."

"Anyway, I'm sure Ken is fond of Bunnie but, well, he sees dollar signs too, and he knows his future is with his wife, come hell or high water. So, as I say, Bunnie doesn't know about some of Ken's little peccadilloes, and I would be the last one to let anything slip."

"Uh-huh."

"You like music, don't you, Monty?"

I wonder if anyone, anywhere, has ever said: "No, I don't like music."

"Yes, I do," I answered.

She uncoiled herself from the love seat and went to the stereo, where she bent way over and searched for something to evoke the mood she wanted. If it was "Bolero," I was out of there. But it was something Middle Eastern: seductive but not cheesy.

"You like?"

"It's good."

"I'll be right back."

When she appeared again she was in a short, translucent nightie in what struck me as a most unappealing shade of peach. But colour was hardly the point. She leaned over me yet again and tried to draw me up by the hand. "I'm going to bed. Are you coming with me? I promise you delights you've never even imagined!"

What? She had body parts other women didn't have?

"See anything you like?"

"Of course I do. You're a babe, Felicia, but I'm leaving."

A look of anger flashed across her face but was quickly masked. "Maybe you'd prefer Ken," she suggested in a needling voice.

"Nope. Ken's the last thing on my mind right now."

"So tell Felicia: what's on Monty's mind right now?"

"Work. And the two of us sitting across from each other in the boardroom." And a whole lot of aggravation I didn't need. And Ed Johnson's laughing face if he could witness this little tableau.

"That just adds to it for me, Monty. Well, you'll certainly have a graphic picture of me when you see me in the boardroom. I'll just have to use my imagination about you, unless —"

"I look like everybody else. Now let me up. I don't want to have to manhandle you out of the way."

"Go ahead!"

After a brief skirmish I made my escape. I put the image of Felicia in her jammies out of my mind and turned my thoughts to Fanshaw and the drug venture. I told myself I would do some digging in the court office in the next couple of days, but researching every trafficking conviction in the past few years was a daunting prospect. I could certainly check Corey Leaman's incarceration history, and made a mental note to do at least that. What were the odds that, of all the drug dealers in the city, Leaman was the one who had hooked up with Ken Fanshaw?

†

It was my week to have the kids, so they arrived on Sunday. I managed to be unavailable when MacNeil dropped them off and I emerged only when her car pulled out of the driveway. Not for the first time I wondered about getting Tommy a good used car so the kids could come without their mother, but I dismissed the idea as something that would set a bad example for my son.

"Hi gang!"

"Hi, Daddy!" Normie reached up, and I lifted her into the air.

"How's my girl?"

"Good. What sharp whiskers you have today!"

"The better to scratch and scrape you with, my dear!"

"I get first dibs on the keyboard," Tom announced, which was enough to propel his sister out of the room and down the stairs. We heard her playing "Big Teddy, Little Teddy."

My son looked me in the eye. "How long are you going to keep this up, Dad?" I didn't insult him by pretending I didn't know what he meant. "You're going to have to deal with her some time, so why not get on with it?"

"Tom, I'm sorry, more sorry than you can imagine, that you have to see all this going on. But I just can't handle it. I think you're old enough to know what this must be like for me. What would you do if Lexie told you she was pregnant with some other guy's baby? How long would you stick around? I wish I could just shrug it off and go on the way we were before, but I can't."

"I know, I know. But I don't think she exactly planned this. You weren't around; you two had split up. So she had a boyfriend. Just like you've had other people in your life. More than she's had, I bet. And this happened. I wish it wasn't happening but it is."

"I'll try, Tom. I know I have to come to terms with it, but —"

"You just did that to get rid of me!" Normie was back. "You wanted to talk to Daddy without me listening in!"

"Well, you're here now, sweetheart."

"Tom wants to invite Lexie over for dinner. Can I invite somebody too?"

"Sure. Who would you like?"

"Kim."

"All right, give her a call. We'll pick her up. How's it going otherwise, Tom? How's school?"

"Great. Do you think there's such a thing as a just war?"

"No idle chat from you today. Are you talking *jus ad bellum* or *jus in bello*?"

"Huh?"

"You haven't looked into it yourself then, I take it."

"I have to do a paper. It's my final, due tomorrow."

"And you haven't started it?"

"Well, I thought you mentioned this topic one time and —"

"No doubt. I did a major paper on it myself in university."

"Yeah, that's what I thought. Do you by any chance —"

"Still have a badly typed copy of it with no updated references to all the unjust wars that have been waged since I was a college student? Is that what you're asking?"

"Uh . . ."

"Get to work! I'll look at it when you're done."

"That's what I thought you'd say. Can I use the car to pick up Lexie?"

"Sure. And get Kim while you're at it. But hit the books first. I take it you have books."

"A few. Well, more like articles."

"Get at it."

"Okay."

Normie sweet-talked me into renovating her bedroom. We cleaned off an old desk and bookcase, and hauled them up from the basement, transferred a worn Aubusson rug from another room, and moved her bed under the window overlooking the water. Then she went downstairs with me to help prepare a dinner of steamed salmon and boiled potatoes. Tom went out to collect Kim and Lexie, and we all sat down at the table when they returned.

"Not sitting for Botticelli today, Lex?" She could have, with the long golden curls and amber eyes.

"I might as well have, Mr. Collins, considering how long I sat and waited for Tom!" She gave him a stern look over the tops of her tiny rimless glasses.

"I'm sorry, Lexie. I got all caught up in this paper I'm doing. You're lucky you're finished with high school."

"Wait till you get into university before you say that."

"Dad, you have to help me. I don't have enough material. This paper is in lieu of an exam, so it's really important. I'll make it up to you, Lexie, I promise."

I looked at the little girl sitting across from me, gnawing on her flaxen braids: "Kim! Are you an expert on 'just war' theory?"

The child stared at me wide-eyed. "I don't think so." Her eyes darted over to my daughter. "Did Miss Dunphy teach us that?"

"No, we haven't learned it yet," Normie replied.

"All right, Kim, dear. You're off the hook. I'll help you, Tom. Eat up, everybody. I slaved away all by myself to put this meal together."

"You did not! It was me as much as you! Don't believe him, Kim!"

Dinner was fun and I thought, for the millionth time, how much I loved the company of my children. As bad as it was sharing them week on, week off, it could have been worse. MacNeil and I had been civilized about this at least. I was thankful that I had limited my drinking the night before, and was feeling chipper.

It was nearly ten before Lexie and Kim went home, and Tom was back at work. I joined him at the dining room table and tried to make sense of the notes and academic articles he had amassed. "Don't you have Walzer?"

"No. Somebody else had the book when I tried at the library

downtown. And the school library didn't have it at all."

"And where are these quotes from? Looks like St. Augustine, but where are the references?"

"I took these quotes secondhand."

"You're usually a little more organized than this, Tommy. Your work has always been top drawer."

"I know."

"Is anything wrong?" Such as the latest disaster on the home front?

"No! Nothing's wrong." A loyal son. Should I keep at him about it? I decided it might do more harm than good. "I just kept putting this off," he admitted.

"What you need here are the original references from Augustine."

"Where am I going to get them at this time of night?"

"Hold on." I went to the phone and dialled a number. Only when the phone was ringing did I remember that things were a little frosty last time I saw my friend Burke. Well, I would act as if nothing had happened; more than likely he would too.

"Hello."

"You don't have St. Augustine over there by any chance, do you?"

"He is with me in spirit, in more ways than I would care to enumerate. Thank you for asking."

"Tommy needs to look at *City of God*. Do you have a copy? If so, I'll take a run in and pick it up."

"Young lads these days don't get enough credit. Though I shouldn't be surprised that *your* son is studying the Doctors of the Church."

"He's doing a paper on just war theory. It's due tomorrow."

"He'll want part of the *Summa* too. And I think I have a couple of short articles on St. Thomas's thought on the matter. Can't do much of a survey without citing Thomas Aquinas."

"True. It's going to be a long night. I'll be there in ten."

"I'll run it out to you."

"No, no."

"Sit tight." Click.

So then it was Brennan, Tom, and I working on the paper, and Normie, in her Paddington Bear pyjamas, peering at us through her glasses and drawing pictures of us in neon colours. Including Brennan's eye. But still: I could feel the tension of the last two weeks melting away. There was nowhere I would rather have been at that moment than home with these three people.

"Where did you get that T-shirt, Father Burke?" Normie asked. "I would kill for, or, well . . ." The shirt was ancient and worn, with the word *Angelicum* on it.

"I always wear it when I commune with St. Thomas." He leaned towards her and whispered: "The Angelic Doctor." She gazed at him with wonder; Thomas Aquinas was someone she might have to work into her research. "When I take you to Rome, Normie, we'll get one a few sizes smaller for you."

"Really?"

"Cross my heart. Was that your doorbell, Monty? Though 'bell' is hardly the word for it. What an ugly sound. Get it replaced."

"I don't think the previous owners chose it for the music, Brennan."

"Well, it's yours now. Do something about it."

I walked to the front of the house, wondering who on earth would be calling at this time of night. I opened the door to a demure-looking woman with black hair. She was dressed in a pale pink sweater with a cream-coloured car coat over it.

"Felicia?"

"Hi." She looked at me briefly, then cast her eyelids downward. What in the hell was she doing here? "May I come in? I'd like to apologize for last night. I had too much to drink and, well, I'm embarrassed." She stepped forward, I stepped back, she was in. "I didn't want to leave it till tomorrow at work. I hope you don't mind. May I?"

I moved aside and gestured with my hand.

"Who is it, Daddy?"

"Oh! You have company."

"My kids."

Normie appeared, and glared owlishly at the interloper.

"This is my daughter, Normie. This is Ms. Morgan."

"Hello."

"Hi there, Normie. How are you?"

"Tired. Bedtime, I guess." She yawned ostentatiously.

Felicia looked around. "What a great house this could be!" She moved in, casing the place as she proceeded. "Think what you could do with this living room. The floors are marvellous. Bird's-eye maple. And the kitchen, all kinds of potential there. I suppose it looks over the water. Yes, and this must be the dining room. Oh! More company."

"My son, Tom. And this is Brennan Burke. Felicia Morgan. One of my colleagues at Stratton Sommers."

Brennan and Tom stood and said hello.

"What are you working on?" She picked up a journal article Burke had brought over: "St. Thomas on War," by Rocco Rosso, OP. "Who's Rocco Rosso, OP?"

"A Dominican," Burke replied. "OP. Order of Preachers."

"I see."

"I'm doing a paper on just war theory," Tommy explained.

"Sounds fascinating. But you know what they say: 'All's fair in love and war.' Are you at Dal?"

"No, still in high school."

"Really! You look older. The girls must all have crushes on you."

"Yeah, in my dreams."

"He has a girlfriend," Normie piped up. "Her name is Lexie and she wears glasses. She's beautiful."

"I'll bet she is. Lucky girl!" She looked at my son as if she might have him for a little late-night snack. "Well, don't let Monty and I interrupt you."

"Monty and *me*," Burke muttered.

"What's that?"

"Don't let Monty and *me* interrupt."

"I see. And what do you do, Brennan? Besides correct other people's failings?"

"That's pretty well it. You might say I'm a corrections officer." The kids looked at each other and tried to suppress their grins.

"It might be fun to be corrected by you. I'll call you next time I do something naughty and need to be punished."

"Feel free," he said, and returned his attention to the *Summa Theologiae*.

"Monty?" She had walked out of the room and seated herself on my couch by the time I entered the living room. "As I said, I wanted to apologize for my behaviour last night. It was out of character. It's just that . . ." She lowered her voice. "I find you so attractive and I know how good we'd be together. But enough of that. I said what I came to say."

She took herself off, expressing warm enthusiasm for seeing me the next day at work. Before she had cleared the steps I was mentally reorganizing my day and planning to divide my time between court and home, avoiding the office altogether.

We got Tom through his paper and Normie into her bed.

"Thanks, Brennan. I appreciate your coming over. I hated to have to admit I didn't have Augustine or the Angelic Doctor on hand."

"That's my job, Monty, to bring the great works of Catholicism to those who haven't had my advantages. So, who's that rossey who came calling at such an unseemly hour?"

"I told you. A lawyer at the firm."

"That's what you told me, yes. She looked as if she was dressed up in somebody else's clothing. I could picture her in something much less ladylike."

"You said a mouthful there."

"Well, hold on to your gonads."

"She's not someone I'm interested in."

"I'd say she's interested in you."

"She'd be interested in that broomstick if it had a promising investment portfolio. And once she got her hands on the money, no more riding around on the broomstick."

†

Tuesday was choir night, and I was just about to leave the office for a quick supper with the kids when my phone rang.

"Monty? This is Gareth Swail-Peddle."

"Oh, yes." I had nearly forgotten the psychologist who had treated Corey Leaman at the Baird Centre, then had a falling out with management.

"You must have been wondering where I've been."

"No, no, not at all."

"I finally got my notes together, relating to my interactions with Corey at the Baird. I would have got them to you sooner but I've been busy with an eating disorders conference in the southern U.S., which I had to attend and prepare for. Then there were some emergencies. Anyway, my wife and I are going to be downtown this evening. I don't know whether you work late, or where you live, but I could drop the notes off."

"I'm just on my way out for dinner now, Gareth. Would you like to join me for something Greek at the Bluenose II?"

"My wife can't tolerate spicy food."

Greek? Spicy? "So how about a lobster sandwich?"

"I'm allergic to shellfish."

"Well, they have everything else, but never mind. I'm going to wind up at the Midtown Tavern later on. If you're downtown, you could meet me there. Or I could come to your office later this week."

"The Midtown! I might enjoy that. Penelope, my wife, has a meeting. I'll pick her up and meet you at the Midtown if she's feeling up to it."

"Sure. I'll be there from about nine-thirty on."

I was looking forward to choir practice, particularly because I had started brooding again about the blow-up with Maura. The music always had the effect of elevating me from my workaday world into another realm. Though I did have to endure the choirmaster's pointed suggestion that I take the music home and learn it more thoroughly. I had been guilty of slacking off. I was pleasantly surprised, however, to see Brennan's brother, Patrick, turn up at the church. We had spent a fair bit of time together earlier in the year, in New York. He was making a one-night stopover in Halifax on his way to Ireland for a conference. The choir was introduced and warned that Father Burke's brother had ears. Any false note, he'd hear it.

Patrick came along to the Midtown afterwards. He was around six feet tall, slightly shorter than Brennan, with sky blue eyes and sandy blonde hair.

"You look more like Monty's brother than Brennan's," Ed Johnson remarked. "Maybe old man Collins crossed the Irish Sea some time during the war for a little R and R."

"Casting aspersions on our sainted mother, are you now?" Brennan said, while raising his hand to the waiter.

"What the hell, it was wartime."

"Not in Ireland, it wasn't."

"Well, you never know now, Brennan," Patrick replied. "Our da was off on manoeuvres of his own in those days."

"True enough."

"Your choir was lovely. The boys sounded angelic."

"They didn't sound too bad, the little Christers. Now if I could just get Collins to do some practising at home."

"This fellow has a big anniversary coming up," Patrick announced. "Are you gentlemen aware of that?"

"Well, it's not a wedding anniversary unless he's even more tight-lipped and mysterious than we think he is. Though I wouldn't put anything past him," Ed said.

"The twenty-fifth anniversary of his ordination."

"Really! I guess I should have known that, Brennan," I said. "Congratulations!"

"Or condolences," Johnson put in. "Which is it?"

"I shall accept whatever greetings you wish to send my way, Edward."

"Oh, I'll think of something. You can count on it."

"Of course, we want him to ourselves for a couple of days. He's coming to New York for his anniversary Mass and a family celebration."

"Shouldn't be hard for us to upstage that."

"You haven't met his family, Johnson. I have. It would take some doing to upstage that crowd. When is it exactly, Brennan?"

"Weekend after next."

"But it's never too early to break out the celebratory cigars," Patrick said, reaching into his pocket and offering them around the table. Ed and I declined. Pat handed one to his brother, fired it up, then lit his own. They puffed contentedly on their stogies until we heard a strangulated cough behind Brennan's chair.

"Monty. Hello." I turned to see Doctor Swail-Peddle standing behind my chair, with a tall, gangly woman in tow. Both were fanning smoke away from their faces.

"Hi, Gareth."

"I brought the diary and my notes."

"Great." I took the papers from him and put them on the table in front of me. "Are you going to join us?"

"Well . . ." He looked at the tall woman with an expression of concern. She wore a long denim jumper over a thick grey cotton shirt. Her frizzy brown hair was tied in a ponytail and half-hidden by a scarf. She had the same enormous eyeglasses as Gareth.

"This is Penelope Swail-Peddle. My wife. Penelope, this is Monty Collins. I don't know these other people."

"Here, Gareth. Grab a couple more chairs. This is Brennan Burke, his brother Patrick, and Ed Johnson." Johnson nodded and picked up his glass. The Burke brothers, as if choreographed, clamped their cigars in their teeth, half rose from their seats and held out their right hands to the newcomers, who shook, then sat down.

The waiter put a draft in front of Penelope, and she looked up at him. "Do you have cranberry juice?"

"'Fraid not. Coke, Seven-Up."

"Oh, I don't want all that caffeine."

"No caffeine in Seven-Up."

"Or in draft," Ed chimed in.

"Seven-Up then. I guess. What are you having, Gareth?"

"I'm going to have a beer!"

"Gareth . . ."

"It's all right, Penelope. It's just one."

"That's what my father used to say."

"Mine never said just one!" Johnson announced. "How 'bout your old man, Brennan?"

"Sure, he'd settle in for a few if he was going to be takin' a drop at all, at all," Brennan answered in an exaggerated Irish brogue.

"Penelope is the child of alcoholic parents," Swail-Peddle explained.

"Aren't we all!" Ed exclaimed. "That describes half the population of the western world."

The Swail-Peddles exchanged a look. Then Penelope announced to her husband: "I didn't wash my hair again today. Five days now."

"Are you okay with it?"

Brennan was not okay with it; he looked at her as if a cockroach had crawled out of her ponytail. But Penelope assured us she was feeling good about herself.

Gareth questioned her gently: "But Penelope. The head scarf? Does that say maybe you're not okay with it?"

"I just like scarves, Gareth. Sometimes a scarf is just a scarf!"

I saw Patrick smile at that.

Gareth turned to us. "Penelope is going to visit her parents tomorrow. We've been doing some work around it."

"You're going to see your parents," Brennan said to her.

"Yes." Her hand went up to her hair.

"I guess they'll be telling you to wash more than your hands before dinner."

Two pairs of humongous spectacles turned to him in shock.

"That's not very helpful, Brendan," Gareth admonished him. "Is that your name?"

"Close enough."

"Penelope feels that her parents put too much emphasis on bodily cleanliness. Bodily denial, one might say."

"Little girls have shiny hair and big, bright smiles!" Penelope sang to us in a voice heard round the room. "And they never bite their fingernails!"

We all looked as one towards her hands, which quickly disappeared beneath the table.

"Penelope's parents were very controlling," Gareth told us.

"And shaming," she added.

"What in the hell are you talking about?" Ed demanded.

Penelope looked down at her fingers. Her husband put his hand under her chin and gently raised it. "Do we look away? Or do we make eye contact and say: 'I am here. I exist'?"

"What's the problem, Penny?" Johnson asked.

Her husband answered for her: "Penelope's parents were verbally abusive. And that can cut just as deeply as physical abuse."

"Oh yeah? I wish somebody had told that to my old man. 'Hey, Vinny. Put your belt back on. You don't have to beat those kids! Just call 'em names instead.'"

"Naming can be harmful!" Penelope protested. "It takes a long time to learn to love yourself after a lifetime of that!"

"Take a page out of my book, Pen. I know I'm a flaming asshole.

But I'm okay with it." The Swail-Peddles sat looking at each other in stunned silence.

"Another round?" Pat said.

"Couldn't hurt, Paddy."

"Bring it on."

"Guess who I saw today, Collins," Ed announced. "Mavis Campbell. And was she tanked! Over at O'Carroll's. Little wonder ole Dice took a header, looking forward to forty more years of liquor bills for her. She mentioned you. She knows we're in the band together. I won't tell you what she said, since we're in such sensitive company. Good old Mavis, still knockin' 'em back. I don't think I've ever seen that woman sober. Don't want to. You've heard the phrase: You're dirty when you're drinkin'. Well, from what I hear about Mavis, it's the other way around. Steer clear if she's running low."

"Gareth, is anything the matter?" Penelope asked, her brow furrowed with anxiety. I looked at the psychologist. He had spilled some of his beer, and his hand was not co-operating in wiping it up.

"No, of course not. I guess all this beer doesn't agree with me."

"No reason to spill it, Gary," Ed commented. "That's a deadly sin in this place. Wouldn't you say so, Brennan?"

"It's a mortaller for sure."

"So, what do you want for your anniversary?" Ed asked. "Coupla hos?"

"That would be grand, Edward. Just the thing."

"Pardon me, Edward, but I see a number of sex-trade workers in my practice and —"

"Me too, Gare, me too."

"And I find the word 'ho' demeaning."

"Lighten up, Gary."

"Excuse me for a moment. Where's the wash — where are the toilets?"

"You mean you've never been here before?" Johnson squawked. I pointed Gareth in the right direction, and he made a hasty retreat.

"When I first started coming here, Paddy, women weren't allowed," Johnson said. "And it took the Midtown a while to warm up to the idea when the law was changed. They took their time about installing a women's toilet. I remember as if it was yesterday: these two girls came in, and every eye in the place was on them. The waiter went over and said: 'We don't have a ladies' washroom, so you may want to go somewhere else.' One of the girls said to him: 'I came here to drink. If I wanted to piss, I'd go to the Pic.' Another place nearby. It was great."

Brennan leaned towards Penelope, saying something we couldn't hear. She put her hand over her mouth and laughed. Then Brennan tapped on the shoulder of a pretty young woman at the next table, said something to her, and both women shared in the humour. Patrick pushed a glass of draft in Penelope's direction, and she reached for it. The hand was withdrawn, and the laughter died, when she saw her husband approaching.

"Can we talk?" Gareth whispered to me.

"Sure."

"Privately."

"Okay. Let's step outside."

"I have to speak to Monty about a confidential matter. I'll be right back." He looked uncertainly at the men at the table, as if wondering whether his wife would survive their conversation without him there to mediate.

When we got outside, Gareth said: "I just remembered something about my diary. I'm so busy these days and I have so much on my mind I didn't think of it earlier. But I was in the process of preparing my diary for you. Finding the relevant passages relating to Corey Leaman. I was whiting out some references to other patients, you know, deleting things that would be confidential about others in the centre. And I was in the middle of this and there was a —" he managed to get a few hairs from his beard into his mouth, and proceeded to gnaw on them "— there was a crisis at home, and I never finished doing the deletions. I just remembered now. Give me the whole bundle; I'll finish editing and bring it to you right away."

"No problem. It's just on the table in there. Take it back and work on it. Why don't you get some White-out tape to cover the irrelevant passages and make a photocopy for me."

"They wouldn't read it, would they?"

"Who?"

"That man Johnson. And his friend Brendan. You said you left it on the table."

"They probably didn't even notice it."

"You know, Johnson has serious issues."

"Yeah, right."

"And I suspect he's in serious denial about them."

"Oh, I doubt that." I couldn't resist a bit of mischief. "What do you make of the other two?"

The psychologist was chuffed to be asked for his professional opinion. "Well, the milder-looking one. Patrick? He strikes me as a bit of an enabler."

"A what?"

"Someone who enables an addict, say an alcoholic or a person addicted to drugs, to continue with the harmful behaviour."

"Why would you say that?"

"Well, there we were, everyone around the table, on the verge of crisis. My wife traumatized by the uncaring tone of the conversation. And Patrick's solution? Not more open dialogue, not working through it, but another round of beer! And then I saw him pushing it on her when I was away from the table."

"Oh, I think Pat is just in a social mood tonight. Being away from the office, seeing his brother, having a good time. Sometimes a round of draft is just a round of draft."

"It would be my guess — and I could be wrong — that he does not have much to get away from at his office, wherever it might be. Nice person, but not too much going on."

"I see. What about Brennan?"

"A bit of a sexual opportunist, I'd say."

"Why would you say that?"

"Didn't you notice? He didn't pay one bit of attention to my wife until I was out of the way. Then, as soon as my back was turned, he intruded into her personal space. I shudder to think what he might have been whispering into her ear."

"It couldn't have been anything too dubious. She was laughing."

"Laughter is a nervous response in Penelope."

"If you say so."

"I do. Everything about Brennan's manner made me uneasy. That eye, for one thing. Looks like an injury from an altercation. As they say, I wouldn't care to see the other guy! I can easily picture this Brendan as the aggressor. My impression of him being something of a sexual opportunist was given ample support when he went right along with Johnson's offer of sex-trade workers for his twenty-fifth anniversary."

"It's just a joke about the hookers. Believe me. Let's go back inside."

The Swail-Peddles left us shortly after that.

"Who are those two flakes?" Johnson asked.

"It's about work."

"After seeing that pair, I'm glad I get my treatment from the bartenders of Halifax, not the psychologists."

"Gareth's a bit of an odd duck. They're not all like that." I turned to Patrick. "What did you think of them, Pat?"

He shook his head. "I'm off duty."

"Off duty as what, Paddy? What do you do?"

"Patrick is a highly respected Manhattan psychiatrist, Johnson. It might be worth your while to commute there once a week."

"No shit. Are you really?"

"I'm a psychiatrist and I work in Manhattan. How much respect I get is open to question." He leaned forward and peered at his brother. "Let me take a closer look at that eye, Bren."

"Leave it, I told you."

Patrick ignored his protestations. "There's some old bruising there and a laceration that hasn't quite healed. And you never had that much of a downturn at the outer corner of that eye."

"Looks good on him. Gives him the appearance of a tragic Irish hero," Johnson put in. "Women will love it."

"Close it, then open it for me. Again. Open it as wide as you can. Now, raise that eyebrow, the way you always do when you're making a point for the rest of us. Well, you can still do that to great effect. But there's a slight downturn to that eyelid, and I think there's some nerve damage. It may repair itself over time. It must have been quite a blow. What happened?"

"It was nothing."

"You see? No respect. My patients think I'm a fookin' eejit who doesn't know where black eyes come from. Of course, I'm admittedly naive about what really goes on in the life of a priest in Halifax, Nova Scotia."

For my part, I didn't know where to look. And I certainly did not want any eye contact with Patrick at that point; he would know the truth in an instant. I thanked Christ in heaven above that Johnson refrained from making any comment about the fact that I had made no comment. The conversation finally turned to other matters, the brothers regaling Johnson with tales from their early years in Ireland and New York. The party broke up at closing time.

I drove the Burkes to the rectory. Brennan hopped out, but Patrick stayed behind, prompting a curious look from his brother. Patrick gestured for him to keep moving.

"What's troubling you, Monty?"

I thought I had presented a fairly trouble-free countenance over the course of the evening. "Oh, there's nothing —"

"Uh-huh." I felt his eyes were able to see right through me. "Well, I'll be back in my office next week. Feel free to call me there or at home. Any time. Here's my card. Or talk to Brennan. You rarely see the priestly side of him, I suppose, but he can be a very good man to talk to."

"He's too close to the situation."

"Which may explain why you clocked him in the eye."

A good rule of engagement when being interrogated is not to deny anything the other person obviously knows. So I didn't even try. "He told you, did he?"

"No. Typically, he gave me the brush-off when I asked him about it. But it doesn't take a respected Manhattan psychiatrist, or an Inspector Morse, to deduce that when Monty Collins refrains from making a smart-arse remark about his friend Brennan's black eye —"

"I know. Is the eye going to get better?"

"Probably. If not, it gives him a certain air, doesn't it? It's not just the eye, Monty. I get the impression you're off kilter. But I'll let you go. Call me if I can help."

"Thanks, Pat. I really do appreciate it."

It was in fact tempting to seek Patrick's help. But he couldn't make the problem go away. Nor could he get me out of the event that was looming the next night. It was an event I wanted to avoid, because Maura was going, but could not avoid, because Ken Fanshaw was putting it on.

†

The event was a black-tie charity dance at the Hotel Nova Scotian for Fanshaw's new shelter for homeless kids. My first opportunity to see him in the same room with some of the people he was purporting to help. Young people he had assisted over the years were going to be servers; others, those still living on the streets, were going to make short speeches or presentations early in the evening. Would there be any veterans of the Colosseum on hand? If so, how could I tell? As for MacNeil, I planned to situate myself so far from her that I'd be able to ignore her entirely. I knew her escort for the evening, an old friend of hers from Cape Breton, a guy I had always liked. My date was Monique LeBlanc, from the office. Her boyfriend, Alyre, had no interest in dressing up and making small talk in a language he barely knew, with a bunch of people he didn't know at all. I could understand that.

I picked Monique up at her apartment on Victoria Road. Alyre was flaked out in front of a baseball game on television, an Alpine brew in one huge hand, the clicker in the other, and a jumbo bag of chips on his lap. He looked at me, in my dinner jacket, with pity. Monique was ravishing in a simple, modest dress of pale yellow silk, which set off her big brown eyes.

"I was going to say I'd have her home before midnight, Alyre, but I'm not sure I'll want to let her go."

"Keep her. It's a double header."

"You're a handsome roué yourself, Monty," she teased. "I'd better watch myself, out with a more experienced older man."

"I'll be the suavest guy there. Just imitate everything I do, from the way I order a martini to the way I wink and cock my finger at everyone as I work the room. You can't go wrong."

When we arrived at the Nova Scotian, we saw our place names with those of Vance "the Undersigned" Blake and some other bores from the office. I switched our cards to a table reserved by a group of

210

Mounties. If they were anything like the RCMP guys I had met over the course of a lifetime, they would be the most enthusiastic partiers in the room. I didn't know what to expect of the band Fanshaw had hired; they promised to give us a sample of music from the 1930s right up to the current hits of 1991. As it turned out, they weren't bad on the old stuff, up to around 1955; after that, the dance floor pretty well emptied out until break time. The recorded music brought people to their feet in droves. I had a few dances with Monique and the other women at our table.

I was accosted by Felicia Morgan, who was tarted up in a black outfit that put me in mind of a spiderweb. "Monty! I'm so glad you could make it."

Was this her event? "Wouldn't miss it for the world."

"I know. It's such a cliché to say it's a worthwhile cause, but that's an understatement in this case. Our young people are our greatest resource, and one young life wasted is one too many. That's what Ken believes, and he's backing up his beliefs with action. And money. This isn't well known, and Ken doesn't want it known, but this shelter is going to be much more costly than the public figures indicate. And the extra funds are coming straight out of Ken's personal savings. That's how strongly he feels."

Her little speech told me two things: one, Felicia would never be convincing in an altruistic role and, two, there had been a sea change in the kind of confidences she saw fit to share about her friend Fanshaw since I saw her Saturday night. What accounted for that? Had she been snooping in my notes on Leaman? Had she heard I was wondering about Fanshaw? Or had he heard about it himself, and commissioned her to do some public relations on his behalf?

When I disentangled myself from her I ran into Murdoch Rankin, my wife's date for the evening, on his way to the bar.

"Monty, *ciamar a tha thu?*"

"*Glé mhath*, Murdoch."

"This is a bit of a queer situation, me here with your wife and you on the opposite side of the room."

"Yeah, well." I shrugged.

"I'd better get her the juice she ordered. And the Captain for me."

"See you later."

I got a beer for myself and a glass of red wine for Monique, and headed to my table. I saw one of the lawyers from Ed Johnson's firm and remembered that Ed and Donna were supposed to attend. No sign of them. There was a Trevelyan family table, with the judge presiding. Ross stood a few paces away from it, in conversation with a rough-looking character who must have been one of the people the event was designed to help. I had to laugh at the expression on John Trevelyan's face as he glowered at Ross and the person he was talking to. Not the sort of company the judge had in mind for his son. I remembered that Ross used to practise criminal law, before joining his father's corporate law firm. Maybe the younger Trevelyan should have stayed with his criminal practice, for no reason other than to stick it to the old man. I noticed that Canon Alastair Scott and Muriel were in attendance, but they didn't see me. Alastair was talking to a man who looked vaguely familiar, and she was staring intently at someone across the room. I followed her gaze and saw Ken Fanshaw holding court near the head table. Muriel Scott grabbed her handbag from the back of her chair and took a step forward, but her husband saw her and caught her arm. He seemed to give her a warning shake of the head. Fanshaw turned to the crowd, stepped up to the microphone, and asked for everyone's indulgence while he said a few words on behalf of his project. I listened with half an ear and kept my attention focused on Muriel Scott, whose eyes never left Fanshaw the whole time he was speaking. Her husband did not so much as glance at the keynote speaker.

Then it was time for speeches by some of the young people who had benefited from the ad hoc programs Fanshaw had helped fund for homeless kids. First up was a commerce student at St. Mary's University; he would never forget what Ken had done for him, and he promised to sign up as a volunteer as soon as the shelter opened. Next came a young woman dressed in a skimpy black shift and a pair of four-inch heels. Her thanks to Fanshaw included a number of anecdotes about how he had kept her on the straight and narrow for the past five years. Her tales, delivered in a voice that seemed unnaturally loud, were interspersed with flirtatious comments, sexy posturing, and attempts at witty bon mots that fell embarrassingly flat. The performance ended with her going up to Ken as if to kiss him, then taking his hand in both of hers and shaking it in the manner of a politician at a meet-and-greet. Fanshaw attempted a grin and a remark about how they do grow up! But he was clearly uncomfortable. I formed a picture of what this girl must have been like five years before, at age fifteen.

There were a few more testimonials, then the band started up again, prompting some desultory dancing by a few determined couples. I saw Muriel Scott make a beeline for Fanshaw. They both knew me, so I could hardly sidle up to them and eavesdrop on their conversation.

"Monique," I whispered. "Do me a favour?"

"Depends!"

"See Fanshaw and that woman walking over to him?"

"Yes."

"Go spy on them for me. Tell me what they say to each other. I'll explain later."

She gave me the odd look my request deserved, but curiosity got the better of her. She casually walked towards them. I kept an eye on my targets while listening to the banter among the Mounties at my table. When Monique came back two minutes later, she reported: "I missed the first part. When I arrived, Mrs. Scott was saying: 'To a child! And that's what he was when it all started, no more than a child! Which makes this charade here tonight all the more —' Then Fanshaw cut her off. His eyes were darting back and forth, as if to see who was listening. To say he was nervous, no — he looked frightened. All he said was: 'It wasn't like that.' And he kind of launched himself past her. So is it her son she's talking about? Did he know Ken Fanshaw? Is this related to Graham Scott's death?"

"There's something she's not telling me about her son. I know he knew Fanshaw; they sailed together. Whatever else happened, I don't know. What I'm really trying to find out is how Corey Leaman came to include Graham Scott in his . . . his suicide. We don't know whether Fanshaw knew Leaman." I did not add that Fanshaw and Dice Campbell were connected through the Colosseum.

"I'm glad this landed in your lap, Monty, not mine," Monique remarked.

She and I drifted over to the Stratton Sommers table to chat with Rowan and Sylvia Stratton. The band shuffled off after an excruciating rendition of "This Diamond Ring," a song I had forgotten completely for twenty years. It was a relief when Janis Joplin came wailing over the sound system. "Kozmic Blues." Yes! An old favourite of mine and, I remembered unfortunately, also of my long-lost and recently unlamented wife. The song had been playing one night when we had patched things up after an agonizing quarrel and separation; we had fallen back into each other's arms, Maura in tears, me trying to make a wisecrack over a lump in my throat, and we swore we would never hurt each other again. We rushed off to the altar shortly afterwards.

No point in dwelling on that. Where was Monique? I felt a tap on my shoulder and turned around. It wasn't Monique. It was Maura, gazing up at me without expression. There was no mistaking the signs of her pregnancy. What the hell was she doing at my firm's table, rubbing it in with all my colleagues present? Revenge for being told off at long last? I looked at her without speaking.

She cleared her throat. "Dance?"

What was I going to do? Turn my back on her in front of everyone? I seized her by the elbow and moved her out to the middle of dance floor, then reluctantly took her in my arms and felt another man's child pressing up against me. The song told me what I already knew: that we still weren't right after all these years and we never would be, so I'd better take what I could get. I listened to "Kozmic Blues" for what I hoped would be the last time ever.

When the music was over, Maura whispered in my ear: "I'm sorry, Monty. I never meant for it to happen. The pregnancy, the scene in Cape Breton, any of it. I'd been hoping we . . . I'm sorry."

I didn't respond; I had already said everything I had to say on the subject. I took her to her own table, then walked away.

When I got to my place Monique put her hand on mine. "Maybe there's a chance you and Maura can work things out, Monty? Alyre can come and pick me up."

"Maybe there's a chance Fidel Castro Ruz will be invited to give the keynote address at the next U.S. Republican convention. Now where were we?"

The night droned on after that, until it was time to make an exit and take my date home to her beau. Alyre was asleep in his armchair when we got there. I gave Monique a double-paw handshake à la Ken

Fanshaw and his over-the-top protégé, and headed for home. But I didn't get there, at least not straight away. I was downtown anyway, so I pulled out from Monique's on Victoria Road, went left on Inglis, left again on Barrington, and pulled up at the Lighthouse Tavern.

A commotion started up at the table beside me just as I ordered my first beer.

"You want my beer bottle? You want my fuckin' beer bottle?"

The man's hair was buzzed short in front and straggled long and dirty down his back. He was face to face across the table with another upstanding citizen, and was trying to shove a bottle down the guy's throat. They were both manhandled out the door by the bar staff.

"What started all that?" I asked a couple of girls who had been at the table until the violence got out of hand.

"Duane don't like nobody peelin' the label off his bottle."

"What?"

"Duane was peelin' the label down with his nail like he always does and then he got up for a piss. When he come back, this other guy was, like, peelin' the rest of the label offa Duane's bottle. So . . ." She shrugged: What can you do?

I spent a few seconds wondering what I was doing there, then returned to my drinking. Once again I boosted the local economy by taking a cab out to Armdale when I could drink no more.

†

I tried to put the personal aspects of the dance, and a brutal hang-over, behind me the next day at the office. I made a phone call to Muriel Scott and asked if I could drop by. I didn't mention Fanshaw. But she put me off. When I suggested other times she put me off again. I was not going to be able to pry any information out of the young victim's mother, at least not for the foreseeable future. The closed look I had seen on her husband's face at the dance led me to believe I would not be any more successful with him.

I sat looking at my notes on the case and saw that I had written a reminder to sort through Leaman's history. His legal troubles began when he was thirteen, and most of them were related to drugs, though he also had convictions for theft, break and enter, and assault.

He did federal time from 1983 to 1985, on a narcotics conviction. This may have been around the time Felicia said Fanshaw paid someone to take a drug rap for him. I would need more evidence before I took the story as gospel. Leaman was admitted to the Wallace Rennie Baird Addiction Treatment Centre in 1985, shortly after his release from Springhill Penitentiary. He entered the Baird Centre again in December 1990, after another string of legal difficulties, and was there until his release in early January, just before his death.

I shoved the file aside and directed my mind to other events coming up that week, most notably the concert our choir was putting on Friday night. I had neglected to practise my parts at home and should do that. But then I lapsed into a funk again and, for the rest of the day and evening, I accomplished absolutely nothing.

Chapter 10

But who may abide the day of His coming?
And who shall stand when He appeareth?
For He is like a refiner's fire.
— Malachi 3:2 (Handel, *Messiah*)

"Boys, you look like angels," the choirmaster declared the night of our concert, when he saw us attired in our white surplices over black cassocks. "See if you can keep up the pretence for the duration of the evening. Sing like the heavenly host."

There had been an extra rehearsal the night before, but I had missed it. Johnson and I had gone to the Seahorse Tavern for supper and a beer. He left for the practice, and I told him I would join him in a few minutes, but I ended up staying at the tavern until it was too late for choir. Ed came back afterwards and let it be known that our choirmaster was not amused by my absence. We stayed till last call, and closed the place by giving our own rendition of Matt Minglewood's "East Coast Blues." I was sick in the morning but recovered in time for the performance; Johnson, by all appearances, had not.

Burke was in a black soutane, the usual square of white at his throat. The nave of St. Bernadette's was filling up below us. "Get yourselves in order for the procession, and remember to keep your places when you get to the altar. Rrrrichard Rrrrobertson, you lead on the left. Matthew, on the right. George and Ed Johnson will be last in their respective columns."

He made the sign of the cross and led us in a short prayer: *"Lauda, Sion, Salvatorem, lauda ducem et pastorem, in hymnus et canticis."* I translated that to mean we were to sing hymns of praise to our Shepherd and King. The prayer had barely left Burke's lips when he leaned towards me and whispered: "You'd better not banjax this on us, Collins, or I'll have your bollocks for bookends. We've worked hard even if you haven't." He returned his attention to the choir of white-robed angels and said: "Move it!"

We processed from the loft and down the aisle with a modicum of dignity. I noted it was pretty well a full house. I caught sight of Normie, Tom, and Lexie, and gave them a discreet wink. Scattered throughout the audience I recognized some of the street people who bedded down regularly in the vicinity of the church. There were a few priests and nuns, and a section reserved for students of the choir school. When we were all in our places, Burke raised his arms, nodded, and we began the twelve-hundred-year-old chant *Veni Creator Spiritus.* The program was organized in chronological order from early medieval times through the Renaissance to the baroque. It was the latter group of pieces that brought our two soloists to the fore. First, young Richard, who was trembling when he stepped forward to do "I Know That My Redeemer Liveth." Burke gave him an encouraging smile, and he started in, gaining confidence as he went along. By the end he was, indeed, singing like a heavenly angel. Burke mouthed the word "beautiful" when he finished, and the applause was warm and prolonged. The little fellow beamed.

We did a couple of other Handel numbers; then it was time for Ed Johnson and "Who May Abide." Johnson got up and was every bit as shaky as Richard, though not for the same reason. I remembered his boozy, croaking vocals of the night before. Would he get through this? He cleared his throat and sang: "But who may abide the day of His coming? And who shall stand, and who shall stand, when He appeareth?" The piece is more than a little threatening, the avenging God burning his way through his kingdom like a purifying flame; Handel wrote in some runs that hammered the point home, and Ed executed them flawlessly, in a magnificent bass voice. He sang like an Old Testament prophet, consumed with righteous fervour. "For He is like a refiner's fire!" When Ed finished, the audience erupted with applause and even a couple of shouts of "all *right!*" and "amen, brother!" The choirmaster was visibly stunned at Ed's performance; finally, he gave him a nod that was more like a bow.

Our concluding number could not have been more of a contrast. We returned to the Middle Ages with the *Salve Regina*, which has been chanted in Catholic churches for nine hundred years. We pleaded with Mary, our sweetness and our hope, to turn her merciful eyes towards us, the poor banished children of Eve.

We were corralled into the inevitable reception in the church basement, where Father Burke graciously accepted tributes for a marvellous concert. I knew there were things he would rather do than nibble on tiny crustless sandwiches, but he was genial as he chatted with his parishioners and others who had come to see the performance.

"I didn't banjax it for you after all, eh, Father?"

"Sure, you were brilliant, Collins. You all were. It exceeded my expectations. In fact, I'm thinking, we may do it again."

"Reverend Burke! Excuse me."

The woman looked familiar. A parent? Yes, I remembered, the mother of Richard Robertson.

"Richard sang beautifully, Mrs. Robertson," Burke said. "I hope he'll —"

"Yes, yes, he did, but that's not why I'm interrupting you and this gentleman. My question is: what kind of security do you have in place here?"

"Security?"

"Yes, security. That's what I want to know."

"Ah. Well, I'm not sure of the need for security at a choral concert, Mrs. Robertson. Some day if we branch out and draw sixty thousand head-bangers to a rock concert, perhaps we'll hire an enforcer."

"I'm sorry you find my concerns amusing, Reverend. I sat there tonight with Mother, who is not well, and we had this person beside us in the pew — jammed in beside us — who made the whole evening unpleasant and distressing for myself and for Mother. She was in fact frightened of the man. You should have seen her arthritic old hands clutching her handbag for fear it might be snatched away from her at any minute. And the smell. It pervaded our nostrils over and above the odour of the incense, which, at the best of times, irritates my sinuses. Anyway, back to this vagrant. There's no other way to say this. The man smelled of liquor. And of urine. That is not what I expect to endure when I attend a concert in a church, even a downtown Cath — or any other event where my son is performing. What do you have to say for yourself?"

"A homeless person, would he have been?"

"I would certainly say so! And mentally ill, to boot. The way he carried on when he heard one of the songs. It scared us. My husband couldn't be with us. He's out of town on business!"

"What was frightening about the fellow?"

"He was fine, aside from the smell, for most of the concert, but when he heard that man singing his solo, he jolted as if he'd been electrified. He grabbed Mother's sleeve — I thought she was going to have a stroke, right then and there. Then the man muttered and argued and I don't know what all. Voices in his head, no doubt. Just between you and me, Reverend, I would have thought the ten-dollar admission charge would have been a deterrent to people of that sort coming in for the evening. Perhaps you should raise the fee next time if these people are wandering the streets with ten-dollar bills to throw around at will."

"Well, the fact is, Mrs. Robertson, we don't charge people who we know can't possibly afford —"

"Aha! There you have it, then. Discontinue that practice in future. I say that as a fee-paying parent at this school! Good evening, Reverend Burke. Richard! Time to go!"

"But Mum! Not now, I'm in line for the brownies!"

"Now, I said. Nanny is tired, and I'm getting one of my headaches." A dejected Richard was marched from the room.

"Dolores!" Burke called to a capable-looking woman hovering over the teapot.

"Yes, Father?"

"Wrap up a couple of those brownies and put them aside for us, would you?"

"I didn't know you had a sweet tooth, Father."

"I'm thinking of a young child with a sugar deficiency."

"Really, Father? What a shame."

"Yes. The brownies should do the trick."

Burke was buying at the Midtown that night. "Ed, when did you get religion?"

"Padre, I don't believe in nuthin'. No God, no soul —"

"And I don't believe there's a bluesman anywhere on the planet who's got no soul," Burke stated placidly, striking a match to light a cigarette. He smiled at Ed through the sulphurous flame. "Not even one by the name of Johnson."

"That was another Johnson. I never had a soul to sell, at the crossroads or anywhere else."

Burke smiled. "If you say so."

"I have no trouble seeing him as an agent of righteous wrath," I chimed in, "avenging and burning his way through the damned and leaving no one standing. He certainly put the fear of God into me."

"Good," Ed replied. "It may come in handy in court someday, if we end up with a couple of losers pointing the finger at each other."

"We're not the only ones who were affected by Ed's performance, Monty. You heard the formidable Mrs. Robertson."

"Robertson?" Ed asked. "Richard's old lady?"

"Yes. A man sitting next to her — one of the less fortunate among God's children — took quite a fright when you did your piece. It was our old friend Vernon," Burke said to me. "I saw him scurrying out of the pew. Vernon's a homeless fellow," he told Ed. "I don't know what happened to him, but he walks with a limp."

"Never heard of him!" Ed stated.

"Well, you're not likely to have *heard* of him, Ed," I answered. "It's not as if he's one of the minor modern poets. He's a street guy, usually hangs out in Cornwallis Park. Maybe you've seen him there."

"Any reason the poor benighted creature should be in fear of you, Johnson?" Burke asked. "You don't put the boots to these down-and-outers when you pass them by, do you? Snatch the coins from their hands and tell them to get a job?"

"Are you serious?"

"No."

"I don't think Johnson's quite *that* miserable, Brennan. And, after all, old Vern didn't cower in fear at the sight of Ed's cruel, mocking face; it was only when he heard the aria that he got a fright. I'd say it was the message, not the messenger."

Ed shrugged. "Right. So. Full house. Pretty good take, I would think. Should pay your salary for another few months, Brennan."

"It should do," Burke agreed. "All slagging aside, Ed, you were magnificent on 'Who May Abide.' I hope you realize you're mine now. Leaving the choir is not an option."

"Thy will be done."

"Good man."

†

It was the beginning of summer vacation for the choir school boys, and the Canada Day long weekend for the rest of us. I put all my cases out of my mind and concentrated on the time I had with the kids over the holiday.

But the shootings claimed my attention again on Tuesday morning. I had established links, of a sort, between Dice Campbell and Corey Leaman; between Kenneth Fanshaw and Roman orgies in Dice's building; and also between Fanshaw and Graham Scott. Graham had been on Ken's yacht at least once, and there was also that scene in which Graham's mother confronted Fanshaw at the charity dance. Had there been more between Graham and Ken than admiring the cut of each other's jib? Felicia had as much as said Ken enjoyed male company now and again. She had also dangled before me the tale of Ken facing a possible drugs conviction and paying someone to take the rap. Was that someone Corey Leaman?

That afternoon I was sitting in the Look Ho Ho Restaurant on Bayer's Road, kitty-corner from the RCMP headquarters, with Keith Nowlan. Keith was big and blonde and had the look of a football player. He had been a narcotics officer for as long as I had been practising law. The Mountie and I often faced off against each other in court, but we were on friendly terms outside the courthouse.

"Does Tim know you're scoring coffee here?" I asked him.

"What do you think?"

"Right. We'll keep it to ourselves."

"Appreciate it."

If word got around that law enforcement was stepping out and having coffee elsewhere, a corporate crisis could ensue at Tim Hortons HQ. Company shares would plummet, causing a panic on Bay Street.

"I'm wondering whether you can help me out with a bit of information from the past, Keith. I'm working on the Leaman and Scott murder-suicide, the lawsuit against the Baird Treatment Centre."

"Right. Not everybody's convinced that was a suicide."

"That's why I'm checking into the background of my victims. I don't have to tell you there was some drug dealing going on in the past."

"Oh, yeah. Your guy was quite the operator. It took us a while before we could catch him at it. But we finally nailed him, not for trafficking but possession for the purpose. He did time, not as much as he should have, but that's always the way. From our point of view."

"So what was the story?"

"The story was weird. We could never get a sighting of the buyer, but we heard it was an otherwise respectable citizen. Rumour had it your guy would score the drugs — cocaine, crack, occasionally heroin — from the usual suspects and then sell it to this most unusual suspect, but we couldn't catch them at it, and it remained a rumour. We also heard that your client, the recently deceased, would charge Mr. Good Citizen premium rates, way above the going street prices. Presumably because the buyer didn't want to take the risk of shopping around. There may have been a whiff of extortion in it too; the buyer was thought to be redistributing it in places where it wouldn't do to be caught with drugs."

He was using it to bribe street people into performing degrading acts at the Colosseum. If Leaman knew that, he could indeed have brought an element of blackmail into the negotiations.

"Do you know the name of the respectable citizen who was making the buys?"

"Sources remain tight-lipped on that one."

"But you know the name."

"We could never prove it; if we had, he'd have been sharing a cell with your client. But that's old news. As far as we know now, the man has been doing nothing but good deeds in the past few years. If he ever slips up, though, we'll have him in cuffs."

I had little doubt that the buyer was Kenneth Fanshaw.

"So how much time did my fellow do?" I asked Keith.

"Three months, first offence. Typical slap on the wrist for a young offender."

"When was this, do you recall?"

"Five, six years ago maybe."

"But Corey was an adult by then."

"Corey?" Nowlan asked.

"Yeah. Corey Leaman."

"Why are we talking about Leaman?" Nowlan asked again.

"Well, all this drug history. With the Chamber of Commerce man."

"That was Scott."

"Scott?" No. No, he couldn't be telling me that Canon Alastair Scott — whom I now pictured in full regalia as a High Anglican priest — was out there on a street corner buying heroin and crack.

"Collins, did I lose you someplace in the conversation here? You asked, and I told you. One of your clients who is now pushing up daisies, Graham Scott, was selling drugs to somebody important, who shall remain nameless until his guilt can be proven, and —"

"Graham Scott!"

"I'm going to call dispatch, Collins. Get you some help."

"I'm sorry, I'm sorry. The whole time I was thinking of Corey Leaman. He had a drug history too. I had no idea that Graham Scott was the one you were talking about."

"I'm talking Graham Scott. Smarmy little bastard with his Topsiders and his top-grade blow."

"All right. So I have two convicted drug dealers lying dead in the parking lot of the Fore-And-Aft." I drained my coffee cup and put it down. I took out my wallet and pulled out a fiver, signalling to Keith that the coffee was on me. "What put you on to Graham Scott? Was he known to you guys?"

"Not to us. We have the city police to thank for the tip. Fellow over there gave us the name."

"I wonder if there would be any point in talking to him."

"Doubt it. He turned in his badge."

"How come?"

"He's taken up another calling."

Warren Tulk. "A kinder, gentler calling?"

Nowlan laughed. "Not necessarily."

"What do you mean?"

"Hey. The guy helped us out. I'm not going to badmouth him now that he belongs to Jesus."

"Keith, I appreciate it."

"Sure, Monty. See you around."

†

It was time to look for someone who could talk to me about Graham Scott, I decided as I drove to my office. Obviously I couldn't ask his parents for a lead. I remembered that he had a sister and two brothers, but any approach to them would be reported to the canon and his wife. Probing into their son behind their backs would not induce in them the tender feelings our firm tried to inspire in its clients. I considered questioning his girlfriend but then thought the better of it; there was no point alerting her at this stage to the possibility that I was looking at someone besides Corey Leaman for the killing. I thought the news reports about Graham's death might provide me with a name or two. After I got back to my desk and made calls on another of my cases, I retrieved the Leaman/Scott file and discovered a few clippings I had glossed over earlier. I came up with two names, a guy and a girl who had spoken about Graham at his funeral. I started making calls until I reached the girl. She agreed to meet me at her place after work. Would I like to speak to her boyfriend at the same time? It turned out he was the other eulogist. Perfect, I told her.

But it was clear two minutes into the conversation at their South Street flat that they had nothing useful to offer. They had been childhood friends of the victim and had more or less been dragooned by his parents into speaking at the funeral. They had fallen out of touch with Graham and had seen very little of him from about grade ten onwards. Without being explicit, they gave me the impression that Graham had turned away from his old friends and started hanging around with a rough crowd. Could they give me any names? They exchanged glances and she said: "Maybe Matty Fuller. If he's around."

"She means if he's not in jail."

"Where does he live, any idea?"

"The Pubs maybe. I'm not sure."

The Pubs were a public housing project close to the Halifax Shopping Centre in the city's west end. I would try to track him down as soon as I had time. I thanked them and left.

†

I then had to make a quick appearance in provincial court. When I got there, I found Ed Johnson grasping the banister upstairs and glaring down at nothing in particular.

"You seem a little tense, Edward. What's the matter?"

"Nothing."

"Well, if it's nothing, why are you —"

"Some Bar Society shit. Nothing to worry about."

"What is it?"

"A client made a complaint about me. With the Barristers' Society."

"So? We all have complaints made about us. They don't come to anything because they're bullshit. Right?"

"Yeah, but —"

"But what?"

"This one may not go away."

"What happened?"

"I kind of roughed this guy up a bit."

"You beat up a client?"

"No, of course not. If I was going to do that, I'd have done it years ago. And done a proper job of it. This guy I just grabbed by the collar and, well . . ."

"Well what?"

"I gave him a shove, and he fell off his chair."

"Was he hurt?"

"No!"

"What brought this on?"

"I had this guy on certificate from Legal Aid because his mother is a long-time Legal Aid client. Family matters, not criminal. Always chasing the kid's father for child support. But the son had a conflict with the mother, so they put him out on certificate and he came to me. Charged with assaulting his mother. He held a knife to her throat and said: 'You don't tell me what to do, bitch.'"

"Is she all right?"

"She was cut. Superficial wound, fortunately."

"What brought this on?"

"Who the fuck knows? I lost it when I had this guy in my office. He sat there, slumped in his seat with a smirk on his face. Instead of the usual rational approach like 'tell me what happened' or 'what's your story,' I said: 'What kind of a man would take a knife to his own mother?' The guy says: 'Bitch deserve it.'

"I just fucking lost it. I grabbed him by his collar and shoved him to the floor. Never touched him again, but I lit into him with words. Was that a manly thing to do? Attacking his mother? Where did he get off, calling his mother a bitch? The woman who gave him life, who changed his shitty diapers, who kept him fed and dressed and took him to school and kissed him when he cried. The only parent who stayed with him. Because the father sure as hell didn't. He fucked off when the kid was two years old and never paid a cent to support him. Why not go after his father, if he was such a tough guy? He's the one who let him down. Fucking dirtbag, I wish I had him here right now. I can't wait to get into that disciplinary hearing! I'll tell them exactly what I just told you."

"You'll tell them nothing of the kind. You'll let your lawyer do the talking."

"Fuck it!"

I talked to him for a few more minutes till he calmed down. Then I made my quick appearance in court and left the building.

†

Matty Fuller was a big hulking guy of around twenty-five. Thursday afternoon I stood with him on the front porch of his townhouse in the Pubs. Fuller was as jumpy as a rabbit; he only half emerged from his door, and his large brown eyes kept darting to the street behind me. I resisted the urge to join him in checking behind my back.

"Thanks for agreeing to see me, Matt."

"No prob'm."

"As I explained, I'm trying to find out something about Graham Scott."

"Like what?"

"Like did he have any enemies that you knew of, or disagreements with anyone in the time leading up to his death?"

"I thought Leaman took him out behind the bar."

"He most likely did. I'm just checking around. So, did you know of anyone who had a grudge against him?"

"Coulda been he pissed off a supplier."

"Do you know whether he did?" Fuller shrugged. "Any other possibilities come to your mind?"

"I gotta go, man."

"All right. But this is important. If there's anything you can tell me —"

"Mighta been those letters."

"Letters?"

"Dude say Scott sendin' him letters."

"What dude?"

Another shrug. "A suit. Seen him on TV."

"Do you know his name?"

He shook his head, stuffed his fists down in his pockets, and rocked back and forth on his heels. "Gotta split."

"How do you know about these letters?"

"Dude show up at Scott's. I was there and seen him."

"Where was Scott living at the time?"

"Robie Street."

"What did the man look like?"

"A suit."

"I know you can do better than that, Matty." I finally got a description out of him that could have covered Kenneth Fanshaw. Of course it could have covered any number of other businessmen as well, but I liked Fanshaw in this role. There was a connection between the two of them, a connection that upset Graham's mother, though she may have got it backwards: maybe it wasn't Fanshaw who had been leading Graham astray. Graham was selling street drugs to Fanshaw at inflated prices. Did Fanshaw turn around and use these drugs to coerce addicts to fight and perform sexual acts for the amusement of the Romans at the Colosseum? If so, it wasn't difficult to predict what the letters might have said.

"What did this man say about the letters?"

"He say: 'If I get any more of this fucking shit in the mail I'll cut your fucking hands off so you can't even deal pencils on the street.'"

"And what did Graham Scott say to that?"

"Graham just laughed and told the guy to suck his dick."

"When was this?"

"I dunno. Long time."

"How long?"

He shrugged.

"Was anything said about the contents of the letters?"

"I don't remember him sayin' nuthin' about that. I gotta get outta here." With that, he pushed past me, jumped down from the porch and disappeared around a corner.

I was left wondering how on earth I could find out more about these letters. Did they constitute blackmail? A motive for murder?

I returned to my office and added my impressions of Matty Fuller to the Scott and Leaman file. Then I skimmed the notes that had been dropped off by Doctor Gareth Swail-Peddle. There wasn't much of interest: a few references to CL — that would be Corey Leaman — needing more treatment, and a lot of pages that were blanked out.

"You're sure you don't want a weekend in New York?"

I looked up, startled. Brennan was standing in the doorway to my office. "I'm on my way to the airport. It won't be all church, you know."

"Don't I know it! I've met your family, after all."

"And they're forever asking after you."

"I'd love to but I just can't. I'm behind the eight ball here, and I made a couple of promises to the kids. Say hello to everyone for me. And don't forget blues night at the Flying Stag when you get back on Monday. It's a fundraiser for some people whose apartment building caught fire out in Sackville. Remember: never dress up for the Flying

Shag. Wear something disposable, just in case."

"In case what?"

"In case of wear and tear happening all of a sudden. Blood spatter, bodily fluids, beer bottles flying across the room, that kind of thing."

"Ah. See you there." On the way out he lifted a couple of CDs from my bookcase.

"What did you take?"

"*Manon Lescaut* and T-Bone Walker."

Opera and blues, the two poles of my musical world.

†

Monday rolled around, and I was at the Flying Shag with the other members of my blues band, Functus.

"Where's Burke?" Ed Johnson was in a state of agitation as we set up our equipment. The place was nearly full, and we were due to go on in half an hour. We had been lifting a few in anticipation, and were starting to feel the effects.

"He said he'd be here, Ed."

"I hope he didn't get so wasted in New York that he forgot about this."

"He's celebrating the twenty-fifth anniversary of his ordination to the priesthood; I don't imagine it was a lost weekend."

"Never know."

"Why are you so worked up about it? You said you're performing a special number for him. If he's late, do it later."

"Can't. It's all set up."

Johnson continued to fret until our attention was distracted by a couple sitting a few tables from the stage. The woman had a lined, pug-nosed face and a mass of dyed black curls; she was sobbing and clutching a bright pink teddy bear. A large, sloppy-looking man leaned across the table towards her.

"Whatsa matter with you?"

"The children, the children," she wailed. "I can't stop thinking about those poor little children."

"What children? What are you blubberin' about?"

"Those poor little children what died in that apartment fire. I can still see their little faces."

"Nobody died in that fire, you dipshit. They're burned out of their apartments, they lost some stolen goods. This deal tonight is raising money to buy them stuff and put them up for a couple of weeks. So stop that moaning, and get off the sauce."

"You fuck off!" the woman roared, and brought her draft glass down on the man's head. He shot out of his seat and grabbed her by the throat. Johnson and I stepped in to help the waiters break it up. A typical night at the Flying Shag.

"Here he is!" Johnson announced. "How was N'Yawk, Padre?"

"It was brilliant. Did I come at a bad time?"

"Nah, business as usual here. Excuse me for a minute. I have to go out and make some calls."

The priest had followed the dress code. He wore an ancient black leather jacket over a T-shirt that said something in Irish.

"How was it, Brennan?"

"Lovely. We had the Mass at St. Kieran's and a reception. Saw a lot of my old cronies, priests I worked with and guys from the sem. They all showed up at the family party that night. Lots of laughs. You'd have enjoyed it. Terry and Patrick patched together a video of my priestly career. Everyone says hello. Bridey said to give you the kiss of peace for her. I'm not going to."

"I'm sorry I missed it. Are they lonesome for you?"

"Who wouldn't be? But I won't be moving back there any time soon."

"Oh?"

"No. I have plans here in Halifax."

"Plans?"

"You'll be hearing a lot more about this later, since you'll be doing the legal work. But, for now, I can tell you I intend to set up a college, or an institution, for the study of the traditional music of the church. To counteract the schlock that's being heard in churches today. A counter-reformation, you might say. I tried for years to get a decision on this idea from the archbishop in New York. Now I have the blessing of the archbishop here. I won't start harping on it tonight. Let's have a pint of porter and listen to some blues."

We did our first set without Johnson. The crowd was into the music so I indulged myself in a longer than usual harp solo on "Blues With A Feeling." I did the vocals on my favourite Muddy Waters tune, "You Can't Lose What You Ain't Never Had," which closed the set. I sat with Burke and the other band members during the break. Then we heard a commotion at the back door, near the stage. The lights went out, but we could dimly see people garbed in black, stumbling around and uttering the occasional curse. There was silence, then Johnson was centre stage with a spotlight on his face.

"This isn't just a regular down and dirty blues night piss-up," he announced. "This is a special occasion for a very special friend of the band and, if I may say so, friend of the Flying Shag. Let's all join in congratulating Father Brennan Burke on the twenty-fifth anniversary of his ordination as a priest of the Roman Catholic Church. Father Burke, take a bow!" The spotlight lurched around until it found Burke, who half stood and gave a wary nod of his head. "And now, please welcome the Flying Shag 'Oh Jesus Yes Yes!' Tabernacle Choir as they join me in a rousing number dedicated to Father Burke. Hit it, sisters!"

The lights went on, and we saw Johnson backed up by a dozen women in what appeared to be barristers' black gowns. Half the faces were black; half were white. Some looked vaguely familiar. In true gospel style, he and the women went back and forth, over and over:

Tell me who's that writing? John the Revelator!
Tell me who's that writing? John the Revelator!
Tell me who's that writing? John the Revelator wrote the book of the seven seals!

The crowd got into the handclapping and swaying and, by about the sixth "who's that writing," we were all on our feet. It was an up-tempo number with lots of Jesus-shouting at the end, and only someone who was stone deaf could have stayed still for it. One of the women had a spectacular voice, which soared and sparred with Johnson's throughout. When it was over, the crowd went wild. Burke was stupefied. When he finally snapped out of it he sprinted to the stage to pump Johnson's hand, and ended up clasping him in a bear hug. Some of the women high-fived the priest and blew him kisses. The crowd demanded an encore; Johnson and his choir were ready with "He's Got the Whole World in His Hands." Burke stayed up with them, clapped and sang along. When it was over and the crowd got back to drinking, the women lined up on stage. In a choreographed move, they tore off their gowns, revealing their street clothes, which ranged from the garish to the barely-there.

"They're all yours, Padre, for another —" Johnson checked his watch "— thirty-five minutes. Extra time negotiable, no doubt."

All I could think was: how much did it cost Johnson to pay a dozen hookers for an hour off the streets, plus rehearsal time? The women descended on our table, and the waiter came over with a complimentary tray of draft.

"Brennan! You think we all sinners and we all be goin' to hell?"

"Brennan, baby! What happened to that eye? Somebody punk you? Did you try to cop a feel off a nun? Man, don't mess with those nuns!"

"Probably a jealous husband, eh, Brennan?"

"You gonna try and get us off the streets and into church? There was this preacher goin' around and tryin' that. But he didn't look nuthin' like you."

"That wasn't no preacher, that was a cop! I can give you a half and half outside, Brennan. Special price."

"You come outside with me and you'll be singing Hallelujah, Praise the Lord!"

"I was Catholic, did you know that, Brennan? Maybe that's why I'm so good at kneeling at the rail!"

He took it all in good grace; in fact, he was having the time of his life. He spent most of his thirty-five minutes talking to the woman with the fabulous voice. I heard her say she had spent ten years singing in the choir of a Baptist church in Preston, an area outside the city. He urged her to take it up again; everybody needs a day off no matter what kind of work they do. But the euphoria couldn't last. Old rivalries surfaced, and two of the women got into a shouting match. One attacked the other over some real or imagined slight, or maybe an old territorial grievance, and three others joined in. Faces were scratched, shins were kicked, foul imprecations were muttered.

Burke, Johnson, and I waded in to break it up.

I gave the skirmish only half my attention because I had heard the name Wanda in a whispered conversation between two of the women who were hanging back, sharing a smoke. Tuning out all the other confusion, I listened in.

"So why's she not back by now?"

"I dunno."

"Well, think about it. How long do these things go on, these conferences or conventions or whatever the fuck it was? Don't they only last a weekend or a few days, then everybody goes home and gets the evil eye from their wife and a shot of penicillin?"

"She didn't say how long she was going to be up there. Just said she was flying up to Montreal, and he would pay her back for the plane ticket when she got there. Guy told her he'd spring for some new clothes too."

"And you're telling me she knew this guy? Was he a regular or what?"

"I don't know. She just said she knew him, or maybe she knew his voice on the phone. Something like that."

"You never heard from her again?"

"No, I never."

"How come you didn't tell anyone?"

"She didn't want nobody to know."

"Come on, girls, drink up," Johnson announced. "I got cabs coming for you."

They all left eventually, some of them kissing Burke goodbye. I saw him deftly avoid one with an incipient cold sore on her lip. When they were gone, he sat down, lit a cigarette, took a deep drag, and expelled the smoke towards the ceiling.

I took Johnson aside: "How the hell did you get them all working together in one room?"

"Diplomacy, Collins. I'm a people person."

"You have abilities I never guessed at. And that's not even counting your talent for gospel music. But what I really want to know is: how did you pay for it all?"

"Well, a bunch of them owed me. Free legal services. I called them on it. I got them all together and did some collective bargaining. It wouldn't do to have one of them find out another one got paid more. Yeah, it cost me a few bucks, but I pulled it off. Can't quite believe it."

I hadn't even sent Burke a card. I wondered whether Maura might have — then brought myself up short. I no longer had a wife to rely on for the things I was too thoughtless to remember on my own.

Ed was the undisputed alpha male after his triumph, and rightly so. Burke was all smiles. "I have to call my brother and tell him this. Even if I do wake him up."

"Which brother are we talking about? Pat?"

"Not the shrink. The barfly. Couldn't you just picture Terry in the middle of this? He'll be destroyed entirely for missing it."

I had met Terry, an airline pilot and raconteur who loved nothing more than sitting on a bar stool telling whopping tales just for the hell of it.

"Say hello for me, and tell him I can't take credit for any of it."

"I'll be telling him every one of those girls knew your name."

"It's your name that's on their lips tonight, Burke."

"So be it."

†

I had heard two things of interest at the anniversary celebration and I congratulated myself on staying semi-sober and alert enough to process the information. One, Wanda Pollard was among the missing. Two, it was confirmed that a preacher-cop was trying to get — or lure — people off the streets. I wanted to know more about the circumstances of Warren Tulk's departure from the police force, so I picked up the phone the next morning and called Phil Riley at HPD. But he was off for the day. I relayed the rumours about Wanda Pollard to the cop on the phone, and left a message for Phil to call me when he got back. Thinking of Phil, and Wanda, brought me back to the first time I had asked about her. I had been talking to Phil somewhere. A charity event, months ago. Kenneth Fanshaw was running it, and I remembered him chatting with Phil. Had Fanshaw overheard me talking about Wanda? There was no way to be sure.

I picked up the phone again, to call Brennan. But he was out at the Correctional Centre, ministering to the inmates. I settled down

to some long-overdue legal work. At the top of the pile was a surveillance report on the plaintiff in a personal injury case. It seemed all
the man did after his injury was hang out at one Tim Hortons or
another. I was unable to determine whether he was capable of lifting
anything heavier than a large double double. Brennan called me back
just as I finished reading.

"Any of your new girlfriends arrested overnight, Brennan?"

"I didn't see anyone I recognized."

"Get in your car and take a drive around tonight. You'll see them."

"I'll keep it in mind."

"I'm wondering if you ever got around to looking through the
phone book for Warren Tulk's friend, Sarah Mac-Something, whatever it was."

"Yes, I did. I meant to fill you in. I thumbed through the directory and found a couple of Sarahs with surnames beginning with
MacL, a considerable number of listings for 'S. MacL,' and scads of
names in which S was one of the initials. Anyway, disguising my
voice and my purpose in ways you would no doubt find amusing, I
think I've narrowed it down. But there's a problem."

"And that is?"

"The woman I think we're after is Sarah MacLeod. She lives in a
place called Barss Corner, but there is no street address given in the
phone book. It simply gives her name and Barss Corner."

"That doesn't surprise me. This place, wherever it is, must be so
small they don't use street addresses. This was the Halifax phone
book?"

"No, it's in Lunenburg County."

"Well! You went beyond the call of duty, didn't you?"

"I'm not just a nine-to-fiver, Collins. So, do you know the place?"

"No, but I can read a map. It shouldn't be too difficult to get a
lead on her once we arrive. Did you call her number?"

"I did, but she wouldn't speak to me. I took that as a sign."

"What? All the other women you reached talked your ear off?
Confessed to you?"

"No, but none was quite as terse — I like to think *mysterious* —
as Sarah of Barss Corner."

A thought occurred to me. "Did you have enough conversation

on the phone, or did you hear enough from her that time in Tulk's shop, to notice whether she had an accent of any kind?"

"Now that you mention it, yes. I can't place it though. I'd say German, but no, that's not quite it."

"Right. A Lunenburg accent. I think we can conclude that her name is not really MacLeod. If her origins are in Lunenburg County, chances are she's an Ernst or a Kaulbach or some other German name. She may be married to a MacLeod of course. Anyway, we'll see what we can find out. What time should I pick you up?"

"Seven?"

"Good. And bring some Bibles."

"Bibles?"

"The Word of the Lord will be our cover story."

"What are you on about?"

"I'll explain later. Oh, and wear a suit."

It was a spectacular July evening as we headed out along Highway 103 to the south shore. Brennan had several maps on his knees. The first map we tried did not show Barss Corner at all; we had more luck with the second. We turned off at Exit 11 and traversed the country-side on winding roads that often ran along crystalline lakes. I filled Burke in on my plan. Following signs for Barss Corner, we arrived at a service station and pulled in. We straightened our ties and made sure we didn't have a hair out of place, then went inside to ask directions to Sarah's place.

"Well now, I don't know," the proprietor said in the German-tinged speech of Lunenburg. The elderly man looked out the window and gave the matter some thought. "If you don't know Sarah well enough to find her on your own, I wonder why you're coming to see her at all. I don't want to be the man to set strangers onto her."

"I understand, Mr. . . ." Brennan paused, and the man gave his name as Kaiser.

Brennan went on in what he no doubt conceived as a rural twang. "We're from the Bible Society and we just want to present Mrs. MacLeod with what we believe is the most faithful, most accurate translation of the Holy Word yet published in the English language. We could show you if you like. Do you have a few minutes? Brother Montague, open the trunk please!" I did my brother's bidding. "This will only take up a few minutes of your time, Mr. Kaiser. Starting with Genesis, you will see the amazing clarity the translators used in —"

"No, no, that's okay," Kaiser said quickly. "You gentlemen go on up to Sarah's. If she wants your Bibles, she'll say so. If she doesn't, she'll say that too." He looked at me standing there with a Bible in each hand and a smarmy smile on my face. "I sure hope you've got more Bibles than that if you're going to Sarah's place."

"Oh, does she still have a crowd of people around?" Brennan asked.

"Far as I know. Nobody ever sees them, but everybody knows they're there." He gave us directions to the house.

"Thank you, sir, and may God bless you."

Brennan's right hand moved upwards out of the habit of a lifetime, and I grabbed it. "Come on, Brother. Let's get on with the Lord's work, and let this gentleman get on with his own appointed task."

We packed our Bibles in the trunk, and got into the car.

"You nearly blew it there, you old Roman heretic," I admonished Burke, as I turned on the ignition.

"Amen, Brother. So, could you understand his dialect enough to find this place of Sarah's?"

"I think so."

As we were pulling out, I looked over and saw Father Burke making a sign of the cross in the direction of the unseeing Mr. Kaiser. Maybe when you start to bless someone you have to follow through. We made a few wrong turns and nearly lost sight of the road in the dust at one point, but we eventually found ourselves on a narrow rutted track lined with overgrown wild rose bushes, which scratched the car as we rumbled along. We came to a padlocked gate with an ancient intercom system mounted on a post. Fifty metres inside, partly obscured by trees, was a white farmhouse distinguished by the large front dormer known as the "Lunenburg bump." It looked to me as if there was bullet-proof glass over the windows.

"Should we try the intercom?" Brennan asked.

"It's either that or skulk around in the woods like a couple of demented bunny killers."

I pressed the button and heard a loud squawk. Then a recorded voice came on and said: "Please enter your code number now." I looked at Burke. He shrugged. I punched in four numbers at random and heard the recorded message again. We waited, but nobody came to speak over the system. We hovered by the gate, uncertain how to proceed. Then we saw the door open a crack, and a pair of binoculars emerged. We could hear strains of music from inside before the binoculars were withdrawn and the door slammed shut. All I could hear of the music was a strong male voice singing the words "in pieces." Then the intercom squawked again, and we heard another recording: "This is private property. Please do not trespass. This is private property."

"What now, Brother Brennan?"

"We can hardly be storming the place."

"No. We have no authority and no convincing reason to be here. At least for now. We'd better take our Bibles and beat a dignified retreat. So, what do you suppose goes on in there?"

"Isn't it obvious? They hunker down behind fortified windows and listen to Handel."

"Handel?"

"Didn't you hear it? The bit from the *Messiah*. 'Thou shalt break them with a rod of iron. Thou shalt dash them in pieces like a potter's vessel.' Some of that scare-the-shite-out-of-'em Old Testament thundering that can be so effective if brandished with conviction."

†

On Wednesday I was in Tim Hortons at the corner of Young and Robie with Constable Phil Riley. I didn't want him to know I was interested in Tulk, so I had brought the paperwork for a case I could legitimately chat about with him. After we had hashed over the file, I brought up the real object of the meeting. Riley provided the segue when he recounted a tale of a car thief who stole a very expensive, noticeable vehicle and drove straight to the nearest Tim Hortons drive-through.

"What kind of a loser comes to Tims in the course of committing an offence?" He shook his head.

"I've even heard of people trying to rob Tim Hortons."

"Are these bozos blind?"

"Is there ever a time when you guys don't have at least one cruiser on the scene?"

"Never been known to happen; it's all co-ordinated from head-quarters," Riley explained.

"Now it's Christian bookstores," I said. "Pretty soon a guy won't be able to stick up one of those, either — I wandered into the His Word bookshop the other day and saw somebody I could swear was one of yours."

"Oh, you mean Tulk."

"Yes, right. He was a cop, wasn't he?"

"Was. Is no more."

"What's the deal?"

"Warren turned into a bit of a zealot."

"So they threw him out?"

"No, he wasn't kicked off the force. Just encouraged to find another line of work. They let him hang on until he had set himself up with something else."

"Which was?"

"He went into a seminary, or whatever it is the Protestants do. He studied to become a minister of some kind. Baptist, maybe. He's a preacher, and he runs that bookstore."

"So he was a zealot."

"So they say. I never worked with him. I heard he had strong views on certain kinds of crime and behaviour. Other crimes, he wasn't so tough on."

"Like what?"

"Well, apparently what turned the tide against him wasn't one of the cases where he came off as a hard-ass. It was the opposite. The department suspected him of soft-pedalling an investigation, holding back evidence. The prosecution collapsed in mid-trial, and the Crown blamed him. That was the beginning of the end for Warren."

"What case was it?"

"Remember that woman who was charged with an assault on her foster child? A spanking case. It was in the papers."

"It sounds vaguely familiar."

"Well, her name was Sybil Kraus. Warren was the investigating officer. After coming down hard on public drinkers, dope smokers, johns, and hookers soliciting in public places, he lightened right up when he got this one. Obviously agreed with her approach to child rearing. Spare the rod, spoil the child. Beat the sin out of them, that kind of thing."

"Or beat it farther in."

Chapter 11

Bless me, Father, for I have sinned.
It has been thirty years since my last confession.

Summer was upon us, the sky was blue, the days were long and hot. I took as much time off as I could during the latter part of July, whenever I didn't have a court appearance or an appointment with a client. The kids and I spent lazy days at the beach, or took short trips out of the city; sometimes we were joined by Lexie, Kim, and Brennan.

But my work schedule overtook me by the first of August, and on Thursday, August 1, I was sitting with a dozen other lawyers in provincial court. It was arraignment day. My client was charged with car theft, dangerous driving, and driving while impaired. I gabbed with my colleagues in the courtroom until the session got under way. I hoped my case would be called early so I could get back to the office; of course, every lawyer in the room felt the same way. I listened without much interest to the roll call of the wicked and the weak, nearly dozing off, until one name caught my attention. Vincent Negus. A name that had come up in my investigation? Vegas Negus, that was it. I perked up and waited for him to make his appearance. But he was a no-show. A lawyer I didn't recognize stood and told the court that Mr. Negus was believed to be out of the country, possibly in Mexico. The

Crown prosecutor asked for an arrest warrant, in a tone of voice that suggested there was little hope of bringing Negus before the court any time soon. The arraignments continued. Then they called a case of Ed Johnson's. He wasn't in the courtroom, either. The prosecutor rose and addressed Judge Ivan Thomas: "I had a call from Mr. Johnson, Your Honour. He was taken ill this morning, and is unable to be with us. His client was arrested and given a promise to appear. He is here today. I understand he has spoken to Mr. Johnson about an adjournment. The Crown has no objection."

"It's rare that Mr. Johnson misses a court date," the judge responded. "I expect we'll see him here next week. We'll adjourn the matter till then. Next?"

My car theft case was called shortly after that, and I was back at my desk fifteen minutes later. What was wrong with Ed? He was never sick. Hungover, yes, but that wouldn't keep him from his work. Well, I was not about to phone and wake him up if he was under the weather.

On Friday afternoon, I got a call from the prothonotary's office, telling me the Court of Appeal had handed down its decision in a case of conspiracy to import narcotics. Just as I left my office building for the Law Courts with my briefcase in one hand and a paper cup filled with coffee in the other, the skies opened, and I was soaked in a matter of seconds. I ditched the coffee in a trash can, hunkered down, and speed-walked to the waterfront court building.

In the reception area, I shook off the water and stood for a moment to catch my breath. I heard someone come in behind me and turned around. Justice John Trevelyan, with not a drop of rain on him, so he must have come from the indoor parking garage. He was the last person I wanted to see. It was his decision I had appealed, and I had enumerated fourteen grounds of appeal in my factum. Grounds of appeal are worded like this: "The appellant submits that the learned trial judge erred in admitting the evidence of so-and-so; the learned trial judge erred in his interpretation of section such-and-such." Trevelyan was a good judge in civil trials, commercial litigation, and the other areas of law that made up his practice before his elevation to the bench, but he was out of his league on the rare occasions he took on a criminal case. I figured my appeal would succeed and his decision would be overturned. But maybe not. He looked tanned, relaxed and, for him, almost cheerful. Had he heard about the decision already? Was it in his favour? Or was he so confident that he just assumed it had gone his way?

"Good morning, Your Lordship."

"Good morning. Mr. Collins, isn't it? Yes, I recognize you."

"That's right."

"Dreadful day out there. But they say the farmers need it, so who are we to complain? Can't expect sun every day."

"You look as if you've had a bit of sun yourself, sir."

"I have indeed. I just got off my boat an hour ago. We sailed to the Bras d'Or Lakes and back. I took two weeks off, had perfect weather and had a marvellous time."

"Great."

I had him in a rare good mood, and I felt emboldened to follow up on something that had slipped my mind until this minute. I wondered whether he remembered the client he had passed on to Dice Campbell years before. Matilda Lonergan, the woman who had spoken up for Corey Leaman at one of his criminal trials. Ross Trevelyan had not mentioned bringing the name up to his father, and I suspected he had never raised the subject at all. He may have forgotten; he was buried in other work. But more likely, Ross saw it as yet another pointless distraction from the damages claim, and not something to pester Trevelyan *père* about. Whatever the case, I had the man himself in front of me.

"Justice Trevelyan, I came across a name that might be familiar to you. Matilda Lonergan."

A couple of seconds went by before he answered: "Miss Lonergan was a former client of mine. Why do you ask?"

"It's just that her name came up in something I'm working on."

He treated me to a probing stare. "I can't imagine how that is possible. The poor woman died in 1981."

"Oh. Well, I could be on the wrong track entirely. Would you happen to recall whether she ever mentioned —"

"Anything she ever mentioned to me would be covered by solicitor-client privilege, but somehow I suspect you have her confused with someone else. I have to go."

He left me and pressed the elevator button. Not going to the pro-thonotary's office? Perhaps he hadn't yet been told that the decision was in. Or he was in no hurry; it was not a matter of concern. I went in to pick up the decision, scanned it and saw that the Court of Appeal had accepted thirteen of my fourteen grounds of appeal. Trevelyan's decision had been reversed, and my client had been granted a new trial. The judge was not going to be a happy man.

I stuffed the decision in my briefcase and left the building. It was still teeming rain, but it looked as if it might be brightening up in the west. Maybe there would be a break in the downpour soon. I decided to stop in at Perks next door for a coffee.

I sat at a table, took out the Court of Appeal decision and read it again. They had come down hard on Trevelyan; phrases like "with the greatest respect" didn't disguise the fact that, in the court's view, he had screwed up.

"What's that?"

I looked up to see Ed Johnson, dripping rainwater on my table.

"Decision from the Appeal Division."

"Good?"

"Good for me, bad for somebody else."

"Who?"

"Trevelyan."

"Serves him right. He never set foot in a criminal court before he was appointed a judge; it was beneath him. So, what else is new?"

"Not much. Good to see you alive and well, Johnson."

"As opposed to?"

"Being too sick to come to court."

"I'm never sick. When was this?"

"Yesterday. Arraignment day. You weren't there."

"Oh, yeah, right." Then his tone sharpened. "You were there?"

"Obviously. That's how I know you weren't. While I have you here, I'll ask you this. A name came up in court, a name I heard in connection with Dice Campbell and the festivities over which he presided. Maybe you know —"

"How the hell would I know? I had nothing to do with . . . with Dicey's excesses, and I am fucking tired of hearing about the guy. Okay?"

"But —"

"Piss off! I have to get to court."

He left Perks without getting anything. A couple of other lawyers I knew came in then, ordered tea and coffee, and sat down for a chat. I looked outside and saw that the rain was letting up, so I said good-bye and headed for the office. I heard footsteps behind me. I turned around to see John Trevelyan, his face like a thundercloud. The holiday was over. I gave him a quick nod, turned and resumed walking. But he caught up.

"There you are, Collins!" He must have come looking for me. "You'd better be letter perfect each and every time you step into my courtroom from this day forward, Collins, or God help you." What, it was my fault he botched the case? I was just doing my job, and doing it well, but I had made an enemy who had the power to make my life hell in any case I tried before him from this day on. He had another message for me as well: "And I don't want to hear the names of any of my former clients uttered in public again. Do you hear me? There are defamation laws in this province, and there's nothing I would rather do than use them against you. Now get out of my way. I'm in a hurry."

What was that about? Was it my simple question concerning Matilda Lonergan? Couldn't be. I hadn't uttered her name in public, and what would be defamatory about it if I had? Or was he warning me, not about his client's reputation, but his own, in case I got oiled up and decided to crow about my triumph all over Halifax? I was pleased with the success of my appeal, but it wasn't my style to strut around the city boasting.

Trevelyan stalked away and turned up George Street. I returned to my office and began the paperwork necessary to get my client his new trial. Then I met with one of the clients in the crumbling condos fiasco. After that I was free and clear.

It was a long weekend and a quiet one for me; Tom and Normie were with their mother. But blues night was coming up on Monday, and I was looking forward to that.

This was the first time Charlie Trenholm had hosted blues night. He had a house full of kids from two marriages, so usually there wasn't any space for a jam session. But tonight the kids were going with his wife, Carrie, to stay with Carrie's sister in the Annapolis Valley. We had the house to ourselves. Except we didn't. When I pulled up at Charlie's, he met me in the driveway. The wife's sister had fallen ill, and the family trip was off. That wasn't a problem for Functus, however, because Charlie had an alternative plan. He had recently bought a big old house in the fishing village of Three Fathom Harbour on the eastern shore. He and Carrie were going to take their time fixing it up. In the meantime it was empty, it had power, it still had all the old furniture, and it was the ideal spot for blues night in the summer. We waited for all the band members to arrive, then headed across the Macdonald Bridge, through Dartmouth and out to Three Fathom Harbour in a convoy.

We stopped at a grocery store, a liquor store, and another spot, which we hoped would remain unknown to police, and loaded up on everything we would need to eat, drink and smoke as we wailed the blues into the wee hours of the morning. Once we started, neighbours got wind of the party and dropped in. Locals and commuters, male and female, young and old, everyone joined in the party. It was a blast.

Ed Johnson seemed to have forgotten whatever had set him off Friday at Perks. He and I spent much of the evening talking to a young woman named Crystal. After complimenting us on our music, she sought our legal advice on a plan to go in with her boyfriend and another guy and girl on the purchase of a house trailer in suburban Dartmouth. Our advice was simple: don't. Ed had a better idea: dump the boyfriend and hook up with Monty Collins. "All his women get a house of their own, so there will be one for you. He can afford to take you around the world and bring you back, he looks damn good when he's dressed up, and if you leave him, he'll play the blues harp under your window so even if you don't want him anymore you'll get a free concert off him." In other words, Johnson was his usual self.

I awoke in the morning in a sleeping bag beneath the rafters of an unfinished attic. Right, I remembered, Charlie Trenholm's house in Three Fathom Harbour. The night came back to me: I had been singing, blowing the harp, drinking, talking to a fisherman, talking to a young girl. My eyes darted around the attic. Nobody here except me and Ed Johnson, snoring away on the other side of the room. Good. No drunken coupling with strange women this time out. I closed my eyes and started to fall asleep again when I heard a pounding downstairs. The door. Charlie would take care of it. But the pounding didn't stop. I heard people running around downstairs, I heard toilets being flushed. What? I got up and looked out the attic window. An RCMP cruiser was parked in the yard. Christ, a raid! Did I have anything on me? I patted my pockets. No. The next thing I knew, Charlie was in the room calling my name.

"Monty!"

I didn't say a word, in case the Mounties were right behind him. But he came in alone.

"RCMP. They're looking for you."

"Me? What for?"

"They won't say."

"Where are they?"

"Downstairs hall."

"Is there anything lying around that shouldn't be here?"

"Not anymore."

All down the toilet. As if the Mounties didn't know what was going on when they approached a house and heard the toilets flushing. I had no choice but to go down and face the music.

A female officer stood in the doorway. I looked out and saw her partner standing by their car. "Montague Collins?" she asked.

"Yes?"

"Could you come with me, please?"

"What's going on?"

We had an audience, composed almost entirely of hungover lawyers.

"I'll explain outside."

I followed her and, when we cleared the house, she said: "A Father Burke called us early this morning to try to locate you."

Oh God, what was it? I felt a spike of fear and demanded to know what was wrong.

"Your wife was rushed to hospital last night. The Grace Maternity. That's all we know. The priest couldn't find you, so he called us."

Jesus, Jesus, Jesus! Of all times. The one and only night I was out of reach. Tom and Normie must be frantic. I thanked the officer, ran into the house and grabbed my keys, told Charlie I'd explain later, got into my car and drove away. The police car followed, then turned off at a crossroads, and I put the accelerator to the floor. This was August; the baby wasn't due till October. As I knew all too well. Damn it to hell! I had never got around to reissuing the divorce papers; I thought I still had plenty of time. But, if the baby wasn't due yet, what was happening? Maybe something had gone wrong. Well, obviously. Maybe there wouldn't be a — I resolutely turned my thoughts from the direction in which they were headed.

I got to the city, roared up to the Grace Maternity Hospital, parked illegally, and ran for the door. I was directed to the floor where Maura had been admitted and, eschewing the elevators, I took the stairs two at a time, not knowing what I was going to find. Or what I wanted to find. I concentrated my mind on my son and daughter, and willed them to be there when I arrived.

The only person I knew was Burke, sitting on the edge of his seat, massaging his temples with his left hand. When he caught sight of me he shoved his right hand into his pocket. But I had seen it. A rosary. His face was grey, and he had dark circles under his eyes.

"Where were you?" he barked at me. "Tommy called in the middle of the night. He couldn't reach you."

"What's going on?" I shouted back.

"She hemorrhaged. They had to —"

"When?"

"After midnight."

"And now?"

"They thought she was going to be all right. I took the kids home. But something went wrong again, and they've got her in surgery."

"What did they say, for Christ's sake? Is she going to be all right?"

"Where in the hell were you, Monty?"

I didn't reply that I'd been partying. I couldn't bear the thought of what the ordeal must have been like for my children. Or how I would make it up to them. And that was without even knowing what was happening to their mother.

"Where are Tom and Normie?"

"Fanny's going over to the house to pick them up. They wanted

249

to be here, but what good would that do? They're better off with Fanny until there's something we can tell them."

"Why are you dressed like that?"

"What?"

"Why are you in your collar?"

He shook his head in disgust at the inanity of the question. But I knew. He hadn't decided at midnight to dress up for the role of a priest visiting the sick. He wore his clerical black so there would be no confusion about his status in the waiting room. He didn't want anyone to pinpoint him as the husband, the lover, the father of the child.

We sat together in silence. The tension was palpable. Then, down the hall, a door flew open. Someone burst out with a bundle in her arms and rushed across the corridor to another room. Burke's black eyes fastened on the corridor, willing it to impart some information. Three people in surgical garb emerged from the first room, removed their masks and conferred in low voices. Heads were shaken and gloves snapped off. Two of them walked away. One turned in our direction and came towards us.

"Mr. MacNeil?" She looked first at Burke, then at me. I stood up. "You have a healthy little — little! — boy. Congratulations. Mum's tired and weak, but she's going to be fine. It will be a while before you can see them, but they're in good hands." The doctor smiled at me and left the waiting room.

Burke slumped in his seat, eyes closed, the very portrait of exhaustion and relief. I could not even begin to plumb the depths of my feelings about the situation. I was overcome with a desperate desire to be out of there.

"I'm going."

Burke's eyes flew open. "You're what?"

"I'm off."

"Are you having me on, Montague? She's just come through —"

"She's fine. Her child is fine. I'm not the father. I don't want to be here."

"But Tom and Normie —"

"I'll go get them, I'll drop them off here, I'll come back and pick them up." I turned and walked away.

When I collected my kids at Fanny's, and gave them the news,

Normie was so excited that I didn't have to think about what kind of a pose to strike for her. Tom was subdued. Aside from casting a couple of glances my way, he did not probe for a reaction. I dropped them off at the hospital, assuring them that I had checked and Mum was fine. Father Burke was there. I had to get home and then to the office; I would see them later. I felt guilty and I felt justified, all at the same time.

I had a trial that day, for a client facing seven years in prison, so I had a good reason to be nowhere near the Grace Maternity. I drove home, showered, went to the office to get my file, and appeared, hungover but presentable in my barrister's gown and tabs, in the Supreme Court of Nova Scotia. Justice Helen Fineberg convicted my client, and he was remanded in custody to await sentencing. I returned to the office.

On my desk were the notes I had taken of my conversation with Constable Riley about the Sybil Kraus case. I didn't have the energy to do anything more than put the notes in the file, but I couldn't find it. Ross Trevelyan must have it, I thought, so I got up and walked to his office.

Ross was talking on the phone and glaring out his window. He didn't see me.

"Dad. Elspeth and I don't have a boat. Nor do we have the resources at this point in our lives to acquire one. So why would we want to join the Royal Nova Scotia Yacht Squadron?" He listened for a moment, then continued. "A social membership without a boat? What would be the point? We know everybody there anyway." He stopped to listen again. "I just got here, remember? I can't expect to be making three hundred thousand dollars my first year at Stratton Sommers. As a matter of fact, though, I have a couple of cases on the go that should bring in a nice return, so . . ."

I didn't want to hear this, and I didn't want Ross to see me loitering in his doorway. But when I tried to melt into the shadows he caught sight of me. I made kind of a wry face and turned to leave. That's when I heard the crash of the telephone receiver and a shout from Ross.

"Collins!" I turned and stared at my law partner. "Get the fuck in here and close the door!"

Normally, I wouldn't take that kind of crap from anyone, no matter where they were in the hierarchy of the firm, but Ross was clearly a man under stress.

"Ross. Settle down. I'm sorry I overheard the conversation. We all have those kinds of hassles sometimes; you should hear me and my wife on the phone! I just stopped by to —"

"How much fucking longer am I going to have to wait for you to get your ass moving on the Leaman and Scott case? Jesus Christ! We've had it for nearly four months and you've been dicking around looking for all kinds of shit that isn't there. The file is full of crazy notes of yours, relating to Dice Campbell and his widow, and all these other red herrings, and for what? My father even said you asked him something about it. He's pissed, and guess who he takes it out on? We stand to make a nice little bundle, and you don't seem to give a damn. Just because you have two houses and not a financial care in the world, and you can take your evenings and weekends off, and spend your time swilling booze and blowing into a harmonica and banging groupies, doesn't mean the rest of us can slack off! I should just start the lawsuit myself and leave you out of it."

"We have lots of time, Ross. I just want to be sure we *have* a case before we start the action, so we won't be faced with a huge award of costs against us if it turns out we've brought the treatment centre into it without justification. And I have to say you've got a highly distorted idea of the kind of life I lead! I've got two kids and —"

"Save it, I don't want to hear it."

"All right, well, let's cool things off a bit, Ross."

"I know, I know. I'm sorry, Monty. What was it you wanted to see me about?"

"I just wanted to get the infamous Leaman file from you."

"It's over there on my table. Get it out of my sight. And I do apologize."

"Forget about it. See you later." I grabbed the file and left his office.

I returned to my desk, shoved the Sybil Kraus notes into the file, and contemplated the rest of the week ahead. I had another criminal trial, and discovery examinations in a case arising out of a multi-vehicle fatal accident that happened during a blizzard three years before. Leaman and Scott would have to wait.

I worked every night that week, and had a couple of stiff drinks when I got home, then collapsed in bed. I checked in with the kids regularly but did not set foot in the Grace Maternity Hospital.

On Saturday, I got a call from Tommy Douglas. "Hi, Dad."

"Hi, Tom. How's it going? Are you sure you don't want me to stay there with you for a couple of days?" I had given them the option of staying at my place, as usually happened when it was my week, or having me move in with them at the Dresden Row house. They wanted to stay there, to be within walking distance of the hospital until their mother was released. Tom had been conscientious in looking after Normie, I knew.

"No, you don't have to move in. Everything's copacetic here. Uh, Mum wants to have the baby baptized right away."

"Why?"

"I don't know. There's nothing wrong with him, aside from being premature. She just . . . I don't know," he finished lamely.

Great. A christening. Who exactly was going to be present? The child's father? Surely not, if I was getting this call. What was my role going to be? Godfather? An image came unbidden to my mind: the unforgettable scene in *The Godfather*: Michael Corleone at the baptism of his sister's child, reciting his vows on the baby's behalf, interspersed with scenes of his men gunning down his enemies as the sacred ritual proceeds.

"Do you renounce Satan?"

"I do renounce him."

"And all his works?"

"I do renounce them."

I snapped myself out of it, only to envision a church filled with family and friends, not knowing what to say to old Monty standing there with a stupid look on his face.

"So it'll just be here at the house."

"Sorry, Tom, what's that again?"

"Just us at the house. And Brennan. She thought you would, well . . ."

My feelings were being spared. She was going to forgo a big

church christening so the kids could have me there but nobody else would be looking on. What choice did I have?

"Sure, Tom. When is it?"

"She thought tomorrow night. She's getting out in the morning. The baby has a name now."

"Oh?"

"Yeah," Tom said. "Dominic. Second name's Alexander."

"After Alec the Trot."

"Granddad. Right."

So. Sunday night I was at the door of my former residence for the christening of my wife's child by someone who wasn't me. Normie greeted me at the door.

"He's so cute, Daddy! And so tiny! I'm only allowed to hold him if I'm sitting down. And you have to keep your hand under his head at all times so it won't flop down. Father Burke isn't here yet. Tommy picked him up and made him cry. Not Father Burke. Obviously. Dominic. He just has to get used to him. Tommy does. Are you coming in?"

"You're in the way!"

"Oh! Sorry."

I stepped inside and there it was: the tableau I had been dreading for weeks. My wife holding her baby. A baby whose paternity I wasn't quite clear on. A baby she loved, presumably, as much as she loved my two children. I suddenly found that notion more wrenching than anything related directly to me. She looked up with trepidation. I couldn't think of anything to say. The baby was small but not inordinately so. He had black hair.

"This will be quick," she said finally. "Brennan's on his way over."

No sooner did she speak than he arrived at the door. He gave Normie a hug and gave me a look over her head, as if to say: "You're not going to ruin this for them."

I stood by as my wife held her child, the priest poured water, and the baby howled. Father Burke made a sign of the cross on the tiny forehead and spoke the words of the sacrament of baptism. I resolutely forced the cinematic images of violent retribution from my mind as we mumbled our vows and our renunciations of evil. After the ceremony Burke picked up the squalling infant and looked lovingly into his face.

The baby calmed down, gave a little burp, and promptly fell asleep. Maura took him away to his crib. She came back and stood uncertainly in the middle of the room.

"Are you all right now?" I asked, finally.

"Oh yes. Tired, but, you know."

"Can I go sit by his cradle, Mum?"

"Why don't you leave him for a little while, Normie. Daddy's here now, so —"

"Daddy! Would you like an ice cream dipped in chocolate? Just like Dairy Queen!"

"Sure. I'd love one."

"Father? Are you allowed to eat chocolate at night?"

"I have a special dispensation from the bishop for tonight, Normie. What luck!"

"Is that what it is, though? Somebody said you can't get married. I already knew that. But they also said you can't go out at night and dip the something — maybe they didn't mean ice cream. But anyway, if the bishop says it's okay . . ."

Burke sat there shaking his head. Tom busied himself with the baby's paraphernalia in the opposite corner of the room. Was he perhaps the author of the overheard, and not clearly understood, wick-dipping remark?

We had our chocolate dips and said our good-nights.

Burke and I stood outside the house, wondering what the protocol was on an evening like this. In other words, could we go for a drink? Would that be sacrilegious somehow? More to the point, would it set me off on a bout of drunken recrimination against a mother and her child? Suddenly I found myself seized by another impulse. And, for some reason, I felt I had no choice but to act upon it.

"Let's sit in your car for a minute," I said to him.

"My car?"

"Yeah."

"All right."

We got in and he sat looking at me. I gestured with my head: "Face front. Don't look at me." He turned and faced the windshield.

"This is something I haven't said in thirty years," I told him. "You know what I mean."

"Yes."

"Do I have to say 'bless me Father for I have sinned,' and all the rest of it?"

He shook his head. His silence, welcome as it was, made it difficult for me to continue.

After a few minutes he said: "What do you want to confess, Monty?"

"Thoughts. About her. Maura. And the baby."

"Yes?"

"After I heard she was in the hospital . . ." The words dried up in my mouth.

"I know. Just tell me."

"It was only for an instant. Before I could even complete the thought, I regretted it. Renounced it. Honestly. I . . ." My voice gave out, and I didn't think I could continue.

"Take your time. I'm not going anywhere."

"I hoped — for an instant, I hoped the baby would die. And if it didn't, that she would die herself. I'm sorry! I don't even know who I'm apologizing to."

"Yes, you do. And you *are* sorry."

"Yes!"

"And you don't feel that way now."

"No. I wish she'd take the child and flee to Egypt. But I don't wish her any harm. Her or the baby."

"I know." He made the sign of the cross over me. *"Ego te absolvo a peccatis tuis in nomine Patris, et Filii, et Spiritus Sancti. Amen."*

Just for a moment, a moment of weakness or of sudden illumination, I was in awe of him. A friend — an acknowledged sinner himself, a guy I drank and had adventures with, someone whose eye I may have irreparably damaged — had the power to take my darkest, most despicable thoughts, deeds, and omissions and strike them from the record. Forgive them and render them of no account in the world beyond. I was relieved when the feeling passed.

Chapter 12

Now the doctor's gonna do all that he can.
But what you're gonna need is an undertaker man.
I ain't had nothin' but bad news.
Now I got the crazy blues.
— Perry Bradford, "Crazy Blues"

I did not go home in the spirit of peace that should have stayed with me after my confession. Instead, I went home and sought oblivion in the depths of a whiskey bottle. Predictably, the alcohol exerted its depressant effect and intensified my misery over my children's new brother on Dresden Row. My mind could not rid itself of the image of Maura and her newborn son. Dominic. What was that? Italian? Or — weren't there Irishmen called Dominic? What was it I had heard recently? The Dominicans? Their initials were "op." What did that stand for, and who gave a shit anyway? Order of Preachers, that was it! Son of a Preacher Man! No, it couldn't be. I didn't want to pursue that thought, or have it pursue me in my dreams, so I went outside and sat in a deck chair, gazing at the waves splashing on the shore. A wind had come up, and rigging banged against the mast of a nearby boat. A bell buoy clanged in the harbour, a lonely sound. I got up and poured one more for the road up to my bedroom, and made a resolution that this would be my last drink for a week. Or even a month. I didn't need the stuff, and I didn't enjoy feeling like crap all day afterwards. That settled, I collapsed in bed.

I had only been asleep for about an hour when my mind came

alive with images — memories — of me finishing a set in a smoke-filled bar; then, back stage, a guitar case filled with pills and tabs of mind-altering chemicals; a young girl; someone bursting into the room, screaming, throwing the guitar case against the wall; people scattering — I forced myself to put this, and the family disaster, out of my mind, or I would not get one more moment of sleep.

My brain then fastened onto the Leaman case. And I had one of those flashes of insight that seem only to come at three in the morning. This time it was: if I couldn't find the connections and conclude once and for all that Leaman's death was really a murder, the lawyers for the other side in the damages suit would not be able to do so either. Of course, the burden was on us as plaintiffs to prove our case. But if the only reasonable conclusion left to draw was that Leaman had wielded the gun, I might as well give up on my investigation, file the claim, and start working towards a profitable resolution. This was obvious, and I wondered why I had not considered it before. After all, the reason I had started digging into it was to reassure myself that our suicide case would not be torpedoed by counsel for the treatment centre. True, we would have to prepare for an attack on the softest spot in our case, that is, that there was no known link between the disadvantaged Corey Leaman and the privileged Graham Scott, so why would Leaman take out Scott before killing himself? But enough was enough. I would get to work first thing in the morning, and file the pleadings with the court. I drifted off to sleep.

I awoke again a couple of hours later, not with the allegations against the treatment centre running through my head, but with strains of Handel drowning out all other thought. "Who may abide the day of His coming" melded into "Thou shalt break them with a rod of iron!" I saw myself at the gated compound in Lunenburg County with Handel's music playing and hostile eyes peering through reinforced windows. What was going on there? The woman who lived in the house was the woman who had been in to see Warren Tulk the day Brennan was in the bookshop. People had seen a couple, one of whom seemed to be a cop, picking up young people in the Tex-Park garage. Another cop — Phil Riley? — told me Tulk had fixed a case. Or at least impeded the prosecution of a woman charged with assault on a child. A spanking case. What was the woman's name? Sybil? Sybil Kraus. But why worry about her? I had made up my mind to file the papers and commence the lawsuit. Well, maybe I'd look into the spanker first.

†

I made a couple of calls that morning, after downing two cups of coffee in a vain effort to clear my head, and found out when the Kraus case had been in court. She had been acquitted, possibly because the investigating officer didn't do his part when the case went to trial. Whatever the situation was, I had the date, so I walked over to the library on Spring Garden Road at lunchtime and went upstairs to search back issues of the *Herald* for clippings about the case. That night I headed to Gottingen Street, armed with a copy of a grainy photo of Sybil Kraus with a scarf around her head and a haunted look in her eyes. There was a cloudburst, and I needed my wipers on top speed to see through the pelting rain. But the person I was looking for was nowhere to be found, so I took a break and went to Tomaso's for a pizza. I scoffed half of it down, took the rest to the car, cruised down Gottingen again, and parked. Half an hour later I saw her getting out of a beat-up old Chev with tinted windows. I waited until it drove away and opened my door.

"Candy!"

"Hey! You looking for a — Mr. Collins. What are you doing up here again? You must be looking for company."

"I'm looking for you. Why don't you get in for a minute."

She climbed in with a sigh, and wiped the rain from her face. She looked exhausted; she was far too thin, and her skin was a mess.

"This life doesn't suit you, Candy. For Christ's sake, get some help."

"You didn't come all the way up here to talk me out of hooking, did you? Because forget it. I know what I'm doing."

"You're going to wind up in a Dumpster."

"Not me. I'm a smart girl, remember my file? So, how can I help you?"

"Have some pizza."

"I'm not hungry."

I shook my head and reached into my pocket. "I have something to show you."

"I just saw one in a different shade. Ha ha."

I ignored that and continued. "It's a news photo. Do you recognize this woman?"

"I don't know. Am I supposed to?"

"Look at it for a few minutes. Think."

"I think it's the lady I saw in that car. The gingerbread lady. She looks skinnier or something here, but I think that's her face. Charged with beating a kid. Figures."

Sybil Kraus, the spanker. Sarah MacLeod, the gingerbread lady. Which aspect of her persona was dominant at the compound in Lunenburg County?

"Can you tell me anything else about her?"

"No. Just that she was with that cop, and they were cruising for young stuff."

†

The next day I was saddled with a most unwelcome obligation, a partners' meeting. Since my synapses had not been firing at optimal levels lately, I had not plotted my customary evasive manoeuvres and could not get out of it. I hadn't even got it together enough to bring my Walkman.

I met Rowan Stratton on the way into the boardroom. "Monty, my dear fellow, you look all in. Come over to the house for dinner soon. Stephen and Janet say they haven't seen you in ages. I'll have Sylvia ring you, shall I?"

"Sure, Rowan. Thanks."

"You'll be pleased to know Sylvia has been taking a French cookery class. Don't worry; we can all order in after she's retired to her room for the evening. Ah. Blake. You're our chairman for the day, I believe. Perhaps we'd better get on with it."

"Yes, Rowan. We have a full agenda, and there are some incidental matters I intend to bring up."

I tuned him out, then remembered I had forgotten to bring the files that were to be discussed at the meeting. I went to fetch them and returned. Vance "the Undersigned" Blake was still droning on. Felicia Morgan glided into the boardroom, sat down opposite me, and gave me what she must have thought was a beguiling smile. Then she busied herself with her stack of files. Before we even got started, however, Felicia's secretary came in and whispered in her ear. Felicia looked annoyed and got up, announcing to the rest of us that she had been called to respond to an emergency chambers application. She pushed the stack of files in Blake's direction and gave him a look. I decided it might be interesting to go through some of her work myself. So I reached for them, but she subtly moved them beyond my grasp while pretending she hadn't seen my hands. Another significant look at Vance Blake, and the files were placed beside his own. Felicia made her exit, and I stood up, leaning over and pulling the stack of folders to my place at the table.

"Collins, do you mind?"

"Not at all, Vance," I replied.

"But she made it quite clear —" he whispered.

"Steady on, Blake," Rowan Stratton growled. "Let's proceed."

Monique LeBlanc was grinning at me from her place down the table. I winked at her in return.

I didn't know how long Felicia would be gone, so I took the opportunity of rifling through her papers while Blake conducted his meeting. But there was little of interest. As I went through the stuff, I wondered why she wanted to keep the files away from me, but then I came upon a family law file with a name I recognized. One of the parties to the divorce was a lawyer I knew, and I had heard he had been involved with Felicia a few years before. If her name was in the record somewhere she might not want me to see it. I guess Vance Blake didn't count; he would rather conduct a meeting than a love affair. But I had no interest in her life, either, so I closed that folder and moved on. She did have something on the Bromley Point development project, but who didn't? She was representing one of the many companies in the massive project. The material was divided into subfiles, but nothing caught my eye. I listened in as Blake wound up his conversation with the lawyer on my left. When it was my turn to discuss my work, I did not mention the Leaman case; the less said the better. Ross Trevelyan was circumspect as well, saying little more than that we hoped to get our claim filed in the next couple of weeks.

I returned my mind to the Bromley Point file in Felicia's stack. It occurred to me that her subfiles had been numbered sequentially from one to eleven. I flipped through the papers. There was no number four or number nine in the folder on the table. I wondered why they had been left out. Blake had reached the part of the meeting dearest to his heart, trolling for new business. Much of my clientele was criminal, and nobody wanted me out beating the streets for any more of that, so I excused myself with the promise of a quick return and went snooping in Felicia's office. Behind her desk, along with several pairs of pricey Italian shoes, I saw a pile of manila envelopes and, underneath those, the missing subfiles. I took them to my office.

Subfile number four contained an informal rating by a Toronto consultant of several local construction firms, a few of which were our clients. Some of the consultant's comments were less than favourable, and I could see why Felicia might not have wanted them passed around. Subfile number nine looked more promising, dealing as it did with man-about-town Ken Fanshaw. We were not his primary law firm but, like many other firms in the city, we did work for him from time to time. There were notes scribbled on the inside of the folder, phone numbers and dates. The initials "MC" caught my eye, though I didn't seriously think Felicia would be writing my initials in her files. The note read: "More 'mail'! K: libel action MC? Cautioned him no, let settle down. Maybe no more now she has int!"

Who was "she"? Ken Fanshaw was being libelled by a woman? What was it about? Was MC the woman? And what did "int" mean? Interest? Interest meaning the earnings from an investment, or interest meaning a share in a property or venture?

The materials in the Bromley Point subfiles were several years old. I was not a corporate lawyer — corporate jargon generally put me in a coma — but I was able to follow the process by which Fanshaw amassed a bigger and bigger piece of the action. So what?

I was about to drift into that corporate-law-induced coma when I saw a few sheets torn from a legal pad. What caught my eye was the name Campbell, then: "DC keen to be in but needs financing. Wants no appearance of confl. w. cli." So Dice Campbell wanted to invest on his own behalf, but would have to borrow the money. He wanted to ensure that his own interest did not appear to conflict with the interests of the client or clients he was representing in connection with the project. The notes went on: "Not saying but imp — pressure fr. ux for more?" This I interpreted as: Dice was not letting on but Felicia's (or Fanshaw's) impression was that Dice was under pressure from his "ux," Latin and legal shorthand for wife, to make a bigger investment. Which brought me back to the scribbles on the folder. Did MC stand for Mavis Campbell? If so, what was she doing to provoke Fanshaw into considering a libel action? What was the "mail" that was the subject of the note? Was she sending him nasty letters? I could see why Felicia had not brought these subfiles to the partners' meeting. I had little doubt that she was aware I was looking for a link between the death of Dice Campbell and the Leaman-Scott shootings; Felicia would not want to draw attention to any connection between her friend Fanshaw and the Campbells.

†

Felicia's files made me curious about Dice Campbell's role in Bromley Point. There was no point in trying to worm anything out of his widow, particularly if she stood to gain a significant sum of money from the development project, and if she had been brewing up mischief for Ken Fanshaw in the pursuit of her ambitions. A lawyer I knew slightly had been a friend of Dice; I called and arranged to meet him at Perks for coffee. Wade Evans and I engaged in some small talk, then I got us on to the subject of the late Mr. Campbell.

"I saw Dice a few days before he died," Wade told me. "He was in a pretty good mood. And I do remember having the impression he had a scheme going, or some kind of plan. Guess it didn't work out."

"Did he say something about a plan?"

"No, it was just an impression. I suggested we go out. We'd gone on a tear a few weeks before that. We started here and ended up in Montreal! Don't ask. Anyway, it turned out Dice didn't have any money on him, and his credit cards were up to their limits, so the weekend was on me. I didn't give a shit, but I could tell it was on Dice's mind. So later on when I suggested a night out, he said: 'Come by and see me in a couple of days, and then we'll go out in style.' He seemed to be saying it would be his treat. But I never saw him again."

"You got the feeling he might have been coming into money."

"I guess so."

"Could this have had anything to do with the Bromley Point development?"

"Oh, he was keen on that, all right. But the project had been halted, so if he was coming into a bag of cash around the time I'm talking about, it wasn't from Bromley Point. Could have been anything, with Dice and Mavis."

"You didn't have Mavis in Montreal with you, I take it."

"Nope. He had Mavis in the detox at the time."

"What?"

"Yeah, he twisted her arm and got her to sign in. Of course, she didn't stay. And those counsellors must have been glad to see the end of her."

"Why do you say that?"

"I heard, on fairly good authority, that she went berserk one night and trashed the place."

"Really!"

"Really. And these people are used to drunks. And crackheads. And all the rest of it. I guess they just weren't prepared for what this well-dressed, well-spoken, middle-class woman would do if she was kept off the sauce too long!"

"What did she do?"

"She was abusive to the staff. Verbally, I mean. Apparently she threatened one of them. Tore down curtains, smashed some glass. A real shitstorm."

"Which detox are we talking about?"

"The Baird Addiction Centre. But, as I say, she wasn't there long."

Mavis in the Baird Centre! Why hadn't this occurred to me before? But, then, why would it? I knew she was a drinker; that didn't mean she was looking for a cure. And if she was, there were several other detoxification centres.

"When was this?"

"Back in 1985."

Wade and I finished our coffee and said goodbye.

Nineteen eighty-five. The year of Leaman's first admission to the centre. Yet again, I was stymied by the fact that I could not talk to anyone on the other side of the case, namely, the doctors and other professionals at the Baird Centre. If the case went to litigation, I would be able to question them on discovery and demand to see their records. But that scenario seemed increasingly unlikely. I did have Doctor Swail-Peddle and his notes. I had skimmed through them with the intention of reviewing them in more detail later. A number of entries in the diary were blanked out, which was only appropriate, because they most likely referred to other patients. Something struck me then about the psychologist. Something had upset him about the diary or the notes the first time he brought them to me. And, for some reason, my mind made a leap from that to Mavis Campbell. I tried to recall what had happened. We were at the Midtown. Ed Johnson was giving Swail-Peddle and his wife a hard time, or at least they must have perceived it that way. But the psychologist had reacted to something else. Then I had it. Ed had mentioned Mavis's name. And it was then that Swail-Peddle's wife noticed her husband had spilled his beer. He took off to the washroom. Then he came back, took me outside, and gave me a big song and dance about needing the diary and notes back, because he hadn't finished editing out the confidential entries. Was it Mavis's name that had set all this in motion? I intended to find out, under the cover of looking for a connection between Mavis and Leaman. What I really wanted was to witness Swail-Peddle's reaction to her name. I gave the psychologist's office a call and set up an appointment.

Gareth Swail-Peddle's office was located in an old brown saltbox house on Fenwick Street. The reception room was painted a sooth-ing shade of pink, and the padded chairs were arranged in groups as if to encourage conversation. The only thing more prominent on the walls than the inspirational and affirmative posters were the framed certificates displaying the psychologist's credentials. His patients may have been the centres of their respective worlds, but he, Swail-Peddle, was the expert.

He peered out from his office, saw me, and beckoned me inside. He was on the phone and made an apologetic face while motioning me to a chair beside his own.

"Penelope, in all fairness, I think I should speak to Theo's teacher myself. You must admit I have some expertise in the area. Theo is gifted. Therefore, he does not need remedial help in reading. If he 'can't read,' as you put it, that says more about the way the school is presenting the material than it does about our son. There are different kinds of 'intelligence.' We've been through this before, and —" I heard a click, and he stared at the receiver as if it had taken it upon itself to terminate the conversation.

"I'm sorry, Montague. Every family has issues. Even that of a trained therapist! Now, how may I help you today? I hope my notes on Corey were helpful."

"Yes. Thanks. I have another question for you, though. Did you ever have any contact with a woman named Mavis Campbell when you worked at the Baird Centre?"

The psychologist's small eyes didn't waver as they met mine, but his left hand darted to his face and shoved a few hairs of his beard into his mouth; he proceeded to gnaw on them.

"Mavis, yes," he said at last, in what was almost a drawl. Then, in a rush, he went on: "But Mavis didn't suffer the same unfortunate fate as Corey Leaman, and therefore I feel a bit hesitant to disclose —"

"Right. She's still alive. But there may have been a connection between Mavis and Corey," I claimed, "and anything you can tell me may help clarify things."

"Well, there's not much I can tell you about Mavis while she was at the Baird." I waited, and he added: "She was there for a very short time before she was either released or transferred to another treatment centre. And although I reached out to Mavis and tried to engage her, she was . . . well, people react to treatment in different ways."

"What was Mavis's reaction?"

"Mavis was resistant to any sort of intervention. Mavis was in denial. And she wouldn't share."

"Wouldn't share what?"

He gave me a puzzled look. "Excuse me?"

"What wouldn't Mavis share?"

"What I mean, Montague, is that she wouldn't share in group. She would not open up in group therapy and share her experiences with the others, and this resistance of course is a stumbling block in her recovery."

"You say 'is.' Have you seen her since her time at the Baird?"

His eyes once more fastened onto mine, in a costly effort to look candid. "Um, no. Or, wait, yes, I have seen Mavis on a couple of occasions. Not professionally."

"Socially?"

"I wouldn't put it that way. We do not travel in the same circles. I have run into her — pardon the aggressive language! — I have seen her casually in various places around the city."

"You said her stay at the treatment centre was short. Exactly how long was she in the Baird Centre?"

"Oh, not long. There was an incident."

"Oh?"

"Mavis had an episode of . . . acting out. She damaged some property. It was decided that her needs could be met more effectively at another centre."

"Had Mavis been drinking when she had this episode?"

"No. She was quite sober."

"Did you witness the incident?"

"No, I wasn't there."

"Did you ever see Mavis and Corey Leaman together at the Baird Centre?"

"Not that I . . . well, there was the time in group when Mavis refused to dialogue. I believe Corey was with us that day. We were doing some grief work."

"Who died?"

"It was not a matter of anyone dying in the sense you mean, Monty, but of the inner child struggling to live again."

I figured there was little point in trying to follow his logic, so I kept quiet. He resumed his narrative.

"Corey shared with us. Shared his experiences, his trauma. Abandonment by his father, a less-than-nurturing environment with his mother. But whether he and Mavis had any conversation together before or after group, I couldn't tell you. He may have been a little angry with her. Everybody may have had feelings of anger that day, not just Corey."

"Why's that?"

"Mavis was less than empathetic with the rest of the group. I saw

her making gestures while the others were sharing. Opening and closing her hand like a mouth or a beak, as if to say 'blah, blah, blah' or
'yak, yak, yak.' Wiping away nonexistent tears, pretending to play a
violin, those sorts of behaviours. Making light of the disclosures of the
other patients, which, to my mind, showed she has a deep-rooted —"

"But you know of no other contact between the two of them?"

"I don't know of anything. That's not to say they weren't
acquainted. It's not a big place."

"Why did you leave the centre?"

"I was unjustly dismissed. Our director considered me a challenge
to his authority and to his orthodoxy. He thought it expedient to
have me removed."

I thanked him for his time and left. I thought it curious that he
had not once asked me why I was inquiring about Mavis Campbell.

†

I was becoming a regular at the bar at the Holiday Inn. Mavis barely
batted an eye when she saw me coming.

"Do you know someone called Gareth Swail-Peddle?" I asked
without preliminaries when I had myself seated.

"Imagine going through life with a handle like that!"

"Do you know him?"

"Never heard of him."

"I don't believe you."

"I know you don't believe me, Collins. That's why it doesn't matter whether I say I don't know him or I say I was sitting on his face
forty minutes before I arrived here."

"Which is it?"

"The truth lies somewhere in between. Dickie! I can barely croak
out a civil word to my inquisitor here, my throat is so parched. Hop
to it, will you?"

"Sure thing, Mave. For you, sir?"

"I'll have a Keith's, thanks, Dick."

"Now, what was it you were interrogating me about?"

"Swail-Peddle."

"Alas, poor Gareth! Poor little putz." She began rocking with laughter and had to wipe her eyes. "The look on his face!"

She brought her hands up on either side of her mouth, like paws. Somehow she made her own broad visage resemble the rather ferrety features of the psychologist, and then did an imitation of him with his eyes bulging out in shock. I couldn't help but laugh. Dick came by with our drinks and asked: "Who're ya doin' now, Mave?"

"Oh, Dick, you don't want to know. You just stay behind the bar here and you'll be doing more good for the world than that little weasel ever did, no matter how hard he tried. Poor old Swail." She was still shaking with mirth. When she got herself under control, she looked at me wearily.

"Why in the hell are you asking me about him?"

"Isn't it obvious?"

"Things that are obvious to me are not necessarily obvious to the rest of humanity. And vice versa. So, why are you here badgering me about Doctor Strangefur?"

"He was at the Baird Centre when you and Corey were there."

"Me and Corey."

"You and Corey Leaman, the second of your acquaintances to die in questionable circumstances."

"Screw you!"

"Talk to me, darling. Help me to understand."

"Screw you, I said. I didn't know this Leaman. If he was there when I was, I don't remember him." She downed her drink and held up her glass. Dick was over in a trice.

"How did you end up in the Baird?"

"Why, I have no idea, Mr. Collins. A case of mistaken identity, I guess. Somebody had me mixed up with a boozehound."

"Did you seek treatment on your own account?"

"Are you *well*?"

"How else did you get in there? Nobody can have you committed against your will."

"My dear, departed husband gave me an ultimatum. If I didn't sign myself into the Baird, he'd walk. He said he was doing it for me. As if me having a few drinks was the cause of all our marital *sturm und drang*. Coincidentally, as soon as he got me locked up in there he went off on a tear himself. Must have been afraid I'd tag along and hog all the booze. That prick. Anyway, yeah, that's where I met Garess."

"Why do you call him Garess?"

"Why do you think?"

"I'd rather not try to second-guess the workings of your mind, Mavis."

"I called him Garess to needle him. So he'd have to correct me by saying 'Gareth.' I sounded right; he sounded like he had a lisp. Had to do something to pass the time in there."

"What did he call you?"

"'Please, please, please! That's what he called me." She let out a squawk of laughter.

"He begged you for something, is that it?"

"Poor old Gareth was determined that I was going to become part of his group. Of course, the last thing I wanted in this world, next to going one more day without a drink, was sitting around with his little group of whiners and mopes, yanging about their problems. Do I have a problem? Sure. And I love my problem. I live for my problem. I intend to feed it and nurture it and make love to it until the day they throw me in the ground. What's to discuss?" She stopped talking to light up a smoke and take another sip of Scotch. "Aah! Bliss! Anyway, Gareth just wouldn't let up. I pissed him off in a couple of his group gropes, and then he wouldn't leave me alone. He'd come to my room at night and want to 'dialogue.' Of course that's not all he wanted."

"What went on during these nocturnal visits?"

"Therapists need love too!" She snickered and took a drink. "You have to wonder what Mrs. Swail was peddling at home, the way this guy sat there gazing at me like a puppy. A bright-eyed little rodent, would be more accurate. On the first of his visits, he said 'hugs!' and glommed on to me, after looking to me for permission of course. He claimed that I was the one who needed a hug. I pressed everything against him, then I broke it off and turned aside, as if tearing myself away from the great passion of my life. 'Garess, I think you'd better go,' I croaked at him. He was all apologies and he scuttled away."

She paused for a swallow of Scotch. "But the next night he was back for more, and he had a plan. He couldn't be more obvious. He began 'sharing' with me some of his own 'issues.' I won't bore you with them. Then he turned the conversation — subtly, he thought — to my relationship with Dice. Was Dice meeting my needs as a person, as a woman? Did I see my drinking as an escape from an unfulfilling marriage? As if I just discovered twelve-year-old single-malt Scotch the first night Dice and I had a tiff. What a fruitcake. I don't know how he got a job there. Or how he hung on to it."

He didn't, I thought, but kept it to myself.

"The next night," Mavis continued, "to move things along, he smuggled some Scotch in for me! To a drunk in a detox! Is there a code of ethics for these people? Gareth had to go on his rounds, and he left me with this alcoholic fluid. Tasted like it came from Wal-Mart. War-Malt, I called it. But of course, I drank it. There was nothing else available. He returned later on, when he figured I'd be blitzed. And he could be forgiven for thinking so, because I was lying on the bed as if I was passed out. So Mr. Smooth makes his move. Starts taking his clothes off. He was down to his shorts when I made my own move. I jumped up from the bed, looked him in the eye and starting undoing my pants. I thought his heart was going to blow up. I turned around, yanked my pants off, and showed him my butt. He made a little choking sound, grabbed his clothes, and fled from my room!"

She smiled as if at a fond childhood reminiscence. "It was an awkward thing to do, but I had managed it. On one butt cheek I had scrawled 'Share,' and 'This' on the other one. And he thought he was setting *me* up!"

"Good for you!" I blurted, forgetting for a moment that I had this woman in the frame as a possible murder suspect. "What happened after that?"

"I heard he took a week off. Family emergency. I'll say. I was gone by the time he was due back."

†

I had another widow in front of me on Wednesday. "I'll only keep you for a minute, Amber." I wanted to see what, if anything, Amber Dawn Rhyno could tell me about Swail-Peddle. "Where's Zachary today?"

"Over at my cousin's."

"All right. What I'd like to know is whether Corey ever mentioned the doctors or therapists at the Baird Centre. If he talked about any one of them in particular."

A canny look came over her face, and I could see her wondering about the implications of my question. She couldn't come up with anything, however, so she just said: "Maybe. Why?"

"Why don't you just tell me what you remember."

She thought for a moment. "Well, there was this one guy who was really mean to him."

"Who was that?"

"I don't know his name."

"What was he? A doctor, psychiatrist, staff member, what?" She shrugged. "How was he mean?"

"I can't remember, just that Corey didn't like him. He . . . was scared of him!"

I decided to play along. "Afraid of him why?"

"This guy was really big. He told Corey he had to do whatever this guy said, or Corey'd never get out! He'd keep him locked up in there forever!"

I cleared my throat. "Amber. Our claim is that they wouldn't let him *stay*. Not that they wouldn't let him *out*. Remember?"

She looked down and didn't answer.

"Now try to recall anything Corey might have said about the people at the centre. Anything at all."

She sat silent for a while, then mumbled: "There was this guy he used to laugh at. But he wasn't scared of him or nuthin'."

"Oh?"

"Yeah, he was, like, this dork. Corey said he seen him the first time he was in there, and he was still there."

"Still there during Corey's most recent admission."

"Yeah."

"What was it Corey used to laugh at?"

"Just that he was a dork and said all these dumb things. And Corey seen him with his pants off."

"Really."

"Yeah, I remember now. Me and Zach were visiting, and this dweeb walked by. Corey told me he seen him standing there one night years ago, all red and sweaty, and he only had his underwear on."

"Where was he standing?"

"Outside some girl's room. Corey could hear her laughing. Like, this geek was pissed 'cause this girl was making fun of him. Every time Corey seen him after that, he'd say, like, 'couldn't get it up, eh?' or 'she thinks you're a jerk-off; she likes me better.' And stuff like that. Maybe this guy got Corey kicked out!"

I would like to have known a great deal more about what went on in the Baird Centre between Swail-Peddle and Leaman; Swail-Peddle and Mavis; and, possibly, Mavis and Leaman. Did the incident in Mavis's room come to the attention of the authorities at the centre? Did Leaman threaten to tell on the psychologist? Did the incident have something to do with Corey's departure from the centre? I was seriously hampered by the fact that the Baird Centre was the opposing party in what might, or might not, turn into a lawsuit. I was not going to get any information out of the people there until — unless — we started our suit and held discovery examinations. I tried to think of someone I might know who would be acquainted with the practices and personnel of the treatment centre. A couple of psychiatrists came to mind, as did Debbie Schwartz, a psychologist who helped me out on occasion with my criminal clients. Debbie's name triggered a memory; I had seen it written somewhere in connection with all this, but where? A file folder, a sheet of paper — I had it. Dice Campbell's files.

I dropped in to Jamie McVicar's office and asked to see the files yet again. It took a few minutes of digging, but I found Dice's scribbled a note: "Asked Debbie Schwartz re: fruitcake from DT; yukked about house call, says don't pay him time & 1/2 or might come back!; name familiar but doesn't know him; suggests try again, call Drug Dependency." Drug Dependency: the detoxification and drug rehabilitation program run by the provincial government. Was Dice trying to get himself off drugs? Was he addicted? Or was it about his wife? He had strong-armed her into the Baird Centre. That hadn't worked; was that what "try again" referred to? What did DT stand for? *Delirium tremens*? That's what you suffered during alcohol withdrawal in the detox. Detox. The fruitcake from the detox. Swail-Peddle. A house call?

†

Mavis was planted at her regular station at the Holiday Inn.

"Dickie! Hit me up, and make it extra strength."

"And the usual for you, sir?"

"Sure, Dick, thanks. Sorry to be such a trial to you, Mavis. What does it say about me that women have to step up their meds when they see me coming?"

"It says you're an interfering, unwelcome asshole who . . . Dickie! What's the difference between a lawyer and a tick?"

"No idea, Mave."

"A tick falls off you when you die."

"Don't die on me, Mavis," I urged her, "not when you have so much to live for."

"Why do I get the impression that is a segue into yet another baseless accusation against me? I think I'll hire a bloodsucker from another firm and sue you for slander."

"I'll save you the trouble and, dare I say it, the expense. If it's just between us, there's no slander. So, just between us —"

I was about to ask for an account of the psychologist's house call but I had another question for the widow, as well, a question about the "mail" Kenneth Fanshaw had been receiving, according to Felicia's notes. Mail that gave rise to thoughts of a libel action against MC. "Mavis, what was the nature of your letters to Kenneth Fanshaw? Around the time the Bromley Point development was getting started."

"Fanshaw!" Her surprise struck me as genuine. "If I was ever going to write anything to Kenneth Fanshaw, it would be 'sex offender' carved into his forehead with my nail file! Other than that I never gave him the time of day. What are you accusing me of now, breaches of etiquette?"

So, if Fanshaw had been receiving nasty letters, they hadn't come from Mavis. I believed her. Had they come from Graham Scott after all? That's what Matty Fuller had told me: Dude say Scott sendin' him letters. I had formed the impression that Fanshaw was the "dude" and the letters might have constituted blackmail.

I realized I'd been had. Felicia must have been keeping an eye on the murder/suicide file Ross and I had started; she must have found the notes I'd made about Fanshaw receiving letters. Perhaps at the instigation of Fanshaw, she had set me up at the partners' meeting, betting that, if she appeared to be subtly but determinedly keeping files out of my reach, I'd go through her office. She'd planted phony subfiles, and I'd fallen for it. Fanshaw didn't want me to know that *he* knew the nasty letters were from Graham Scott. Blackmail and the threat of exposure by Scott constituted a possible motive for Fanshaw to want Scott out of the way. To deflect my suspicion, he pretended he thought they came from Mavis Campbell. This ruse put Fanshaw squarely in my sights again. But now I had Mavis before me.

"You know, Mavis, I think I'll settle in for the night. I like it here. The fact that you haven't changed watering holes suggests to me that this is as good for you as it is for me."

"What kind of fantasy world do you live in, Collins?"

"I live in a nightmarish world where nothing is what it seems, and respectable widows have secrets that they keep from the most benign questioner."

"What now?"

"Why don't you tell me about Doctor Swail-Peddle showing up at your place. Which you neglected to mention last time we 'shared.'"

"Why don't you tell me something instead. Like how you earned the God-given right to come aboard me whenever you feel like it, and demand to know everything about my life."

"I just find it odd that you told me all about how you humiliated this poor devil but neglected to tell me the sequel. Why would that be?"

"Because it's none of your business? Could that be it, do you suppose? You know I'm getting pretty goddamned tired of you, Collins. I have a good mind to call the police and tell them you're harassing me."

"You don't really want to attract the interest of the police, do you, Mavis? I know I wouldn't if I were you."

"If you really think I killed my husband, Monty, aren't you afraid I'll come after you some night? They say if you kill once, it's a lot easier the second time."

"Would it only be the second time for you, though, Mavis? I'm wondering whether there was something going on between you and Corey Leaman."

"I didn't even know Leaman. I told you that."

"Keeping track of your stories, are you? I see a lot of that on the stand. 'I left at eleven-thirty. Like I told you before.'"

"Oh, cut the crap."

"What happened when Swail-Peddle turned up at your house?"

"Dicey came home."

"All right, back up. When exactly did this happen?"

"Well, I got out of the detox in July '85. So it was within a week of that."

"Okay. Tell me about Gareth's arrival."

"*Gareth* showed up on my doorstep very late one night. He probably figured I was alone because there was only one car in the driveway. Or maybe he was watching the house. Anyway, I went to the door and there he was. There was nothing 'sharing and caring' about him this time. He was in a snit. Anyone else, I'd call it a rage. He pushed his way past me and told me to sit down and keep my mouth shut. Yeah, like Mavis Campbell is gonna keep her mouth shut! I started to needle him. 'Got any cheap hooch tonight, Doc?' That kind of thing. He told me to shut the fuck up or I'd be sorry. I just laughed and offered him a drink. He started to tell me that I was a deeply disturbed woman, that my behaviour that night was very revealing — I let out a squawk at that, and he turned beet red. He went on and on. I guess I was supposed to draw the conclusion that if I told anyone what happened I would just be letting them know how sick and fucked up I was. I started in on him, that I had been a patient there, that his boss might not look too favourably on his bringing booze to an alcoholic who was supposed to be recovering in his treatment centre, and trying to seduce her in the most ham-handed way. His face, or what you could see of it behind the fur, was nearly purple. He moved towards me as if he was going to hit me. I think I could have pounded the crap out of him if it came to that. But it didn't. Because that's when Dice walked in.

"'Who the fuck are you?' Dicey bellowed at him. Gareth just stood there, his eyes popping out of his head.

"'This is my boyfriend, darling. Gareth, meet my husband, Dice.'

"'Like hell he's your boyfriend. What do you want?'

"'Maybe we should all sit and calm down,' Doctor Swill says then. He sits, but nobody else does.

"'Mavis, get me a drink,' Dicey says.

"'We're all out.'

"'If we were all out, I'd have had to swerve to miss you outside because you'd be crawling away from the house with your tongue hanging out. But never mind. I can do without. Unlike some. Now, what are you doing in my house at this time of night, Gareth or whatever your name is?'

"Swail looked over at me and then back at Dice. He didn't know whether to shit or go blind. Finally he comes up with: 'There was an incident at the treatment centre. I'm a clinical psychologist there. Your wife needs help, Mr. Campbell, er, Dice.'

"'Go to the top of the class, Gary! My wife needs to be transported, blindfolded, to a detox in central Saudi Arabia. But so what?'

"'Well, as I was saying . . .' Poor Gare was shitting bricks. 'There was an incident. The details are confidential and I am not permitted to disclose them to you.' His beady little eyes darted over to me. 'But there is something we call alcoholic psychosis, in which the patient loses touch with reality, and hallucinates —'

"'The day I start hallucinating about scrawny little men stripping off in front of me in a detox centre is the day I'll swear off the stuff for good and start pouring Kool-Aid at the Baptist church picnic!'

"'What's this about him stripping off?' Dicey asks.

"Gareth jumps in: 'I was not of course unclothed. This is part of the hallucinatory process that I was describing to you.'

"'Bullshit. What happened, Mave?'

"So I told him. Every detail, finishing up with me flashing my big butt at Gareth with the words 'share this' emblazoned on it. Gareth was rocking back and forth in his chair by this time, hyperventilating. Then Dice just lets go with a roar of laughter. I think that was the happiest I had ever made Dice since the first night I ever . . . Anyway, he got up, gave me a slap on the rump, then wrapped his arms around me and said: 'That's my babe!' He gave me a great big kiss. Affection from Dice wasn't a common occurrence those days. Men! You never know what's going to set them off. Then he remembered that little shit, Swail-Peddle, sitting there. So he made a big show of rubbing his hands all over every part of me and saying he couldn't wait to tear my clothes off. Et cetera, et cetera. 'Oh, sorry,' he says to Gareth. 'I forgot you were here. I'll be in touch later this week.'

"'About what?' Gareth croaks.

"'About my refund from the detox. Your treatment didn't work, especially seeing how you got her drinking while she was in there. Oh, and there may be a lawsuit. You could counterclaim against Mavis. I don't know what the cause of action would be: sexual humiliation? You'll need independent legal advice on that. Who do we serve the papers on over there? What's the executive director's name at the centre? Never mind, I'll get it. Don't let me keep you. I gotta lay a bad lovin' on my wife here. Run along now.'

"I never saw anything so pathetic in my life as that little man scuttling out the door. Is there such a thing in law as sexual humiliation? Because if so, he had it. And he brought it on himself. I didn't start it!"

I wasn't sure sexual humiliation qualified as grounds for a lawsuit. But I wondered whether it could provoke someone to murder. Especially if Dice Campbell had been about to go public by filing a complaint with Swail-Peddle's employer.

"You know how sick this life is, Monty?" She clutched the drink Dickie had placed in front of her, then picked it up and downed it. "I'll tell you. That ridiculous incident led to one of the happiest nights of my marriage to Dice."

"This was how long before his death exactly?"

But she had tuned me out. "And it didn't mean a fucking thing to him. What the hell is the matter with men?" I was surprised to see tears falling from Mavis's eyes.

"Is there anything I can do for you, Mavis?"

"You can go away and leave me alone."

I did. I went away wondering yet again about Mavis's role in her husband's death. Was it, in the end, a crime of passion? This territory was all too familiar to me, after the flame-out of my own marital reconciliation. I could understand perfectly how Dice Campbell's wife might have been in such a state of heartbreak and rage that she could push him off the balcony of his tenth-floor office and stand there watching as he crashed to earth on Barrington Street. And did Leaman fit in somehow? Two apparent suicides: Leaman killed by Dice's gun. Dice had a clipping about one of Leaman's criminal convictions — even though Corey's name was not mentioned, the blender assault had been his doing. And Dice had done some work for Leaman's elderly neighbour, Matilda Lonergan, who had gone to the trouble of testifying on Leaman's behalf.

And then there was Gareth. On my way to the office, I recalled joking with Ross Trevelyan about the psychologist coming forward to offer assistance, like a criminal insinuating himself into the investigation. Swail-Peddle certainly merited another look now that I knew about his humiliation at the hands of Mavis and Dice Campbell. I had given his diary and notes a cursory glance before leaving them in Ross's office. I decided to go through them more carefully, then use them as an excuse for another chat with the psychologist. When I went over the evening with Gareth and his wife at the Midtown, I remembered he had felt uneasy with Brennan Burke: reason enough to bring Brennan along for the interview. I picked up the phone and asked to speak to Doctor Swail-Peddle. He had gone for the day, so I left my number.

Back to Matilda Lonergan. What exactly had I found out about her? Hadn't Justice Trevelyan threatened me with a defamation suit for mentioning his former client? Of course, his attitude towards me had rapidly soured as the result of the Court of Appeal's ruling against him. But I knew he had handed off Mrs. Lonergan's little assignment to a younger, still-keen Dice Campbell.

Who was the woman I had spoken to about Matilda? I looked through my file to find her name. Mrs. Pottie. Yes, she had lived in the Sackville neighbourhood too, and had spoken to me from her nursing home. My notes didn't tell me much: Mrs. Pottie had known of Leaman as a local ne'er-do-well and obviously thought Mrs. Lonergan's affection for him was misplaced. The two women used to chat at the bus stop, though I saw I had written "TL could have afforded cab." Yet she took the bus to her doctor and to some other place. The food bank. Why a food bank if she could afford to take taxis? I must have had it wrong. I didn't have much hope of finding out anything useful about Mrs. Lonergan, and even less hope of explaining to myself why it mattered, but I decided to call Mrs. Pottie again.

"Oh, yes, I remember you. You were asking me about Matilda. Why was it you were asking again?"

"I'm working for the family of Corey Leaman, you know, the

young man who was found dead of gunshot wounds."

"Leaman, yes, yes, I remember. It's a wonder you don't find more of these people lying around with bullets in them, the way they carry on."

"I realize Mr. Leaman wasn't a favourite of yours, but Mrs. Lonergan seemed fond of him."

"Tilly Lonergan was moved by the Holy Spirit! And she thought the Holy Spirit was moving in every human creature on the planet! Hmph! Sometimes I wondered if Tilly ever picked up a newspaper. There's nothing holy about the world today, in my opinion! But she felt differently, God love her, going in there three or four days a week to work with those layabouts and punks. You wouldn't catch me in there! Turn your back on one of them for an instant, and they'd have you by the throat."

"Who?"

"The young bums and drug addicts at that hostel where she spent her days. I know the Good Book says feed the poor and visit the sick and the prisoners, but I don't think it means you have to take your life in your hands. Or risk having your purse snatched."

"So Mrs. Lonergan did volunteer work, is that it? With young people?"

"Young people old before their time! Thieves and reprobates!"

"What was the name of this place, do you know?"

"Oh, something that wouldn't give you any inkling of what was really going on. Primrose House. That was it; sounded like a gardening shop. They let them hang around there all day and night. Fed them, clothed them, tried to teach them how to spell and do their sums. How to live among decent people. I wonder how many successful graduates they had."

"I don't think I've ever heard of it. Is it in Halifax?"

"I think it's in Dartmouth, because I used to take the number eighty-four bus right into town, but Tilly used to get off and transfer before we got to the bridge. Why she didn't take taxis or even buy herself a little car, I don't know. Though I suppose she didn't want to drive in that kind of neighbourhood."

"So Mrs. Lonergan would have had the financial resources for more convenient transportation."

"Her husband died long ago, and they had no children. So Tilly had money. Yet she wouldn't think of spending it on herself! I would if it were me, I'll tell you that. But, no, Tilly wasn't one for pampering herself when there were others in need. Well, you'll see if you're keen on visiting that youth place, Primrose House. It must look like the Taj Mahal these days!"

"What do you mean? Had she helped fix the place up?"

"Fix it up? I imagine they have a whole new building by now, considering how much money she left them! She had no family, so —"

"So she provided for the hostel in her will?"

"I'll say!"

"Would Mr. Leaman have attended the program at the hostel, do you know?"

"Who knows? Though if there was anything in it for him, you can be sure he was there with his hand out."

"Mrs. Pottie, thanks again for your information."

"Any time. Nothing else to do in this place, except watch a bunch of nincompoops braying for money on the game shows, and another bunch of nincompoops egging them on from the recreation room in here."

I had never heard of Primrose House. I was familiar with a great many government programs, shelters, group homes, halfway houses, church-run charities, and other outfits, but this was a new one to me. I got out the phone directory and looked it up. I found a listing, with an address on Primrose Street in Dartmouth. I had never been on the street in my life, so I consulted my city map. I would head over there tomorrow. A new Taj Mahal should be easy to spot.

†

Shortly after I arrived at the office on Thursday, my secretary rang to tell me Doctor Swail-Peddle was on the line. He offered to meet me in his office that afternoon but I thought he might be a little too comfortable there, so I suggested a drink after work. He sounded doubtful, but he came around in the end. I called Brennan and lined him up for the outing as well, then went into Ross's office to pick up the diary and notes the psychologost had given us. Ross looked at me over a stack of case reports teetering on his desk. He seemed more harried and stressed out than ever.

"Monty! Do I dare even ask if we're any closer to filing our claim for Leaman and Scott?"

"That's why I'm here. I want to go over Swail-Peddle's notes again."

"Glad to hear it. I think you'll find them helpful. It looks to me as if Leaman was a prime candidate for the longer rehab program, but Swail-Peddle couldn't persuade his colleagues at the Baird to go along. So Leaman was out, and we know how that ended." He got up and found the papers. "Here. Photocopies of the diary and notes on our deceased client. Happy reading."

"Thanks."

I returned to my desk and sat down with the photocopied pages. The psychologist had done a lot of editing. There were entire pages in his diary on which there were only two or three lines of handwriting. I could not help but wonder how many of these blanked-out entries had been about Mavis Campbell. The diary certainly went back to 1985, the year she was in the program; there were brief references to "CL" at that time. There was nothing to indicate whether Mavis and Corey had spent any time together.

Corey's most recent admission was more regularly documented. There were a couple of sessions in which Gareth reviewed Corey's progress and advised him of the Phase Two program, which offered an extended stay and more intensive therapy. Gareth also noted his efforts to meet with Doctor Edelman, the director, to present his case for a longer course of treatment. According to Gareth's notes, Edelman barely gave him the time of day. This looked straightforward to me, but one could never be sure. After all, I had discovered something Gareth did not want me to know: the painfully embarrassing scene with Mavis, and Gareth's further humiliation in front of her husband. Dice Campbell and Corey Leaman, two supposed suicides, connected in several ways. One of the links was Gareth Swail-Peddle.

I pictured the walls of his office, festooned with certificates attesting to his qualifications. Many professionals were touchy about their credentials; Swail-Peddle was obviously one of those. I had already formed an impression of him as a man who craved recognition for his expertise. His pleasure in being right was obvious; his embarrassment at being wrong could be equally strong. How far would he go to prevent Dice Campbell from revealing the Mavis incident to his superiors at the centre? Had Corey Leaman, six years later, threatened to tell what he had seen?

†

Brennan and I were seated at a table in Ryan Duffy's when Swail-Peddle arrived. His mouth went into a little twitch when he spotted Burke, but he nodded and sat down. The large wing chair nearly swallowed him up when he sat back, and he quickly moved to perch himself on the edge of the seat. Burke ordered three pints of Guinness. Swail-Peddle looked at his as if it might be poison. Or truth serum.

"How are you?" he asked Burke.

"Flying. And yourself?"

"Forgive me. I can't recall your name."

"Brennan Burke."

"Oh, yes. And you have a brother. He seemed like an amiable chap. Will he be joining us?"

"No, he's back in New York."

"New York. Really. A harsh environment. What does he do there?"

"Paddy's a psychiatrist."

"Oh! I see." Swail-Peddle seemed distracted during the next round of small talk, perhaps trying to recall whether he had said or done anything revealing in Patrick's presence. I could have answered that for him. But I wanted to bring him around to the subject at hand, which was, ostensibly, Leaman. He did not have much to add to what I'd read in his diaries.

We ordered a second round and listened to the therapist discuss his patients without giving away their identities and without letting up on the touchy-feely jargon. When he finished his second pint he smirked at Brennan.

"So. Brendan. How was your anniversary? Your twenty-fifth? Do I have that right?"

"You do."

Swail-Peddle was childishly pleased to have his recollection confirmed. I wondered whether his inability to recall Burke's name was a bit of play-acting. His face was pink, and I concluded that he did not have a large capacity for alcohol.

"I also seem to recall that your friend — Ed, was it? — offered you rather an unorthodox gift to help you celebrate." The psychologist leaned forward with an arch smile playing about his lips. "We're all adults here. Did he come through with a couple of sex-trade workers for the occasion?"

"Yes, he did. Well, not a couple."

"Not a couple. I see. Just as well, perhaps!"

"A dozen, by my count."

Swail-Peddle's tiny eyes seemed to bulge behind his spectacles. "Come now, Brendan, surely this constitutes a bit of male braggadocio!"

"No, no, not at all," Burke said.

"Well, where was your partner while this anniversary was being celebrated so uninhibitedly?"

"Partner?"

"Brendan, forgive me if I'm overstepping. But do you think it's possible that you are engaging in patriarchal behaviours and denying your wife the empowerment that a woman —"

"I don't have a wife."

"Excuse me?"

"I'm not married."

"This anniversary, then . . ."

"Johnson hired the women for my twenty-fifth anniversary as a priest. Sure, after all that time, couldn't I do with a rub of the relic?"

Swail-Peddle goggled at him across the table. Burke sent me an almost imperceptible wink as he lifted his pint to his mouth.

"Gareth, did you ever meet Mavis Campbell's husband, Dice?" I said then.

"Eh?" His eyes were those of a startled rabbit.

"Dice Campbell. Did you ever meet him?"

"I'm not following you here, I'm afraid," he said, stalling for time.

"The question sounded simple enough to me," Burke put in.

I leaned towards the little bearded man. "Dice Campbell died, an apparent suicide. Corey Leaman died, an apparent suicide, only this time the 'suicide' was committed with Dice Campbell's gun. You knew Corey, you knew Mavis. Did you also know Dice?"

"What are you saying?" His voice was overly loud, and had gone up in pitch. He stole a glance at Burke, who regarded him impassively with his black eyes half shut.

"I'm just wondering if you can help me here, Gareth," I prompted.

"You are being very aggressive, Monty. I wonder why."

"You are being very evasive, Gareth. I wonder why."

"Now you are being sarcastic and accusatory. I suspect your occupation as a lawyer tempts you at times to take on an intimidating posture. Well, this may disappoint you, but you won't find me very enabling."

"Are you going to answer my question?"

"Your question was what again?"

"Did you ever meet Dice Campbell?"

"Oh. Right. Yes, Mr. Campbell and I met once or twice while his wife was in recovery. I cannot imagine why my work with Mrs. Campbell or her husband has anything to do with my efforts to assist you in the claim for Corey Leaman."

He was going to bluff it out. As much as he feared I might know about the gonad-shrivelling incidents with Mavis and Dice Campbell, he could not bring himself to acknowledge them. And who could blame him for that? I really had no desire to rub his nose in it. From his point of view, too, there was always a chance that I was bluffing and knew nothing about what had happened. I decided to keep him in the dark, and off balance, about what I knew. The psychologist was someone I wanted to investigate further, but I had nothing to gain by antagonizing him.

"I'm sorry, Gareth," I lied. "It's just that all these people were connected somehow, and I can't find anyone who can help me piece it together." Had I ever told Gareth I had met Mavis? Had Johnson said something about her knowing me, that night at the Midtown? I was pretty sure I had never alluded to my conversations with her. I made a face I hoped would pass as a thoughtful expression: "Perhaps Mavis Campbell herself . . . I should see if I can track her down. Shouldn't be hard to do."

"I wouldn't bother, if I were you," he said quickly.

"Why not?"

"I'll be frank. Mavis Campbell is delusional. You'd be surprised at some of the things she used to say to me, in the full expectation that I would believe her." He gave a condescending little laugh. "You and I, Monty, are trained professionals. We know a lie when we hear one. Or several! And her husband wasn't any better, from the little I saw of him. It was my impression that they lived in a state of dysfunctionality and co-enablement, and they were both in denial about their issues. Sad, I know. Terribly sad. But you won't get a word of truth out of poor Mavis Campbell."

Chapter 13

You know, you know how it is with me, baby,
You know I just can't stand myself
And it takes a whole lot of medicine
For me to pretend that I'm somebody else.
— Randy Newman, "Guilty"

I stayed on at Ryan Duffy's for a couple more drinks after Swail-Peddle and Burke left the bar. But I didn't want to leave my car downtown, particularly since it was parked at the family home down the street, so I got up to leave when I was still relatively unimpaired. On my way down the stairs to Dresden Row, I heard footsteps behind me. A soft but grating voice sang: "I'm going back to New Orleans to wear that ball and chain."

I turned to look when I got to the bottom of the stairs but, before I realized what was happening, I was grabbed, pushed outside and shoved up against the building.

"Montague Collins. Imagine meeting you outside a bar in downtown Halifax."

"Kenneth Fanshaw. Imagine you casting aspersions on anyone else's behaviour."

Fanshaw was practically standing on my toes; his face was about six inches from mine.

"Do you know anything about the defamation laws in this province, Collins?"

"I do. That's why I am always meticulous about not contravening those laws in any way."

"You'd better be fucking meticulous. And stop poking around where you have no right to poke around."

"Speaking of poking around, you wouldn't be making reference to private files in my law office, would you? Files that are covered by solicitor-client confidentiality?"

"I don't give a fuck about your law office."

"That doesn't cause me any great anguish, but I know someone who would be most dismayed if she heard you say that."

"Never mind anyone else. Let's talk about you. About a U.S. road trip and a flight from the American authorities."

"This sounds like pillow talk from Felicia Morgan."

"Felicia Morgan isn't the only one in this town who's heard about your escapades, Collins. Though maybe the Bar Society hasn't been advised of them yet. Sounds pretty bad. A whole rock band, a bag of mind-altering drugs, and one underage girl."

"My blues band had nothing to do with the girl, although some regular patrons of a particularly seedy nightclub did."

"If it was all a big misunderstanding, why the jailbreak?"

I was not about to give Fanshaw the details of the incident, the all-too-bluesy incident that occurred when I was on a road trip with an American band called Busted Flat. I had indeed been involved in a jailbreak. If Tyrone Jackson and I had not knocked that guard unconscious and broken out of the jailhouse in Trou de Boue, Louisiana, I'd still be sitting in there, serving as a punching bag for Sheriff Salaud. And Tyrone would have fared even worse. We had no involvement with the young girl — nobody in the band did — and we weren't going to stick around and face Louisiana justice. I didn't have any identifying information on me and I hitched rides, jumped on boxcars, and got up to the border and crossed over at night. I'd always believed the other guys on our bus got rid of my papers and said they had no idea who I was. Nobody had served any extradition papers on me. From what I heard, the party-gone-wrong was the girl's idea, but she was too young to give legal consent. The fact that she was the daughter of one of the state troopers down there did not redound to the advantage of those of us who were wrongly accused.

All I said to Fanshaw was: "There was no wrongdoing on my part or that of the band."

"Yeah, sure. You didn't lay a hand on her."

"I have not touched an underage girl since I was an underage boy. Can you say the same?"

"You know, I find your story hard to believe —"

"You would."

"— and I suspect others would find it hard to believe, too."

"Speaking of blackmail, Ken, did you ever have any experience along that line? On the receiving end, I mean. Letters, threats of exposure, that sort of thing? My own response to blackmail would be: 'Publish and be damned.' Of course it's easier for me, being innocent. Others, not so lily-white, might be tempted to silence the blackmailer at all costs, and perhaps in the process —"

Fanshaw leaned even closer to me. "Fuck you, Collins. And get the fuck out of my life. People who cross me sometimes find themselves in unenviable circumstances. That's not a threat; that's just a description of economic reality in this town. Don't make me come looking for you again."

I gave him a shove, and he stumbled. He regained his balance and came towards me, but a group of people came out of the bar at that moment, and he quickly walked away. I escaped to my car. Who had told Fanshaw about the road trip? Felicia was the obvious suspect, but how did she know about it? The woman was a sponge when it came to picking up dirt about other people. The fact that I was innocent was small consolation at the moment. My most immediate worry was what Fanshaw might do with the information. My only hope was that he knew the secret would become useless as a threat if he revealed it.

†

On Friday morning I intended to check out Primrose House, the group home or shelter Mrs. Pottie had described to me as a beneficiary of Matilda Lonergan's generosity. Just before my departure, I got a call from Constable Phil Riley.

"You may be interested in this, Monty. Remember the spanker, Sybil Kraus?"

I did indeed. Sybil Kraus, also known as Sarah MacLeod, the gingerbread lady of Lunenburg County.

"Yes, I remember."

"She's going to be arraigned this morning on fraud charges."

"No!"

"Yeah. She wrote a couple of bad cheques — for food! Couple of massive grocery orders. I guess times are tough."

"What's the story?"

"I don't know. One of the other guys is handling the case, and he's left for the courthouse."

"Thanks, Phil. I'll check it out."

I sprinted to Spring Garden Road and took a seat upstairs in the courtroom, where I watched the usual sad parade of the misguided, the misanthropic, and the misbegotten. What was the story on Sybil Kraus? First the spanking charges, now this. After an hour of other cases, Sybil's name was called. A lawyer popped up and went to the door, returning with a plump, round-faced woman with curly grey hair. The gingerbread lady did not look like a child beater to me, or a fraud artist, but I had learned long ago not to bet the farm on a sweet face. Her lawyer conferred with the Crown prosecutor, who then asked the judge for an adjournment. He made a reference to Community Services involvement, and he was not even in his seat again before the judge moved on to the next matter.

I got up and made sure I was out the door before Sybil Kraus. She emerged alone; her counsel must have had another client on the docket.

"Excuse me, Ms. Kraus."

"No comment," she said, brushing past me to go down the stairs.

"I'm not a reporter."

"I have nothing to say no matter who you are. Excuse me."

What was I going to do? Grab her and have her charge me with assault? And what would I say to her anyway? *Your friend, the Reverend Warren Tulk, raided a party at the Colosseum; the host of the party was later dispatched to hell. You were charged with spanking a child, and Tulk booted the case. You and Tulk were seen cruising for young people in the Tex-Park garage. You have a reinforced compound out in the country. And I'm making this my business.* I could not make it my business without a clear connection to my case. I stood and watched her walk out of the courthouse. She crossed Spring Garden and walked up Grafton Street. Was she headed to Tulk's shop? I debated following her but, just as I was about to leave, I was hailed by a former Legal Aid colleague who was now a judge; he wanted to speak to me about the scheduling of one of my cases. By the time I got away, Sybil Kraus was nowhere in sight. But I went over to Blowers Street and peered in the window of the His Word bookshop. There was no sign of Sybil, or of Tulk. A young girl stood beside the cash register, talking animatedly into the phone. The shop had a sale on, advertised by a poster done in elaborate calligraphy: "Ask and it shall be given!" If only it were that simple. I walked down the street to my office.

I had two clients waiting so I dealt with them, then got in my car and headed for Dartmouth via the old bridge. I knew at least one person who refused to drive on this, the Macdonald, bridge because of "the curse" supposedly placed on it by a young Micmac in the early years of the city. Legend has it the dispute arose when two men fell in love with the same woman. Some things never change.

Three times o'er these waves a bridge shall rise,
Built by the pale face, so strong and wise,
Three times shall fall like a dying breath,
In storm, in silence, and last in death.

The first two predictions came true in the late 1800s. They didn't take any chances when they built the bridge for the third time; they had the Grand Chief of the Micmac on hand to lift the curse during the opening ceremonies in 1955. But, take note: half a dozen men died building it.

I got over safely for the thousandth time, and found my way to Primrose Street. The streetscape was composed of small apartment buildings and mean-looking bungalows. I saw nothing that had been recently built, or even repaired, to offer a home to troubled kids. Perhaps the youth shelter had relocated. Or maybe I had the wrong address. I turned at the end of the street and drove out again. Only then did I see a two-storey house with a small sign on the door. I parked and got out to look. Primrose House, sure enough. The house was done up in beige plastic siding; its large picture window was covered with Plexiglas, which had been scratched and spray-painted with graffiti. A brave little window box was crammed with purple and yellow pansies. I rang the bell.

"Yes?" A small, tired-looking woman in her sixties peered up at me.

I offered her a cover story about Corey Leaman and a possible connection with the shelter, and she invited me in. She introduced herself as Connie. The place was clean but worn. I could hear rock music coming from the upper floor, and voices murmuring in the back of the house.

"Thanks for seeing me, Connie. I'm trying to track down any information I can find about Corey Leaman's life. He may have come to Primrose House but I'm not sure. The reason I think he may have been here is that Mrs. Lonergan seems to have helped him out at times. I understand she was a volunteer."

"Dear, sweet Mrs. Lonergan! Matilda. Yes, she spent several days a week here with us. I'll just go back into the office and see if I can find Corey's name."

"Thank you."

She left the room and stood aside in the hall as a heavy, and heavily tattooed, young girl passed by with a baby over her shoulder.

"How's Chelsea? Has her rash cleared up?"

"All gone," the girl replied. "You were right. All it took was water! They were telling me I had to get this really expensive medicine but they were just trying to rip me off."

"Oh, yes, sometimes all a baby's skin needs is cool, soothing water. I'm glad she's better. Will you be in for dinner tonight?"

"Yup. I'll put Chelsea down and help you peel the potatoes."

"Thank you, Megan. Take your time."

A young guy with buzzed hair and a Maltese cross dangling from his ear came into the room and stared at me without speaking. His head rocked in time to the music upstairs. Connie came back and smiled at him; he mumbled a "hi" and backed out of the room.

"I can't find any record of Corey's having been here. I'm sorry. But I remember Matilda speaking of him, and of her hopes that he would get himself straightened out. I recognized his name from the news stories."

Looking around me, I wondered what had become of the building plans mentioned by Mrs. Pottie. Of course, that may have been an inference she had drawn herself. I readied myself for a bit of tactful probing.

"I suppose it's difficult to keep a place like this running. Maintenance costs, heat, food for the residents, and all that."

"Oh, we're on a shoestring budget, no question. But that's the way of the world when you're a not-for-profit organization. We get by. We have our supporters, and we're most grateful to them. And some of the young people sell their artwork."

"I had been under the impression that perhaps Mrs. Lonergan might have —"

"Oh, she did! Matilda was forever helping us cover expenses, and buying little extras for the place, or for a young person in trouble."

"When she died, did she perhaps leave anything for Primrose House in her will? Somebody mentioned that, but I could be mistaken."

A slight blush crept up Connie's cheeks. "Well, that had always been our understanding. Matilda had indicated to me that when the time came . . . Such a generous lady! I suspect that, when she became ill, perhaps family members came to her assistance, and she found them to be in need. I didn't know she had family — the death notice mentions only very distant relatives — but however Matilda settled her affairs in the end, you can be sure she did it in a way that would do the most good. And we're getting along just fine here."

"Was it fairly close to the time of her death that she intimated to you that she hoped to leave a bequest?"

The blush again. The poor woman must have thought it unseemly to have been hoping to inherit under the will. "It wasn't long before. Certainly in the year before her death. But, as I say, things change and people respond in the best way they can."

"When was it that she died?"

"It was May, 1981."

"You didn't contest the will, I take it."

"Of course not! Good heavens! We're not family members, and we certainly didn't think it was any of our business to question Tilly's intentions."

"No, no, I understand. You said something about the death notice; you don't happen to have a copy, do you? I mean, do you keep files relating to your volunteers?"

"Oh, yes, we keep records of their hours, little mementoes, honours they've received for their work, that sort of thing. We still have Tilly's. I couldn't bring myself to throw it away. Would you like to see it?"

"Can't hurt."

She disappeared into the office again and I heard the sound of papers, followed by the whirr of a photocopier. "There you go, Monty. Though I can't imagine how it will help you with Corey's case."

"You're probably right," I said, folding it carefully and slipping it into my jacket pocket. "I won't take up any more of your time, Connie. Thanks."

So. The will that went missing from Dice Campbell's files had been changed in the year before Matilda's death in May 1981. Who got the money?

I could not say who got the money, but my files told me that the first zoning applications relating to the Bromley Point project were filed within three months of Mrs. Lonergan's death. And if Dice got the money, and put it into the project, it was worth a lot more now that it had been when he got his hands on it. Of course, it was the widow Mavis who would reap what Dice had sown when he went to work on poor old Tilly Lonergan. He could not, of course, have done anything so obvious, and open to challenge, as have the woman bequeath money to him directly. He could not have witnessed the will if he was a beneficiary. But I had little doubt that with a bit of digging I would discover someone or something — a corporate entity perhaps — with an obscure connection to Dice Campbell, and a sudden influx of cash in 1981.

†

"Is Ed still in?" I had scooted over to Johnson's office on Hollis Street late that afternoon.

The receptionist stole a glance at one of the secretaries who was standing nearby. "Well, he's in, but —"

"But what?" The look again.

"He's not feeling well."

"So I'll take him up to the Grafton Street Clinic; I think he needs plenty of fluids." I walked ahead to Johnson's office and knocked on his door.

"Get lost!"

I opened the door and went in. "Going to knock off soon? I thought we could have a steak at the Midtown or — Jesus! Are you all right?"

"No. Yes. I had a hard night. And morning. I crashed here at six a.m. or something. Fuck." He was pale and shaky, head propped up on one hand while the other arm dangled down the side of his desk.

"You coming for a steak or not?"

"No, no! Maybe. It might be just what I need. A hair of the dog, you know how it goes."

When we were seated in the tavern I asked him again if he was all right. "Have you been hitting the bottle harder than usual? Is there anything wrong?"

"Everything I touch turns to shit."

"Like what?"

He waved a hand and picked up his beer with the other. "The Bar Society complaint. Clients pissing me off. Shit like that. I should just hang it up. Find something else to do with my life. Drink all day and sponge off Donna."

"Listen. I want to ask you about Dice Campbell."

"Why do you keep asking me about Campbell? You seem to think I was a Siamese twin with the guy, or something. I only saw him at a few —"

"You knew him. I didn't."

"What about him?"

"Do you know if he ever set up any kind of corporation?"

"Why?"

"Never mind why. Just, did he?"

"No idea. How does this tie in with Leaman?"

"I'm not sure."

"Well, what the hell —"

"I think there was a connection between the two of them, and anything I can find out about Campbell may help me find the link."

"My advice to you is: stop rooting around in all this old crap. Stick to the point, which is that Leaman killed himself and Scott, and you're going for the payoff. Forget Campbell."

I shrugged. Johnson eventually returned to the subject of the client who had filed a complaint against him; he muttered darkly about that, and the other aggravations of running a legal practice, for the rest of the night.

It was drizzling when we left the Midtown; I slipped on the rain-slicked pavement and grabbed Johnson for support. We looked like a pair of Vaudeville drunks. My companion thundered at a passing cab, and it pulled over. Ed passed out beside me, and I had to shake him when we got to his condo. Staging had been set up along one wall of his building, and I wondered idly what it would be like to be part of a condominium when costly repairs were required. At least this building was being maintained, unlike the crumbling condos that my clients had slapped together. Who had sent me a warning about that? No, nobody. Drunken reasoning. I was losing brain cells at a rapid rate. That was the Colosseum postcard I was thinking about. I had thought somebody was making a point about ruins, but really it was a tip-off about Campbell and the Colosseum. "Ask," the person had written. Well, I had done a lot of asking since then . . . Wait a minute! "Ask and it shall be given!" The same writing, done with a calligraphy pen. Warren Tulk's bookshop. It was Tulk who had sent the postcard. I realized Ed was mumbling something as he struggled from the car; he was telling me to pay the fare. I paid when I got home; the cabbie had to shake me awake when we pulled up to the house.

I hadn't got anywhere with Johnson about whether Dice Campbell may have set up a corporation as a dodge for the acquisition of Mrs. Lonergan's money. And I didn't even remember my interest in the subject till eleven o'clock Saturday morning, then immediately pushed it from my mind.

I spent a dreary day doing long-neglected chores around the house, accompanied by loud rock music on the stereo, which I hoped would be more effective than booze in drowning out thoughts of Maura and her baby. Nevertheless, I picked up the phone and made arrangements to take Tom and Normie to Lawrencetown Beach for a few hours of body-surfing on Sunday. Even in the middle of August, the water temperature at Lawrencetown was only 13 degrees Celsius but, as always, we eschewed the wetsuits favoured by the surfers there and had a grand old time in the waves. Of course, with our body temperatures so low afterwards, we were the only ones in the entire city driving home with our windows up and the heater on. Small price to pay.

†

First thing Monday morning I called Dice Campbell's friend, Wade Evans.

"Hey, Monty."

"Another question about Dice. Do you know whether he ever set up a corporation of any kind?"

"Yes, but I don't think he did anything with it. Just got it registered and let it sit there."

"What was the company name, do you know?"

"Yeah, something unusual. Spirit Safe Limited."

Spirit Safe. What was the company going to do? Sell safes? Spirits? Did it matter? I took it upon myself to do some corporate research. By the end of the day I had the paperwork showing that Spirit Safe Limited was established in 1978 with Darren Dice Campbell as president and Mavis as vice. Nothing was done with the company, but it was reactivated in 1981. I called Ed Johnson's number; maybe the name Spirit Safe would trigger his memory.

"Ed."

"What?"

"I found out the name of Campbell's company." Silence. "Ed?"

"What?"

"It was Spirit Safe."

"So?"

"What was the company set up for?"

"Who cares? Go bark up another tree, for Christ's sake!"

"Do-you-know-what-the-company-was —"

"I think Dicey wanted to open a bar. Scotch bar. Never got it done. That obviously has nothing to do with your case, so forget about it. I'm tired of all this old shit. And I'm late for court." Click.

It took me a while after that to get through to the woman identified in Matilda Lonergan's obituary, namely, Matilda's late husband's brother's niece by marriage. Martha Fielding lived in Arizona. It was a steamy hot August day in Halifax, so I prompted her to tell me the temperature where she was — 101 degrees Fahrenheit — which cooled me off a bit. I explained why I was calling. Sure enough, she had been the recipient of the contents of Matilda's house, or at least the few residual items that had not been willed to other people. I asked if she had the will. I did not mention the fact that the solicitor's copy had disappeared from Campbell's files not long after I discovered it. She went to check.

"There are two wills here!" Martha announced when she came back. "Aren't you supposed to destroy the old one when you make a new one?"

"The new one supersedes the old. Could you go through the later one — you can skip the teacups and butter knives — and tell me if there is a bequest to something called Spirit Safe Limited?"

"Yes, she left them eight hundred eighty thousand dollars."

"What are the names of the witnesses on the last page?"

"Tracy MacKay and Irene Fowler."

Tracy had been Dice Campbell's secretary. Irene may have been a woman working in the same building, called in to be one of the two required witnesses.

"Now, could you look at the earlier will? What was the date of the first one?"

"August 14, 1977."

"Who did she leave the eight hundred thousand to at that time?"

"Just a second. Here it is. She left eight hundred thirty thousand to something called Primrose House Foundation."

As expected. The very archetype of the sleazy lawyer, preying upon a well-heeled, and well-intentioned, elderly widow. I could picture Dice at her bedside, speaking of the charitable organization he had founded, Spirit Safe. Its purpose was undoubtedly noble: providing shelter for runaway children to keep them safe, or to keep their spirits alive. How did he get away with it? What role, if any, did

Mavis play in the scheme?

"Thanks, Martha. I wonder if you could make copies of both wills and send them to me in Halifax. I'll be happy to reimburse you for your expenses."

"No need of that. But I'm leaving for a short vacation. If I don't get them in the mail before then, I certainly will when I come back."

"Thanks again. Oh, before you go, are there any other beneficiaries named?"

"Let me look here. Yes. She left fifty thousand dollars to someone by the name of Corey Leaman."

I absorbed the news in silence.

"Monty?"

"Yes, sorry. Which will is he in?" As if I didn't know.

"The old one, but not the new one."

I gave her my address and rang off.

What did I have? A wealthy and generous woman who seemed not to have spent any money on herself, but who saved and planned to leave it where it could do the most good for the cause dearest to her heart: troubled young people without resources of their own. Including Corey Leaman. She had made out a bequest in 1977 to Primrose House, in a multi-page will that listed every trinket and bauble she owned. The amount suggested that she envisioned either a magnificent new building or, more likely, a modest house and a fund for future expenses. John Trevelyan had been her lawyer at the time. When Trevelyan had become too busy — or too high and mighty — to drive out to Sackville and listen to a sick old lady dither about her Royal Doultons, he had made the fatal mistake of palming her off on a young lawyer on the lookout for any work he could get. Fatal for whom? Leaman? Dice Campbell? Could Leaman have found out that Dice had cut him out, pushed Dice off the balcony of his office, then stolen his gun? I could easily see fifty thousand dollars as a motive for murder. I had any number of clients who risked long years in prison for a few bucks and a pack of smokes. And Dice Campbell considered fifty thousand a princely enough sum to take the risk of cutting Leaman out and adding it to the sum bequeathed to his own company, Spirit Safe.

Did Mavis know about this, or at least suspect it? If she was in on the plan to divert Mrs. Lonergan's money to the family business, did she also know there had originally been a bequest to someone named Leaman? If she suspected that Dice was killed by Leaman, had she delayed her revenge on Leaman until now? Had she bided her time all these years to divert suspicion away from the will scam? I had no trouble at all thinking of Mavis as a woman with complicated motives. I had recently convinced myself she had a motive to kill Dice herself.

I fished around in my desk drawer and found the paperwork I had obtained showing the details of Dice Campbell's company. Ed Johnson said Dice intended to open a Spirit Safe bar but never got around to it. I formed a mental picture of Mavis tarted up as a bar wench. The corporate documents said the company was incorporated in 1978, with Dice and Mavis as its officers and directors. It was allowed to lapse, and then was reactivated right around the time Dice altered Matilda Lonergan's will. Yes, here it was again in 1981 with the directors' names — I looked at the paper, blinked, and looked again. No. It couldn't be.

"I have to go to the Law Courts!" I announced to the receptionist, as I flew from the office.

I ran down the hill to Lower Water Street, turned left and kept running till I reached the Supreme Court building. I took the stairs to the third floor. I knew which courtroom he was in; if he had to face the judge's wrath for holding up the proceedings, so be it. That would be the least of his problems.

"You look like you've seen a spook, Collins. What's your problem?"

I found myself unwilling to blurt out the only thing that was on my mind. I had to catch my breath and decide how to handle this. "Are you here for the Bromley Point chambers hearing?"

"Yeah, me and half the bar of Nova Scotia. The rest of them are inside, but it's going to take a while before I get my turn." He peered at me. "You look a little jumpy. There's a cure for that, but it ain't pretty."

"What's the cure?" I said, barely listening as I surveyed the area to see who else was around.

"Detox, Collins. How about the Baird Centre?"

"I don't need to be detoxified, Johnson. But you do. Your hand is shaking."

"Oh, I should be in there, no question. The place gives me the willies, though. Makes people shoot themselves in the head. I'm glad to see you finally filed that lawsuit. You want to get the ball rolling before the young widows both find rich husbands, and there goes your dependency claim."

"I didn't file anything."

"Somebody did. I heard about it downstairs."

"There's not going to be a lawsuit, Ed."

"No?"

"No."

"Let's cut the crap, Monty. We both know why you're here."

"Do we?"

"But you're going to be disappointed. The old man didn't show. I think he's out of the country."

"The old man?"

"There's a warrant out for his arrest. Story of his life."

I decided to play for time. "Why would I want to see the old man?"

He laughed, and it was not a joyful sound. "So you could hear the story first-hand, right? He's shameless enough to tell it. I'd rather die than tell it — in some moods, I'd rather kill than tell it — and he'd spill it like it happened every day."

"I don't —"

"Sure you do. It's right there on the docket. *R. v. Negus*. Theft over. Judge alone." Ed wrenched open his briefcase and rummaged through his papers.

My mind latched on to the name Negus. Vincent "Vegas" Negus. Right. Vernon, the homeless guy, had remembered the name.

"There." Ed waved the Crown sheet in front of my face. "Satisfied? You saw the docket, like you saw the docket on arraignment day that time over in provincial court. You saw my old man's name on it. Which I have no doubt you uncovered in your relentless investigations into that fucking Colosseum. The ruin that stands for all time! Nobody knew I was related to that bottom-feeder because at the earliest opportunity I changed my name from Negus to Johnson, my mother's name. Then, after one of his many stints in the bin with the rest of the trash, the old man blew into town and got wind of the orgy going on at Dice Campbell's back in '85. And he was in there. Hoping to sit at the table and gamble for human flesh. When did you piece it all together, Collins?"

"I —"

"When that old bum freaked out at the sound of my voice at the choir concert, right? Or at least that came back to you when the rest of it . . . ah, fuck it."

"But if it was your father at the Colosseum, how would your voice —"

"My voice probably still resounds in their heads, at least the ones who are alive. 'Do a dance for us, boys. Give us a song. Then maybe we'll let you go.'"

"What do you mean about singing? I don't follow."

"I'd heard about this party that had been going on all weekend, and was out of control. I knew my father was there, and my only fear — I didn't care if they brought in wild animals to tear him apart — my only fear was that he'd let slip in front of everyone that I was his son. I couldn't have that. So I pulled a ball cap over my head, took a pair of Donna's old eyeglasses, and tried to make myself look like someone else. I got myself in there — never mind how — and tried to drag old Vinny out. He was at the bottom of the heap as usual. A gladiator, fodder for the amusement of his betters, and he was beating up on some smaller guy. Maybe it was that guy, Vernon. I grabbed the old man and tried to get him out. He started to fight me off. He said: 'Well, if it isn't the little crooner.' About my singing in the band. But he didn't say I was his son. The Romans cheered and laughed and made wagers on the outcome of the fight between me and him. I knocked the old man's head against a table, and he slumped to the floor. But the guy at the door wouldn't let me take him out. The guy had Dicey's gun. Dicey was in his office with the door closed, with some girl. The rest of them all started to stomp their feet and demanded a song: 'You're a crooner, eh? Sing us a tune! Sing us a tune!' On and on. I didn't want to make it any worse and I didn't want to stay and let them find out who I was, so I — fuck!" Ed's voice broke, and he slashed at his eyes with the back of his hand.

"You knew this, you fucker. You must have had a good laugh picturing the scene. Me singing for the likes of Ken Fanshaw and his hangers-on! I was born in a lousy stinking flophouse and we were starving half my childhood. We had old Negus beating the shit out of us, but I made it out of there and got my law degree. And there I was, back at the bottom of the pile with the rest of the poor white trash. I sang a few bars of 'The Gambler,' and tried to pretend I thought it was a big joke. That tramp, Vern, must have been the guy in the fight, and he heard my voice.

"All you had to do was file that lawsuit and maybe, just maybe, collect the winnings. But, no. You decided to lift up the rocks and see what came crawling out from underneath. Like me. Well, here we are. What happens now? If you think I'm going to —"

I turned when I heard the elevator open. It was Ross Trevelyan, arriving late for his chambers hearing, trying to balance his briefcase and adjust his gown and tabs at the same time.

"Ross!"

He seemed startled to see me. "Hi, Monty. I don't have time to chat. I have to see the client before we go in there."

"Go down to the prothonotary's office and tell them to —"

"What are you talking about?"

"Leaman and Scott. You commenced the action. Now un-commence it."

"It's going ahead, Monty. I decided it was time to fish or cut bait. You weren't getting anything done, just raising a whole lot of dust. Dust that was obscuring the light at the end of the tunnel. And that is, for me and for you and for the firm as a whole, the payoff for the survivors of Leaman and Scott, and our thirty percent of the take. You were losing sight of that. I decided it was time to get you focused. Starting the litigation will do that."

"There's not going to be any litigation, Ross. There's going to be a murder trial."

"You're crazy. The police put it down as a suicide. End of story."

"The police don't know what we know, do they, Ross?"

I heard Ed moving behind me, and I whirled around. "Don't move, Ed. Stay where you are."

When I turned again, Ross had bolted. I heard him pounding

down the staircase.

"Ed! Watch where he goes! I'm calling the police."

†

Three days later, we got the news: Ross Trevelyan, while on remand awaiting three charges of murder, committed suicide in his cell at the Halifax County Correctional Centre. Under his body was an envelope addressed to me. It took some persuading, but the prison authorities provided me with a copy of the letter. I opened it and started to read. There was a lot of crossing out, and the handwriting was shaky.

I'm telling you up front, Monty: this is a real suicide. No need to look for a smoking gun. You have the peanut shells! In morbid moments, or times of extreme stress, I always thought of my allergy as my own personal cyanide capsule. Why have I written this? Because I don't know how my father will spin the story after I'm gone. So let the record show I did it for him.

Things were going well at Dad's office when I was there, but not well enough. He had overextended himself and was going to have to cut some of the associates loose, maybe even me. But he kept putting it off; how would it look on his application for a judgeship if he couldn't even keep a mid-size practice going? Then the old lady called. Matilda Lonergan. This was ten years ago. She wanted to change her will. Dad asked me to look after her. So I sat her down, and she dictated who was to get the Belgian lace tablecloth, the grape shears, the Hummel figurines. I saw she had left a bundle to this youth shelter, Primrose House. And I had a brainwave. I knew of a better charity to leave her money to, something my father had been working at for years, or so I claimed. Old Matilda thought the world of Dad. But I had to make sure it was done right. No way our names were going on that will if our charity was going to benefit. So I thought of Dice Campbell. I knew he was in a financial tailspin, and he wasn't afraid to get his hands dirty.

I told her I would, in all conscience, have to send her for independent legal advice so she could be sure she was doing what she thought best. I worked the conversation around to Campbell, and

304

set it up. Dice and I put our heads together and decided to resurrect this defunct corporation he had started a few years before: Spirit Safe Limited. Such an all-purpose name. Really it refers to a piece of equipment used in the distillation of Scotch whisky. So we made up a story about a Holy-Spirit-inspired charity that helps abandoned kids all around the world, with my illustrious *pater* as chairman of the board. I kicked back twenty percent to Dice. He wanted more, but I told him if it wasn't for me, he'd be getting zero, so like it or lump it. I talked Tilly out of leaving fifty K to Corey Leaman, some loser she'd lost contact with. I said he'd only piss it away on drugs. But Trevelyan and Associates, out of the goodness of our hearts, would try to find Leaman and set up a trust for him. Oops, we never managed to find him before the old lady croaked. Anyway, we revived Spirit Safe Limited, this time with me and my old man as the company officers. Which you apparently saw when you looked at the corporate records.

Yes, I had seen the names John and Ross Trevelyan when I finally looked at the records for the company's second incarnation; in its first run, Dice and Mavis had been the officers, and I had wrongly assumed their names would be there again. I read on.

So when old Matilda died — of natural causes — Spirit Safe acquired a small fortune. That meant a small fortune for John and Ross Trevelyan, and their suddenly thriving law firm. Dad thought it was all above board, that the Lonergan woman had really come up with the idea herself. Why not? Everyone else thinks the world of him. And of course I was the blue-eyed son, because I had got the job done legitimately, having found another upstanding member of the bar to shepherd the deal through. The sun rose and shone out of my ass, as far as the old man was concerned. I finally had his gratitude and admiration. But even though he thought it was legit, he did not want it known — outside a limited circle — that he had benefited so directly from an elderly client. Somebody might think he had influenced her improperly. God forbid. He spent the money discreetly, expanded the firm gradually, and eventually got his appointment to the bench. Everything was coming up roses.

Then, last January, there was a disturbance at the reception desk of Trevelyan and Associates. A young lout was demanding to see John Trevelyan. John had gone on to bigger and better things, so the receptionist called me. Turned out this was the very Corey Leaman I had cut out of Mrs. Lonergan's will. Leaman had been in the Baird Centre, and his mother had been in Kingston Penitentiary. So, with one thing and another, Leaman had only the night before found a letter from Mrs. Lonergan. The letter had been stashed, unread, in a box of papers at his mother's house in Sackville. Old Matilda had had a soft spot for Corey, who used to help her around the house. She had written a letter encouraging him to rise above his difficulties and become the man she knew he could be. To help him along, she had named him in her will, and he was to go see her trusted lawyer, John Trevelyan, when the time came. With Corey's luck, by the time he saw the letter and began wondering why he had never been contacted about his windfall, John T was on the bench, the will had been changed, and Corey was out of the money.

He ranted and raved, and I came up with a story to calm him down. I won't bore you with the details but, basically, I told him I would be out drinking that night with somebody who could help him find his money. And if he kept his mouth shut until then, he'd be able to get most of it back. He was to meet me beside the Baird Centre. If he was found dead on the Baird grounds, it would support my suicide cover story. And it was dark around there. I waited across the street by the Fore-And-Aft. Leaman showed up and I started across, but he came running over to the parking lot of the bar, bellowing about his money. I panicked and yelled at him to shut up. Then I got myself under control. I beckoned him over as if to whisper in his ear. Then I took out the gun — Dicey's gun — and put a bullet in Leaman's head. He dropped. Perfect. I was just getting him arranged and planting the gun on him when this other guy came flying around the side of the bar, zipping his pants up. Turned out he was getting serviced by a hooker who couldn't keep her mouth shut, in more ways than one. This guy obviously heard the shot and, poor schmuck that he was, came running to see what was happening. This was Graham Scott, who I later learned was peddling drugs to half the hookers in town. Though I didn't know him from Adam when I blew him away. He didn't feel a thing. My advice to anyone who hears gunshots is: run the other way.

The Luger. We have to go back in time again for that. This was 1985, a few years after the will fraud, but way before Corey made his ill-fated appearance in my office. Dice got greedy. Or maybe just desperate. He had big gambling debts, and his law practice was going south. Then, in the middle of all this darkness, a light went on in his head. He called one night and told me to meet him at his office, pronto; there was a problem. I knew exactly what the problem would be, but I wasn't too worried. If he wanted money from me, he'd have to wait till I could produce it, and I couldn't do that in the middle of the night. I went to the meet to keep him happy till I figured out how to handle him.

So I go up to Dice's office on Barrington Street. As predicted, he tries to blackmail me about the will scam. If I don't pay him one hundred K he'll call the Bar Society. Then he pulls a gun to bring the point home! I start laughing. 'Come on, Dice, let's not be cowboys here. We can work something out.' He was half-corked as usual and he looked kind of sheepish. He started to shove the gun back in his pocket, and I made a dive for it. Even as I was going for it, I was thinking: 'This is stupid; it probably isn't loaded.' But he looked so terrified I knew the fucking gun really was loaded. I also knew this was the best and maybe the only chance I would ever have to silence the one person who knew about the will. Remember, this was years before Corey Leaman showed up. As long as Dice Campbell was alive, I would have to live with the fear of blackmail. With him dead, my secret was safe.

What you have to understand, Monty, is that I could never, ever let this dirty deed come out in the open. I could never let my father know that his good fortune, which looked to the world like a natural outgrowth of his own accomplishment, had in fact come from a fraud perpetrated by his own son. What would that do to his chance of a seat on the Supreme Court of Canada? What would that do to his feelings for *me*? I don't know what your relationship with your father was like, Monty, but mine was such that letting this story come out was simply unthinkable. Couldn't be done. I'd kill to make sure that didn't happen. Which I wouldn't have had to do, if people hadn't got so greedy.

Let's just say Dice played his own death card. I forced him at gunpoint to jump off his own balcony. Dice was crying and begging and pleading but, really, he had left me with no choice. I thought it might be useful to keep his gun. Which turned out to be forward thinking on my part. I was ready when Leaman showed up six years later. Poor Graham Scott, I didn't want to do that. He was just in the wrong place at the wrong time.

The hooker, Wanda, didn't get a look at me, but she knew Leaman wasn't alone out there. Wanda got promoted. Out of province. Comes in handy to have a criminal clientele, doesn't it, Monty? I gave up criminal law years ago and was glad of it, but some of my old clients are still around. Always in need of pocket money, these guys. Can't seem to hold down a steady, seventy-hour-a-week job. Maybe they never had a father to give them a guiding hand. I call my old client the odd jobs man. Need somebody to break in and steal a bunch of papers from a house in Sackville? Need an escort for a young lady flying up to Montreal? As far as I know, Wanda's paralyzed with fear of coming back to Halifax. Otherwise, she's healthy.

At this point, Ross's writing was barely legible. The last few lines were a scrawl: "I can't do another night in this place. I can't face the old man. I can't face a trial. I can't face Elspeth. My next note is for her. Make sure she gets it."

†

The next day, Friday, I saw Ed Johnson in the plaza outside the Law Courts.

"Ed! Hold on."

"What do you want?"

"How about a lobster sandwich at the Bluenose II?"

"Are you out of your fucking mind?"

"What?"

"I don't want you around anymore, Collins. Not after all the stuff I blurted out the other day. I was so worked up about it all, I just couldn't believe you didn't already know. So there I was, blubbering away about how I made an ass of myself at that party. The

Colosseum. And thus made an ass of myself all over again in front of you. About the most humiliating experience of my adult life. Every time I see your face, I'll know that you know."

"*You've* been humiliated? Those so-called Romans were people you have zero respect for, and with good reason. And to this day they don't know it was you." He didn't have to hear that Felicia Morgan claimed to have "dirt" on him; that could be anything. "I, on the other hand, know something about real humiliation. I sat down in a room full of people I do care about — my son, my daughter, my in-laws, my friend Burke — I sat there grinning like a lovesick teenager at my faithless wife, who then told the whole room that she was pregnant with another man's child. Now she has that child for all the world to see. You don't *know* humiliation, Johnson. If you and I were to sit down and pen a twelve-bar blues on our stories, mine would have 'em cryin' in their beer. Yours wouldn't even be heard over the drunken chatter in the bar. Now, Ross and John Trevelyan, there's a father-son story that *really* went out of control! So let's forget all about it, and have a sandwich and a beer at the Bluenose."

No reply.

"Ed. Let's eat."

"All right, all right."

As we waited for the light at Hollis Street, I said: "Tell me something. Was Mavis Campbell there that night?"

"No. Mavis wasn't one of the Romans. She wouldn't go in for any of that filth."

Chapter 14

*In the park I saw a daddy with a laughing
little girl that he was swinging
And I stopped beside a Sunday school and
listened to the songs that they were singing.
Then I headed down the street, and somewhere
far away a lonely bell was ringing
And it echoed through the canyons like the
disappearing dreams of yesterday.*
— Kris Kristofferson, "Sunday Mornin' Comin' Down"

I, along with the other members of the Stratton Sommers law firm, spent the last week of August dealing with fallout from Ross Trevelyan's arrest and suicide. The meetings spilled over into Saturday, and some of us ended up drowning our sorrows in time-honoured fashion downtown. The phone rang at the crack of dawn Sunday morning. No, not dawn; it was nine-thirty.

"I know you've been preoccupied, Collins. But it's a mortal sin to miss Mass on Sunday; have you forgotten?"

"I thought they changed that. It's not a sin anymore."

"*They* are just telling you that to make you feel good about yourself. *He* hasn't changed. He is unchangeable. Immutable. Eternal."

"There now, Father. At least I haven't missed the sermon."

"Get used to early mornings. I'm thinking about having the men's choir sing the early Mass, in Latin."

"Every week?"

"Negotiable. But don't let me keep you; you still have time to catch the eleven o'clock. The reason I called —"

"Saving my soul was not the reason?"

"Ah, no. I wondered whether you saw the piece in the paper yesterday about our friend Sarah MacLeod. She's also known as Sybil Kraus."

"Right. No, I didn't see the article. She was charged with fraud, and I meant to follow it up."

"No need. I'm on the case. She entered a guilty plea in return for an absolute discharge. She was desperate for food for her foster home, which was not registered with the authorities. There's a bit of a row with the government about that. She and Warren Tulk have been taking in young people from the streets, promising them anonymity, protecting them from abusive parents, vengeful pimps, and God knows what all. She has so many under her roof she can't feed them. The place we saw out in the country is a rescue mission, not a house of corruption. Or of correction."

"She hasn't been meting out punishment to them?"

"No, she says she's changed her ways. She offers them unconditional love — what Christian love is supposed to be, but so rarely is. She does insist that they make their beds, help with the dishes and other chores, and read a chapter of the Bible every day. Now, about the Colosseum —"

"Everything we know is recorded in my files."

"Good. I went to see Tulk in his bookshop again. Turns out the Colosseum has been part of his mission. He's been working on it for years, gathering evidence from young people who were involved. Apparently, it was one long party extending over several nights in 1985. The so-called Romans have been doing damage control ever since. One of the participants went on to become Minister of Justice."

"Tolliver."

"Tolliver made sure the information Tulk brought to the prosecutors, when he was a cop, was discredited. Tulk was made to look like a religious kook. This Tolliver apparently extracted money and even good works out of Kenneth Fanshaw for the city, in the district he represented! Homeless shelters and that sort of thing. I don't know how they kept it as quiet as they did."

"Well, the Romans — the lawyers and other upstanding citizens — would be terrified of admitting they knew about it. And the street people must have been kept in line with booze, drugs, and threats."

"Tulk is determined to see that justice is done."

"Good. I'll go talk to him."

"Yes. He sent you the postcard but he didn't want to show his hand otherwise, because he didn't know if you might end up representing Dice Campbell's estate in some way. He wasn't sure what you were looking into."

"That makes two of us!"

"Anyway, I imagine Mr. Fanshaw is in for a surprise."

And I would have to gamble that, by the time the police arrived at the drawbridge of Fanshaw's château, Fanshaw would realize it was too late to gain anything by spreading the story of my misadventures in New Orleans. To Burke, I said: "I'll ask Tulk how close he is to handing his information over to the police, then I'll have a word with Phil Riley, my pal on the force." But I would not be giving them the name Vegas Negus. I couldn't do that to Ed Johnson. With any luck, the police would see no reason to talk to Burke. Vernon might or might not recall the name Negus, might or might not repeat it if he did. Either way, I didn't think anybody would be able to prove Ed had been there. The Romans would be busy denying that they had been there themselves.

I realized Burke was winding up his call. "Don't let me hold you up. See you at eleven." Click.

Why not? A little spiritual refreshment would not go amiss. I showered, shaved, and dressed in a shirt and sports jacket. On my way downtown I came up with the idea of stopping in and seeing if the kids might like to join me. But when I drove down Dresden Row I saw a sight that stopped me cold. There, turning left at the corner of Dresden and Morris Street, was my family: Maura pushing the baby carriage, Normie holding on at the side, and Tommy walking behind. I knew that picture would stay with me as clearly as if I had it framed and hung on the wall across from my bed. They were dressed up enough that I knew where they were headed: St. Bernadette's Church. That put paid to my appearance at Mass there. I turned the car around, went up the street to Clyde and turned left.

†

When I got to the address I wanted on Tower Road, I rang the bell and waited. The place was not what I would have expected; it was one of the beautiful Victorian houses with an Italianate storm porch on the front. I was just about to give up when a pale but bravely painted Mavis Campbell came to the door.

"You again."

"Me again. Nice place. I expected something a little more flashy."

"I'm just an old-fashioned girl at heart. But you wouldn't know that. Are you ever going to go away and leave me alone? Now that you know I didn't kill my husband?"

"You'll never see me again."

"Really?"

"Really."

"Oh." She stood staring at me. "Would you like to come in? Have a drink?"

"I thought maybe I could take you out for breakfast. Or lunch."

"As long as it's licensed."

"How about walking over to Barrington Street. The Athens."

"All right. I keep hearing rumours they're going to move."

"No! Where to?"

"I heard Quinpool Road."

"Hmm."

We walked up Tower Road, cut through the Victoria General Hospital parking lot, and headed east on Spring Garden. A cold fog had settled over the city; the occasional foghorn broke the silence of the morning. Nobody was out, except for the odd panhandler. My mind kept replaying the image of my children with their mother and their new baby brother. But I turned to the subject at hand.

"Mavis, you now know Dice was murdered. By Ross Trevelyan."

"I know. But none of it makes any sense to me!"

"Trevelyan wasn't working with us then. In fact, he joined our firm for one reason: to control the lawsuit against the Baird Centre, so he could cover up the fact that he killed Dice and then killed Leaman to keep the Dice killing under wraps. Graham Scott was shot because he arrived on the scene before Trevelyan could get away."

"Why?" She stopped walking; her face had gone a deathly white. "Why did he kill Dice? Was he involved in the . . . Tell me."

I recounted the story of her husband's death.

Tears streamed down her face; she made no effort to wipe them away.

"Mavis, I'm sorry. About Dice. About everything. Truly."

"Well, at least I know," she said, struggling to get her voice under control. "After all these years. And, as much as it sticks in my craw, I have you to thank for taking the trouble to find out what happened. I know it would have been tempting for you to have stuck to the Leaman suicide theory and gone for the payoff."

"Mavis, you know I'm going to have to tell the police about that party. The Colosseum. I understand that you weren't part of it."

"Good. Nail them. I wanted to call the police myself. But . . . I couldn't do it. Kept telling myself the things I heard could not be true. Even Dice felt guilty. He didn't let on — he never mentioned that Colosseum business to me — but I knew. It had an effect on him. He'd hold forth about the Hobbesian view of man, that life was nasty, brutish, and short. I just stayed blind drunk all the time so I could be oblivious."

"It won't be good for Dice's reputation."

"It can't hurt him now. He's dead."

We walked in silence, lost in our thoughts. Then I said: "Well, as promised, as soon as we finish lunch I'm out of your life."

"Now that I'm finally going to be rid of you, I'm not sure I like the idea. Is there a woman in your life these days?"

I ended up spilling the whole sorry tale to her as we walked through the fog.

"Is she in love with this other man?"

"If it's who I think it is, this Giacomo, then no, I don't think she is."

"Well, then."

"Well, then, what?"

"The love of your life is still breathing. Mine isn't. Try to imagine yourself grieving for someone and then, in the middle of that grief, you're brought up short by the fact that the person didn't love you. Was seeing someone else right up until he died. Try to imagine what that's like, Monty. Plus those other things . . . I have a friend who's an arch-Catholic; she'd probably tell me there's a prayer for uncomplicated grief! Too late for me, if there is. And you think *you* have problems. My advice to you, Monty, is get over it and get on with it."

"I'm not sure I can."

"It's up to you. You have to decide whether you want to spend the rest of your allotted time on earth with her. Or without her."

I couldn't answer.

After a moment she looked at me and said: "I guess you don't want to take up with an alcoholic!"

"I don't want to become one, Mavis; it scares the hell out of me."

"It hasn't hurt me."

"No, of course it hasn't, sweetheart."

We passed the Basilica and were nearly knocked over by a blast of wind from the Maritime Centre as we turned the corner onto Barrington Street. I took my friend's arm and slipped it through mine. We huddled together against the wind as we headed north.

Chapter 1

I

Father Burke appeared ready to burst into song, or at least into chant, as he tacked Saint Thomas's words to a bulletin board at the entrance to the building. He said, simply: "Let our work begin."

"Our work" was the inaugural session of the new Schola Cantorum Sancta Bernadetta, under the directorship of the Reverend Father Brennan Xavier Burke, BA (Fordham), STL (Pontifical Gregorian), STD (Angelicum). The schola was a kind of choir school for grown-ups, who would be learning or relearning the traditional music of the Roman Catholic Church. Gregorian chant and Renaissance choral music had been largely shunted aside over the past thirty years. For the church, the cataclysmic event of the 1960s was the Second Vatican Council, popularly known as Vatican II. It was a meeting of bishops and theologians from around the world, called together by Pope John XXIII for the purpose of opening the windows of the church to the modern world. When you open a window, fresh air may blow in, but something else may get blown out. In the opinion of Father Burke, the great musical heritage of the church went out the window after Vatican II. In setting up his schola cantorum, he intended to do his part to recover what had been lost.

My law firm, Stratton Sommers, had done the legal work for the schola, but my involvement went far beyond that. My family and I — my estranged wife Maura, son Tommy Douglas, and daughter Normie — had been privy to Father Burke's anticipation, his anxiety, and his all-night planning sessions as he worked towards the realization of his dream. It was a lot of work but we were happy to assist in any way we could. We knew that if he succeeded in establishing the school, he would be making a permanent home in Halifax. Burke had spent much of his childhood in Ireland, most of his adult life in New York, and the past few years here in Nova Scotia. By this point we felt wedded to him, for better or for worse, and I know the lights would dim if he walked out of our lives. Not surprisingly, then, I was on hand for the introductory session.

"Now, Father, be mindful of the possibility that others in the group may have, em, views that differ from your own." The gentle warning came from Burke's pastor, Monsignor Michael O'Flaherty, a slight, white-haired priest who spoke with a lilting Irish brogue. "I know this is your show, but a bit of advice from your elders may not go amiss. Just remember to be patient, forbearing, courteous, and open to the variety of —"

"Michael," Burke interrupted, "when have I ever failed to be patient and forbearing?"

The older priest — who really was patient and forbearing, and who answered to "Michael" or "Mike" as cheerfully as to "Monsignor" — sent me a knowing glance, which I returned. He knew as well as I did that when the meek inherited the earth, Father Brennan Burke would not be among those on the podium taking a salute.

"Besides," Burke was saying, in a clipped Irish voice that could never be described as lilting, "these people know what they've signed up for. The fact they are here says to me that they have certain views on the Mass and on music that accord with my own."

"Oh, I wouldn't make that assumption now, Brennan. Not necessarily. Just keep caution in mind, my son." Michael turned to me. "Any advice for him, Monty, before he goes up there?"

"Somehow I suspect my words would be wasted, Michael," I answered.

We had reached the gymnasium of St. Bernadette's choir school, where the schola had its headquarters and the students were already gathered. Monsignor O'Flaherty and I took seats in the back. Burke went to the front of the gym and took his place at the lectern. Tall, with black eyes and black hair threaded with silver, Burke was a commanding figure in his clerical suit and Roman collar. He faced his inaugural class of just under sixty students. They were priests, nuns, friars, and a smattering of laymen and women from all over North America, Europe, and Japan. The term was originally intended to begin in September and wind up before Christmas. But, owing to the meddling of the priests' housekeeper, Mrs. Kelly, the notices and registration forms were several weeks late going out. The housekeeper, who had never quite approved of the worldly Father Burke and was not skilful enough to mask her disapproval, wrongly believed the papers had to be seen and endorsed by the bishop. By the time Burke discovered the error and set her straight in a blast that nearly blistered the paint off the walls, he had missed a number of publication deadlines. The first session had to be delayed, throwing the whole year's schedule off.

But the big day had arrived. It was Monday, November 18, 1991. Burke began his opening address: "Welcome to the first session of the schola cantorum. I am Father Burke, and I look forward to meeting each of you when we begin our work this afternoon. Your presence here suggests to me that you are looking for something deeper, something richer, something more, shall we say, mature than the liturgy and music you may be encountering in your home parish. I have heard the term 'do-it-yourself Mass' and that pretty well —"

"The phrase 'do-it-yourself' raises a red flag to me, Father! It suggests that you disparage anything but the old, conservative liturgy that held sway before the Second Vatican Council." The speaker was a heavy-set woman of middle age, with a large wooden cross hanging from a strip of leather around her neck.

"Well, you're right in part. There is much that has crept into the church today that I disparage. But people have the wrong idea when they blame Vatican II. None of that was envisioned by the Council —"

"Oh, I think you're being too kind there, Father, too kind altogether." An elderly priest struggled to his feet with the aid of a cane; he faced Burke, then turned to address the crowd. "In fact we can put the blame squarely on the Second Vatican Council for destroying the very essence of Catholic worship; some would say the very essence of Catholicism itself."

The first speaker was back before Burke could respond. "So some liturgical practices are not as good as others? Is that what you're saying, Father Burke? Are you admitting you're an elitist?"

Many a schoolteacher would have envied Father Burke at that moment; he may have been under siege, but he had the attention of every student in the room.

"We are members of the Roman Catholic Church," Burke countered. "That is not an institution founded on relativism, moral or otherwise. We need look no further than Saint Thomas Aquinas, who speaks of degrees of perfection. *Gradibus in rebus*, gradations in things. Thomas says some things are better, truer, finer than others. And that is certainly true of music. When you compare Mozart with, well, some of the tripe —"

"I was right," the woman asserted. "An elitist. Well, that approach leaves out great segments of our community, I'm afraid, Father. Not everyone can appreciate —"

"Who's being an elitist now?" Burke snapped. I was surprised he had held his temper this long. "I refuse to talk down to my congregation, as if the people are simpletons who 'don't get' the great music. I refuse to insult their intelligence with childish, jaunty, sentimental little tunes —"

"So we're going to be stuck with all the old music? I thought we were going to dialogue and workshop together to create some music of our own. There's a group of us here who have been sharing ideas for some new compositions for the Mass."

Burke's customary deadpan expression gave way to one of horror. How had someone who proposed composition by committee found her way into his schola, a bastion of traditional music?

He eventually got back on track and continued his address. The vast majority of the group were attentive and silent, but he was going to have his hands full with the disgruntled minorities in the student body. If things proved dull in the criminal courts, where I spent most of my days, I'd make a point of dropping in to the schola to observe the fireworks!

✝

That evening found me in Father Burke's church, where I was a well-established member of the St. Bernadette's Choir of Men and Boys. There were sixteen of us in the choir. The trebles and altos were young boys; the tenor and bass sections were made up of guys in their teen years or well beyond, like me. I was something of a crossover artist, since I usually did my singing with a bunch of scruffy characters who shed their day jobs at five o'clock, donned old frayed shirts and porkpie hats, lit up smokes, and did their wailing in my blues band, known as Functus.

The church, at the corner of Morris and Byrne streets, was a couple of blocks south of the city's downtown shopping area, and about a minute's walk from the waterfront. St. Bernadette's was a small neo-Gothic church with arched stained-glass windows. The Victorian-era rectory, three storeys high, stood beside it. Across the way on the west side of Byrne was a large stone building in the Second Empire style with a mansard roof, dormers, a crucifix on top, and a more recent brick extension. Wide stone steps led up to the double front doors. This building was home to the new schola cantorum; it also housed the children's choir school and a parish youth centre. I entered the church and took my place with my fellow choristers in the loft.

"*Gloria in excelsis Deo!*" The voice of an accomplished operatic tenor filled the church, and the entire membership of the St. Bernadette's Choir of Men and Boys moved to the rail of the choir loft to gape at the exotic figure below. The man wore an elaborate-looking soutane, the close-fitting ankle-length black robe traditionally worn by priests of the Catholic Church. It was unusual to see one these days. Over the soutane he had some sort of shoulder cape; the cape's lining flashed a lighter coloured silk as he extended his arms, turned, and intoned the "Gloria" again. He stopped to listen as the sound reverberated off the church's stone walls. A jewel flashed on his left hand as he raised it to his head. He was wearing an old-style flat black hat with a large round brim, a type of headgear I had never seen on a local priest. He whipped the hat off and shook out black and grey curls that swept back from a widow's peak. A prominent nose and curved lips gave the impression that he had stepped out of a Florentine portrait from Renaissance times. Father Burke emerged from the sacristy in his stark black suit and Roman collar. He greeted the man, and they seemed to be conferring on the subject of the church's superb acoustics. Burke pointed up to the loft, and the operatic priest bowed towards us with a flourish, then left the building.

Our choirmaster joined us. Burke did not allude to the stranger in our midst, but proceeded to open the rehearsal as he always did with a Latin prayer. He then announced that the choir would be joining the schola group for solemn vespers on November 22.

"As the boys from the choir school know, vespers is the church's evening prayer of thanksgiving. We chant or sing hymns, psalms, and antiphons. This will take place on the feast day of Saint Cecilia."

Burke looked at a little fellow named Richard Robertson, who was a bit of a rogue, which may have been why Burke was particularly fond of him. "Who is Cecilia, Richard?"

"The patron saint of church musicians, Father."

"Right. Now, we can't have the service here at St. Bernie's because there's a wedding that evening, so we're going to Stella Maris. A great old stone hulk of a church."

"It's spooky there, Father!" Richard said. "Me and my friend snuck over to that church one night because we heard there were rats there, and we wanted to shoot them with a BB gun. We didn't see them but we heard noises."

"Well, you'll be hearing the 'Magnificat' at vespers. About as far as you can get from the squeak of rodents. But you're right. It's quite deserted around there; the church is scheduled for demolition. I guess there are no parishioners nearby. All right, now, open your books to the 'Sanctus XVIII.' This probably dates back fifteen hundred years; some say longer than that. I'd like the full choir to sing it just to the 'Benedictus.' I want you young fellows in the front row — you're supposed to be in the front row, Richard, get down here — to carry on from there. The words are among the most beautiful in the Mass: *Benedictus qui venit in nomine Domini.* What's it mean, Ian?"

"Blessed is He who comes in the name of the Lord."

"Precisely. Let's hear those clear, young voices." He raised his arms and conducted the piece. The little boys sounded like angels as their pure voices soared to the heavens.

"Lovely. A little lighter on the higher notes. Let's hear it again." It was even more beautiful the second time. The priest favoured us with a rare smile, and gave credit where credit was due: *"Deo gratias!"*

When the rehearsal wound up an hour and a half later, Burke and I retired to the Midtown Tavern on Grafton Street. At the Midtown you got draft, you got steak, you got fries; nothing came with, say, a light mango-chutney mayonnaise on the side. The priest had shed his clerical collar, as he always did when we headed out for the night. He lit up a cigarette and sucked the smoke deep into his lungs.

"Big day for you, Brennan," I said. "How's it going so far?"

"O'Flaherty was right," he said. "How did he know all these malcontents would show up?"

"Monsignor O'Flaherty is a wise man. But, really, what's surprising about it? Ever since the Vatican Council wrapped up in 1965, preconciliar and postconciliar Catholics have been squabbling about whether it was good or bad for the church, whether it modernized things too much or not enough. Some of the more authoritarian aspects of the church needed reform. And surely not all the music composed in the past twenty-five years is bad."

"Of course not. I've heard some compositions and some choirs that are excellent. But there's an overwhelming amount of rubbish as well. If we don't do something about it, generations of Catholics are going to grow up without knowing anything better."

"Well, try not to fret too much about the students at the schola. There are just a few grumblers. And they're not all of the same stripe. You'll be attacked from the conservative side when they find out how liberal you are about everything except music and the Mass."

"This is about the sacraments, not politics! It's about beauty: the beauty of music, of language, of ritual. I've wanted this for so long and now . . ." He drained his beer and signalled for another. "What have I got myself into?"

I felt a bit guilty thinking it, but this was going to be fun to watch.

II

Et antiquum documentum novo cedat ritui
O'er ancient forms departing newer rites of grace prevail
— Saint Thomas Aquinas, "Tantum Ergo"

"'The most beautiful thing this side of heaven,'" Burke said to his class the next day. I had a chance to drop in to the schola between an early morning court appearance and my first appointment of the day. "That is Father Frederick Faber's timeless description of the traditional Latin Mass."

"So why did Vatican II outlaw the Latin Mass?" The voice was unmistakably American.

"Vatican II did no such thing," Burke replied. "Many changes were made, which were in fact not promoted, authorized, or envisioned by the Council. The only things that are official are those contained in the Council documents. Here's what the documents really say, and I'm quoting from *Sacrosanctum Concilium,* the *Constitution on the Sacred Liturgy*: '. . . care must be taken that any new forms adopted should in some way grow organically from forms already existing. . . . Particular law remaining in force, the use of the Latin language is to be preserved in the Latin rites.' Vatican II made that point in a paragraph all by itself. There is a subsection that opens the door to local languages in some parts of the Mass, but it is worded with great caution. Latin is the official language of the church. It is the sacral language of our faith, just as Hebrew is the sacral language of the Jewish faith. Active participation in the Mass was considered back in 1903 by Pope Saint Pius x to mean the congregation should be singing Gregorian chant. Subsequent popes agreed. Now let us observe two versions of the Mass."

The room darkened and a screen lit up before us, showing the exterior of a building shaped something like a saddle. The scene shifted and we were inside the low-ceilinged structure. A spindly cross was the only evidence that the place was a church. Two giant quilts depicting wheat sheaves hung on either side of what must have been the sanctuary. An earnest-looking man and woman stood at a microphone with guitars. A third woman raised her hands and urged everybody to sing the "gathering hymn." Few did, but the words came through loud and clear from the leaders of song:

Come into the love! Come into the new day!
His room is for all, a true meeting place.
We are the ones He has called to the new way,
We bring our light to the whole human race!

All we in the love, all we in His peace,
Will shake hands today with a peace that will bind
All brothers and sisters. Divisions will cease.
We are the light of all humankind!

Well, that wasn't going to get anyone inducted into the songwriters' hall of fame. They'd have to come up with something better than that if they wanted to be seen as light to the whole human race. But my attention was wrenched from the music to the centre aisle of the church on the screen, where I saw a procession of . . . clowns! Everyone in the procession, including the cross bearer and the priest himself, was, incredibly, dressed in the red, yellow, and green costume of a clown. They were carrying balloons and stopping to pass them out to children in the pews. We all sat, stunned, as the elderly clown-priest read the gospel, gave a sermon, changed the bread and wine to the body and blood of Christ. Every one of the priest's gestures reflected excruciating embarrassment.

Then I heard the ancient tones of Gregorian chant, and the screen was filled with the rich blues and golds of a magnificent church, with marble floors and stained-glass rose windows. The priest approached the altar wearing gold-trimmed white vestments and a biretta, a square black cap with three ridges and a tuft on top. He looked very European, yet familiar. A younger, somewhat heavier Brennan Burke without a trace of grey in his pitch-black hair, his handsome face less hawkish than it was now. In the film he followed a procession of altar boys dressed in black cassocks under lacy white surplices. One carried the crucifix; the others brought candles. In the priest's hands was a chalice covered with a cloth. I should have remembered the names of the items from my days as an altar boy. Purificator? Chalice veil?

When he arrived at the foot of the elaborate high altar, the Father Burke on the screen removed his biretta and handed it to an altar boy. He prayed *sotto voce*, then made a profound bow and recited the "Confiteor," striking his breast three times at the *"mea culpa, mea culpa, mea maxima culpa."* Incense rose to the heights of the vaulted ceiling, and bells rang out at the consecration. In a universally known ritual essentially unchanged since the days of Saint Gregory in the year 600, the Mass proceeded to the sound of Latin prayers and solemn chant.

When the morning class was over the present-day Burke stopped to chat with me in the corridor before the schola's next session began. The composition-by-committee woman, whose name tag read "Jan Ford," came up to him with a question: "Am I right? Were you the presider at the liturgy we just saw on tape, Father?"

"I was the priest singing the Mass, if that's what you're asking."

"Right," Jan Ford said, nodding, and she moved off down the hall.

"As if I'd sign up for a life of celibacy to be a *presider*," Burke remarked to me.

"I didn't see anyone leap to the defence of the clown Mass, Brennan. I've been to a lot of very beautiful and dignified Masses since the Council, so I assume you're using an extreme example of post-Vatican II experimentation."

"An abomination. Shows how far things can go if unchecked. It happened on more than one occasion, believe it or not. There were basketball Masses, cowboy Masses, all sorts of liturgical chaos."

"The Latin Mass was magnificent, of course, as I well remember from my altar boy days."

"You still have the look of an altar boy, Montague. The blondy hair, the boyish face, the baby blue eyes. You don't always behave like one, of course, but . . ."

"Yeah, yeah. I nearly didn't recognize you, though."

"It was a few years ago. When I was doing my graduate work in Rome. I'll be teaching the rubrics of the Latin rite to the younger priests who missed out on it; no doubt it will be a refresher for some of the older fellows as well."

"*Buongiorno*, Brennan! I am sorry to have missed this morning's sessions. I would explain but I do not wish to be indelicate. It is enough to say I was not feeling well." The man spoke with a strong Italian accent. It was the elaborately attired priest I had seen in the church just before the choir rehearsal. He and Brennan exchanged a few words in Italian, then turned to me. The stranger extended his hand, and Brennan made the introductions.

"Monty Collins, meet Father Enrico Sferrazza-Melchiorre."

"*Piacere, Signor* Collins."

"My pleasure. I saw you in the church. Where are you from, Father Sferrazza-Melchiorre?"

"Mississippi."

"*What?* Forgive me. I don't speak Italian so whatever you said sounded like —"

"You heard me correctly, *signore*. I live in rural Mississippi."

"Impossible!"

"Yes. It is impossible and yet, *è vero*, like the resurrection. It is the truth."

"You're not native to the southern United States," I insisted to the flamboyant European. "Surely I haven't got that wrong."

"I am a native of Rome. My mother's family is from Sicily."

"And what exactly did you do in Rome?"

"I worked for many years in the Roman Curia — the bureaucracy of the universal church — and taught at the Lateran University also."

"My question remains: what did you *do*? To get posted to the American south?"

"It is such a long story."

"I'm sure. Leaving that story — whatever it is — aside for now, what are the demographics down there? I wouldn't have thought the Catholic population was very large."

"Oh! You are right, of course. Only five percent of the entire state is Catholic. Even less so where I work, in Mule Run. Eh! What can you do?" He shrugged.

"Fit in well with the locals, do you?"

"Let us say there was a process of adjustment. There was, I recall, some confusion at the first seminar I conducted in the church hall. I thought it might be helpful to give people a little history of the Catholic Church. To dispel some false ideas. Striving for a popular touch, I advertised it as 'Introduction to AAA.' I was encouraged when I peered outside and saw many large vehicles roaring up to the building. But my set piece on Augustine, Aquinas, and Abelard was not well received by those assembled." He sighed. "I hope we shall meet again, *signore*." He turned and was off in a swirl of luxurious fabric.

I raised an eyebrow at Burke.

"Later," was all he said.

III

Great was the company of the preachers.
— Handel, "Messiah," from Psalm 68

"This is some information the insurance company requires," I told Brennan when I returned to St. Bernadette's rectory after work that day. "You're already covered, but they need this form completed and signed."

"Why? In case somebody arrives home and claims he wasn't taught the difference between a *punctum* and a *podatus* in chant notation? He's going to sue me for failure to deliver the goods?"

"No, it's in case somebody *doesn't* arrive home. Never makes it out of your course alive! Or goes home on crutches because you didn't clear the steps after the first snowfall. Typical liability insurance."

Burke scribbled his answers on the insurance form.

I was stuffing the paperwork back in my briefcase when Monsignor O'Flaherty came in and announced that he was going to the airport. "To pick up our final guest. Student, I suppose I should say, though it seems odd to apply the word student to people in middle age!"

"We could call them scholars but that sounds a little grand," Brennan said. "Or disciples, but I wouldn't presume . . ."

"Good of you, my lad."

"So, who is it you're picking up?"

"A Father Stanley Drew. Do you know him?"

"No."

"He's an American, apparently. Working overseas. That's all I know."

"Thanks for fetching him, Michael."

✝

That evening at the Midtown, the waiter had just placed our glasses of draft on the table, and Brennan had lit up his first cigarette, when Monsignor O'Flaherty appeared before us again.

15

"Brennan!" O'Flaherty was all out of puff. "Hello to you, Monty. Brennan, you'll be hard put to believe me!"

"Evening, Michael. Have a seat, and let us treat you to a draft."

"Thank you. I've an awful drouth on me, all the talking I've just been doing."

"How did you ever know to find me here, Monsignor?"

"Amn't I after following a star in the east? But no, all coddin' aside. Wait till I tell you! Thank you. Ah. Goes down like liquid gold." He smiled and put his glass on the table, then looked at each of us in turn. "You'll never guess in a million years who our latest student is!"

"Stanley Drew," Burke replied in a deadpan voice, "an American who's been working overseas —"

"No! Drew is just a pseudonym for —" Monsignor O'Flaherty paused for dramatic effect, then blurted out his news "— Reinhold Schellenberg!"

"You're having me on!" Brennan exclaimed.

It wasn't often I saw a dumbstruck look on the face of Brennan Burke. They stared at each other in amazement.

"How could we not have known he was coming? Why the false name?" Brennan asked.

"Security reasons!"

"What do you mean?"

Here O'Flaherty looked uncertain. "I don't know exactly. He wasn't all that forthcoming on the subject. But he's a lovely man."

"So what did he say when you met him? Did he identify himself right away?"

"No. Not till we were alone in the car coming into town. But you know, there was something familiar about him. I just didn't twig to it. He hasn't been in the public eye for a long time. He used to sport a beard, but that's gone now. He has only the slightest accent; his English is perfect. You wouldn't know right off who he was. Did you ever meet him, Brennan, during your time in Rome?"

"I attended a couple of lectures he gave, and saw him at a conference or two, but I never had a conversation with him."

"Gentlemen."

"Yes, Monty?" O'Flaherty turned to me.

"Who is Reinhold Schellenberg?"

"Do I take it that theology was not among the subjects in which you excelled during your illustrious academic career, young Collins?"

"You wouldn't be wrong in drawing that conclusion."

"Father Schellenberg is a noted theologian who became quite famous — infamous might be the better word — in the years immediately following the Second Vatican Council. He was a figure of some controversy in controversial times. It apparently got too much for him and he entered a monastic order. He hasn't been heard from in public since — what would it be, Brennan? — the early 1980s, or thereabouts. Ten years or so."

"What kind of controversy are we talking about?"

"His theological positions didn't sit well with some in the church."

"Didn't sit well with whom? Liberals or conservatives?"

"It's never that simple, Monty, but, em, he attracted criticism from both ends of the spectrum."

"How did he manage that?"

"He started off as what we'll call a liberal, at the time of the Council in the 1960s," Brennan replied, "pissing off traditionalists and other conservatives. Then he did an apparent about-face, renounced his liberal positions of the past, and pissed off his former adherents. But his ability as a theologian has never been in doubt."

"And now he's here to learn at the feet of the Reverend Doctor Brennan Burke at the Schola Cantorum Sancta Bernadetta."

"You find that surprising in some way, Collins?" Burke demanded.

"Not at all, Father."

"I thought not. Well, we'll have to make his visit a memorable one."

IV

Hora novissima, tempora pessima sunt, vigilemus.
These are the latter times, not the better times.
Let us stand watch.
— Bernard of Cluny, *De Contemptu Mundi*

Everything I had heard about the students of the schola and the controversies swirling around them made me keen to catch some of the show. So I popped in to the school two days later, on Thursday, when a client failed to show up for my last appointment of the afternoon. I headed down the hall and turned left, on my way to find Brennan or Michael, or perhaps the famous and now reclusive Schellenberg. Someone had set up a table and chessboard in a little alcove off the corridor, where two men were engaged in silent combat. They appeared to be in their late fifties. One had very pale blue eyes and greying blonde hair in a short military-looking cut. His opponent was a priest with fluffy white hair and rimless spectacles reflecting the light from the window at the end of the hall. The priest gave me a pleasant, if absent, nod as I stopped momentarily to observe the match. The man with the military appearance looked up, kept me in his gaze for a few seconds, then returned to the game without any change of expression. I felt I had been scanned, comprehended, and committed to memory.

I continued on my way and found Father Burke leading a seminar billed simply as "The Great Latin Hymns." I pushed the door open and took a seat in the back.

"The 'Dies Irae,' the Day of Wrath, is attributed to a Franciscan friar in the twelve hundreds. Walsh's book on the thirteenth century contains a description of the 'Dies Irae' as 'the greatest of all hymns, and one of the greatest of all poems . . . nearly or quite the most perfect wedding of sound to sense that they know.' The author concludes that perhaps no one with the exception of Dante or Shakespeare has ever equalled the 'Dies Irae' as poetry. Two verses will suffice to show he's right:

Recordare, Jesu pie,
quod sum causa tuae viae:
ne me perdas illa die.

Quaerens me, sedisti lassus:
redemisti crucem passus:
tantus labor non sit cassus.

"As for melody, Walsh tells us the creators of the great Gothic cathedrals developed music worthy of those magnificent temples. He means of course Gregorian chant.

"Now let's hear what is on offer in the hymn books of today:

The lowly ones, they come to sup.
The rich man, shamed, is drawing near.
The lame, the leper, all are here
To share His brimming, saving cup!

Burke gave a shudder, then turned a new page.

Share the courage of the songfest.
Join His dance around the table.
If the proud ones come among us,
Call them forth if you are able.

"Does that make any sense at all? Woe betide anyone I catch doing the shimmy around the altar in my church. This sort of goofiness is everywhere in the hymn books now. Along with all those songs in which the members of the congregation congratulate themselves endlessly about being the light of the world, and aren't we grand? All this is yet another selective interpretation of the documents of the Second Vatican Council, in this case *Lumen Gentium*, Light of Nations. Which in reality did not replace worship of God with worship of ourselves.

"Ah. Mr. Collins. Thank you for drawing near. Come forth if you are able. May I present to you Mr. Collins," he said to the class. "You may have seen him around. Not only is he the schola's wise legal counsel; he is also a member of the St. Bernadette's choir." I nodded to the group.

After the lecture I saw Monsignor O'Flaherty standing alone by the chessboard, looking down at the pieces.

"Are you a chess player, Mike?"

"Alas no, Monty, I can't even win at checkers."

"Who are the two men I saw playing chess here?"

"You haven't met Father Schellenberg yet, have you? That's who you would have seen at the chessboard. And a fellow by the name of Bleier, who's actually Colonel Bleier. He's a German policeman, *'Oberst der VP.'* The *Volkspolizei*! Retired now, apparently. They live in Berlin. She teaches there."

"She?"

"Doctor Jadwiga Silkowski is Bleier's wife. She's a leading authority on moral theology." He leaned forward, a mischievous look in his eyes "She told me she got in trouble on a couple of occasions. Ran afoul of the authorities."

"Government authorities?" I asked.

"Well, now that you mention it, she may have got herself in the soup there as well, considering that it was East Berlin they were living in till the wall came down. But I meant the church authorities. Some of the positions she has taken from time to time have not gone down well in Rome."

"I don't suppose the colonel could help her there."

"No."

"I wonder why Colonel Bleier and Father Schellenberg weren't in the seminar."

"Who knows?"

V

I called Brennan Friday morning to ask where the choir would be meeting for vespers that evening.

"We'll all go directly to Stella Maris. That way we don't have to arrange drives for all the little lads."

"That's what you have insurance for."

"Spoken like a true lawyer. We have insurance but we don't have the vehicles. So the parents will drop the boys off. We'll meet outside and have a procession. Put on a little show for Saint Cecilia."

"Right. She's the patron saint of . . . music, is it?"

"Church musicians. This is her feast day, November 22. Oh, and wear your surplice. You got it from the choir loft?"

"Yes, I did. I feel like an altar boy again."

"Good. That means I'm doing my job."

"When do I get an introduction to the great man?" I asked.

"We have a surfeit of great men here, Monty. To whom are you referring?"

"Not to you, you pompous arsehole."

"Ah. Could it be Father Schellenberg then? If so, you're in luck. Mike O'Flaherty charmed him into giving a lecture this afternoon. He had to be cajoled and he made it clear he does not want to speak on the subject of the Second Vatican Council. His topic will be the divine office of the Latin rite, the prayers sung at various hours of the day. Matins, lauds, vespers, compline, and so on. Schellenberg is a Cistercian-Benedictine monk, so he knows whereof he speaks. And after his lecture you, too, will be qualified to speak on the matter. If ever you're asked."

"Good. Some new opening lines for my next visit to a pickup joint. Hey, baby, have you heard this one? A lawyer and a monk go into a bar. Only it's time for compline, so the monk says —"

"It's always worked for me."

"I'm sure."

"Anyway, O'Flaherty had lined up a bus trip for the group, to Peggy's Cove; the tour will be postponed for an hour or two so people can hear Schellenberg first. Be here at two o'clock."

I returned to my office on Barrington Street, dictated some letters on a medical malpractice case, and tried to line up my witnesses for an upcoming drug trafficking trial. Then, just before two, I headed over to the schola for the lecture by Reinhold Schellenberg. But I was out of luck. I would not be meeting the renowned theologian after all.

"Father Schellenberg came to see me," Monsignor O'Flaherty explained. "He was most apologetic. But something came up, and he had to go out. Where he'd have to go, and him a stranger in town, I don't know. I didn't ask. Anyway, he promised he'd give his talk next week. So I called the bus company and got the Peggy's Cove trip back on schedule. I packed them all onto the bus, and they're gone. But, Monty, you'll meet Schellenberg this evening at vespers."

"Yes, our choir's first performance for the schola."

"A beautiful ceremony, the peaceful closing of the day."

†

Stella Maris Church had not been used, as a church at least, for fifteen years. It was the scene of occasional manoeuvres by the police, putting the run to squatters who used the place for their own purposes. The massive ironstone building, with its twin Gothic spires, sat high on the northwest tip of the Halifax peninsula, above what is now the Fairview Container Terminal. Overlooking the waters of the Bedford Basin, the church had been built in the late nineteenth century to assert the Catholic presence in the city; it was a landmark visible to those approaching by boat or by train from the north. Now, commuters coming in on the Bedford Highway could see only the tips of the spires, behind the massive structures of the container terminal. Very few people lived in the area; it was strictly industrial.

The church's day was nearly done. Stella Maris was scheduled for demolition the following week, and in fact a twentieth-century addition at the back had already been torn down, except for one jagged stone wall. The stained-glass windows would be saved, as would the pews, the font, and all the other fittings. Brennan had mentioned his desire to have the ornate old altar transferred to St. Bernadette's, where it would be used for the weekly Tridentine Mass.

Now, in the dark of a moonless November night, robed figures gathered before the blackened wooden doors of the church. The scene was indistinguishable from one that might have taken place in the early Middle Ages. We were far away in time from modern-day Halifax. Priests in vestments, monks in cowls, nuns in habits, choirboys in white surplices, we processed into the nave and down the aisle. A candle in red glass flickered on the altar; our golden candles were the only other light. The only warmth. Incense wafted back to us from the front of the procession. Two by two we genuflected before the Blessed Sacrament present on the altar and took our places in the sanctuary for the Office of Vespers, by which we would consecrate the end of the day to God. Father Burke chanted the opening prayer:

> *APERI, Domine, os meum ad benedicendum nomen sanctum tuum: munda quoque cor meum ab omnibus vanis, perversis et alienis cogitationibus.*
>
> OPEN my mouth, O Lord, to bless thy holy name: cleanse also my heart from all vain, evil and distracting thoughts.

In the company of friars who sang Gregorian chant as part of their everyday lives, choir and clergy made their voices one; the ancient psalms floated upwards like the incense. All vain, evil, and distracting thoughts melted away, and I felt myself at peace in a way I had never known.

The peace was shattered by a scream.

We all whirled towards the sound. One of the sisters stood clutching her heart; her other hand groped wildly for support. Her mouth hung open; her eyes were fixed on the south wall of the sanctuary.

"Mother of God, Mother of God," she whispered over and over.

"What is it?" Burke demanded, making all too clear his annoyance at the breaking of the spell.

"He's dead! He's been . . ." Her voice faltered but her trembling finger pointed to the scene.

With a swish of robes, the whole group rushed to see. There, slumped against the wall, was a figure in white vestments and a Roman collar, drenched with blood. The blood was everywhere, on the wall, the floor, and all over the man's body, which had been nearly severed from his head. What was that on his leg? I shifted slightly to get a better view in the dim light. There were three or four cards showing hearts pierced with arrows — valentine cards! And something else; it appeared to be a swizzle stick for stirring drinks. The top of it was shaped like an anchor. I saw no sign of a murder weapon.

"It's Father Schellenberg!" a woman cried behind me. "Oh God in heaven! Who would do this?"

A few feet shuffled towards the scene, and someone said: "He should be given the last —"

"Stop! Do not approach the body!" The voice was German. Colonel Bleier, the former East German police officer. Bleier's voice was calm, and it carried the weight of authority, but his face was ashen. "Everyone move back to your places," he instructed. "We will not further interfere with the scene. Is there a working telephone in the building?"

"There wouldn't be, no," Burke answered distractedly. He turned towards the dead man and began to pray aloud in Latin.

"Does anyone have a car telephone?" Bleier demanded. Nobody in the group was on the cutting edge of 1990s technology. "One of you will go and call the authorities. You will exit the same way you entered, and return that way also."

I was already on my way. "I'm going for the police." I turned to make sure I'd been heard; I saw Bleier making a count and writing something down — names? — in a small spiral notebook.

I got into my car and drove at top speed to Jenny's Place Beverage Room on Lady Hammond Road, where I used the phone to alert the Halifax Police Department. When I returned to the church, I saw that the traumatized group had broken into small clusters, though, in strict obedience to the resident officer of the *polizei*, none had left the sanctuary. Some, such as Father Sferrazza-Melchiorre, knelt in prayer; others sat with eyes downcast as if in shame. An aggressive-looking man with red hair stood with his hands gripping the pew in front of him; he stared at the body and seemed to be unaware of anything else. It was too late to mark anyone's immediate reaction to the discovery. If someone had made a ham actor's effort to look surprised, I had missed it. We had all been gaping at the dead man. I joined Father Burke and Monsignor O'Flaherty, who were on their feet, eyeing the scene and conferring with Colonel Bleier.

"Ah. Monty," O'Flaherty said. "We were just saying that there's a swath of clean floor leading from the body to the sacristy. The killer must have wiped up after himself."

"I wonder how long the body has been there. Any idea?"

"I would say a number of hours," Bleier answered. "Was the church door locked when you arrived, Father Burke?"

"I can't say for sure because I was given a key to the side door and used it. I was able to push open the front doors — they have those bars you push down — so I don't know whether they were locked when I pushed on the bar or not."

"I came in the front just now. It wasn't locked. Or, at least, it hadn't locked behind us when we all came in."

"I see. When was the last time you were here, before this evening, Father?"

"Yesterday afternoon. I brought the . . . the Blessed Sacrament and placed it in the tabernacle. The place was bathed in light, and there was nothing amiss."

"The church is not used, am I correct?"

"That's right. It's going to be knocked down next week. Young people, homeless people, sleep in here sometimes. But the place was empty when I was here yesterday. I looked around and I locked up."

"Would there be tools in the basement, I'm wondering, Brennan?"

"Don't know, Michael. I'd say not. I imagine everything's been removed."

The local police arrived then and took charge, securing the scene, examining the body and surroundings, and taking our statements. Colonel Bleier and a tall, balding man I had not met watched the police activity with interest. Monsignor O'Flaherty tended to the flock of schola students, reassuring them that the killer would be brought to justice and that counsellors would be available for anyone who would like to use their services. The schola's director, Father Burke, was too shell-shocked to respond. Even if he were his usual self, he would not have thought of counselling. And he would undoubtedly have sworn to bring the killer to justice himself. For everyone on the scene, it was a long night.

I went to the rectory with Burke and O'Flaherty after the police were finished with us. We stood together in the parking lot of St. Bernadette's before I headed home.

"Let us hope and pray this slaughter had nothing to do with our work here," O'Flaherty pleaded. "Some other motive was in play, surely —"

"It happened on the feast of Saint Cecilia, Michael. Patron saint of church musicians."

"That could be coincidence, Brennan. The killer knew we would be going to Stella Maris and so —"

"Nothing about this looks like coincidence to me, as much as I would like to go along with you, Mike."

"How did Saint Cecilia die?" I asked. "Was she a martyr?"

"She was indeed," O'Flaherty replied. "She didn't die a happy death, God rest her soul. Now, as for details . . . Let me do some quick research. I have a number of works on the saints' lives. Are you coming in, Monty?"

"No, it's long past my bedtime."

"I'll be back in a jiffy."

O'Flaherty's face told half the tale when he returned. "Not a happy death, indeed not. Saint Cecilia's killers —"

"Who were they?" I interrupted.

"The Roman authorities of the second or third century. The true date is unknown. They tried to suffocate her in her bath. But she survived that attempt. They then sent a soldier to cut off her head! Three times he hacked at her neck, yet he couldn't separate her head from her body. They left her like that, the poor young girl. She lived for three days before she finally succumbed!"

"Nearly, but not quite, decapitated. Just like Reinhold Schellenberg."